"Action-packed...an enjoyable thrill ride of a summer read."—*Library Journal*

"Fresh prose, a smart and amusing husband-and-wife team, interesting history and science...wildly imaginative."
—*Publishers Weekly*

"When the going gets tough, I read Clive Cussler, for no one can spin a yarn that's so thoroughly spellbinding and entertaining as he can." —**Harold Coyle**

In *Spartan Gold* and *Lost Empire*, Clive Cussler brought readers into the world of husband-and-wife team Sam and Remi Fargo, whose passion and instinct for treasure hunting have led to extraordinary discoveries and perilous journeys. Their next adventure, however, might be their most astonishing yet.

THE KINGDOM

The Fargos are used to hunting for treasure, not people. But then a Texas oil baron contacts them with a personal plea: an investigator friend of the Fargos was on a mission to find the oil baron's missing father—and now the investigator is missing too. Sam and Remi are willing to look for them both—even though something about the situation doesn't quite add up.

What they find will be beyond anything they could have imagined. On a journey that will take them to Tibet, Nepal, Bulgaria, India, and China, the Fargos will find themselves embroiled with black-market fossils, a centuries-old puzzle box, the ancient Tibetan kingdom of Mustang, a balloon aircraft from a century before its time . . . and a skeleton that could turn the history of human evolution on its head.

PRAISE FOR THE FARGO ADVENTURES

"A spunky Nick and Nora for the twenty-first century . . . Fans of Matthew Reilly and James Rollins will revel in this treasure-hunting adventure." —***Booklist***

"Engaging . . . This adventure thriller is sure to please new fans and old." —***Publishers Weekly***

DIRK PITT® ADVENTURES BY CLIVE CUSSLER

Crescent Dawn
(WITH DIRK CUSSLER)
Arctic Drift
(WITH DIRK CUSSLER)
Treasure of Khan
(WITH DIRK CUSSLER)
Black Wind
(WITH DIRK CUSSLER)
Trojan Odyssey
Valhalla Rising
Atlantis Found
Flood Tide
Shock Wave
Inca Gold
Sahara
Dragon
Treasure
Cyclops
Deep Six
Pacific Vortex!
Night Probe!
Vixen 03
Raise the Titanic!
Iceberg
The Mediterranean Caper

FARGO ADVENTURES BY CLIVE CUSSLER
WITH GRANT BLACKWOOD

The Kingdom
Lost Empire
Spartan Gold

ISAAC BELL ADVENTURES BY CLIVE CUSSLER

The Spy
(WITH JUSTIN SCOTT)
The Wrecker
(WITH JUSTIN SCOTT)
The Chase

CHILDREN'S BOOKS BY CLIVE CUSSLER

The Adventures of Hotsy Totsy
The Adventures of Vin Fiz

KURT AUSTIN ADVENTURES BY CLIVE CUSSLER

AND GRAHAM BROWN

Devil's Gate

WITH PAUL KEMPRECOS

Medusa

The Navigator

Polar Shift

Lost City

White Death

Fire Ice

Blue Gold

Serpent

OREGON® FILES ADVENTURES BY CLIVE CUSSLER

WITH JACK DU BRUL

The Jungle

The Silent Sea

Corsair

Plague Ship

Skeleton Coast

Dark Watch

WITH CRAIG DIRGO

Golden Buddha

Sacred Stone

NONFICTION BY CLIVE CUSSLER AND CRAIG DIRGO

Built for Adventure: The Classic Automobiles of Clive Cussler and Dirk Pitt

The Sea Hunters II

The Sea Hunters

Clive Cussler and Dirk Pitt Revealed

· THE ·

KINGDOM

CLIVE CUSSLER

WITH GRANT BLACKWOOD

BERKLEY BOOKS
New York

THE BERKLEY PUBLISHING GROUP
Published by the Penguin Group
Penguin Group (USA) Inc.
375 Hudson Street, New York, New York 10014, USA
Penguin Group (Canada), 90 Eglinton Avenue East, Suite 700, Toronto, Ontario M4P 2Y3, Canada (a division of Pearson Penguin Canada Inc.) • Penguin Books Ltd., 80 Strand, London WC2R 0RL, England • Penguin Group Ireland, 25 St. Stephen's Green, Dublin 2, Ireland (a division of Penguin Books Ltd.) • Penguin Group (Australia), 250 Camberwell Road, Camberwell, Victoria 3124, Australia (a division of Pearson Australia Group Pty. Ltd.) • Penguin Books India Pvt. Ltd., 11 Community Centre, Panchsheel Park, New Delhi—110 017, India • Penguin Group (NZ), 67 Apollo Drive, Rosedale, Auckland 0632, New Zealand (a division of Pearson New Zealand Ltd.) • Penguin Books (South Africa) (Pty.) Ltd., 24 Sturdee Avenue, Rosebank, Johannesburg 2196, South Africa

Penguin Books Ltd., Registered Offices: 80 Strand, London WC2R 0RL, England

THE KINGDOM

A Berkley Book / published by arrangement with Sandecker, RLLLP

PUBLISHING HISTORY
G. P. Putnam's Sons hardcover edition / June 2011
Berkley premium edition / June 2012

Cover illustration by Tom Hallman.
Cover typographic styling by Lawrence Ratzkin.

ISBN: 978-0-425-24808-9

BERKLEY®
Berkley Books are published by The Berkley Publishing Group,
a division of Penguin Group (USA) Inc.,
375 Hudson Street, New York, New York 10014.
BERKLEY® is a registered trademark of Penguin Group (USA) Inc.
The "B" design is a trademark of Penguin Group (USA) Inc.

PRINTED IN THE UNITED STATES OF AMERICA

10 9 8 7 6 5 4 3 2 1

PROLOGUE

A Land Forgotten

Of the original one hundred forty, could I be the last Sentinel? The grim thought swirled through Dhakal's mind.

The invaders' main force had overrun his country from the east eight weeks earlier with brutal speed and cruelty. Cavalry and foot soldiers poured from the hills and swarmed into the valleys, razed the villages to the ground, and slaughtered all who stood before them.

Along with the armies came elite bands of soldiers tasked with a single mission: locate the sacred Theurang and bring it to their King. Having foreseen this, the Sentinels, whose duty was to protect the holy relic, removed it from its place of reverence and spirited it away.

Dhakal slowed his horse to a trot, slipped off the trail through a break in the trees, and stopped in a small shaded clearing. He climbed from the saddle, allowing his horse to wander to a nearby stream and bend its head to drink. He moved behind the horse to check the series of leather bands that secured the cube-shaped chest to the animal's rump. As always, his cargo was held fast.

The chest was a marvel, so solidly built that it could withstand a high fall onto a rock or repeated bludgeoning without showing the slightest crack. The locks were many, hidden and ingeniously designed to make them all but impossible to open.

Of the ten Sentinels in Dhakal's cadre, none had the resources or ability to open this unique chest, nor did any of them know whether its contents were genuine or a substitute. That honor, or perhaps curse, belonged solely to Dhakal. How he had been chosen was not revealed to him. But he alone knew that this sacred chest carried the revered Theurang. Soon, with luck, he would find a safe place to hide it.

For nearly the past nine weeks he'd been on the run, escaping the capital with his cadre just hours ahead of the invaders. For two days, as the smoke from their burning homes and fields filled the sky behind them, they raced south on horseback. On the third day they split up, each Sentinel heading in his predetermined direction, most heading away from the invaders' line of advance, but some back toward it. These brave men were either already dead or suffering at the hands of their enemy who, having captured each Sentinel's decoy cargo, were demanding to know how to gain access to his chest. As designed, this was an answer none of them could give.

As for Dhakal, his orders had taken him due east, into the rising sun, a direction he'd maintained for the past sixty-one days. The land in which he now found himself was very different from the arid, mountainous terrain in which he was raised. Here there were mountains too, but they were covered in thick forest and separated by lake-pocked valleys. It made staying hidden much easier, but it had also slowed his progress. The terrain was a double-edged sword: skilled ambushers could be upon him before he had a chance to run.

Thus far he'd had many close calls, but his training had seen him through each one. Five times he'd watched, hidden, as his pursuers rode within feet of him, and twice he'd fought a pitched battle with enemy cavalry squads. Though outnumbered and exhausted, he'd left these men dead, their bodies and equipment buried and their horses scattered.

For the past three days he'd not seen or heard any sign of his pursuers. Nor had he come across many local people; those he did encounter paid him little attention. His face and stature were similar to theirs. His instincts told him to ride on, that he hadn't put enough distance between himself and—

From across the stream, perhaps fifty yards away, came the crack of a branch in the trees. Anyone else would have dismissed it, but Dhakal knew the sound of a horse pushing through heavy brush. His own horse had stopped drinking, its head raised and ears twitching.

From the trail, another sound, the scuff of a horse's hoof on the gravel trail. Dhakal pulled the bow from the sheath on his back and an arrow from the quiver, then crouched down in the knee-high water grass. Partially blocked by the horse's legs, Dhakal peeked under the animal's belly, looking for signs of movement. There was nothing. He turned his head right. Through the trees he could just make out the narrow trail. He watched, waited.

Then, another hoof scuff.

Dhakal nocked an arrow and drew the bow slightly, taking up the tension.

A few moments later a horse appeared on the trail, cantering slowly. The horse stopped. Dhakal could see only the rider's legs and his black-gloved hands resting on the saddle's pommel, reins gripped loosely in his fingers. The hand moved, jerked the reins slightly. Beneath him, the horse whinnied and stamped its hoof.

An intentional move, Dhakal realized immediately. A distraction.

The attackers would be coming from the forest side.

Dhakal drew the bow fully, took aim, and let fly the arrow. The point pierced the man's leg in the crease between his upper thigh and hip. He screamed, clutched his leg, and toppled off his horse. Instinctively, Dhakal knew his aim was true. The arrow had punctured the leg artery; the man was out of the fight and would be dead within minutes.

Still crouching, Dhakal spun on his back heel while retrieving three more arrows from his quiver; two he planted in the ground before him, the third he nocked. There, thirty feet away, were three attackers, swords drawn, creeping through the underbrush toward him. Dhakal took aim on the trailing figure and fired. The man went down. In rapid succession he fired twice more, catching one man squarely in the chest, the next in the throat. A fourth warrior let out a war cry and charged from behind a copse of trees. He almost reached the edge of the stream before Dhakal's arrow dropped him.

The forest fell silent.

Four? Dhakal thought. They had never sent fewer than a dozen before.

As if in answer to his puzzlement, the pounding of horses' hooves sounded on the trail behind him. Dhakal spun, saw a line of horses galloping down the trail past their fallen comrade. Three horses . . . four . . . seven . . . Ten horses and still they came. The odds were overwhelming. Dhakal mounted his horse, nocked an arrow, and turned in his saddle in time to see the first horse galloping through the gap between the trees and into the clearing. Dhakal fired. The arrow plunged into the man's right eye. The force drove him backward, over his saddle, where he bumped off the rump of his horse and into the next rider, whose horse reared, backpedaling, creating a choke point. Horses began slamming into one another. The charge stalled.

Dhakal kicked his heels into his horse's flanks. The animal leapt off the bank into the water. Dhakal brought its head around, heeled the horse, and charged downriver.

He realized this was no chance ambush. His pursuers had been covertly following him for some time and had managed to surround him.

Over the splashing of his horse's hooves in the shallow water he could hear them now: riders crashing through the forest to his right and hooves on the gravel trail to his left.

Ahead, the stream curved to the right. The trees and undergrowth were thicker here, crowding the bank, all but blotting out the sun and leaving him in twilight. He heard a shout and glanced over his shoulder. Four riders were in pursuit. He looked right, saw dark horse shapes slipping in and out of the trees, paralleling his course. They were flushing him, he realized. But to where?

His answer came seconds later as the trees suddenly parted and he found himself in a meadow. The stream's width quadrupled; the color of the water told him the depth had increased as well. On impulse, he veered his horse left, toward the sandy bank. Directly ahead, a line of five riders burst from the tree line, two of them bent low, pikes held horizontally before them, the other three riding upright, bows drawn. He laid his body across his horse's neck and jerked the reins to the right, back into the water. On the opposite bank, another line of riders had emerged from the trees, these too armed with pikes and bows. And to complete the ambush, directly behind, galloping down the stream toward him, was yet another line of cavalry.

As if on cue, all three groups slowed to a trot, then

stopped. Pikes still at the ready and arrows nocked, they watched him.

Why aren't they following? he wondered.

And then he heard it, the deafening rush of water. Waterfall.

I am caught. Trapped.

He reined back and let the horse walk until they reached a bend in the river. He stopped. Here the water was deeper and moving fast. Fifty yards ahead Dhakal could see the mist plume billowing over the surface, could see the water boiling over the rocks at the rim of the cataract.

He turned in his saddle.

His pursuers had not moved save a single rider. The man's armor told Dhakal this was the leader of the group. The man stopped twenty feet away and raised his hands to his shoulders, signaling he was unarmed.

He shouted something. Dhakal did not understand the language, but the tone was clear: placation. *It is over,* the man was surely saying. *You have fought well, done your duty. Surrender, and you will be treated fairly.*

It was a lie. He would be tortured and eventually killed. He would die fighting before he would let the Theurang fall into the hands of his accursed enemy.

Dhakal turned his horse until he was facing the pursuers. With exaggerated slowness, he drew the bow from his back and tossed it into the river. He did the same with his quiver, followed by his long sword and short sword. Finally the dagger in his belt.

The enemy leader gave Dhakal a nod of respect, then turned in his saddle and shouted something to his men. Slowly, one by one, the riders raised their pikes and sheathed their bows. The leader turned back to Dhakal and raised his hand, gesturing for him to come forward.

Dhakal gave him a smile and a shake of his head.

He jerked his reins hard to the right, whipping his horse around, then heeled it hard in the flanks. The horse reared, coiled its legs beneath it, and began thrashing toward the spray rising above the deep waterfall.

FRONTIER WASTELANDS
OF XIZANG PROVINCE, QING
EMPIRE, CHINA, 1677

Giuseppe saw the dust cloud on the eastern horizon before his brother did. A mile wide and confined by the walls of a narrow valley, the swirling brown wall of dirt and sand was headed directly for them.

Eyes fixed on the spectacle, Giuseppe tapped his older brother on the shoulder. Francesco Lana de Terzi of Brescia, Lombardy, Italy, turned from his kneeling position, where he'd been studying a sheaf of blueprints, and looked in the direction Giuseppe was pointing.

The younger Lana de Terzi whispered nervously, "Is it a storm?"

"Of sorts," Francesco replied. "But not the kind you

mean." Behind that dust cloud was not another wind-whipped sandstorm, the kind they'd grown so accustomed to over the last six months, but rather hundreds of pounding horses' hooves. And atop the horses, hundreds of elite and deadly soldiers.

Francesco gave Giuseppe a reassuring clap on the shoulder. "Do not worry, brother, I have been expecting them—though, I admit, not this early."

"It is him?" Giuseppe croaked. "He is coming? You did not tell me that."

"I didn't want to frighten you. Worry not. We still have time."

Francesco raised a flattened hand to shield his eyes from the sun and studied the approaching cloud. Distances were deceptive here, he had learned. The vastness of the Qing Empire lay far behind the horizon. In the two years they'd spent in this country, Francesco and his brother had seen a wild variety of terrain—from jungles to forests to deserts—but of all of them, this place, this territory that seemed to have a dozen different pronunciations and spellings, was the most godforsaken.

Composed mostly of hills, some rolling and some jagged, the land was a vast canvas painted in only two colors: brown and gray. Even the water of rivers that gushed through the valleys was a dull gray. It was as though God had cursed this place with a swipe of his mighty hand. On days when the clouds parted, the startlingly blue sky seemed only to accent the ashen landscape.

And then there was the wind, Francesco thought with a shudder. The seemingly endless wind that whistled through the rocks and drove eddies of dust along the ground and that seemed so animated the locals often treated the phenomena like ghosts come to snatch away their souls. Six months ago, Francesco, a scientist by nature and training, had scoffed at such superstitions. Now he wasn't so sure. He had heard too many strange sounds in the night.

Another few days, he consoled himself, and we will have the resources we need. But it wasn't simply a matter of time, was it? He was making a bargain with the devil. The fact that he was doing it for the larger good was something he hoped God would remember when Judgment Day came.

He studied the approaching wall of dust a few seconds more before lowering his hand and turning to Giuseppe. "They are still twenty miles away," he estimated. "We have another hour, at least. Come, let us finish."

Francesco turned back around and shouted to one of the men, a squat, powerful figure in a roughly woven black tunic and trousers. Hao, Francesco's primary liaison and translator, jogged over.

"Yes, sire!" he said in heavily accented but passable Italian.

Francesco sighed. Though he'd long ago given up trying to get Hao to call him by his first name, he had hoped that at least by now the man would have ceased with the formality.

"Tell the men to finish quickly. Our guest will be arriving soon."

Hao cast an eye to the horizon and saw what Giuseppe

had pointed out a few minutes earlier. His eyes widened. He nodded curtly, said, "It will be done, sire!" then turned around and began barking orders to the dozens of local men milling around the hilltop clearing. He scurried off to join in.

The clearing, which measured a hundred paces square, was in fact the roof of a gompa's interior courtyard. On all sides of the clearing, its turreted walls and watchtowers followed the hill's ridges down to the valley floor like spines on a lizard's back.

While Francesco had been told a gompa was primarily a fortified center for education, the residents of this particular stronghold seemed to practice only one profession: soldiering. And for that, he was grateful. As evidenced by the frequent raids and skirmishes that took place on the plains below, it was clear he and his men were living on this realm's frontier. It was no accident that they had been transported here to complete work on the machine—what their benefactor had dubbed the *Great Dragon.*

The clearing now echoed with the overlapping pounding of mallets on wood as Hao's workers hurried to drive the final stakes into the rocky soil. All across the clearing, plumes of brown dust rose into the air, only to be caught by the wind and whipped into nothingness. After another ten minutes the mallets fell silent. Hao scrambled back to where Francesco and Giuseppe stood.

"We are done, sire."

Francesco backed up a few steps and admired the structure. He was pleased. Designing it on paper was one thing; to see it come to life was something else altogether.

Standing forty feet tall, occupying three-quarters of the clearing, and constructed of snow-white silk, with curved exterior bamboo braces painted bloodred, the tent seemed like a castle built of clouds.

"Well done," Francesco told Hao. "Giuseppe?"

"Magnificent," the younger Lana de Terzi murmured.

Francesco nodded, and said softly, "Now, let us hope what is inside is even more impressive."

Though the gompa's hawkeyed lookouts had certainly spotted the visitors approaching even before Giuseppe had, the alert horns did not sound until the retinue was but minutes away. This, as well as the riders' direction of approach and early arrival, was a tactical decision, Francesco guessed. Most of the enemy's outposts lay to the west. By coming in from the east, the party's dust cloud would be obscured by the hill on which the gompa sat. This way, roving ambush parties would have no time to intercept the new arrivals. Knowing their benefactor as he did, Francesco suspected they had been covertly watching the gompa from a distance, waiting for the wind direction to change and enemy patrols to move on.

A cunning man, their patron, Francesco reminded himself. Cunning and dangerous.

Less than ten minutes later Francesco heard the crunching of leather and armored boots on the spiral gravel path below the clearing. Swirling dust rose above the rock-lined border of the clearing. Then, suddenly, silence. Though Francesco was expecting it, what came next startled him all the same.

With a single barked command from an unseen mouth, a cadre of two dozen Home Guard soldiers double-timed into the clearing, each syncopated footstep punctuated by a rhythmic grunt. Grim-faced, eyes fixed on the horizon, their pikes held horizontally before them, the guards spread out through the clearing and began herding the awestruck workers to its far side and out of sight behind the tent. Once done, they took up stations along the clearing's perimeter, spaced at regular intervals, facing outward, pikes held diagonally across their bodies.

Again from the path below, another guttural command, followed by armored sandals crunching on gravel. A diamond-shaped formation of royal bodyguards in red-and-black bamboo armor marched into the clearing and headed directly toward where Francesco and Giuseppe stood. The phalanx stopped suddenly, and the soldiers foreside stepped to the left and right, opening a human gate, through which a single man strode.

Standing three hand widths taller than his tallest soldiers, the Kangxi Emperor—the Ruler of the Qing Dynasty, the Regent of the Mandate of Heaven—wore an expression that made the grimness of his soldiers' faces seem positively exuberant.

The Kangxi Emperor took three long strides toward Francesco and came to a stop. Through squinted eyes, he studied the Italian's face for several seconds before speaking. Francesco was about to call for Hao to translate, but the man was already there, standing at his elbow and whispering in his ear: "The Emperor says, 'Are you surprised to see me?'"

"Surprised, yes, but pleased nonetheless, Your Majesty."

The question was not a casual inquiry, Francesco knew. The Kangxi Emperor was paranoid in the extreme; had Francesco not seemed sufficiently surprised at the Emperor's early arrival he would have fallen under immediate suspicion of being a spy.

"What is this structure I see before me?" the Kangxi Emperor asked.

"It is a tent, Your Majesty, of my own design. It serves not only to protect the *Great Dragon* but also to shield it from prying eyes."

The Kangxi Emperor nodded curtly. "You will provide the plans to my personal secretary." With a raised fingertip, he commanded the secretary to step forward.

Francesco said, "Of course, Your Majesty."

"The slaves I provided you have performed adequately?"

Francesco winced inwardly at the Emperor's question but said nothing. Over the past six months he and Giuseppe had worked and lived with these men under hardship conditions. They were friends now. He did not confess this aloud, however. Such an emotional attachment would be a lever the Emperor would not hesitate to use.

"They have performed admirably, Your Majesty. Sadly, though, four of them died last week when—"

"That is the way of the world, death. If they died in service to their Emperor, their ancestors will greet them with pride."

"My foreman and translator, Hao, has been especially invaluable."

The Kangxi Emperor flicked his eyes at Hao, then back to Francesco. "The man's family will be released from prison." The Emperor raised his finger above his shoulder; the personal secretary made a notation on the parchment he cradled in his arms.

Francesco took a deep, calming breath and smiled. "Thank you, Your Majesty, for your kindness."

"Tell me: when will the *Great Dragon* be ready?"

"Another two days will—"

"You have until dawn tomorrow."

With that, the Kangxi Emperor turned on his heel and strode back into the phalanx, which closed in behind him, did a synchronized about-face, and marched from the clearing, followed moments later by the Home Guard soldiers from around the perimeter. Once the clomp of footsteps and the rhythmic grunting faded away, Giuseppe said, "Is he crazy? Tomorrow at dawn. How can we—"

"We will make it," Francesco replied. "With time to spare."

"How?"

"We have only a few more hours of work left. I told the Emperor two days, knowing he would demand the seemingly impossible. This way, we can give it to him."

Giuseppe smiled. "You are a crafty one, brother. Well done."

"Come, let us put the finishing touches on this *Great Dragon.*"

Under the glow of pole-mounted torches and the watchful gaze of the Emperor's personal secretary, who stood just inside the tent's entrance, arms folded inside his tunic, they worked through the night, with Hao, their ever-reliable foreman, playing his part perfectly, haranguing the men to hurry, hurry, hurry. Francesco and Giuseppe did their part as well, walking through the tent, asking questions, bending down here and there to inspect this or that . . .

Ox-sinew guylines were unlashed, reknotted, then checked for tension; bamboo stays and cross braces were sounded with mallets to search for cracks; silk was closely examined for the slightest imperfections; the rattan-woven undercarriage underwent a mock attack with sharpened sticks to gauge its battle-readiness (finding it lacking, Francesco ordered another coat of black lacquer be applied to the walls and bulwarks); and finally the artist Giuseppe had hired finished the bow mural: a dragon's snout, complete with beaded eyes, bared fangs, and a protruding forked tongue.

As the sun's upper rim rose above the hills to the east, Francesco ordered that all work be quickly finished. Once this was done, he slowly circled the machine from bow to stern. Hands on his hips, head tilting this way and that, Francesco studied the ship's every surface, its every feature, looking for the slightest flaw. He found none. He returned to the bow and gave the Emperor's personal secretary a firm nod.

The man ducked under the tent flap and disappeared.

An hour later came the now familiar clomping and grunting of the Emperor's retinue. The sound seemed to fill the clearing before suddenly falling silent. Now dressed in a simple gray silk tunic, the Kangxi Emperor stepped through the tent's entrance, followed by his personal secretary and his chief bodyguard.

The Emperor stopped in his tracks, eyes wide.

In the two years he had known the Emperor, this was the first time Francesco had seen the potentate taken aback.

With the sun's pinkish orange light streaming through the tent's white silken walls and roof, the interior was bathed in an otherworldly glow. The normally earthen floor had been covered in jet-black rugs that left the attendees feeling as though they were standing at the edge of an abyss.

Scientist though he was, Francesco Lana de Terzi had a bit of showman in him.

The Kangxi Emperor stepped forward—unconsciously hesitating as his foot touched the edge of the black rug—then strode to the bow, where he gazed at the dragon's face. Now he smiled.

This was another first for Francesco. He'd never seen the Emperor without his characteristic dour expression.

The Emperor spun to face Francesco. "It is magnificent!" came Hao's translation. "Unleash her!"

"At your command, Majesty."

Once outside, Francesco's men took their stations around the tent. At his command, the tent's guylines were cut. Weighted along their upper hems, as Francesco had designed them, the silken walls collapsed straight down. Simultaneously, on the rear side of the tent, a dozen men heaved the tent's roof backward, which rose up and billowed open like a great sail before being hauled down and out of sight.

All was silent save the wind whipping through the gompa's turreted walls and windows.

Standing alone in the center of the clearing was the Kangxi Emperor's flying machine, the *Great Dragon*. Francesco cared nothing for this moniker; while he of course humored his benefactor, to Francesco the scientist the machine was merely a prototype for his dream: a true lighter-than-air Vacuum Ship.

Measuring fifty feet long, twelve feet wide, and thirty feet tall, the ship's upper structure was composed of four spheres of thick silk contained inside cages of finger-thin bamboo braces and animal sinew. Running from bow to stern, each sphere measured twelve feet in diameter and was equipped with a valve port in its belly; each of these ports was connected to a vertical copper stovepipe engirdled in its own lattice of bamboo and sinew. From the valve port, the stovepipe descended four feet to a thin bamboo plank to whose bottom was affixed a wind-shielded charcoal brazier. And finally, affixed by sinew to the spheres above was the black-lacquered rattan gondola, long enough to accommodate ten soldiers in a line, along with supplies, equipment, and weapons, as well as a pilot and navigator.

The Kangxi Emperor strode forward alone until he was standing beneath the fore sphere, facing the dragon's mouth. He raised his hands above his head as though he were beholding, Francesco thought, his own creation.

It was at this moment that the gravity of what he'd done hit him. A wave of sadness and shame washed over him. Truly, he had made a pact with the devil. This man, this cruel monarch, was going to use his *Great Dragon* to murder other human beings, soldiers and civilians alike.

Armed with *huǒ yào*, or gunpowder, a substance that Europe was only now using with moderate success and which China had long ago mastered, the Kangxi Emperor would be able to rain fire down upon his enemies using matchlock muskets, bombs, and fire-spitting devices. He could do all of this while out of reach in the sky and moving faster than the swiftest horse.

The truth had come too late, Francesco realized. The death machine was in the Kangxi Emperor's hands now. There was no changing that. Perhaps if he were able to make a success of his true Vacuum Ship, Francesco could balance out the evil to come. Of course, he would know that only on Judgment Day.

Francesco was shaken from his reverie as he realized the Kangxi Emperor was standing before him. "I am pleased," the Emperor informed him. "Once you have shown my generals how to build more of these, you will have all you require to pursue your own venture."

"Majesty."

"Is it ready to fly?"

"Give the command and it will be done."

"It is given. But first, a change. As planned, Master Lana de Terzi, you will pilot the *Great Dragon* on her test flight. Your brother will remain here with us."

"Pardon me, Majesty. Why?"

"Why, to ensure you return, of course. And to save you when you are tempted to hand over the *Great Dragon* to my enemies."

"Majesty, I would not—"

"And now we will be certain you will not."

"Majesty, Giuseppe is my copilot and navigator. I need him—"

"I have eyes and ears everywhere, Master Lana de Terzi. Your vaunted foreman, Hao, is as well trained as your brother. Hao will accompany you—along with six of my Home Guard, should you need . . . assistance."

"I must protest, Majesty—"

"You must not, Master Lana de Terzi," the Kangxi Emperor replied coldly. The warning was clear.

Francesco took a calming breath. "Where will you have me go on this test flight?"

"Do you see the mountains to the south, the great ones touching the heavens?"

"I do."

"You will travel there."

"Your Majesty, that is enemy territory!"

"What better test for a weapon of war?" Francesco opened his mouth to protest, but the Kangxi Emperor continued. "In the foothills, along the streams, you will find a golden flower—Hao knows the one I mean. Bring that flower back to me before it wilts and you will be rewarded."

"Your Majesty, those mountains are"—Forty miles away, Francesco thought. Perhaps fifty—"too far for a maiden voyage. Perhaps—"

"You will bring the flower back to me before it wilts or I will mount your brother's head on a spike. Do you understand?"

"I understand."

Francesco turned to his younger brother. Having heard the entire exchange, Giuseppe's face had gone ashen. His chin trembled. "Brother, I . . . I'm scared."

"No need. I'll be back before you know it."

Giuseppe took a breath, set his jaw, and squared his shoulders. "Yes. I know you are right. The craft is a wonder, and there is no one better at piloting it. With luck, we'll be sharing dinner together tonight."

"Good spirit," Francesco said.

They embraced for several seconds before Francesco pulled away. He turned to face Hao, and said, "Order the braziers stoked. We lift off in ten minutes!"

· 1 ·

Sunda Strait, Sumatra,
The Present Day

Sam Fargo eased back on the throttle, taking the engine to idle. The speedboat slowed, gliding to a stop in the water. He shut off the engines, and the craft began rocking gently from side to side.

A quarter mile off the bow their destination rose from the water, a thickly forested island whose interior was dominated by sharp peaks, plummeting valleys, and thick rain forest; below these, a shoreline pockmarked with hundreds of pocket coves and narrow inlets.

In the speedboat's aft seat, Remi Fargo looked up from her book—a little "escapist reading" entitled *The Aztec Codices: An Oral History of Conquest and Genocide*—pushed her sunglasses onto her forehead, and gazed at her husband. "Trouble?"

He turned to her and gave her an admiring stare.

"Just enjoying the scenic view." Then Sam gave an exaggerated wiggle of his eyebrows.

Remi smiled. "A smooth talker." She closed the book and placed it on the seat beside her. "But Magnum P.I., you're not."

Sam nodded at the book. "How is it?"

"Slow reading, but the Aztecs were fascinating people."

"More than anyone ever imagined. How long until you're finished with that one? It's next on my reading list."

"Tomorrow or the next day."

As of late, each of them had been saddled with a daunting amount of homework, and the island to which they were headed was largely the cause. In any other circumstances, the speck of land between Sumatra and Java might be a tropical getaway, but it had in the last few months been turned into a dig site crawling with archaeologists, historians, anthropologists, and of course a plethora of Indonesian government officials. Like all of them, each time Sam and Remi visited the island, they had to negotiate the tree house–like rope city the engineers had strung above the site lest the ground collapse below the feet of the people trying to preserve the find.

What Sam and Remi had discovered on Pulau Legundi was helping to rewrite Aztec and U.S. Civil War history, and as the directors of not only this project but also two others, they had to stay current on the mountain of data coming in.

It was for them a labor of love. While their passion was treasure hunting—a decidedly hands-on, field-intensive avocation based as much on instinct as it was on research—each of them had come to it from a scientific background, Sam a Caltech-educated engineer, Remi an anthropology and history major from Boston College.

Sam had fallen fairly close to the familial tree: his father, now passed away, had been one of the lead engineers on NASA's space programs, while his mother, Eunice, now seventy-one, lived in Key West, the sole proprietor, captain, and chief bottle washer of a snorkeling and deep-sea-fishing boat. Remi's mother and father, a custom homebuilder and a pediatrician/author respectively, were both retired and living the good life in Maine, raising llamas.

Sam and Remi had met in Hermosa Beach at a jazz bar called The Lighthouse. On a whim, Sam had stopped in for a cold beer, and he found Remi and some colleagues letting off steam after spending the past few weeks hunting for a sunken galleon off Abalone Cove.

Neither of them were starry-eyed enough to remember their first meeting as instant love, but the spark was undeniable; talking and laughing over drinks, they closed down The Lighthouse without noticing the hours slipping by. Six months later, they were married there in a small ceremony.

With Remi's encouragement, Sam had been pursuing an idea he'd been tinkering with, an argon laser scanner designed to detect and identify alloys at a distance, through soil and water alike. Treasure hunters, universities, corporations, mining outfits, and the Department of Defense came begging for licenses, checkbooks open, and within a couple years Fargo Group Ltd was turning a seven-figure profit. Four years later they accepted a buyout offer that left them undeniably wealthy, set for the rest of their lives. Instead of sitting back, however, they took a monthlong vacation, then established the Fargo Foundation, and set out on their first joint treasure hunt. The wealth recovered went to a long list of charities.

Now the Fargos stared in silence at the island before them. Remi murmured, "Still a little hard to fathom, isn't it?"

"Indeed it is," Sam agreed.

No amount of education or experience could have prepared them for what they'd found on Pulau Legundi. The chance discovery of a ship's bell off Zanzibar had mushroomed into discoveries that would occupy the attention of generations of archaeologists, historians, and anthropologists.

Sam was shaken from his reverie by the double whoop of a marine horn. He turned to port; half a mile away, a thirty-six-foot Sumatran Harbor Patrol boat was headed directly for them.

"Sam, did you forget to pay for gas back at the rental place?" Remi asked wryly.

"No. Used the counterfeit rupiah I had lying around."

"That might be it."

They watched as the boat closed the gap to a quarter mile, where it turned first to starboard, then to port in a crescent turn that brought it alongside them a hundred feet away. Over a loudspeaker, an Indonesian-accented voice said, in English, "Ahoy. Are you Sam and Remi Fargo?"

Sam raised his arm in the affirmative.

"Stand by, please. We have a passenger for you."

Sam and Remi exchanged puzzled glances; they were expecting no one.

The Harbor Patrol boat circled them once, closing the distance, until they were three feet off the port beam. The engine slowed to idle, then went silent.

"At least they look friendly," Sam muttered to his wife.

The last time they'd been approached by a foreign naval vessel had been in Zanzibar. There it had been a patrol boat equipped with 12.7mm cannons and crewed by angry-looking sailors bearing AK-47s.

"So far," Remi replied.

On the boat's afterdeck, standing between two blue-uniformed police officers, was a petite Asian woman in her mid-forties with a lean angular face and a hairdo that bordered on being a crew cut.

"Permission to come aboard?" the woman asked. Her English was almost flawless, with only the barest trace of an accent.

Sam shrugged. "Permission granted."

The two policemen stepped forward as though preparing to help her cross the gap, but she ignored them, taking a single fluid stride that vaulted her off the gunwale and onto the Fargos' afterdeck. She landed softly, cat-like. She turned to face Sam and Remi, who was now standing at her husband's side. The woman stared at them a moment with a pair of impassive black eyes, then handed them a business card. It said simply "Zhilan Hsu."

"What can we do for you, Ms. Hsu?" asked Remi.

"My employer, Charles King, requests the pleasure of your company."

"Our apologies, but we're not familiar with Mr. King."

"He is waiting for you aboard his private aircraft at the private charter terminal outside Palembang. He wishes to speak with you."

While Zhilan Hsu's English was technically flawless, there was a disconcerting stiffness to it, as though she were an automaton.

"That part we understand," Sam said. He handed the card back to her. "Who is Charles King and why does he want to see us?"

"Mr. King has authorized me to tell you it concerns an acquaintance of yours, Mr. Frank Alton."

This got Sam's and Remi's attention. Alton was not just an acquaintance but rather a close, longtime friend, a former San Diego police officer turned private detective Sam had met in judo class. Sam, Remi, Frank, and his wife, Judy, had a standing monthly dinner date.

"What about him?" Sam asked.

"Mr. King wishes to speak to you directly regarding Mr. Alton."

"You're being very secretive, Ms. Hsu," Remi said. "Care to tell us why?"

"Mr. King wishes to—"

"Speak with us directly," Remi finished.

"Yes, that is right."

Sam checked his watch. "Please tell Mr. King we will meet him at seven o'clock."

"That is four hours from now," said Zhilan. "Mr. King—"

"Is going to have to wait," Sam finished. "We have business we need to attend to."

Zhilan Hsu's stoic expression flashed to anger, but the look was gone almost as soon as it appeared. She simply nodded and said, "Seven o'clock. Please be on time."

Without another word, she turned and leapt gazelle-like off the deck to the Harbor Patrol boat's gunwale. She pushed past the policemen and disappeared into the cabin. One of the policemen tipped his cap to them. Ten seconds later the engines growled to life and the boat pulled away.

"Well, that was interesting," Sam said a few seconds later.

"She's a real charmer," Remi said. "Did you catch her choice of words?"

Sam nodded. "'Mr. King has authorized.' If she understands the connotation, then we can assume Mr. King is going to be just as genial."

"Do you believe her? About Frank? Judy would have called us if anything had happened."

While their adventures often led them into dicey situations, their daily lives were fairly calm. Still, Zhilan Hsu's unexpected visit and mysterious invitation had both their internal warning alarms going off. As unlikely as it seemed, the possibility of a trap was something they couldn't ignore.

"Let's find out." Sam said.

He knelt down by the driver's seat, retrieved his backpack from under the dashboard, and pulled out his satellite phone from one of the side pockets. He dialed, and a few seconds later a female voice said, "Yes, Mr. Fargo?"

"Thought this was going to be the lucky call," Sam said. He had a running bet with Remi that someday he'd catch Selma Wondrash off guard, and she'd call either of them by the first name.

"Not today, Mr. Fargo."

Their chief researcher, logistical guru, and keeper of the inner sanctum, Selma was a former Hungarian citizen who, despite having lived in the United States for decades, still retained a trace of an accent—enough that it gave her voice a slight Zsa Zsa Gabor lilt.

Selma had managed the Library of Congress's Special Collections Division until Sam and Remi lured her away with the promise of carte blanche and state-of-the-art resources. Aside from her hobby aquarium and a collection of tea that occupied an entire cabinet in the workroom, Selma's only passion was research. She was at her happiest when the Fargos gave her an ancient riddle to unravel.

"Someday, you'll call me Sam."

"Not today."

"What time is it there?"

"About eleven." Selma rarely went to bed before midnight and rarely slept past four or five in the morning. Despite this, she never sounded anything less than wide awake. "What have you got for me?"

"A dead end, we're hoping," Sam replied, then recounted their visit from Zhilan Hsu. "Charles King comes off like the anointed one."

"I've heard of him. He's rich with a capital *R*."

"See if you can dig up any dirt about his personal life."

"Anything else?"

"Have you heard any news from the Altons?"

"No, nothing," replied Selma.

"Call Judy and see if Frank's out of the country," Sam requested. "Look into it discreetly. If there is a problem, we don't want to alarm Judy."

"When do you meet King?" Selma asked.

"In four hours."

"Got it," Selma said with a laugh in her voice. "By then, I'll know his shirt size and his favorite flavor of ice cream."

2

Palembang, Sumatra

Twenty minutes early for their meeting, Sam and Remi pulled their scooters to a stop beside the hurricane fence bordering Palembang Airport's private terminal area. As Selma had predicted, they found the tarmac before the hangars crowded with a handful of private planes, all of them either single- or twin-engine prop models. Save one: a Gulfstream G650 jet. At sixty-five million dollars, the G6 was not only the world's most expensive executive jet but also the fastest, capable of nearly a Mach 1 top speed, with a range of over eight thousand miles and a ceiling of fifty-one thousand feet—ten thousand feet higher than commercial jets.

Given what Selma had discovered about the mysterious Mr. King, the presence of the G6 was of little surprise to Sam and Remi. "King Charlie," as he was known to his close friends and enemies alike, was currently ranked eleventh on *Forbes*'s Richest People list, with a net worth of 23.2 billion dollars.

Having started out in 1964 as a sixteen-year-old wildcatter in the oil fields of Texas, King had by the age of twenty-one started his own drilling company, King Oil. By twenty-four, he was a millionaire; by thirty, a billionaire. Through the eighties and nineties, King expanded his empire into mining and banking. According to *Forbes*, if King spent the rest of his life playing checkers in his penthouse office in Houston, he would still be earning a hundred thousand dollars an hour in interest.

For all that, however, King was in his daily life unostentatious to a fault, often tooling around Houston in his 1968 Chevy pickup and eating at his favorite greasy spoon. And while not quite at the same level as Howard Hughes, he was rumored to be something of a recluse and a stickler for privacy. King was rarely photographed in public, and when he did attend events, whether business or social, he usually did so virtually via webcam.

Remi looked at Sam. "The tail number matches Selma's research. Unless someone stole King's jet, it appears the man himself is here."

"The question is, why?"

In addition to giving them a brief biography of King, Selma had done her best to trace Frank Alton, who, according to his secretary, was out of the country on a job. While she hadn't heard from him for ten days, she was unconcerned; Alton often dropped from communication for a week or two if the job was particularly complex.

They heard a branch snap behind them and turned to find Zhilan Hsu on the other side of the fence only five feet away. Her legs and lower torso were hidden by foliage. She regarded the Fargos with her black eyes for a few seconds, then said, "You are early." Her tone was slightly less severe than that of a prosecuting attorney.

"And you're light on your feet," Remi said.

"I've been watching for you."

Sam said with a half smile, "Didn't your mother ever tell you it's not nice to sneak up on people?"

Zhilan's face remained stoic. "I never knew my mother."

"I'm sorry—"

"Mr. King is ready to see you now; he must depart promptly at seven-fifty. I will meet you at the gate on the eastern side. Please have your passports ready."

With that, Zhilan turned, stepped into the bushes, and disappeared.

Eyes narrowed, Remi stared after her. "Okay, it's official: she's creepy."

"Seconded," Sam said. "Let's go. King Charlie awaits."

They pulled their scooters into a spot beside the cross-barred gate and walked up to a small outer building where Zhilan was standing beside a uniformed guard. She stepped forward, collected their passports, and handed them to the guard, who glanced at each before handing them back.

"This way, please," Zhilan said, and led them around the building, through a pedestrian gate, then to the Gulfstream's lowered stairs. Zhilan stepped aside and gestured for them to continue on. Once aboard, they found themselves in a small but neatly appointed galley. To the right, through an archway, was the main cabin. The bulkheads were covered in lustrous walnut inlaid with silver teacup-sized Texas Lone Star emblems, the floor in thick burgundy carpet. There were two seating areas, one a grouping of four leather recliner-type seats around a coffee table, the second, aft, a trio of overstuffed settees. The air was crisp and air-conditioned. Faintly, through unseen speakers, came Willie Nelson's "Mammas Don't Let Your Babies Grow Up to Be Cowboys."

"Oh, boy," Remi muttered.

Somewhere aft, a voice with a Texas twang said, "I think the fancy word for all this is 'cliché,' Mizz Fargo, but, heck, I like what I like."

From one of the backward-facing leather recliners a man rose and turned to face them. He was six foot four, two hundred pounds—nearly half was muscle—with a tan face and thick, carefully styled silver-blond hair. Though Sam and Remi knew Charles King was sixty-two, he looked fifty. He smiled broadly at them; his teeth were square and startlingly white.

"Once Texas gets into your blood," King said, "it's near impossible to get it out. Believe me, I've had four wives do their damnedest, with no luck."

Hand outstretched, King strode toward them. He wore blue jeans, a faded powder blue denim shirt, and, to Sam's and Remi's surprise, Nike running shoes rather than cowboy boots.

King didn't miss their expressions. "Never liked those boots. Uncomfortable as hell, and impractical. Besides, all the horses I got are for racin', and I ain't exactly jockey-sized." He shook Remi's hand first, then Sam's. "Thanks so much for comin'. Hope Zee didn't put you off. She ain't much for small talk."

"She'd make a good poker player," Sam agreed.

"Hell, she is a good poker player. Took me for six thousand bucks in ten minutes the first—and last—time we played. Come on in, take a seat. Let's get you somethin' to drink. What'll you have?"

"Bottled water, please," Remi said, and Sam nodded for the same.

"Zee, if you don't mind. I'll have the usual."

From close behind Sam and Remi, Zhilan said, "Yes, Mr. King."

They followed him aft to the settee area and sat down. Zhilan was only seconds behind them with a tray. She placed Sam's and Remi's waters before them and held out a whiskey-rocks to King. He did not accept the tumbler but simply stared at it. He scowled, glanced at Zhilan, and shook his head. "How many ice cubes in there, honey?"

"Three, Mr. King," Zhilan said hastily. "I'm sorry, I—"

"Don't give it a second thought, Zee, just plop another one in there, and I'll be fine." Zhilan hurried off, and King said, "No matter how many times I tell her, she still forgets sometimes. Jack Daniel's is a fickle spirit; gotta get the ice just right or it ain't worth a damn."

Sam said, "I'll take your word for it."

"You're a wise man, Mr. Fargo."

"Sam."

"Suit yourself. Call me Charlie."

King stared at them, a pleasant smile fixed on his face, until Zhilan returned with his now correctly cubed drink. She stood at his side, waiting as he tasted it. "That's my girl," he said. "Run along, now." To the Fargos: "How goes your dig on that little island? What's it called?"

"Pulau Legundi," Sam replied.

"Yeah, that's right. Some kind of—"

"Mr. King—"

"Charlie."

"Zhilan Hsu mentioned a friend of ours, Frank Alton. Let's save the small talk for now; tell us about Frank."

"You're also a direct man. You share that quality too, I'm guessin', Remi?"

Neither of them replied, but Remi gave him a sweet smile.

King shrugged. "Okay, fair enough. I hired Alton a few weeks ago to look into a matter for me. Seems he's up and disappeared. *Poof!* Since you two seem to be good at findin' what ain't easily found, and you're friends of his, I thought I'd touch base with you."

"When did you last hear from him?" Remi asked.

"Ten days ago."

"Frank tends to be a bit independent when he's working," Sam said. "Why do you—"

"Because he was to check in with me every day. That was part of our deal, and he stuck to it until ten days ago."

"Do you have any reason to think something's amiss?"

"You mean, aside from him breakin' his promise to me?" King replied with a hint of annoyance. "Aside from him takin' my money and disappearin'?"

"For argument's sake."

"Well, the part of the world he's in can be a tad hairy sometimes."

"And that is?" Remi asked.

"Nepal."

"Pardon? You said—"

"Yep. Last I heard, he was in Kathmandu. Sort of a backwater burg, but it can be tough if you ain't got your wits about you."

Sam asked, "Who else knows about this?"

"A handful of folks."

"Frank's wife?"

King shook his head, took a sip of whiskey. He screwed up his face. "Zee!"

Zhilan was at his side five seconds later. "Yes, Mr. King?"

He handed her the tumbler. "Ice is meltin' too fast. Get rid of it."

"Yes, Mr. King."

And then she was gone again.

Scowling, King watched her walk away, then turned back to the Fargos. "Sorry, you were sayin'?"

"Have you told Frank's wife?"

"Didn't know he had one. He didn't give me emergency contact info. Besides, why worry her? For all I know, Alton's taken up with some Oriental woman and is gallivantin' around down there on my dime."

"Frank Alton wouldn't do that," Remi said.

"Maybe, maybe not."

"Have you contacted the Nepalese government?" asked Sam. "Or the American embassy in Kathmandu?"

King gave a dismissive wave of his hand. "Backward, all of 'em. And corrupt—the locals, that is. As for the embassy idea, I considered it, but I ain't got the months it would take for them to get their butts in gear. I've got my own people on the ground there workin' on another project, but they ain't got the time to spend on this. And, like I said, you two have got a reputation for findin' what other folks can't."

Sam said, "First of all, Charlie, people aren't things. Second, hunting for missing persons isn't our specialty." King opened his mouth to speak, but Sam raised his hand and went on: "That said, Frank's a good friend, so of course we'll go."

"Fantastic!" King slapped his knee. "Let's talk nuts and bolts: how much is this gonna cost me?"

Sam grinned. "We're going to assume you're kidding."

"About money? Never."

"Because he's a good friend, we'll foot the bill," Remi said with a little edge to her voice. "We'll need all the information you can give us."

"Zee's already put together a file. She'll give it to you on the way out."

"Give us the condensed version," Sam said.

"It's a bit of a wheels-within-wheels situation," King said. "I hired Alton to hunt down someone who'd disappeared in the same region."

"Who?"

"My dad. When he first disappeared, I sent a string of folks out to look for him, but nothin' came of it. It's like he fell off the face of the earth. When this latest sighting came up, I beat the bushes for the best private eye I could find. Alton came highly recommended."

"You said 'latest sighting,'" Remi observed. "What does that mean?"

"Since my dad disappeared, there've been rumors of him popping up from time to time: a dozen or so times in the seventies, four times in the eighties—"

Sam interrupted. "Charlie, exactly how long has your father been missing?"

"Thirty-eight years. He disappeared in 1973."

Lewis "Bully" King, Charles explained, was something of an Indiana Jones type, but long before the movies came out: an archaeologist who spent eleven months out of the year in the field; a globe-trotting academic who'd visited more countries than most people knew existed. What exactly his father was doing when he disappeared, Charles King didn't know.

"Who was he affiliated with?" Remi asked.

"Not sure what you mean."

"Did he work for a university or museum? Perhaps a foundation?"

"Nope. He was a square peg, my pop. Didn't go for all that stuff."

"How did he fund his expeditions?"

King offered them an aw-shucks smile. "He had a generous and gullible donor. To be fair, though, he never asked for much: five thousand here and there. Workin' alone, he didn't have much overhead, and he knew how to live cheap. Most of the places he traveled, you could live for a few bucks a day."

"Did he have a home?"

"A little place in Monterey. I never sold it. Never did anything with it, in fact. It's still mostly the way it was when he went missin'. And, yeah, I know what you're gonna ask. Back in '73 I had some people go through his house lookin' for clues, but they didn't find nothin'. You're welcome to look for yourselves, though. Zee'll get you the info."

"Did Frank go there?"

"No, he didn't think it'd be worth it."

"Tell us about the latest sighting," Sam said.

"About six weeks ago a *National Geographic* crew was doing some spread on an old city out there—Lo Manta somethin' or another—"

"Lo Monthang," Remi offered.

"Yeah, that's the place. Used to be the capital of Mustang."

Like most people, King pronounced the name as he would the horse.

"It's pronounced Moos-tong," Remi replied. "It was also known as the Kingdom of Lo, before it was absorbed by Nepal in the eighteenth century."

"Whatever you say. Never did like that sort of stuff. Fell kind of far from the tree, I guess. Anyway, in one of the photos they took there's this guy in the background. A dead ringer for my dad—or at least how I think he'd look after nearly forty years."

"That's not much to go on," Sam said.

"It's all I've got. Still wanna take a crack at it?"

"Of course we do."

Sam and Remi stood up to leave. They shook hands all around. "Zee's got my contact info in there. You'll be giving her updates. Let me know what you find. I'd appreciate regular reports. Good huntin', Fargos."

Charles King stood in the doorway of his Gulfstream and watched the Fargos return through the gate, mount their scooters, then disappear down the road. Zhilan Hsu came walking back through the gate, trotted up the plane's stairs, and stopped in front of King.

"I do not like them," she said.

"And why is that?"

"They do not show you enough respect."

"I can do without that, darlin'. Just as long as they

live up to their reputation. From what I've read, those two have a real knack for this kind of thing."

"And if they go beyond what we ask of them?"

"Well, hell, that's why I've got you, ain't it?"

"Yes, Mr. King. Shall I go there now?"

"No, let's let things unfold natural-like. Get Russ on the horn, will ya?"

King walked aft and dropped into one of the recliners with a grunt. A minute later Zhilan's voice came over the intercom. "I have him ready for you, Mr. King. Please stand by."

King waited for the warbled squelch that told him the satellite line was open. "Russ, you there?"

"I'm here."

"How's the dig goin'?"

"On track. Had some problems with a local making a fuss, but we took care of him. Marjorie's in the pit right now, cracking the whip."

"I'll bet she is! She's a pistol. Just keep a sharp eye out for them inspectors. They ain't supposed to show up outta the blue. I'm paying outta my ears as it is. Anything extra I'm takin' outta your salary."

"I've got it under control."

"Good. Now, tell me somethin' good. Find anything juicy?"

"Not yet. But we came across some trace fossils that our expert says are promising."

"Yeah, well, I've heard that before. You forgettin' about that con man in Perth?"

"No, sir."

"The one who told you he had one of them Malagasy dwarf hippo fossils? He was supposed to be an expert too."

"And I handled him, didn't I?"

King paused. His scowl faded, and he chuckled. "That you did. But listen up, son. I want one of them *Calico* whatchamacallits. A real one."

"Chalicotherium," Russ corrected.

"I don't give a damn what it's called! Latin! God save me. Just get me one! I already told that no-good Don Mayfield I got one comin', and I got a space all ready for it. We clear?"

"Yes, sir, we're clear."

"Okay, then. New business: just met with our newest recruits. Sharp operators, the both of 'em. I imagine they ain't gonna waste much time. With any luck, they'll probably have a poke around the Monterey place, then head your way. I'll let you know when they're in the air."

"Yes, sir."

"Make sure you keep a tight leash on 'em, you hear me? If they get away from you, I'll have your hide."

3

Goldfish Point, La Jolla,
near San Diego, California

After parting company with King, Sam and Remi had returned to Pulau Legundi, where, as expected, they found Professor Stan Dydell surveying the site. Remi's former teacher at Boston College had taken a sabbatical to participate in the multiple excavations. After hearing their news about Alton, Dydell agreed to oversee the dig until they returned or found a permanent replacement.

Thirty-six hours and three connections later they landed in San Diego at noon local time. Sam and Remi had driven straight to the Alton home to break the news to Frank's wife. Now, with their luggage deposited in their own home's foyer, they'd made their way downstairs to Selma's domain, the workroom.

Measuring two thousand square feet, the high-ceilinged space was dominated by a twenty-foot-long maple-topped worktable lit from above by halogen pendant lamps and surrounded by high-backed stools. Along one wall was a trio of half cubicles—each equipped with a brand-new 12-core Mac Pro workstation and a thirty-inch Cinema HD Display—a pair of glassed-in offices, one each for Sam and Remi, an environmentally controlled archive vault, a small screening room, and a research library. The opposite wall was dedicated to Selma's only hobby: a fourteen-foot, five-hundred-gallon saltwater aquarium filled with a rainbow-hued assortment of fish. Its soft gurgling lent the workroom a mellow ambience.

Above the first-floor work space, the Fargos' home was a three-story, twelve-thousand-square-foot Spanish-style house with an open floor plan, vaulted ceilings, and enough windows and skylights that they rarely had their lights on for more than a couple hours a day. What electricity they did draw was primarily supplied by a robust array of newly installed solar panels on the roof.

The top floor contained Sam and Remi's master suite. Directly below this were four guest suites, a living room, a dining room, and a kitchen/great room that jutted over the cliff and overlooked the ocean. On the second floor was a gymnasium containing both aerobic and circuit training exercise equipment, a steam room, a HydroWorx endless lap pool, a climbing wall, and a thousand square feet of hardwood floor space for Remi to practice her fencing and Sam his judo.

Sam and Remi took a pair of stools at one corner of the worktable. Selma joined them. She wore her traditional work attire: khaki pants, sneakers, a tie-dyed T-shirt, and horn-rimmed glasses complete with a neck chain. Pete Jeffcoat and Wendy Corden wandered over to listen. Tan, fit, blond, and easygoing, Selma's assistants were quintessential Californians but far from beach bums. Jeff had a degree in archaeology, Wendy in social sciences.

"Judy's worried," Remi now said. "But did a good job of hiding it, for the kids. We told her we'd keep her updated. Selma, if you could touch base with her every day while we're gone . . . ?"

"Of course. How was your audience with His Highness?"

Sam recounted their meeting with Charlie King. "Remi and I discussed this on the plane. He says all the right things and has the ol' country boy routine down pat, but something doesn't sit right about him."

"His girl Friday, for one thing," Remi said, then described Zhilan Hsu. While outside King's presence, the woman had a thoroughly unnerving demeanor, her behavior aboard the Gulfstream had told a different story. King's displeasure over the number of ice cubes in his Jack Daniel's and her mortified reaction told them not only that she was frightened of her employer but that he was a domineering control freak.

"Remi's also got an interesting hunch about Ms. Hsu," Sam said.

Remi said, "She's his mistress. Sam's not so sure, but I'm positive. And King's grip on her is ironfisted."

"I'm still preparing a biography of the King family,"

Selma said, "but, so far, still no luck on Zhilan. I'll keep working. With your permission, I may call Rube."

Rube Haywood, another friend of Sam's, worked at the CIA headquarters in Langley, Virginia. They'd met, of all places, at the CIA's infamous Camp Peary covert operations training facility when Sam was with DARPA (the Defense Advanced Research Projects Agency) and Rube was an up-and-coming case officer. While "The Farm" was a prerequisite course for someone like Rube, Sam was there as part of a cooperative experiment: the better engineers understood how case officers worked in the field, DARPA and the CIA proposed, the better they would be able to equip America's spies.

"If you need to, go ahead. Another thing," Sam added. "King claims he has no idea what his father's area of interest was. King claims he's been searching for him for almost forty years and yet he knows nothing about what drove the man. I don't buy it."

Remi added, "He also asserts that he hasn't bothered contacting either the Nepalese government or the U.S. embassy. Somebody as powerful as King would get action with just a few phone calls."

"King also claimed Frank wasn't interested in his father's Monterey house. But Frank's too thorough to have ignored that. If King had told Frank about it, he would have gone."

"Why would King lie about that?" Pete said.

"No idea," replied Remi.

"What does all that add up to?" Wendy asked.

"Somebody who's got something to hide," replied Selma.

"Our thoughts exactly," Sam said. "The question is, what? King also has a tinge of paranoia. And, to be fair, as wealthy as he is, he's probably got scammers coming at him in droves."

"In the end, none of that matters," Remi said. "Frank Alton is missing. That's where we need to focus our attention."

"Starting where?" asked Selma.

"Monterey."

MONTEREY, CALIFORNIA

Sam took the corners slowly as the car's headlights probed the fog that swirled over the ground and through the foliage that lined the winding gravel road. Below them, the lights of the cliff-side houses twinkled in the gloom, while farther out the navigation beacons of fishing boats floated in the blackness. Remi's window was open, and through it they could hear the occasional mournful gong of a buoy in the distance.

Tired though they were, Sam and Remi were anxious to get started on Frank's disappearance, so they'd caught the evening shuttle flight from San Diego to Monterey's dual-runway Peninsula Airport, where they'd rented a car.

Even without seeing the structure itself, it was clear

Lewis "Bully" King's home was worth millions. More accurately, the property on which it sat was worth millions. A view of Monterey Bay did not come cheap. According to Charlie King, his father had purchased the home in the early fifties. Since then, appreciation would have worked its magic, turning even a tar-paper shack into a real estate gold mine.

The car's dashboard navigation screen chimed at Sam, signaling another turn. As they rounded the corner, the headlights swept over a lone mailbox sitting atop a listing post.

"That's it," Remi said, reading the numbers.

Sam pulled into a driveway lined with scrub pine and a rickety no-longer-white picket fence that seemed to be held erect only by the vines entangling it. Sam let the car coast to a stop. Ahead, the headlights illuminated a thousand-square-foot saltbox-style house. Two small boarded-up windows flanked a front door, below which was a set of crumbling concrete steps. The facade was painted in what had likely once been a deep green. Now what hadn't peeled away had faded to a sickly olive color.

At the end of the driveway, partially tucked behind the house, stood a single-car garage with drooping eaves troughs.

"That's a nineteen-fifties house, all right," said Remi. "Talk about no frills."

"The lot must be at least two acres. It's a wonder it's stayed out of the hands of developers."

"Not considering who owns it."

"Good point," Sam said. "I have to admit, this is a little spooky."

"I was going to say a lot spooky. Shall we?"

Sam doused the headlights, then shut off the engine, leaving the house illuminated only by what little pale moonlight filtered through the mist. Sam grabbed a leather valise from the backseat, then they climbed out and shut the car's doors. In the silence, the double thunk seemed abnormally loud. Sam dug his micro LED flashlight from his pants pocket and clicked it on.

They followed the walkway to the front door. Probing with his foot, Sam checked the stability of the stairs. He nodded to Remi, then mounted the steps, slipped the key Zhilan had provided them into the lock, and turned. With a snick, the mechanism opened. He gave the door a gentle shove; the hinges let out a predictable squelch. Sam stepped across the threshold, followed by Remi.

"Give me a little light," Remi said.

Sam turned and shone the beam on the wall beside the doorjamb, where Remi was hunting for a switch. She found one and flipped it. Zhilan had assured them that the home's power would be on, and she'd been true to her word. In three corners of the room, floor lamps glowed to life, casting dull yellow cones on the walls.

"Not as abandoned as King made it sound," Sam observed. Not only did the bulbs in the lamps work but there wasn't a trace of dust to be seen. "He must have the place cleaned regularly."

"Doesn't that strike you as strange?" Remi asked. "Not only does he keep the house for almost forty years after his father disappeared, he doesn't change a thing, and he has it cleaned while the yard goes to seed?"

"Charlie King himself strikes me as strange, so, no, this doesn't surprise me. Give the guy germ phobia and hide his fingernail clippers, and he's halfway to Howard Hughes territory."

Remi laughed. "Well, the good news is, there's not much ground to cover."

She was right. They could see most of Bully's house from where they stood: a twenty-foot-square main room that appeared to be a den/study, the east and west walls dominated by floor-to-ceiling bookcases filled with books, knickknacks, framed photos, and display cases containing what looked to be fossils and artifacts.

In the center of the room was a butcher-block kitchen table that Lewis had been using as a desk; on it, an old portable typewriter, pens, pencils, steno pads, and stacks of books. On the south wall were three doorways, one leading to a kitchenette, the second to a bathroom, and the third to a bedroom. Beneath the tang of Pine-Sol and mothballs, the house smelled of mildew and old wallpaper paste.

"I think the ball's in your court, Remi. You and Bully were—or are—kindred spirits. I'll check the other rooms. Holler if you see a bat."

"Not funny, Fargo."

Remi was a trouper through and through, never afraid to get her hands dirty or to jump into danger, but she loathed bats. Their leathery wings, tiny claw hands, and pinched pig faces struck a primal chord in her. Halloween was a tense time in the Fargo household, and vintage vampire movies were banned.

Sam stepped back to her, lifted her chin with his index finger, and kissed her. "Sorry."

"Accepted."

As Sam stepped into the kitchenette, Remi scanned the bookcases. Predictably, all of the books appeared to have been written prior to the 1970s. Lewis King was an eclectic reader, she saw. While most of the books were directly related to archaeology and its associate disciplines—anthropology, paleontology, geology, etcetera—there were also volumes on philosophy, cosmology, sociology, classic literature, and history.

Sam returned to the den. "Nothing of interest in the other rooms. How about here?"

"I suspect he was a—" She paused, turned around. "I guess we should decide on a tense for him. Do we think he's dead or alive?"

"Let's assume the latter. Frank did."

Remi nodded. "I suspect Lewis is a fascinating man. If I had to wager, I'd say he'd read most of these books, if not all of them."

"If he was in the field as much as King said, when would he have had the time?"

"Speed-reader?" Remi suggested.

"Possible. What's in the display cases?"

Sam shone his flashlight on the one nearest Remi's shoulder. She peered into it. "Clovis points," she said, referring to the now universal name for spear and arrow tips constructed from stone, ivory, or bone. "Nice collection too."

In turn, they began checking the rest of the display cases. Lewis's collection was as eclectic as his library. While there were plenty of archaeological artifacts—pot shards, carved antlers, stone tools, petrified wood splinters—there were pieces that belonged in the historical sciences: fossils, rocks, illustrations of extinct plants and insects, scraps of ancient manuscripts.

Remi tapped the glass of a case containing a parchment written in what looked like Devanagari, the parent alphabet of Nepali. "This is interesting. It's a reproduction, I think. There's what looks like a translator's notation: 'A. Kaalrami, Princeton University.' But there's no translation."

"Checking," Sam said, pulling his iPhone from his pocket. He called up the Safari web browser and waited for the 4G network icon to appear in the phone's menu bar. Instead, a message box appeared on the screen:

```
Select a Wi-Fi Network
1651FPR
```

Frowning, Sam studied the message for a moment, then closed the web browser and brought up a note-taking application. He said to Remi, "I can't get a connection. Take a look."

Remi turned to look at him. "What?"

He winked. "Take a look."

She walked over and looked at his iPhone's screen. On it he had typed a message:

```
Follow my lead.
```

Remi didn't miss a beat. "I'm not surprised you couldn't get a signal," she said. "We're in the boondocks."

"What do you think? Have we seen everything?"

"I think so. Let's go find a hotel."

They shut off the lights, then walked out the front door and locked it behind them. Remi said, "What's going on, Sam?"

"I picked up a wireless network. It's named after this address: 1651 False Pass Road." Sam recalled the message screen and showed it to Remi.

"Could it be a neighbor?" she asked.

"No, the average household signal won't carry beyond fifty yards or so."

"Curiouser and curiouser," Remi said. "I didn't see any modems or routers. Why would a supposedly abandoned house need a wireless network?"

"I can think of only one reason, and, given who we're dealing with, it's not as crazy as it sounds: monitoring."

"As in, cameras?"

"And/or listening devices."

"King's spying on us? Why?"

"Who knows. But now my curiosity is piqued. We

have to get back in there. Come on, let's have a look around."

"What if he's got exterior cameras?"

"Those are hard to hide. We'll keep an eye out."

Shining his flashlight along the home's facade and soffit, he walked up the driveway toward the garage. When he reached the corner of the house, he paused and took a peek. He pulled back. "Nothing," he said. He walked to the garage's side door and tried the knob. It was locked. Sam took off his Windbreaker, balled it around his right hand, and pressed his fist against the glass pane above the knob, leaning hard until the glass shattered with a muffled pop. He knocked the remaining glass shards clear, then reached in and unlocked the door.

Once inside, he took only a minute to find the electrical panel. Sam opened the cover and studied the configuration. It was an old fuse type. Some of the fuses appeared relatively new.

"What now?" asked Remi.

"I'm not messing with fuses."

He tracked his flashlight beam from the panel down to the wooden sole plate, then left to the next stud, where he found the electricity meter. Using his pocketknife, he ripped away the lead wire, then opened the cover and flipped off the main power switch.

"Providing King doesn't have a generator or backup batteries hidden somewhere, that should do the trick," Sam said.

They returned to the front step. Remi pulled out her

iPhone and checked for the wireless network. It had disappeared. "Clear," she said.

"Let's go see what Charlie King's hiding."

Back inside, Remi went straight back to the case containing the Devanagari parchment. "Sam, can you get my camera?"

Sam opened the valise, which he'd placed on a nearby armchair, retrieved Remi's Canon G10, and handed it to her. She began taking pictures of the case. Once done, she moved on to the next. "Might as well document everything."

Sam nodded. Hands on hips, he surveyed the bookcases. He did a quick mental calculation: there were five hundred to six hundred volumes, he estimated. "I'll start flipping pages."

It quickly became evident that whoever King had hired to clean the house had paid scant attention to the cases; while the books' spines were clean, their tops were covered in a thick layer of dust. Before removing each volume, Sam examined it with the flashlight for fingerprints. None appeared to have been touched for a decade or more.

Two hours and a hundred sneezes later they returned the last book to its slot. Remi, who had finished photographing the display cases an hour earlier, had helped with the last hundred volumes.

"Nothing," Sam said, backing away from a bookcase and wiping his hands on his pants. "You?"

"No. I did find something interesting in one of the cases, though."

She powered up her camera, scrolled to the relevant picture, and showed Sam the display. He studied it for a moment. "What are those?"

"Don't hold me to it yet, but I think they're ostrich egg shards."

"And the engraving? Is it a language? Art?"

"I don't know. I took them out of the case and photographed each individually as well."

"What's the significance?"

"For us in particular, probably nothing. In a larger context . . ." Remi shrugged. "Perhaps a lot."

In 1999, Remi explained, a team of French archaeologists discovered a cache of two hundred seventy engraved ostrich shell fragments at the Diepkloof Rock Shelter in South Africa. The shards were engraved with geometric patterns that dated back between fifty-five thousand and sixty-five thousand years ago and belonged to what is known as the Howiesons Poort lithic cultural period.

"The experts are still debating the significance of the engravings," Remi continued. "Some argue it's artwork; others, a map; still others, a form of written language."

"Do these look similar?"

"I can't recall, offhand. But if they're of the same type as the South African shards," Remi finished, "then they predate the Diepkloof find by at least thirty-five years."

"Maybe Lewis didn't know what he had."

"I doubt it. Any archaeologist worth his or her salt would recognize these as significant. Once we find Frank and things get back to normal"—Sam opened his mouth to speak, and Remi quickly corrected herself—"normal for us, I'll look into it."

Sam sighed. "So for now, all we've got that is even remotely related to Nepal is that Devanagari parchment."

4

Kathmandu, Nepal

Sam and Remi awoke to the sound of the pilot announcing their final approach to Kathmandu's Tribhuvan International Airport. After having spent the majority of the past three days in the air, it took a solid thirty seconds before either of them was fully awake. Their United–Cathay Pacific–Royal Nepal flight had taken nearly thirty-two hours.

Sam sat up, stretched his arms above his head, then reset his watch to match the digital clock on his seat-back screen. Beside him, Remi's eyelids fluttered open. "My kingdom for a good cup of coffee," she murmured.

"We'll be on the ground in twenty minutes."

Remi's eyes opened the rest of the way. "Ah, I'd almost forgotten."

In recent years, Nepal had gotten into the coffee

business. As far as the Fargos were concerned, the beans grown in the country's Arghakhanchi region produced the best black gold in the world.

Sam smiled at her. "I'll buy you as much as you can drink."

"My hero."

The plane banked sharply, and they both stared out the window. In the minds of most travelers, the name Kathmandu evokes exotic visions of Buddhist temples and robed monks, trekkers and mountaineers, incense, spice, ramshackle huts, and shadowed valleys hidden by Himalayan peaks. What doesn't occur to the first-time visitor is the image of a bustling metropolis of 750,000 people with a ninety-eight percent literacy rate.

Seen from the air, Kathmandu seems to have dropped neatly into a crater-like valley surrounded by four towering mountain ranges: the Shivapuri, Phulchowki, Nagarjun, and Chandragiri.

Sam and Remi had been here on vacation twice before. They knew that despite its population, Kathmandu, on the ground, felt like a conglomeration of medium-sized villages shot through with veins of modernism. On one block you might find a thousand-year-old temple to the Hindu Lord Shiva, on the next a cell phone store; on major thoroughfares, sleek hybrid taxis and colorfully decorated rickshaws competing for fares; in a square, located directly across from each other, an Oktoberfest-themed restaurant and a curbside vendor selling bowls of *chaat* to passersby. And of course, tucked into the mountain slopes and atop the craggy peaks surrounding the city, hundreds of temples and monasteries, some older than Kathmandu itself.

Experienced travelers that they were, Sam and Remi were well prepared for customs and immigration and were passed through with a minimum of fuss. Soon they found themselves outside the terminal, standing on the ground transportation sidewalk beneath a modern curved awning. The terminal's facade itself was done in pristine terra-cotta, with a deeply sloped roof adorned with hundreds of rectangular insets.

"Where did Selma book us?"

"The Hyatt Regency."

Remi gave her nod of approval. On their last visit to Kathmandu, in hopes of immersing themselves in Nepali culture, they'd stayed in a hostel that happened to be located next to a yak-breeding corral. Yaks, they discovered, had little concern for modesty, privacy, or sleep.

Sam stepped to the curb to hail a taxi. Behind them came a male voice: "Would you be Mr. and Mrs. Fargo?"

Sam and Remi turned and found themselves facing a man and woman, both in their early twenties and both near-duplicate images of not only each other but Charles King as well—save one startling difference. While the King children had been blessed with their father's white-blond hair, blue eyes, and big smile, their faces also bore subtle yet distinct Asian characteristics.

Remi gave Sam a sideways glance that he immediately and correctly interpreted: her hunch about Zhilan Hsu had been at least partially right. However, unless the Fargos were assuming too much, her relationship went far beyond that of a common mistress.

"We would be," Sam replied.

The man, who also shared his father's height but not his corpulence, stuck out his hand and gave each of them a vigorous handshake. "I'm Russell. This is my sister, Marjorie."

"Sam . . . Remi. We weren't expecting a reception."

"We decided to take the initiative," Marjorie said. "We're here on some business for Daddy, so it's no trouble."

Russell said, "If you've never visited Kathmandu before, it can be a bit disconcerting. We've got a car. We'll be happy to take you to your hotel."

The Hyatt Regency was two miles northwest of the airport. The ride went smoothly, if not quickly, inside the King children's Mercedes-Benz sedan. Inside its sound-controlled interior and tinted windows, Sam and Remi found the trip a tad surreal. At the wheel, Russell navigated the confusing narrow streets easily while Marjorie, in the front passenger's seat, gave them a running travelogue over her shoulder with all the charm of a canned tour guide script.

At last they pulled up to the Hyatt's covered lobby turnaround. Russell and Marjorie were out of the car and holding open the backseat doors before Sam and Remi had touched the handles.

Like the airport terminal's, the Hyatt Regency's architecture was a blend of old and new: a sprawling six-story facade in terra-cotta and cream topped by a pagoda-style roof. The lush manicured grounds occupied twenty acres.

A bellman approached the car, and Russell barked something in Nepali. The man nodded vigorously and forced a smile, then retrieved the luggage from the trunk and disappeared into the lobby.

"We'll let you get settled in," said Russell, then handed them each a business card. "Give me a call later, and we can discuss how you'd like to proceed."

"Proceed?" Sam repeated.

Marjorie smiled. "Sorry, Daddy probably forgot to tell you. He asked us to be your guides while you look for Mr. Alton. See you tomorrow!"

With almost synchronized smiles and waves, the King children climbed back into the Mercedes and pulled away.

Sam and Remi watched the receding car for a few seconds. Then Remi murmured, "Is anyone in the King family normal?"

Forty-five minutes later they were settled into their suite and enjoying their coffee.

After spending the afternoon lying around the pool relaxing, they returned to their suite for cocktails. Sam ordered a Bombay Sapphire Gin Gibson, and Remi asked for a Ketel One Cosmopolitan. They finished reading the dossier Zhilan had given them at the Palembang Airport. While on the surface it seemed thorough, they found little of substance with which they could start their hunt.

"I have to admit," Remi said, "the combination of Zhilan Hsu's and Charlie King's genes produced . . . interesting results."

"That's very diplomatic of you, Remi, but let's be honest: Russell and Marjorie are scary. Combine their appearance with their over-the-top friendliness and you've got a pair of Hollywood-born serial killers. Did you see specific traces of Zhilan in them?"

"No, and I'm half hoping there aren't. If she's their mother, that means she was probably eighteen or nineteen when she had them."

"Which would've put King in his mid-forties at the time."

"Did you notice the lack of Texas accents? I think I caught a trace of Ivy League in some of their vowels."

"So Daddy shipped them out of Texas and off to college. What I want to know is, how did they know what flight we were on?"

"Charlie King flexing his muscles? Showing us he's well connected?"

"Probably. That might also explain why he didn't tell us to expect the Wonder Twins. As powerful as King is, he probably fancies himself a master at keeping people off guard."

"I'm not fond of having them shadow us everywhere."

"Neither am I, but let's play along tomorrow and see what they know about Frank's activities. I have a sneaking suspicion the King family knows a lot more than they're letting on."

"Agreed," Remi replied. "It all adds up to one thing, Sam: King is trying to play the puppet master. The question is, why? Because he's a control freak or because he's hiding something?"

The door chimes rang. As he moved to the door to retrieve an envelope that had just been slid under it, Sam said, "Ah, confirmation of our dinner reservations."

"Really?"

"Well, only if you can be ready to leave in thirty minutes," replied Sam.

"Love to, and where are we going?"

"Bhanchka and Ghan," responded Sam.

"How did you remember?"

"How can you forget such memorable food, the ambience, and the finest Nepalese cuisine in Nepal!"

Twenty-five minutes later Remi had changed into Akris slacks and a top, with a matching jacket thrown over her arm. And Sam, freshly shaved, wearing a blue Robert Graham shirt and dark gray slacks, ushered her out the door.

Remi was only marginally surprised to awaken at four a.m. to find her husband not in bed but rather in an armchair in the suite's sitting area. When something was badgering Sam Fargo's subconscious, he rarely could sleep. She found him under the soft glow of a lamp reading the dossier Zhilan had given them. Using her hip, Remi gently shoved aside the manila folder. Then she settled into his lap and wrapped her long La Perla silk robe tightly around her.

"I think I found the culprit," he said.

"Show me."

He flipped through a series of paper-clipped pages. "The daily e-mail reports that Frank was sending King. They start the day he arrived here and end the morning he disappeared. Do you notice anything different about the last three e-mails?"

Remi scanned them. "No."

"He signed each one 'Frank.' Look at the ones prior."

Remi did so. She pursed her lips. "Simply signed 'FA.'"

"That's how he signed e-mails to me too."

"What's it mean?"

"Just speculating. I'd say either Frank didn't send the last three e-mails or he did and was trying to embed a distress signal."

"I think that's unlikely. Frank would have found a more clever code."

"So that leaves us with the other option. He disappeared earlier than King believes."

"And someone was posing as him," Remi concluded.

THIRTY MILES NORTH OF
KATHMANDU, NEPAL

In the predawn gloom, the Range Rover pulled off the main road. Its headlights swept over green terraced fields as it followed the winding road to the bottom of the valley, where it intersected another road, this one narrower and rutted with mud. The Rover bumped along the track for several hundred yards before crossing a bridge. Below, a river churned, its dark waters lapping at the bridge's lowermost girders. On the opposite bank the Rover's headlights briefly illuminated a sign. In Nepali, it read "Trisuli." Another quarter mile brought the Rover to a squat gray-brick building with a patchwork tin roof. Beside a wooden front door, a square window glowed yellow. The Rover coasted to a stop before the building, and the engine shut off.

Russell and Marjorie King climbed out and headed for the door. A pair of shadowed figures emerged from behind each corner of the building and intercepted them. Each man carried an automatic weapon diagonally across his body. Flashlights clicked on, panned over the King children's faces, then clicked off. With a jerk of the head, one of the guards gestured for the pair to enter.

Through the door, a single man was sitting at a wooden trestle table. Aside from this and a flickering kerosene lantern, the room was barren.

"Colonel Zhou," Russell King grunted.

"Welcome, my nameless American friends. Please sit."

They did so, taking the bench across from Zhou.

Marjorie said, "You're not in uniform. Please don't tell us you're afraid of Nepalese Army patrols."

Zhou chuckled. "Hardly. While I'm sure my men would enjoy the target practice, I doubt my superiors would look kindly on my crossing the border without going through proper channels."

"This is your meeting," Russell said. "Why did you ask us here?"

"We need to discuss the permits you have requested."

"The permits we've already paid for, you mean?" replied Marjorie.

"Semantics. The area you wish to enter is heavily patrolled—"

"All of China is heavily patrolled," Russell observed.

"Only part of the area in which you wish to travel falls under my command."

"This has never been a problem in the past."

"Things change."

"You're squeezing us," Marjorie said. Her face was expressionless, but her eyes were hard, mean.

"I don't know that expression."

"Bribery."

Colonel Zhou frowned. "That's harsh. The truth is, you are right: you have already paid me. Unfortunately, a restructuring in my district has left me with more mouths to feed, if you understand my meaning. If I do not feed those mouths, they will begin talking to the wrong people."

"Perhaps we should be talking to them instead of you," said Russell.

"Go ahead. But do you have the time? As I recall, it took you eight months to find me. Are you willing to start from the beginning again? You were lucky with me. Next time, you might find yourself imprisoned as spies. It could still happen, in fact."

"You're playing a dangerous game, Colonel," Marjorie said.

"No more dangerous than illegally crossing into Chinese territory."

"And, I suppose, no more dangerous than not having your men search us for weapons."

Zhou's eyes narrowed, darted toward the door, then back to the King twins. "You wouldn't dare," he said.

"She would," Russell said. "And so would I. Bet on it. But not now. Not tonight. Colonel, if you knew who we were, you would think twice about extorting more money from us."

"I may not know your names, but I know your kind, and I have a hunch about what you are after."

Russell said, "How much to feed these extra mouths?"

"Twenty thousand—in euros, not dollars."

Russell and Marjorie stood up. Russell said, "You'll have the money in your account before day's end. We'll contact you when we're ready to cross."

He could tell from the chill in the night air, the utter lack of traffic sounds, and the nearby and frequent clanking of yak bells that he was fairly high in the foothills. Blindfolded as soon as he'd been shoved into the van, he had no way of knowing how far from Kathmandu they'd taken him. Ten miles or a hundred, it didn't really matter. Once outside the valley in which the city rested, the terrain could swallow a person whole—and had done so, thousands of times. Ravines, caves, sinkholes, crevasses . . . a million places in which to hide or die.

The floor and walls were made of rough planking, as was the cot. His mattress was a straw-filled pad that smelled vaguely of manure. The stove was an old potbellied model, he guessed, from the sound of the kindling hatch banging shut whenever his captors entered to stoke the fire. Occasionally, over the tang of wood smoke, he caught the faint smell of stove fuel, the kind used by hikers and mountaineers.

He was being held in an abandoned trekkers' hut, somewhere far enough off the regular trails that it received no visitors.

His captors had spoken fewer than twenty words to him since his abduction, all of them gruff commands given in broken English: sit, stand, eat, toilet . . . On the second day, however, he'd caught a snippet of conversation through the hut's wall, and while his grasp of Nepali was virtually nonexistent, he knew enough to recognize it. He'd been taken by locals. Who, though? Terrorists or guerrillas? He knew of none operating within Nepal. Kidnappers? He doubted it. They hadn't forced him to make any ransom recordings or letters. Nor had they mistreated him. He was fed regularly, given plenty to drink, and his sleeping bag was well suited for subzero temperatures. When they handled him, they were firm but not rough. Again he wondered, who? And why?

So far, they'd made only one major mistake: while they'd bound his wrists securely with what felt like climbing rope, they'd failed to check the hut for sharp edges. In short order, he'd found four of them: the legs of his cot, each of which jutted a few inches above the mattress. The roughly cut wood was unsanded. Not exactly saw blades, but it was a place to start.

5

Kathmandu, Nepal

As advertised, Russell and Marjorie pulled into the Hyatt's turnaround precisely at nine a.m. the next morning. Bright-eyed and smiling, the twins greeted Sam and Remi with another round of handshakes, then ushered them toward the Mercedes. The sky was a brilliant blue, the air crisp.

"Where to?" Russell asked as he put the car in gear and pulled away.

"How about the locations where Frank Alton seemed to be spending most of his time?" Remi asked.

"No problem," replied Marjorie. "According to the e-mails he was sending Daddy, he spent part of his time in the Chobar Gorge area, about five miles southeast of here. It's where the Bagmati River empties out of the valley."

They drove in silence for a few minutes.

Sam said, "If it was your grandfather that was photographed in Lo Monthang—"

"You don't think it was?" Russell said, glancing in the rearview mirror. "Daddy thinks it was."

"Just playing devil's advocate. If it was your grandfather, do you have any idea why he would have been in that area?"

"Can't think of a thing," replied Marjorie flippantly.

"Your father didn't seem familiar with Lewis's work. Are either of you?"

Russell answered, "Just archaeology stuff, I suppose. We never knew him, of course. Just heard stories from Daddy."

"Don't take this the wrong way, but did it occur to you to learn what Lewis was up to? It might have helped in the search for him."

"Daddy keeps us pretty busy," Marjorie said. "Besides, that's why he hires experts like you two and Mr. Alton."

Sam and Remi exchanged glances. Like their father, the King twins seemed only marginally interested in the particulars of their grandfather's life. Their detachment felt almost pathological.

"Where did you two go to school?" Remi asked, changing the subject.

"We didn't," Russell answered. "Daddy had us homeschooled by tutors."

"What happened to your accents?"

Marjorie didn't answer immediately. "Oh, I see what you mean. When we were about four, he sent us to live with our aunt in Connecticut. We lived there until we finished school, then moved back to Houston to work for Daddy."

"So he wasn't around much when you were growing up?" Sam asked.

"He's a busy man."

Marjorie's reply was without a trace of rancor, as though it were perfectly normal to bundle your children off to another state for fourteen years and have them raised by tutors and relatives.

"You two ask a lot of questions," Russell said.

"We're curious by nature," Sam replied. "Comes with the job."

Sam and Remi expected little to come of their visit to Chobar Gorge, and they weren't disappointed. Russell and Marjorie pointed out a few landmarks and offered more canned travelogue.

Back in the car, Sam and Remi asked to be taken to the next location: the city's historical epicenter, known as Durbar Square, which was home to some fifty temples.

Predictably, this visit was as unrevealing as the first. Shadowed by the King twins, Sam and Remi walked around the square and its environs for an hour, making a show of taking pictures, checking their map, and jotting notes. Finally, shortly before noon, they asked to be taken back to the Hyatt.

"You're done?" Russell asked. "Are you sure?"

"We're sure," said Sam.

Marjorie said, "We're happy to take you anywhere you'd like to go."

"We need to do some research before we continue," Remi said.

"We can help with that too."

Sam put a little steel in his voice: "The hotel, please."

Russell shrugged. "Suit yourself."

From inside the lobby, they watched the Mercedes pull away. Sam pulled his iPhone from his pocket and checked the screen. "Message from Selma." He listened to it, then said, "She's dug something up on the King family."

Back in their room, Sam speed-dialed Selma's number and put the phone on speaker. After thirty seconds of crackling, the line clicked open. Selma answered with, "Finally."

"We were on a tour with the King twins."

"Productive?"

"Only in that it reinforced our urge to get away from them," said Sam. "What've you got for us?"

"First, I've found someone who can translate the Devanagari parchment you found at Lewis's house."

"Fantastic," Remi said.

"It gets better. I think it's the original translator—the A. Kaalrami from Princeton. Her first name is Adala.

She's almost seventy and is a professor at . . . Care to guess?"

"No," Sam said.

"Kathmandu University."

"Selma, you're a miracle worker," Remi said.

"Normally, I would agree, Mrs. Fargo, but this was dumb luck. I'm e-mailing you Professor Kaalrami's contact info. Okay, next: after hitting dry hole after dry hole in researching the King family, I ended up calling Rube Haywood. He's sending me information as he gets it, but what we've got so far is interesting. First of all, King isn't the family's true surname. It's the anglicized version of the original German: Konig. And Lewis's first name was originally Lewes."

"Why the change?" asked Remi.

"We're not entirely sure at this point, but what we do know is Lewis immigrated to America in 1946 and got a teaching job at Syracuse University. A couple years later, when Charles was four years old, Lewis left him and his mother and started his globe-trotting."

"What's next?"

"I found out what business Russell and Marjorie are handling there. One of King's mining concerns—SRG, or Strategic Resources Group—acquired permits from the Nepalese government last year to conduct, and I quote, 'exploratory studies related to the exploitation of industrial and precious metals.'"

"Which means what, exactly?" Remi asked. "That's an awfully vague mission statement."

"Intentionally vague," Sam said.

Selma replied, “The company isn’t publicly traded, so information is hard to come by. I found two sites that are being leased by SRG. They’re to the northeast of the city.”

“A tangled web,” Remi said. “We’ve got the King twins overseeing a family mining operation in the same place and at the same time Frank disappears while looking for King’s father, who may or may not have been ghosting around the Himalayas for the past forty years. Am I forgetting anything?”

“That about covers it,” Sam said.

Selma asked, “Do you want the particulars on the SRG sites?”

“Hold on to it for now,” Sam replied. “On the surface it seems unrelated, but, with King Charlie, you never know.”

After asking the Hyatt’s concierge to arrange a rental car, they took to the road, with Sam driving and Remi navigating, a Kathmandu city map flattened against the dashboard of the Nissan X-Trail SUV.

One of the few lessons they’d learned (and had since forgotten) from their last visit to Kathmandu some six years earlier came rushing back to them soon after leaving the hotel.

Except for major thoroughfares like the Tridevi and the Ring Road, Kathmandu’s streets rarely bore names, either on maps or signs. Verbal directions were given relative to landmarks, usually intersections or squares—known as *chowks* or *toles* respectively—and occasionally to temples or markets. Anyone unfamiliar with such reference points had little choice but to rely on a regional map and a compass.

In Sam and Remi's case, they were lucky. Kathmandu University lay fourteen miles from their hotel in the foothills on the extreme eastern outskirts of the city. After spending twenty frustrating minutes finding the Arniko Highway, they made smooth progress and arrived at the campus only an hour after setting out.

Following signs in both Nepali and English, they turned left at the entrance, then drove up a tree-lined drive to a brick-and-glass building fronted by an oval plot brimming with wildflowers. They found a parking spot, walked through the glass entrance doors, and found an information desk.

The young Indian woman sitting at the counter spoke Oxford-tinged English. "Good morning, welcome to Kathmandu University. How may I help you?"

"We're looking for Professor Adala Kaalrami," said Remi.

"Yes, of course. One moment." The woman tapped on a keyboard below the counter and studied the monitor for a moment. "Professor Kaalrami is currently meeting with a graduate student in the library. The meeting is scheduled to end at three." The woman produced a campus map, then circled their current location and that of the library.

"Thank you," Sam said.

Kathmandu's campus was small, with only a dozen or so main buildings centered atop a rise. Below were miles and miles of green terraced fields and thick forests. In the distance they could see Tribhuvan International Airport. To the north of this, just visible, were the pagoda-style roofs of the Hyatt Regency.

They walked a hundred yards east down a hedge-lined sidewalk, turned left, and found themselves at the library's entrance. Once inside, a staff member directed them to a second-floor conference room. They arrived as a lone student was leaving. Inside, seated at a round conference table, was a plump elderly Indian woman in a bright red-and-green sari.

Remi said, "Excuse me, would you be Professor Adala Kaalrami?"

The woman looked up and scrutinized them through a pair of dark-rimmed glasses. "Yes, I am she." Her English was thickly accented with a lightly musical quality common to many Indian English speakers.

Remi introduced herself and Sam, then asked if they could sit down. Kaalrami nodded to the pair of chairs opposite her. Sam said, "Does the name Lewis King mean anything to you?"

"Bully?" she replied without hesitation.

"Yes."

She smiled broadly; she had a wide gap between her front teeth. "Oh, yes, I remember Bully. We were . . . friends." The glimmer in her eyes told the Fargos the relationship had gone beyond mere friendship. "I was affiliated with Princeton but had come to Tribhuvan University on loan. That was long before Kathmandu University was founded. Bully and I met at a social function of some kind. Why do you ask this?"

"We're looking for Lewis King."

"Ah . . . Ghost hunters, are you?"

"I take that to mean you believe he's dead," Remi said.

"Oh, I do not know. Of course I've heard the stories about his periodic manifestations, but I have never seen him, or any genuine pictures of him. At least, not in the last forty years or so. I'd like to think if he were alive, he would have come to see me."

Sam pulled a manila folder from his valise, pulled out a copy of the Devanagari parchment, and slid it across the table to Kaalrami. "Do you recognize this?"

She studied it for a moment. "I do. That is my signature. I translated this for Bully in . . ." Kaalrami pursed her lips, thinking. "Nineteen seventy-two."

"What can you tell us about it?" Sam asked. "Did Lewis tell you where he found it?"

"He did not."

Remi said, "To me, it looks like Devanagari."

"Very good, my dear. Close, but incorrect. It is written in Lowa. While not quite a dead language, it is fairly rare. At last estimate, there are only four thousand native Lowa speakers alive today. They are mostly found in the north of the country, up near the Chinese border, in what used to be—"

"Mustang," Sam guessed.

"Yes, that's right. And you pronounced it correctly. Good for you. Most Lowa speakers live in and around Lo Monthang. Did you know that about Mustang or was it a good guess?"

"A guess. The only current lead we have on Lewis King's whereabouts is a photograph in which he supposedly appears. It was taken a year ago in Lo Monthang. We found that parchment at Lewis's home."

"Do you have this picture with you?"

"No," Remi said, then glanced at Sam. Their shared expression said, Why didn't we ask for a copy of the picture? Rookie mistake. "I'm sure we can get it, though."

"If it is not too much trouble. I like to think I would recognize Bully if it were truly him."

"Has anyone else come to see you recently about King?"

Kaalrami hesitated again, tapping an index finger on her lip. "A year ago, perhaps a bit longer than that, a pair of kids were here. Strange-looking pair—"

"Twins? Blond hair, blue eyes, Asian features?"

"Yes! I did not particularly like them. I know that is not a charitable thing to say, but I must be honest. There was just something about them . . ." Kaalrami shrugged.

"Do you remember what they asked you?"

"Just general questions about Bully—if I had any old letters from him or remember him talking about his work in the region. I could not help them."

"They didn't have a copy of this parchment?"

"No."

Sam asked, "We never found the original translation. Would you mind?"

"I can give you the essence of it, but a written translation will take a while. I could do that tonight, if you'd like."

"Thank you," said Remi. "We'd be most grateful."

Professor Kaalrami adjusted her glasses and centered the parchment before her. Slowly she began tracing her finger down the lines of text, her lips moving soundlessly.

After five minutes, she looked up. She cleared her throat.

"It is a royal edict of sorts. The Lowa phrase does not translate well to English, but it is an official order. Of that, I'm certain."

"Is there a date?"

"No, but if you look here, at the upper left corner, there's a piece of text missing. Was it on the original parchment?"

"No, I photographed it exactly as it appeared. Do you remember if the date was on the original you saw?"

"No, I'm afraid not."

"Would you care to venture a guess?"

"Do not hold me to this, but I would estimate between six and seven hundred years old."

"Go on, please," Sam prompted.

"Again, you must wait for the written version . . ."

"We understand."

"It is an order to a group of soldiers . . . special soldiers called Sentinels. They are instructed to carry out a plan of some kind—something detailed in another document, I suspect. The plan is designed to remove something called the Theurang from its place of hiding and transport it to safety."

"Why?"

"Something to do with an invasion."

"Does it explain what the Theurang is?"

"I do not think so. I am sorry, most of this is only vaguely familiar to me. This was four decades ago. I remember the word because it is unusual, but I do not think I followed up on it. I am a classics teacher. However, I have no doubt there is someone on staff here who would be of more help with the word. I can check for you."

"We'd appreciate that," Sam replied. "Do you remember Lewis's reaction when you gave him the translation?"

Kaalrami smiled. "He was elated, as I recall. But, then again, Bully never lacked for enthusiasm. He lived life to its fullest, that man."

"Did he say where he found the parchment?"

"If he did, I don't remember. Perhaps tonight, while I'm translating this, more will come back to me."

"One last question," Remi said. "What do you remember about the time Lewis disappeared?"

"Oh, yes, I remember. We spent the morning together. We had a brunch picnic along a river. The Bagmati, on the southwestern side of the city."

In unison, Sam and Remi leaned forward. Sam asked, "Chobar Gorge?"

Professor Kaalrami smiled and tilted her head at Sam. "Yes. How did you know?"

"Lucky guess. And after the picnic?"

"Lewis had his backpack with him—that was more common than not for him. He was always on the move. It was a beautiful day, warm, not a cloud in the sky. As I recall, I took pictures. I had a new camera, one of those first instant Polaroid models, the ones that folded up. Back then, it was a marvel of technology."

"Please tell us you still have those pictures."

"I may. It will depend on my son's technical skills. If you'll excuse me." Professor Kaalrami got up, walked to the side table, picked up a phone, and dialed. She spoke in Nepali for a couple minutes, then looked over to Sam and Remi and covered the phone's mouthpiece. "Do you have mobiles with e-mail access?"

Sam gave her his address.

Kaalrami spoke on the phone for another thirty seconds, then returned to the table. She sighed. "My son. He tells me I need to come into the digital age. Last month he started scanning—is that the right word?—all my old photo albums. He finished the ones from the picnic last week. He's sending them to you."

"Thank you," Sam said. "And to your son."

Remi said, "You were saying, about the picnic . . . ?"

"We ate, enjoyed each other's company, talked, then—in the early afternoon, I think—we parted company. I got in my car and drove away. The last I saw of him, he was crossing the Chobar Gorge bridge."

· 6 ·

KATHMANDU, NEPAL

Their second drive to Chobar Gorge went quickly as they first headed west, back toward the city on Arniko Highway. On the outskirts they turned south on the Ring Road and followed it along Kathmandu's southern edge to the Chobar region. From there it was a simple matter of following two signs. An hour after leaving Professor Kaalrami, they pulled into Manjushree Park, overlooking the gorge's northern cliff, at five p.m.

They got out and stretched their legs. As he had been doing for the past hour, Sam checked his iPhone for incoming mail. He shook his head. "Nothing yet."

Hands on hips, Remi surveyed the surroundings. "What are we looking for?" she asked.

"A giant neon marquee with 'Bully Was Here' flashing on it would be nice, but I'm not holding my breath."

The truth was, neither of them knew if there was anything to find. They'd come here based on what might be little more than a coincidence: both Frank Alton and Lewis King had spent their final hours here before disappearing. However, knowing Alton as they did, it was doubtful he'd come here without a good reason.

Aside from a pair of men eating an early dinner on a nearby bench, the park—itself little more than a low hill covered in brush and bamboo and a spiral hiking trail—was deserted. Sam and Remi walked down the gravel entrance drive and followed the winding track to the head of the Chobar Gorge. While the main bridge was built of concrete and wide enough to accommodate cars, the gorge's lower reaches and opposite bank were accessible only via three plank-and-wire suspension bridges, all set at different heights and all reached by hiking trails. On both sides of the gorge, small temples were set into the hillside, partially hidden by thick trees. Fifty feet below, the Bagmati frothed and crashed over clusters of boulders.

Remi walked to an information placard attached to the bridge's facade. She read aloud the English version:

"'Chovar Guchchi is a narrow valley formed by the Bagmati River, the only outlet of the entire Kathmandu Valley. It is believed that Kathmandu Valley once held a giant lake. When Manjusri first came upon the valley, he saw a lotus on the surface. He sliced open this hillside to drain the water from the lake and make way for the city of Kathmandu.'"

Sam asked, "Who is Manjusri?"

"I'm not sure exactly, but, if I had to guess, I would say he was a bodhisattva—an enlightened person."

Sam was nodding as he checked his e-mail. "Got it. Professor Kaalrami's son came through."

He and Remi walked to a nearby tree to get out of the setting sun. Sam called up the pictures, five in all, and scrolled through them. While they had been digitized well enough, the photos had that old Polaroid feel: slightly washed out, the colors a bit unnatural. The first four photos were of young Lewis King and Adala Kaalrami, each reclining or sitting on a blanket, plates and glasses and picnic supplies laid out around them.

"None of them together," Remi remarked.

"No timer," Sam replied.

The fifth photo was of Lewis King, this time standing, facing the camera in three-quarters profile. On his back was an old frame-style backpack.

They studied the photos a second time. Sam exhaled heavily and said, "Shouldn't have gotten our hopes up."

"Don't speak too soon," Remi said, leaning closer to the iPhone's screen. "You see what he's holding in his right hand?"

"An ice ax."

"No, look closer."

Sam did so. "A caver's ax."

"And look at what's clipped to his back, to the left of his sleeping bag. You can just make out the curve of it."

Sam kept his eyes fixed on the screen. A smile spread

on his face. "I don't know how I missed that. I'll be damned. It's a hard hat."

Remi nodded. "Equipped with a headlamp. Lewis King was going spelunking."

Not knowing for sure what they were looking for but hoping they were correct, they took only ten minutes to find it. Near the opposite shore's bridgehead was a roofed, open-fronted kiosk with wooden slots containing informational brochures. They found a recreational map of the gorge and scanned the numbered dots and description labels.

A mile upriver from the bridge, on the northern bank, was a dot labeled "Chobar Caves. Closed to the Public. No Unauthorized Access."

"It's a long shot," Remi said. "For all we know, Lewis was headed into the mountains and Frank was simply lost."

"Long shots are what we do," Sam reminded his wife. "Besides, it's either this or we spend another day with Russell and Marjorie."

This did the trick. Remi said, "What are the odds Kathmandu has an REI outlet?"

As expected, the odds were nil, but they did find a Nepalese Army surplus shop a few blocks west of Durbar Square. The equipment they purchased was far from modern but of decent quality. While neither of them were remotely convinced an exploration of the Chobar Caves would further their cause, it felt good to be taking action. This had become one of their mottos: when in doubt, do something. Anything.

Shortly before seven they pulled back into the Hyatt's parking lot. As Sam climbed out he spotted Russell and Marjorie standing beneath the turnaround awning.

Sam muttered, "Bandits at three o'clock."

"Oh, yuk."

"Don't open the tailgate. They'll want to go with us."

Russell and Marjorie jogged over to them. "Hey," Russell said, "we were getting worried about you. We came by to see how you were doing, and the concierge said you'd rented a car and left."

Marjorie asked, "Everything okay?"

"We were mugged twice," Remi replied, deadpan.

"And I think I was tricked into marrying a goat," Sam added.

After a few seconds, the King children broke into smiles. "Oh, you're kidding," Russell said. "We get it. Seriously, though, you shouldn't wander off—"

Sam cut him off. "Russell, Marjorie, I want you to listen to me. Do I have your attention?"

He got two nods in return.

"Between the two of us, Remi and I have traveled in more countries than either of you can probably name—combined. We appreciate your help, and your . . . enthusiasm, but from this point on, we'll call you if we need you. Otherwise, leave us alone and let us do what we came here to do."

Mouths hanging half open, Russell and Marjorie King stared at him. They glanced at Remi, who simply shrugged. "What he says, he means."

"Are we clear?" Sam asked them.

"Well, yes, sir, but our father asked us—"

"That's your problem to solve. If your father wants to talk to us, he knows how to reach us. Any more questions?"

"I don't like this," Russell said.

Marjorie added, "We're just trying to help."

"And we've thanked you. Now you're testing our limits of politeness. Why don't you two run along. We'll call if we get into trouble we can't handle."

After a few moments' hesitation, the King children turned and walked back to their Mercedes. They pulled out and slowly passed Sam and Remi, staring hard at them through Russell's rolled-down window before accelerating away.

"If looks could kill," Remi said.

Sam nodded. "I think we may have just seen the true faces of the King twins."

7

Chobar Gorge, Nepal

They set out shortly before four the next morning, hoping to arrive at the gorge before sunrise. While they had no idea how strictly the Chobar Caves' no-trespassing rule was enforced—or whether the area was even patrolled by the police—they didn't want to take any chances.

At five, they pulled into Manjushree Park and found a spot under a tree not visible from the main road. Headlights off, they sat in silence for two minutes, listening to the tick-tick-tick of the Nissan's engine cooling down, before climbing out, opening the tailgate, and gathering their gear.

"Did you really expect them to tail us?" Remi asked, settling her pack over her shoulders.

"I don't know what to think anymore. My gut tells me they're bad to the core, and I know without a doubt King didn't ask them to help us. He ordered them to keep an eye on us."

"I agree. Hopefully, your heart-to-heart with them will do the trick."

"Bad bet," Sam said, and slammed the tailgate.

Led by the glow of the rising sun, they walked down to the bridgehead. As advertised on their map, twenty yards to the east of the bridge, behind a copse of bamboo, they found the trail. With Sam in the lead, they headed upriver.

The first quarter mile was an easy hike, the path three feet wide and covered in well-groomed gravel, but this soon changed as the grade steepened. The trail narrowed and began going through a series of switchbacks. The foliage closed in, forming a partial canopy over their heads. To their right and below, they could hear the river gurgling softly.

They reached a fork. To the left, the trail headed due east, away from the river; to the right, down toward the river. They paused only a few moments to double-check their map and Sam's iPhone compass, then took the right-hand path. After another five minutes of walking, they came to a forty-five-degree slope into which rough steps had been cut. At the bottom, they found themselves facing not a trail but a rickety suspension bridge, its left side affixed to the cliff by lag bolts. Vines had overrun the bridge, so tightly twisted around the supports and wires that the structure looked half man-made, half organic.

"I have the distinct feeling that we're looking down the rabbit hole," Remi murmured.

"Come on," Sam said. "It's quaint."

"With you, I've come to equate that word with 'hazardous.'"

"I'm crushed."

"Can you see how far it goes?"

"No. Keep ahold of the cliff side. If the span goes, the vines will probably hold."

"Another lovely word, 'probably.'"

Sam took a step forward, slowly shifting his weight onto the first plank. Aside from a slight creaking, the wood held firm. He took another cautious step, then another, and another, until he'd covered ten feet.

"So far, so good," he called over his shoulder.

"On my way."

The bridge turned out to be a mere hundred feet long. On the other side the trail continued, spiraling first down the slope, then up. Ahead, the trees began thinning out.

"Round two," Sam said to Remi.

"What?" she replied, then stopped short behind him. "Oh, no."

Another suspension bridge.

"I sense a trend," Remi said.

She was right. On the other side of the second span they found another section of trail, followed by yet another bridge. For the next forty minutes the pattern continued: trail, bridge, trail, bridge. Finally, on the fifth section of trail, Sam called a halt and checked his map and compass. "We're close," he murmured. "The cave entrance is below us somewhere."

They spread out, searching up and down the trail for a way down. Remi found it. On the river side of the trail, a rusted cable ladder affixed to a tree trunk dangled in space. Sam dropped to his belly and, with both of Remi's hands wrapped around his belt, scooted forward through the underbrush. He wriggled back.

"There's a rock shelf," he said. "The ladder stops about six feet above it. We'll have to drop."

"Of course we will," Remi replied with a tight smile.

"I'll go first."

On her knees, Remi leaned forward and kissed Sam. "Bully King's got nothing on you."

Sam smiled. "On either of us."

He shed his pack and handed it back to Remi, then crab-walked through the underbrush. He wrapped his arms around the tree trunk, then slowly lowered himself, legs dangling and feet probing, until he found the ladder's top rung.

"I'm on," he told Remi. "Starting down."

He disappeared from view. Thirty seconds later he called, "I'm down. Drop the packs over the edge." Remi crawled forward and dropped the first one.

"Got it."

She dropped the second pack.

"Got it. Come on down. I'll talk you through it."

"On my way."

When she had reached the second-to-last rung and her lower body was hanging in space, Sam reached out and wrapped his arms around her thighs. "I've got you."

She let go, and Sam lowered her to the shelf. Remi adjusted her skewed headlamp, then looked around. The shelf on which they were standing was six feet wide and jutted several feet over the river. In the cliff face was a roughly oval-shaped cave entrance, closed off by hurricane fencing screwed into the rock. The bottom left corner of the fence had sprung free from the rock. A red-on-white sign written in both Nepali and English was affixed to the rock:

DANGER
NO TRESPASSING
DO NOT ENTER

Below the words was a crudely painted skull and crossbones.

Remi smiled. "Look, Sam, it's the universal symbol for 'quaint.'"

"Funny lady," he replied. "Ready to spelunk?"

"Have I ever said no to that question?"

"Never, bless your heart."

"Lead on."

Their suspicion that the cave had been sealed off to keep curiosity seekers from getting lost or injured was confirmed seconds after they crawled through the gap in the fence. While pushing himself to his feet, Sam's arm slipped into a fissure in the floor barely larger than his forearm. Had he been moving even at a modest pace, he would have broken a bone; had he been walking, it would have been his ankle.

"Bad omen or fair warning?" he asked Remi with a half smile as she helped him to his feet.

"I'm going with the latter."

"Reason 640 why I love you," he replied. "Ever the optimist."

They shone their flashlights around the tunnel. It was wide enough that Sam could almost spread his arms to their full breadth but only a few inches taller than Remi, forcing Sam to stand stoop-shouldered. The floor was rough, like stucco magnified a hundred times.

Sam turned his head, sniffing. "Smells dry."

Remi ran her palm over the ceiling and wall. "Feels dry."

With luck, moisture was out of the equation, or almost. Spelunking in a dry cave was dicey enough; water made it hazardous, with floors, ceilings, and walls that could collapse at the slightest disturbance. Even so, they knew that unseen tributaries of the Bagmati River could be running beneath their feet, so the cave's composition could change with little or no warning.

With Sam in the lead, they started forward. The tunnel veered sharply left, then right, then suddenly they found themselves standing before their first obstacle, this one also man-made: a set of vertical iron bars running from wall to wall, drilled into the floor and ceiling.

"They're not kidding around," Sam said, shining his flashlight over the rusted steel. How many curiosity seekers had triumphantly squeezed through the hurricane fence at the entrance only to find themselves thwarted here? Sam wondered.

Remi knelt before the bars. One by one, she gave each a shake. On the fourth try, the metal let out a grating sound. She smiled over her shoulder at Sam. "The beauty of oxidation. Give me a hand."

Together they began working the bar back and fourth until slowly it began to loosen in its socket. Stone chips and dust rained down from the ceiling. After two minutes' work the bar fell free, striking the floor with a clang that echoed through the tunnel. Sam grabbed the bar and dragged it back through the gap. He examined the ends.

"It's been cut," he murmured, then showed it to Remi.

"Acetylene torch?"

"No scorch marks. Hacksaw, would be my guess."

He shone his flashlight into the bar's empty floor

socket and could see, a few inches down, a stub of metal.

Sam looked at Remi. "The plot thickens. Somebody's been here before."

"And didn't want anyone to know about it," she added.

After taking a moment so Sam could get a bearing on his compass and sketch a rough map in his moleskin notebook, they squeezed through the gap, refitted the bar in its upright position, and continued on. The tunnel began zigzagging and narrowing, and soon the ceiling was at four feet, and Sam's and Remi's elbows were bumping along the walls. The floor began sloping downward. They put away their flashlights and turned on their headlamps. The floor steepened until they were sidestepping their way down a thirty-degree grade, using rock protrusions as hand- and footholds.

"Stop," Remi said suddenly. "Listen."

From somewhere nearby came the gurgling of water.

Sam said, "The river."

They descended another twenty feet, and the tunnel flattened out into a short corridor. Sam shimmied ahead to where the floor began sloping upward again.

"It's nearly vertical," he called back. "I think if we're careful, we can free-climb—"

"Sam, take a look at this."

He turned around and made his way back to where

Remi was standing, her neck craned back as she stared at the wall. In the beam of her headlamp, an object about the size of a half-dollar bulged from the rock.

"It looks metallic," Sam said. "Here, climb aboard."

Sam knelt down, and Remi climbed on his shoulders. He slowly stood up, allowing Remi time to steady herself against the wall. After a few seconds she said, "It's a railroad spike."

"Say again?"

Remi repeated herself. "It's buried in the rock up to the cap. Hold on . . . I think I can . . . There! It's tight, but I managed to slide it out a few inches. There's another one, Sam, about two feet up. And another one. I'm going to stand up. Ready?"

"Go."

She rose to her full height. "There's a line of them," she said. "They go up about twenty feet to what looks like a shelf."

Sam thought for a moment. "Can you slide out the second one?"

"Hold on . . . Done."

"Okay, climb back down," said Sam. Once she was back on the ground, he said, "Good show."

"Thanks," she said. "I can think of only one reason they'd be that high off the ground."

"So they'd go unnoticed."

She nodded. "They look fairly old."

"Circa 1973?" Sam wondered aloud, referring to the year Lewis King disappeared.

"Could be."

"Unless I miss my guess, it looks like Bully, or some other phantom spelunker, built himself a ladder. But to where?"

As Sam's words trailed off they panned the beams of their headlamps up the wall.

"One way to find out," Remi replied.

· 8 ·

Chobar Gorge, Nepal

As a ladder, the vertical alignment of the spikes would make Sam's ascent awkward—if, in fact, he was able to reach the first rung. To that end, he uncoiled his rope, tied a slipknot in one end, and spent two minutes trying to lasso the second spike. Once done, he used a bit of parachute chord to secure a stirrup-like prusik knot to the rope to climb-and-slide his way up the wall.

With one foot perched on the lowermost rung and his left hand wrapped around the second rung, he untied the slipknot and clipped it to his harness. He then reached up, slid out the third spike, and started upward. After five minutes of this he reached the top.

"Not that I'd care to try it," Sam called down, "but there are just enough handholds to make the ascent without the spikes."

"It would have taken some skill to set them, then."

"And strength."

"What do you see?" Remi called.

Sam craned his neck around until his beam shone over the rock shelf. "Crawl space. Not much wider than my shoulders. Hang on, I'll drop you a line."

He withdrew the second-to-last rail spike and replaced it with a SLCD (spring-loaded camming device), which locked itself into the hole. To this he attached first a carabiner, then the rope. He dropped the coil down to Remi.

"Got it," she said.

"Wait there. I'm going to scout ahead. There's no sense in both of us being up here if it's a dead end."

"Two minutes, then I'm coming after you."

"Or if you hear a scream and a thud, whichever comes first."

"No screaming or thudding allowed," Remi warned.

"Be back in a flash."

Sam adjusted his position until both his feet were perched on the uppermost spike and his arms were braced against the rock ledge. He took a breath, coiled his legs, and pushed off while levering with his arms, launching his torso onto the ledge. He inchwormed forward until his legs were no longer dangling in air.

Ahead, Sam's headlamp penetrated only ten to twelve feet. Beyond that, blackness. He licked his index finger and held it upright. The air was perfectly still, not a welcome sign. Getting into caves was usually the easy part, getting out often harder, which was why any spelunker worth his salt was always on the lookout for secondary exits. This was especially true of unmapped systems like this one.

Sam brought his watch to his face and started the chronometer. Remi had given him two minutes, and knowing his wife as he did, at two minutes and one second she'd be on her way up the rope.

He started crawling forward. His gear clanked and rasped over the rock floor, sounding impossibly loud in the cramped space. "Tons." The word appeared, unbidden, in his mind. There were countless tons of rock hanging over his body at this very moment. He forced the thought from his mind and kept going, this time more slowly, the primal part of his brain telling him: *Tread carefully, lest the world collapse around you.*

He passed the twenty-foot mark and stopped to check his watch. One minute gone. He kept crawling. The tunnel curved left, then right, then began angling upward, gently at first, then more steadily, until he had to use a modified chimney crawl to keep moving. Thirty feet gone. Another time check. Thirty seconds to go. He crossed over a hump in the floor and found himself in a wider, flat area. Ahead, his headlamp swept over an opening almost twice as wide as the crawl space.

He craned his neck and called over his shoulder, "Remi, are you there?"

"I'm here!" came the faint reply.

"I think I've got something!"

"On my way."

He heard her crawling up behind him as her headlamp washed over the walls and ceiling. She gripped his calf and gave it an affectionate squeeze. "How're you doing?"

While Sam wasn't clinically claustrophobic, there were moments in particularly tight spaces when he had to exert strict control over his mind. This was such a time. It was, Remi had told him, the downside of having a fertile imagination. Possibilities became probabilities, and an otherwise stable cave became a death trap ready to collapse into the bowels of the earth at the slightest bump.

"Sam, are you there?" Remi asked.

"Yep. I was mentally practicing Wilson Pickett's 'In the Midnight Hour.'"

Sam was a fair hand at the piano, and Remi at the violin. Occasionally, when time permitted, they practiced duets. While composer Pickett's music didn't readily lend itself to classical instruments, as lovers of vintage American soul, they enjoyed the challenge.

"What've you found?" Remi asked.

"That it's going to take a lot more practice. And my blues voice needs more—"

"I mean, ahead?"

"Oh. An opening."

"Lead on. This crawl space is too tight for my liking."

Unseen by Remi, Sam smiled. His wife was being kind. While Sam's male ego wasn't a fragile thing, Remi also knew that offering a little face-saving was a woman's prerogative.

"Here we go," Sam replied, and started crawling forward.

It took only thirty seconds to reach the opening. Sam inched forward until his head was through. He looked around, then said over his shoulder, "A circular pit about ten feet across. I can't see the bottom, but I can hear water gurgling—probably a subterranean offshoot of the Bagmati. Directly across from us is another opening, but about twelve feet higher."

"Oh, joy. How are the walls?"

"Diagonal stalagmites, the biggest about as thick as a baseball bat, the rest about half that."

"No conveniently placed spike ladders?"

Sam took another look, panning his headlamp along the pit's walls. "No," he called back, his voice echoing, "but dangling directly over my head is a spear."

"Pardon me? Did you say—"

"Yes. It's affixed to the wall by what looks like a leather cord. There's a piece of cord hanging below the spear with a shard of wood attached."

"Trip wire," Remi commented.

"My guess as well."

They'd seen similar traps—designed to foil intruders—in tombs, fortresses, and primitive bunkers. However old this spear trap was, it had likely been contrived to plunge into the neck of an unsuspecting interloper. The question, Sam and Remi knew, was what had the booby trap been intended to protect?

"Describe the spear," Remi said.

"I'll do you one better." Sam rolled over on his back, braced his feet against the ceiling, and wriggled forward until his upper torso was jutting through the opening.

"Careful . . ." Remi warned.

". . . is my middle name," Sam finished. "Well, this is interesting. There's only one spear but two more attachment points. Either the other two spears fell away or they found victims."

He reached up, grasped the spear's shaft above the point, and pulled. Despite its half-rotted appearance, the leather was surprisingly strong. Only after Sam wriggled the shaft back and forth did the cordage give way. He maneuvered the spear around, twirling it like a baton, then slid it back along his body toward Remi.

"Got it," she said. A few seconds later: "This doesn't look familiar. I'm no weapons expert, mind you, but I've never seen a design like this before. It's very old—at least four hundred years, I imagine. I'll get some pictures in case we can't come back for it."

Remi retrieved her camera from her pack and took a dozen shots. While she was doing this, Sam took a closer look around the pit. "I don't see any more booby traps. I'm trying to imagine what it must have looked like by torchlight."

"'Terrifying,' is the word," Remi replied. "Think of it. At least one of your friends had just taken a spear to the back of the neck and plummeted into a seemingly bottomless pit, and all you've got is a flickering torch to see by."

"Enough to turn away even the bravest of explorers," Sam agreed.

"But not us," Remi replied with a smile Sam could hear in her voice. "What's the plan?"

"Everything depends on those stalagmites. Did you bring up the rope we left behind?"

"Here."

Sam reached back until he felt Remi's outstretched hand, grabbed the carabiner, and pulled the coil up to him. He tied first a slipknot into the loose end, followed by a stopper knot; to this, for weight, he clipped the carabiner. He maneuvered his body until his arms were free of the opening, then tossed the line across the pit, aiming for one of the larger stalagmites a few feet below the opposite tunnel opening. He missed, retrieved the rope, tried again, this time laying the slipknot over the tip of the protrusion. He jiggled the line until the knot slid down to the base of the stalagmite, then cinched the knot tight.

"Care to help me with a stress test?" Sam asked Remi. "On three, pull with everything you've got. One . . . two . . . three!"

Together, they heaved on the rope, doing their best to rip the stalagmite from the wall. It held steady. "I think we're okay," Sam said. "Can you find a crack in the wall and—"

"I'm looking . . . Found one."

Remi slid a spring-loaded cam into the crack and fed the rope through it, then through a ratchet carabiner. "Take up the slack."

Sam did so, heaving on the rope as Remi slid the carabiner up to the cam until the line was taut. Sam gave it a test pluck. "Looks good."

Remi said, "I suppose it goes unsaid—"

"What, be careful?"

"Yes."

"It does. But it's nice to hear anyway."

"Luck."

Sam wrapped both hands around the rope and shimmied forward, slowly transferring his weight onto the line. "How's the cam look?" he asked.

"Steady."

Sam took a steadying breath, then pulled his lower legs free of the crawl space. He dangled in the air, not daring to move, gauging the sag in the rope and listening for the sound of cracking rock, until ten seconds had passed. He then pulled his legs up, hooked his ankles over the line, and began inching across the pit.

"Holding steady on this end," Remi called when Sam reached the halfway point.

Sam reached the opposite wall, transferred first one hand, then the other, to the stalagmite, then swung his legs up and braced his right heel against another protrusion. Testing his weight as he went, he contorted his body until he was sitting perched atop the stalagmite. He took a moment to catch his breath, then slowly stood up until he was level with the opening. A quick boost with his hands and a shove off the stalagmite, and he was inside the crawl space.

"Be right back," he called to Remi, then scrabbled

inside. He was back thirty seconds later. "Looks good. It widens out farther on."

"On my way," Remi answered.

In two minutes she was across, and Sam was pulling her into the opening. They lay still together for a few moments, enjoying the feeling of solid rock beneath them.

"This reminds me a lot of our third date," Remi said.

"Fourth," Sam corrected her. "The third date was horseback riding. The fourth was the rock climbing."

Remi smiled, kissed him on the cheek. "And they say guys don't remember those things."

"Who's 'they'?"

"They who haven't met you." Remi shone her head-lamp around. "Any sign of booby traps?"

"Not yet. We'll keep a sharp eye, but if your estimate on the age of that spear is accurate, I doubt any trip mechanisms would still be working."

"Famous last words."

"You have my permission to put it on my tombstone. Come on."

Sam started crawling, with Remi right behind him. As Sam had promised, a few seconds later the crawl space opened into a kidney-shaped alcove roughly twenty feet wide and five feet tall. In the opposite wall were three vertical clefts, each no wider than eighteen inches.

They stood up and stoop-walked to the first cleft. Sam shone his headlamp inside. "Dead end," he said. Remi checked the next: another dead end. The third cleft, while deeper than its neighbors, also petered out a half dozen paces inside.

"Well, that was anticlimactic," Sam said.

"Maybe not," Remi murmured, then started toward the right-hand wall, her headlamp pointing at what looked like a horizontal slash of darker rock where the wall met the ceiling. As they drew closer, the slash seemed to grow taller, rising into the ceiling, until they realized they were looking at a slot-like tunnel.

Standing side by side, Sam and Remi peered into the opening, which rose away from them at a forty-five-degree angle for twenty feet before rounding over a jagged bump in the floor.

"Sam, do you see what—"

"I think I do."

Jutting over the ridge in the floor was what appeared to be the sole of a boot.

9

Chobar Gorge, Nepal

The lack of treads on the boot's sole told Sam and Remi they weren't looking at a modern piece of footwear, and the skeletal toe poking through a rotted patch in the boot told them the owner had long since departed the earthly plane.

"Is it strange that this sort of thing doesn't shock me anymore?" Remi said, staring at the foot.

"We've stumbled across our fair share of skeletons," Sam agreed. Such surprises were part and parcel of their avocation. "See any trip wires?"

"No."

"Let's take a look around."

Sam braced his legs against one wall, his back against the other, and let Remi use his arm to pull herself up. He made his way up the slope and over the hump in the floor. After panning his headlamp around the space, he called, "All clear. You're going to want to see this, Remi."

She was beside him in an instant. Kneeling together, they examined the skeleton.

Protected from the elements and predators, and entombed in the relative dryness of the cave, the remains had partially mummified. The clothes, which appeared to be made mostly of laminated and layered leather, remained largely intact.

"I don't see any obvious signs of trauma," Remi said.

"How old?"

"Just speculating . . . at least four hundred years."

"In the same range as the spear."

"Right."

"This looks like a uniform," said Sam, touching a sleeve.

"Then that makes more sense," replied Remi, pointing. Jutting from what had once been a belt sheath was the hilt of a dagger. She panned her headlamp around the space, then murmured, "Home sweet home."

"Home, perhaps," Sam replied, "but sweet? . . . I suppose everything's relative."

A few paces from the flat area on which the skeleton lay, the tunnel widened into an alcove of roughly a hundred square feet. In several hand-carved niches in the rock walls were the stubs of crude candles. At the base of one wall, nestled in a natural hollow, were the remains of a fire; beside it, a pile of small animal bones. At the far end of the alcove were the remains of what looked like a bedroll, and, beside it, a sheathed sword, a half dozen crudely honed spears, a compound bow, and a quiver containing eight arrows. A scattering of miscellaneous items occupied the remainder of the floor: a pail, a coil of half-rotted rope, a leather pack, a round wood-and-leather shield, a wooden chest . . .

Remi stood up and began walking around the space.

"He was definitely expecting unfriendly company," Sam observed. "This has all the signs of a last stand. But to what end?"

"Maybe it has something to do with this," Remi said, and knelt down beside the wooden chest. Sam walked over. About the size of a small ottoman, the chest was a perfect cube made of a dark, heavily lacquered hardwood, with leather carrying straps on three sides and double shoulder straps on the fourth. Sam and Remi could find no hinges, no locking mechanisms. The seams were so well formed, they were nearly invisible. Engraved into the top of the chest were four intricate Asian characters in a two-by-two grid pattern.

"Do you recognize the language?" Sam asked.

"No."

"This is remarkable," Sam said. "Even with modern woodworking tools it takes incredible skill to create something like this."

He rapped on the side with his knuckles and got a solid thud in return. "Doesn't sound hollow." Gently he rocked the chest from side to side. From within came a faint rattling sound. "But it is. Fairly light too. I don't see any other markings. You?"

Remi leaned down and from side to side, examining it. She shook her head. "Bottom?" Sam tipped it. Remi checked, then said, "Nothing there, either."

"Somebody went to a lot of trouble to build this," said Sam, "and it looks like our friend here was prepared to give his life to protect it."

"It may be more than that," Remi added. "Unless we've stumbled onto the mother of all coincidences, I think we may have found what Lewis King was looking for."

"If so, how did he miss this? He was so close."

"If he didn't make it across the pit," Remi replied, "could he have survived?"

"Only one person knows the answer to that."

They turned their attention to documenting the contents of the cave. Not knowing how soon they would return, and unable to take with them but a fraction of the artifacts, they would have to rely on digital photographs, drawings, and notes. Luckily, Remi's background and training made her well equipped to do just this. After two hours of painstaking work, she proclaimed the job done.

"Wait," Remi said, then knelt beside the shield.

Sam joined her. "What is it?"

"These scratches . . . the light caught them. I

think . . ." She leaned over, took a deep breath, and blew on the shield's leather surface. An accumulation of rotted leather dust scattered.

"Not a scratch," Sam observed, and blew clear some more dust, then again and again until the shield's surface was exposed.

As Remi had suspected, the scratches were in fact an etching burned into the leather itself.

"Is that a dragon?" Remi asked.

"Or a dinosaur. Probably his crest or that of his unit," Sam guessed.

Remi took a couple dozen shots of the etching, and they stood up. "That'll do it," she said. "What about the chest?"

"We have to take it. My gut tells me it was why our friend had barricaded himself in here. Whatever's inside was something he thought worth dying for."

"I agree."

It took only a few minutes for Sam to jury-rig a web of straps that allowed him to piggyback the chest on his own pack. They took a last look around the cave, nodded a good-bye to the skeleton, and departed.

In the lead, Sam crawled up to the lip of the pit and peeked over. "Now, that's a problem."

"Care to be more specific?" Remi said.

"The rope's given way at the other end. It's dangling into the pit."

"Can you rig a—"

"Not with any confidence. We're above the other opening. At this angle, if I try to cinch the slipknot into place, it'll just slide off. There'd be no way to take up the slack."

"That leaves only one option, then."

Sam nodded. "Down."

It took but a minute for Sam to secure himself to the line. As he did, Remi set up a second belay point by hammering a piton into a crack just below the opening. Once it was set, Sam began a slow rappel, walking himself over and around the jutting stalagmites, while Remi kept watch from above, occasionally telling him to pause and adjust position to minimize the rope chafing on the protrusions.

After two minutes of careful work, he stopped. "I've reached the other cam. Good news: the cam tore free."

If the rope had parted, they would have had to splice their remaining line onto the loose end. Now he had sixty feet of line beneath him. Whether that would be enough to reach the bottom was still an unknown. If what awaited them was the icy-cold water of the Bagmati River, they would have fifteen minutes at most to find a way out before succumbing to hypothermia.

"I'll take that as a good omen," replied Remi.

Foot by foot, careful step by careful step, Sam kept descending, his headlamp receding into a small rectangle of light.

"I can't see you anymore," Remi called.

"Don't worry. If I fall, I'll be sure to give out an appropriately terrified scream."

"I've never heard you scream in your life, Fargo."

"And, cross fingers, you won't this time."

"How're the walls?

"More of the— Whoa!"

"What?"

No response.

"Sam!"

"I'm okay. Just lost my footing for a second. The walls are getting icy. Must be mist from the water below."

"How bad?"

"Just a thin coating on the walls. Can't trust any of the stalagmites, though."

"Come back up. We'll figure out another way."

"I'm continuing on. I've got another thirty feet of rope to play with."

Two minutes passed. Sam's headlamp was a mere pinpoint now, jostling back and forth in the pit's darkness as he maneuvered around the stalagmites.

Suddenly, there came the sound of shattering ice. Sam's headlamp began spinning, winking up at Remi like a strobe light. Before she could open her mouth to call to him, Sam shouted, "I'm okay. Upside down but okay."

"More description, if you please!"

"Got turned around in my harness and flipped. Good

news, though: I'm staring at the water. It's about ten feet below my head."

"I hear a 'but' coming."

"The current's fast—three knots at least—and it looks deep. Waist high, probably."

Though three knots was slower than a fast walking pace, the depth and temperature of the water multiplied the hazard. Not only would it take only one minor misstep to be swept away but the exertion it would take to stay upright would speed up the hypothermia process.

"Come back up," Remi said. "No arguments."

"Agreed. Give me a second to . . . Hold on."

From the darkness came more cracking of ice, followed by splashes.

"Talk to me, Fargo."

"Give me a second."

Another thirty seconds of cracking, then Sam's voice: "Side tunnel!"

After ten minutes of detailed work, Sam shouted, "It's good-sized. Almost tall enough to stand in. I'm going in. Give me a minute to set up a belay." If Remi went into the subterranean river, this measure would give Sam a fighting chance to reel her back in—provided there weren't rocks downriver ready to bash Remi into pulp.

Once this was done and Sam was braced and ready to take slack, Remi started her descent. Lighter and a bit more agile than her husband, she covered the distance in less time, pausing only to allow Sam time to take up slack through the piton's belay point.

At last she descended into view and stopped even with the side tunnel's entrance. Headlamps shining into one another's faces, they shared a relieved smile.

"Fancy meeting you here," Sam said.

"Damn!"

"What?"

"I had a mental bet you were going to go with 'What's a nice girl like you doing in a nearly bottomless pit like this?'"

Sam laughed. "Okay, you're going to have to go Superman in your rig and push off the opposite wall. I'll catch you."

Remi took a few moments to catch her breath and then made the appropriate adjustments to her harness until she was hanging perpendicular in the pit. Flexing her body, she slowly built up a swing until she could toe-push off the opposite wall. Three more of these allowed her to fully coil her legs and push off. Arms extended, she swung forward, hands grasping. The side wall rushed toward her face. She ducked her head. Her arms slipped into the tunnel. Sam's hands clamped on hers, and she jolted to a stop.

"Got you!" Sam said. "Wrap both hands around my left wrist."

She did, and Sam used his right arm to slowly release some slack in the rope so Remi could climb up his arm. Once her torso was inside the tunnel, Sam began back-crawling until her knees were also inside. He fell back and let out a relieved sigh.

Remi started laughing. Sam raised his head and looked at her.

"What?"

"You take me to the nicest places."

"After this, a nice hot bubble bath—for two."

"You're singing my song."

Though twice as wide as their shoulders and tall enough to allow them to walk stooped over, the tunnel's floor was Swiss cheese—so riddled with potholes that they could glimpse the river's roiling black surface rushing beneath their feet. Plumes of cold air and ice crystals shot up through the gaps, creating a fog that glittered and swirled in their headlamps. Like the pit behind them, the tunnel's walls and ceiling were coated in a membrane of ice. As they walked, pencil-thin icicles broke from the ceiling and shattered on the floor like sporadic wind chimes. Though mostly clear of ice, the heavily rutted floor forced them to brace themselves as they walked, adding to the exertion.

"Not to be a wet blanket," Remi said, "but we're assuming this leads somewhere."

"We are indeed," Sam replied over his shoulder.

"And if we're wrong?"

"Then we turn back, scale the opposite side of the pit, and leave the way we came in."

The tunnel twisted and turned, rose and fell, but, according to Sam's compass bearings, it maintained a rough easterly bearing. They took turns counting steps, but without a GPS unit to measure their overall progress, and only Sam's sketched map to go by, they had no idea how much distance they were actually covering.

After what Sam guessed was a hundred yards, he called another halt and found a relatively solid section of tunnel and plopped to the ground. After sharing a few sips of water and a quarter of their remaining jerky and dried fruit, they sat in silence, listening to the rush of the water beneath their feet.

"What time is it?" Remi asked.

Sam checked his watch. "Nine o'clock."

While they had told Selma where they were heading, they'd also asked her not to press the panic button until the following morning local time. Even then, how long would it take the authorities to arrange a rescue party and mount a search? Their only saving grace was that this tunnel had not branched; if they chose to turn back, they'd have no trouble finding the pit again. But at what point did they make that decision? Was an exit around the next bend, or miles away, or nonexistent?

Neither Sam nor Remi spoke of any of this. They didn't need to. Their years together, and the adventures they'd shared, had put them on the same wavelength.

Facial expressions were usually enough to convey what each was thinking.

"I'm still holding you to that hot bubble bath promise," Remi said.

"Forgot to tell you: I've added a relaxing massage to the pot."

"My hero. Shall we?"

Sam nodded. "Let's give it another hour. If a red carpet exit doesn't materialize, we'll turn back, have a rest, then tackle the pit."

"Deal."

Accustomed to hardship, of both the mental and the physical variety, Sam and Remi fell into a rhythm: walk for twenty minutes, pause for two minutes to rest, take a compass bearing and update the map, then onward again. The remaining time of their journey passed quickly. Left foot, right foot, repeat. To conserve light, Remi had long ago turned off her headlamp, and Sam had set his to its lowest setting, so they found themselves moving in the faintest of twilights. The cold air gushing through the floor seemed colder, their footing harder to maintain, the tinkle of falling icicles jarring to their numbed brains.

Suddenly Sam stopped. Her reactions at half speed, Remi bumped into him. Sam whispered, "Do you feel that?"

"What?"

"Cold air."

"Sam, it's—"

"No, in our faces. Ahead. Will you dig the lighter out of my pack?"

Remi did so and handed it to him. Sam took a few steps forward, looking for a solid section of floor between plumes. He found a suitable spot, stopped, and clicked on the lighter. Remi squeezed herself in next to Sam and peered around his arm. Flickering yellow light danced off the icy walls. The flame wavered, then steadied and stood straight up.

"Wait." Sam murmured, eyes on the flame.

Five seconds passed.

The flame wobbled, then shot sideways, back toward Sam's face.

"There!"

"Are you sure?" Remi asked.

"The air feels warmer now too."

"Wishful thinking?"

"Let's find out."

They walked for ten feet, stopped, checked the lighter's flame. Again it angled backward, this time more strongly. They proceeded twenty more feet and repeated the process, with the same result.

From Remi: "I hear whistling. Wind."

"Me too."

Another fifty feet brought them to a fork in the tunnel. Lighter held before him, Sam proceeded down the left tunnel without luck, then down the right.

The flame quavered, then a sudden gust nearly blew it out.

Sam shed his pack. "Wait here. I'll be back in a flash."

He switched his headlamp to its brightest setting and disappeared into the tunnel. Remi could hear his feet scuffing along the floor, the sound growing fainter by the second.

Remi checked her watch, waited ten seconds, checked it again.

"Sam?" she called.

Silence.

"Sam, answer—"

Ahead in the darkness his headlamp reappeared.

"Sorry," he said.

Remi let her head drop.

"No red carpet," Sam continued. "But would daylight do?"

Remi raised her head, took in Sam's wide smile. She narrowed her eyes at him and gave him a punch in the shoulder. "Not funny, Fargo."

As Sam had promised, there was no red carpet, but after twenty feet of walking he brought her to something even better: a set of natural steps winding up a shaft at whose top, some fifty feet away, was a fuzzy patch of sunlight.

Two minutes later Sam pushed himself off the top step and found himself peering down a short sideways tunnel. Instead of rock, the sides and floor were earth. At the far end, through a tangle of grass, was sunlight. Sam crawled toward it, shoved his arms through the opening, then dragged himself out. Remi appeared a few moments later, and together they lay back in the grass, smiling and staring up at the sky.

"Almost noon," Sam remarked.

They'd been underground all morning.

Suddenly, Sam sat up, his head turning this way and that. He leaned over to Remi and whispered, "Radio static. A portable radio."

Sam rolled over, crawled to a berm a few feet away, and peeked his head over the side. He ducked down and crawled back. "Police."

"A rescue party?" Remi asked. "Who would've called them?"

"Just a guess, but I'd say our erstwhile exploratory escorts, the King twins."

"How—"

"I don't know. Maybe I'm wrong. Let's play it safe."

They stripped themselves of anything that would indicate where they'd been and what they'd been doing—helmets, headlamps, backpacks, climbing gear, Sam's map, Remi's digital camera, the box they'd retrieved from the tomb—and shoved it all back into the tunnel, then packed grass over the entrance.

With Sam in the lead, they headed east, following a ravine and ducking between trees, until they'd put a quarter mile between themselves and the tunnel. They stopped and listened for radio static. Sam tapped his ear and pointed north. A hundred yards away they could see several figures moving through the trees.

Sam whispered, “Put on your best forlorn face.”

“Not much of a stretch at this point,” replied Remi.

Sam cupped his hands around his mouth and shouted, “Hey! Over here!”

10

Chobar Gorge, Nepal

The cell door creaked open. A guard peeked inside, scrutinized Sam for a moment as though he were about to make a dash for freedom, then stood aside. Clothed in a baggy light blue jumpsuit, auburn hair pulled back in a ponytail, Remi stepped into the room. Her face was pink, freshly washed.

The guard said in broken English, "Please sit. Wait," then slammed shut the door.

Clothed in a similar jumpsuit, Sam stood up from the table, walked over to Remi, and gave her a big hug. He pulled back and looked her up and down and smiled. "Ravishing, simply ravishing."

She smiled. "Idiot."

"How're you feeling?"

"Better. Amazing what a few minutes with a washcloth and hot water can do. Not quite a warm shower or a hot bath, mind you, but a close second."

Together, they sat down at the table. The space in which the Kathmandu police were keeping them wasn't so much a cell as it was a holding room. The cinder-block walls and the floor were painted a light gray, and the table and chairs (all bolted to the floor) were made of heavy aluminum. Before them, across the table, was a four-foot-wide mesh-embedded window through which they could see the squad room. A half dozen uniformed officers were going about their business, answering phones, writing reports, and chatting. So far, except for a few polite but firm commands in rough English, no one had spoken to them in the two hours since they'd been "rescued."

Riding in the back of the police van, Sam and Remi had watched the passing scenery, looking for the slightest clue as to where they had emerged from the cave system. Their answer had come almost immediately as they crossed over the Chobar Gorge bridge and turned northeast toward Kathmandu proper.

Their underground march to freedom had brought them to the surface a mere two miles from where they'd entered. This realization brought first a smile to Sam's and Remi's lips and then, to the bewilderment of the two police officers in the front seat, a gale of laughter that lasted a full minute.

"Any clue as to who raised the alarm?" Remi now asked Sam.

"None. As far as I can tell, we're not under arrest."

"We have to assume they're going to question us. What's our story going to be?"

Sam thought for a moment. "As close to the truth as possible. We came out here a little before sunrise for a day hike. We got lost and wandered around until they found us. If they push, just stick with 'I'm not sure.' Unless they found our equipment, they can't prove otherwise."

"Got it. And providing we don't get thrown into a Nepali prison for some obscure crime?"

"We'll need to retrieve the—"

Sam stopped talking, his eyes narrowed. Remi followed his gaze through the window to the far left side of the squad room near the door. Standing at the threshold were Russell and Marjorie King.

"I wish I could say I was surprised," Remi muttered.

"Just as we suspected."

Across the squad room, the sergeant in charge spotted the King twins and hurried over to where they were standing. The trio began talking back and forth. Though neither Sam nor Remi could hear the conversation, the sergeant's mannerisms and posture told the tale: he was subservient, if not a little frightened. Finally the sergeant nodded and hurried back into the squad room. Russell and Marjorie stepped back into the hallway.

A few moments later Sam and Remi's door opened,

and the sergeant and one of his underlings stepped inside. They took the seats opposite the Fargos. The sergeant spoke Nepali for a few seconds, then nodded to his underling, who said in heavily accented but decent English, "My sergeant has asked that I translate our conversation. Is this acceptable?"

Sam and Remi nodded.

The sergeant spoke, and a few seconds later the translation came: "If you would, please confirm your identities."

Sam replied, "Have we been arrested?"

"No," the officer replied. "You are being temporarily detained."

"On what grounds?"

"Under Nepali law, we are not required to disclose the answer to that question at the present time. Please confirm your identities."

Sam and Remi did so, and for the next few minutes they were taken through a series of routine questions—Why are you in Nepal? Where are you staying? What prompted your visit?—before getting down to substance.

"Where were you going when you got lost?"

"Nowhere in particular," Remi responded. "It seemed like a lovely day for a hike."

"You parked your car at Chobar Gorge. Why?"

"We heard it was a beautiful area," said Sam.

"What time did you arrive?"

"Before dawn."

"Why so early?"

"We're restless souls," Sam replied with a smile.

"What does that mean?"

"We like to stay busy," said Remi.

"Please tell us where your hike took you."

"If we knew that," Sam said, "we probably wouldn't have gotten lost."

"You had a compass with you. How did you lose your way?"

"I flunked out of Boy Scouts," said Sam.

Remi chimed in. "I only sold cookies in the Girl Scouts."

"This is not a laughing matter, Mr. and Mrs. Fargo. Do you find this funny?"

Sam put on his best chastised expression. "Apologies. We're exhausted and a little embarrassed. We're grateful you found us. Who alerted you we might be in trouble?"

The officer translated the question. His sergeant grunted something, then spoke again. "My sergeant asks that you restrict yourselves to answering his questions. You said you planned to go on a daylong hike. Where were your backpacks?"

"We didn't expect to be gone that long," Remi said. "We're not the best planners, either."

Sam nodded sadly to emphasize his wife's point.

The officer asked, "You expect us to believe you went on a hike with no equipment whatsoever?"

"I had my Swiss Army knife," Sam said drily.

At this translation, the sergeant glanced up and glared at Sam, then Remi, then stood up and stalked from the room. "Please wait here," the officer said, and left the room.

Not surprisingly, the sergeant walked straight through the squad-room door to the hallway. Sam and Remi could see only his back; Russell and Marjorie were out of view. Sam stood up, walked to the far-right side of the window, and pressed his face against it.

"Can you see them?" Remi asked.

"Yep."

"And?"

"The twins look unhappy. Not a smarmy smile in sight. Russell's gesturing . . . Well, this is interesting."

"What?"

"He's mimicking the shape of a box—a box that looks remarkably like the same size as the chest."

"That's good. I imagine they've searched the area in which they found us. Russell wouldn't be asking for what's already been found."

Sam stepped back from the window and hurried back to his seat.

The sergeant and his officer stepped back into the room and sat down. The questioning resumed, this time with a bit more intensity, and in a roundabout fashion designed to trip up Sam and Remi. The gist of the queries remained the same, however: we know you had to have had belongings, where are they? Sam and Remi took their time and stuck to their story, watching as the sergeant's frustration grew.

At last the sergeant resorted to threats: "We know who you are and what you do for a living. We suspect you have come to Nepal in search of black market antiquities."

"On what do you base your suspicions?" Sam asked.

"Sources."

"You've been misinformed," said Remi.

"There are several statutes under which you can be charged, all of which carry serious penalties."

Sam leaned forward in his chair and fixed the sergeant's gaze. "Charge away. Right after we're booked we'll want to talk to the legal attaché at the U.S. embassy."

The sergeant held Sam's eyes for a long ten seconds, then leaned back and sighed. He said something to his underling, then stood up and left the room, banging the open door against the wall as he left.

The underling translated, "You are free to go."

Ten minutes later, back in their own clothes, Sam and Remi were out the front door of the police station and walking down the steps. Dusk was falling. The sky was clear, and a scattering of diamond-speck stars began to shine. Streetlights illuminated the cobblestoned street below.

"Sam! Remi!"

Expecting this, neither of them were surprised when they turned to see Russell and Marjorie hurrying down the sidewalk toward them.

"We just heard," Russell said, trotting up. "Are you okay?"

"Tired, a little embarrassed, but no worse for wear," Sam replied.

They'd already decided to stick to their got-lost-on-a-hike story with the King twins. It was a precarious dance; everyone knew Sam and Remi were lying. What would Russell and Marjorie do about it? Better question: as it now seemed clear that Charlie King had a wholly different agenda than the one he'd shared with Sam and Remi, how would they proceed? What was King after, and what was the true story behind Frank Alton's disappearance?

"We'll take you to your car," Marjorie said.

"We'll collect it in the morning," replied Remi. "We're going back to the hotel."

"Better we get it now," Russell said. "If you've got gear inside—"

Sam couldn't help but smile at this. "We don't. Good night."

Sam took Remi's arm, and together they turned and started walking in the opposite direction. Russell called, "We'll call you in the morning!"

"Don't call us, we'll call you," Sam replied without turning.

HOUSTON, TEXAS

"Hell, yes, I'd say they're off the reservation," Charles King barked, reclining in his plush office chair. Behind him, the cityscape filled his floor-to-ceiling window.

Half a world away, Russell and Marjorie King said nothing over the speakerphone. They knew better than to interrupt their father. When he wanted to know something, he would ask a question.

"Where the hell were they all day?"

"We don't know," Russell replied. "The man we hired to follow them lost them southwest of the—"

"Hired? What d'ya mean, hired?"

"He's one of our . . . security men at the dig site," Marjorie said. "He's trustworthy—"

"But incompetent! How about gettin' somebody with both those glowin' attributes? Ever consider that? Why'd you hire someone? What were you two doin'?"

"We were at the site," said Russell. "We're getting ready to ship the—"

"Never mind. Doesn't matter. Could the Fargos have been in that cave system?"

"It's possible," replied Marjorie, "but we've been through it. There's nothing to find."

"Yeah, yeah. The question is, if they were, how'd they find out about it? You gotta make sure they're gettin' only the info we want them to get, understand?"

"Yes, Dad," replied Marjorie and Russell in unison.

"What about their belongin's?"

"We went through them," said Russell. "And their car. Our man in the police department questioned them for an hour, but no luck."

"Did he twist their arms, for God's sake?"

"As far as he could."

"The Fargos were unfazed, he said."

"What'd they say they'd been doin'?"

"They claimed they got lost on a hike."

"Bull crap! This is Sam and Remi Fargo we're talkin' about. I'll tell you what happened: you two screwed up somehow, and the Fargos got suspicious. They're runnin' circles around you two. Put a bunch of people on 'em. I want to know where they're goin' and what they're doin'. You got that?"

"You can count on us, Dad," said Marjorie.

"That'd be a nice change," grumbled King. "In the meantime, I'm not takin' any more chances. I'm sendin' reinforcements."

King leaned forward and stabbed the speakerphone's Disconnect button. Standing on the other side of the desk, her hands folded before her, stood Zhilan Hsu.

"You are hard on them, Charles," she said quietly.

"And you coddle 'em!" King shot back.

"Until this latest incident with the Fargos, they've done well for you."

King frowned, and gave an annoyed shake of his head. "I s'pose. Still, I want you to get out there, make sure this thing don't go too far off the rails. Somethin's got the Fargos' backs up. Take the Gulfstream and get out there. Fix 'em. That Alton character too. He's useless now."

"Can you be more specific?"

"Get the Fargos to play their part. Failin' that . . . Nepal's a big place. Plenty of room for people to disappear."

11

Hyatt Regency Hotel,
Kathmandu, Nepal

In the early morning, the phone on Remi's nightstand was ringing. "Sam, did you do this on purpose? A wake-up call. Do you know what time it is?"

Sam picked up the phone and said, "We'll be there in forty-five minutes."

"Be where?" Remi demanded.

"As I promised. A Himalayan hot stone massage for you and a deep tissue massage for me."

"Fargo," said Remi with a wide smile, "you're a treasure."

She slid out of bed and dashed to the bathroom as Sam answered a knock on the door. Room service delivered the breakfast he'd ordered the night before: Remi's favorite, corned beef hash and poached eggs, and, for him, scrambled eggs with salmon.

He'd also ordered coffee and two glasses of pomegranate juice.

While they ate, they turned their attention to the mysterious chest that sat on the couch across from their table. Remi poured a second cup of coffee as Sam dialed up Selma.

"Do you think King had Alton kidnapped?" Selma asked.

"To get us here," Remi offered, taking a sip of coffee.

Selma chimed in, "Get you there on the pretext of looking for Frank and then . . . what?"

"False flag," Sam murmured, then explained: "It's an espionage term. An agent is recruited by an enemy posing as an ally. The agent thinks his mission is one thing, but it's actually something altogether different."

"Oh, great," Remi remarked.

"It's a house of cards," Sam agreed. "If that's what King is up to, his ego wouldn't let him entertain the idea of the plan derailing."

"Then you don't know if you're actually looking for Lewis King or not. Or whether there was even a sighting of him."

"Charlie doesn't strike me as the sentimental type. If I had to guess, I'd say it's not so much his father Charlie is chasing but perhaps what his father was chasing."

"The chest you found?" Selma suggested.

"As I said, a guess," replied Sam.

The night before, rather than returning to the hotel, Sam and Remi had walked south of the police station until they were out of view, then turned north and flagged a cab. Sam ordered the driver to meander around the city for ten minutes as he and Remi watched for signs of surveillance. They had little doubt the King twins intended to follow them, and they were giving them no time to set up.

Once certain they were not being followed, Sam ordered the driver to take them to a rental car agency on the southern outskirts of Kathmandu, where they hired a battered green Opel. An hour later they pulled into a motel parking lot a half mile from Chobar Gorge, where they left the car and walked the remaining distance.

Having memorized landmarks while being driven away by the police, they took less than an hour to find their exit tunnel. Their gear was still inside and apparently untouched.

"We're sending it to you via FedEx," Remi told Selma.

"If it is what King is after, better we get rid of it. Besides, Selma, you like puzzles; you're going to love this one. Solve it, and we'll buy you that fish for your tank . . . the, uh—"

"Aquarium, Mr. Fargo. A tank is something you

put in a child's bedroom. And the fish is a type of cichlid. Very rare. Very expensive. Its scientific name is—"

"In Latin, I'm sure," Sam finished with a chuckle. "Open our Nepali puzzle box, and it's yours."

"You don't need to bribe me, Mr. Fargo. This is part of my job."

"Then call it an early birthday present," Remi replied. She and Sam shared a smile: Selma did not enjoy celebrating birthdays, especially her own.

"By the way, I heard back from Rube," Selma said, rapidly changing subjects. "He looked into Zhilan Hsu. He said she's—and I quote—'all but invisible.' No driver's license, no credit cards, no public records of any kind save one: her immigration record. According to it, she emigrated here on a work visa from Hong Kong in 1990 at the age of sixteen."

"Let me guess," Sam said. "Employed by King Oil."

"Correct. But here's the kicker. She was six months pregnant at the time. I've done the math. Her due date roughly coincides with the birth date of Russell and Marjorie."

"It's official," Remi said. "I doubly don't like Charlie King. He probably bought her."

"A safe bet," Sam agreed.

Selma asked, "What's your next step?"

"Back to the university. We got a voice mail from Professor Kaalrami. She's finished the translation of the Devanagari parchment—"

"Lowa," Remi corrected. "She said it was written in Lowa."

"Right. Lowa," Sam replied. "With any luck, her colleague can shed some light on the tomb we found—or at least rule out a connection."

"And what about Frank?"

"Assuming King's behind his kidnapping, our only chance to get him back is leverage. If King thinks we have something he wants, we'll be in a better position to bargain. Until then, we can only hope King is smart enough not to kill Frank."

KATHMANDU UNIVERSITY

After making certain they were not being followed, Sam and Remi found a FedEx office and mailed the chest. It would take two days and six hundred dollars, the agent told them, but the package would be on a plane by early evening. A bargain, Sam and Remi decided, knowing the chest would be beyond Marjorie and Russell's reach—provided it was, in fact, of interest to King. Anyway, they had neither the time nor the resources to devote to opening the chest. It was better off in the hands of Selma, Pete, and Wendy.

Sam and Remi reached the university campus shortly after one o'clock and found Professor Kaalrami in her office. After exchanging pleasantries, they settled around her conference table.

"This was challenging," Professor Kaalrami began. "The translation took me nearly six hours."

"We're sorry it took so much of your time," Remi replied.

"Nonsense. It was better than spending the evening watching television. I enjoyed the brain exercise. I have a written translation for you." She slid a typewritten sheet of paper across the table to them. "I can confirm the essence of the document. It is a military decree ordering the evacuation of the Theurang from the capital city of Lo Monthang, in the Kingdom of Mustang."

"When?" asked Sam.

"The decree does not say," said Professor Kaalrami. "The man we are going to meet after this—my colleague—may be better equipped to answer that. There may be some clue in the text that I missed."

"This Theurang . . ." Remi prompted.

"Aside from it also being referred to as the 'Golden Man,' I'm afraid I found no explanation. But as I said, my colleague may know. I can tell you the reason the decree was issued: an invasion. An army was approaching Lo Monthang. On behalf of the Royal House, the leader of the Mustang Army—I gather the position is similar to that of a marshal or chief of staff—ordered that the Theurang be carried from the city by a special group of soldiers known as Sentinels. There is no description beyond that. Just their name."

"Evacuated to where?" asked Sam.

"The decree does not say. The phrase 'as ordered' is

used several times, which suggests the Sentinels may have received a separate, more specific briefing."

"Anything else?" Remi asked.

"One item that caught my attention," Professor Kaalrami replied. "The decree praises the Sentinels' willingness to die in order to protect the Golden Man."

"Fairly standard military language," Sam said. "A pep talk by the general before—"

"No, I'm sorry, Mr. Fargo. I used the wrong word. The praise was not for their willingness to give their lives in the line of duty. The language used was one of certitude. Whoever wrote this document fully expected the Sentinels to die. None of them were expected to return to Lo Monthang alive."

Shortly before two o'clock, the time Professor Kaalrami had arranged for them to meet with her colleague Sushant Dharel, they left her office and walked across campus to another building. They found Dharel—a pencil-thin man in his mid-thirties, wearing khaki pants and a short-sleeved white shirt—finishing a class in a wood-paneled classroom. They waited until all the students had filed out, and then Professor Kaalrami made the introductions. Upon hearing Kaalrami's description of Sam and Remi's interest, Dharel's eyes lit up.

"You have this document with you?"

"And the translation," Professor Kaalrami replied, and handed them over.

Dharel scanned both, his lips moving wordlessly as

he absorbed the contents. He looked up at Sam and Remi. "Where did you find this? In whose possession was—" He stopped suddenly. "Forgive my excitement and my bad manners. Please, sit down."

Sam, Remi, and Professor Kaalrami took chairs in the first row. Dharel pulled a chair from around his desk and sat before them. "If you would . . . Where did you find this?"

"It was among the belongings of a man named Lewis King."

"A friend of mine from long ago," Professor Kaalrami added. "It was long before your time, Sushant. I believe my translation is fairly accurate, but I could not give Mr. and Mrs. Fargo much context. As our resident expert on Nepalese history, I thought you might help."

"Of course, of course," Dharel said, eyes again scanning the parchment. After a full minute he looked up again. "Do not be offended, Mr. and Mrs. Fargo, but for the purposes of clarity, I will assume you have no knowledge of our history."

"A safe assumption," Sam replied.

"I should also admit that much of what I am about to tell you is considered by many as more legend than history."

"We understand," Remi said. "Please go on."

"What you have here is known as the Himanshu Decree. It was issued in the year 1421 by a military commander named Dolma. Here at the bottom you can see his official stamp. It was common practice then. Stamps and seals were meticulously crafted and closely guarded tools. Often, high-ranking personnel—both military and governmental—were accompanied by soldiers whose sole purpose was to guard official seals. Given time, I can confirm or refute the provenance of this stamp, but at first glance I believe it to be genuine."

"Professor Kaalrami's translation suggests the decree was ordering the evacuation of an artifact of some kind," Sam prompted. "The Theurang."

"Yes, quite right. It is also known as the Golden Man. This is where history becomes muddled with myth, I'm afraid. The Theurang is said to have been a life-sized statue of a man-like creature or, depending on whom you ask, the skeleton of the creature itself. The story behind the Theurang is similar to that of Genesis from the Christian Bible in that the Theurang is said to be the remains of the earth's . . ." Dharel's voice trailed off as he searched for the correct phrase. "Life giver. The Mother of Mankind, if you will."

"That's quite a job title," Sam said.

Dharel's brows furrowed for a moment, then he smiled. "Oh, yes, I see. Yes, a heavy burden to carry, that of the Theurang. At any rate, whether real or mythological, the Golden Man became a symbol of reverence for the people of Mustang—and for much of Nepal, for that matter. But the legendary home of the Theurang is said to have been Lo Monthang."

"This 'life giver' moniker," Remi said. "Is it believed to be metaphorical or literal?"

Dharel smiled, shrugged. "As with any religious story, the interpretation is in the mind of the believer. I think it is safe to say that at the time this decree was issued, there were more literal believers."

"What can you tell us about these Sentinels?" asked Sam.

"They were elite soldiers, the equivalent of today's Special Forces. According to some texts, they were trained from youth for one purpose: to protect the Theurang."

"Professor Kaalrami mentioned a phrase in the decree—'as ordered'—in relation to the evacuation plan the Sentinels were supposed to carry out. What are your thoughts?"

"I have no knowledge of the specific plan," Dharel replied, "but as I understand it, there were only a few dozen Sentinels. Upon evacuation, each of them was to leave the city carrying a chest, a chest designed to confuse invaders. In one of the chests was to be the disassembled remains of the Theurang."

Sam and Remi exchanged sideways smiles.

Dharel added, "Only a select few in the military and government knew which Sentinel carried the genuine remains."

Sam asked, "And inside the other chests?"

Dharel shook his head. "I do not know. Perhaps nothing, perhaps a replica of the Theurang. At any rate, the plot was designed to overwhelm any pursuers. Equipped with the best weapons and the fastest horses, the Sentinels would race from the city and separate in hopes of dividing the pursuers. With luck and skill, the

Sentinel carrying the Theurang would escape and hide it in a predetermined location."

"Can you describe the weapons?"

"Only generally: a sword, several daggers, a bow, and a spear."

"There's no account of whether the plan succeeded?" asked Remi.

"None."

"What did the chest look like?" said Remi.

Dharel retrieved a pad of paper and pencil from his desk and sketched a wooden cube that looked remarkably similar to the chest they recovered from the cave. Dharel said, "As far as I have found, there is no description beyond this. The chest was said to have been of an ingenious design, the hope being that each time an enemy recovered one of them he would spend days or weeks trying to open it."

"And in the process, buy more time for the other Sentinels," said Sam.

"Exactly so. Similarly, the Sentinels had no family, no friends an enemy could use against them. They were also trained since youth to withstand the worst kinds of torture."

"Amazing dedication," Remi remarked.

"Indeed."

"Can you describe the Theurang?" asked Sam.

Dharel nodded. "As I mentioned, it is said to have man-like features but an overall . . . beastly appearance. His bones were made of the purest gold, his eyes made of some kind of gem—rubies or emeralds, or the like."

"The Golden Man," Remi said.

"Yes. Here . . . I have an artist's rendering." Dharel stood up, walked around to his desk, and rummaged through the drawers for half a minute before returning to them with a leather-bound book. He flipped through pages before stopping. He turned the book around and handed it to Sam and Remi.

After a few seconds, Remi murmured, "Hello, handsome."

Though highly stylized, the book's rendering of the Theurang was nearly identical to the etching on the shield they had found in the cave.

An hour later, back at the hotel, Sam and Remi called Selma. Sam recounted their visit to the university.

"Amazing," Selma said. "This is the find of a lifetime."

"We can't take credit for it," Remi replied. "I suspect Lewis King beat us to it, and rightly so. If he had, in fact, spent decades hunting for this, it's all his—posthumously, of course."

"You're assuming he's dead, then?"

"A hunch," Sam replied. "If anyone else had found that tomb before us, it would have been announced. An archaeological site would have been set up and the contents removed."

Remi continued: "King must have explored the cave

system, set those railroad spikes, discovered the tomb, then fell while trying to recross the pit. If that's what happened, Lewis King's bones are scattered along some underground tributary of the Bagmati River. It's a shame. He was so close."

"But we're getting ahead of ourselves," Sam said. "For all we know, the chest we found was one of the decoys. It would still be a significant find, but not the grand prize."

Selma said, "We'll know if—when—we get it open."

They chatted with Selma for a few more minutes, then disconnected.

"What now?" asked Remi.

"I don't know about you, but I've had enough of the creepy King twins."

"You even have to ask?"

"They've been nipping at our heels since we got here. I say it's time we turn the tables on them—and on King Senior himself."

"Covert surveillance?" Remi said with a gleam in her eye.

Sam stared at her a moment, then smiled thinly. "Sometimes, your eagerness scares me."

"I love covert surveillance."

"I know you do, dear. We may or may not have what King is after. Let's see if we can convince him we do. We'll shake the tree a little bit and see what falls out."

12

KATHMANDU, NEPAL

Knowing the King twins were in Nepal minding one of their father's mining concerns, Selma took but a few hours to ferret out the details. Working under the banner of one of King's many subsidiaries, the exploratory dig camp was located north of Kathmandu in the Langtang Valley.

After another trip to the surplus store, Sam and Remi packed their gear into the back of their newly rented Range Rover and set out. Though it was nearly five o'clock and nightfall less than two hours away, they wanted to get far away from the King twins, who Sam and Remi felt certain weren't about to leave them alone.

As the crow flies, the mining camp was not quite thirty miles north of the city. By road, it was over three times that distance—a short drive in any Western country but a daylong odyssey in Nepal.

"Judging by this map," Remi said in the passenger's seat, "what they call a highway is actually a dirt road that's a bit wider and slightly better maintained than a cow path. Once we pass Trisuli Bazar, we'll be on secondary roads. God knows what that means, though."

"How far to Trisuli?"

"With luck, we'll be there before nightfall. Sam . . . goat!"

Sam looked up to see a teenage girl escorting a goat across the road seemingly oblivious to the vehicle bearing down on them. The Range Rover skidded to a stop in a cloud of brown dust. The girl looked up and smiled, unfazed. She waved. Sam and Remi waved back.

"Lesson relearned," Sam said. "No crosswalks in Nepal."

"And goats have the right-of-way," Remi added.

Once clear of the city limits and into the foothills, they found the road bracketed by terraced farm fields, lush and green against the otherwise barren and brown slopes. To their immediate left, the Trisuli River, swollen with spring runoff, churned over boulders, the water a leaden gray color from scree and silt. Here and there, they could see clusters of shacks nestled against the distant tree line. Far to the north and west stood the higher Himalayan peaks, jagged black towers against the sky.

Two hours later, just as the sun was dipping behind the mountains, they pulled into Trisuli Bazar. Tempted as they were to stay in one of the hostels, Sam and Remi had decided to err on the side of slight paranoia and rough it. However unlikely it was that the Kings would think to look for them here, Sam and Remi decided to assume the worst.

Following Remi's directions, Sam followed the Range Rover's headlights out of the village, then turned left down a narrow service road to what the map described as a "trekker's waypoint." They pulled into a roughly oval clearing lined with yurt-like huts and rolled to a stop. He doused the headlights and turned off the ignition.

"See anyone?" Sam said, looking around.

"No. It looks like we have the run of the place."

"Hut or tent?"

"Seems a shame to waste the ugly patchwork pup tent we paid so much money for," Remi said.

"That's my girl."

Fifteen minutes later, under the glow of their headlamps, they had their camp set up a few hundred yards behind the huts in a copse of pine. As Remi finished rolling out their sleeping bags, Sam got a fire going.

Sorting through their food supply, Sam asked, "Dehydrated chicken teriyaki or . . . dehydrated chicken teriyaki?"

"Whichever one I can eat the fastest," Remi replied. "I'm ready for bed. Got a terrible headache."

"It's the thin air. We're around nine thousand feet. It'll be better tomorrow."

Sam had both food packets ready in minutes. Once they finished eating, Sam brewed a couple cups of oolong tea. They sat before the fire and watched the flames dance. Somewhere in the trees an owl hooted.

"If the Theurang is what King is after, I wonder about his motivation," Remi said.

"There's no telling," Sam replied. "Why all the subterfuge? Why the heavy-handedness with his children?"

"He's a powerful man, with an ego the size of Alaska—"

"And a domineering control freak."

"That too. Maybe this is how he operates. Trust no one and keep an iron thumb on everything."

"You may be right," Sam replied. "But whatever is driving him, I'm not inclined to hand over something as historically significant as the Theurang."

Remi nodded. "And, unless we've misjudged his character, I think Lewis King would agree—alive or dead. He'd want it handed over to Nepal's National Museum or a university."

"Just as important," Sam added, "if for whatever twisted reason King had Frank kidnapped, I say we do our level best to make sure he pays for it."

"He won't go down without a fight, Sam."

"And neither will we."

"Spoken like the man I love," Remi replied.

She held up her mug, and Sam put his arm around her waist and drew her close.

They were up before dawn the next day, fed and packed and back on the road by seven. As they gained altitude and passed through hamlet after hamlet with names like Betrawati, Manigaun, Ramche, and Thare, the landscape changed from green stair-step fields and monochromatic hills to triple-canopied forest and narrow gorges. After a brief lunch at a scenic overlook, they continued on and reached their turnoff, an unmarked road just north of Boka Jhunda, an hour later. Sam stopped the Rover at the intersection, and they eyeballed the dirt road before them. Barely wider than the Rover itself and hemmed in by thick foliage, it looked more like a tunnel than a road.

"I'm having a bit of déjà vu," Sam said. "Weren't we on this road a few months ago, but in Madagascar?"

"It bears an eerie resemblance," Remi agreed. "Double-checking."

She traced her index finger along the map, occasionally checking her notes as she went. "This is the place. According to Selma, the mining camp is twelve miles to the east. There's a larger road a few miles north of here, but it's used for camp traffic."

"Best to sneak in the back window, then. Do you have a signal?"

Remi grabbed the satellite phone from between her feet and checked for voice messages. After a moment she nodded, held up a finger, and listened. She hung up. "Professor Dharel from the university. He made some calls. Evidently there's a local historian in Lo Monthang who is considered the national expert on Mustang history. He's agreed to see us."

"How soon?"

"Whenever we get there."

Sam considered this and shrugged. "No problem. Providing we don't get caught invading King's mining camp, we should make Lo Monthang in three or four weeks."

He shifted the Rover into drive and pressed the accelerator.

Almost immediately the grade steepened and the road began zigzagging, and soon, despite an average speed of ten miles per hour, they felt like they were on a roller-coaster ride. Occasionally through the passing foliage they caught glimpses of gorges, surging rivers, and jagged rock outcroppings, soon gone, absorbed by the forest.

After nearly ninety minutes of driving, Sam came around a particularly tight bend. Remi shouted, "Big trees!"

"I see them," Sam replied, already slamming on the brakes.

Looming before the windshield was a wall of green.

"Tell me it isn't so," Sam said. "Selma made a mistake?"

"No chance."

They both climbed out, ducking and weaving their way through the foliage surrounding the Rover until they reached the front bumper.

"And no valet, either," Sam muttered.

To the right, Remi said, "I've got a path."

Sam walked over. As promised, a narrow, rutted trail disappeared into the trees. Sam dug out his compass, and Remi checked their bearing against the map.

"Two miles down that trail," she said.

"So, translated to Nepalese distances . . . ten days, give or take."

"Give or take," Remi agreed.

The trail took them through a series of down-sloping switchbacks before bottoming out beside a river. Flowing from north to south, the water crashed over a series of moss-covered boulders, sending up plumes of spray that left Sam and Remi dripping wet in a matter of seconds.

They followed the path south along the river to a relatively calm section, where they found a wooden suspension bridge barely wider than their shoulders. The canopy from both banks spanned the water; vines and branches draped over the bridge and obscured the other side.

Sam shed his pack and, with both hands clenched on the rope side rails, crept onto the bridge's head, probing with his foot for cracks or loose planks before transferring his weight. When he reached the bridge's midpoint, he tried a test hop.

"Sam!"

"Seems sturdy enough."

"Don't do that again." She saw the half smile on his face, and her eyes narrowed. "If I have to jump in after you . . ."

He laughed, then turned and walked back to where she was standing. "Come on, it'll hold us."

He donned his pack and led the way back on the bridge. After two brief pauses to let the bridge's swaying slow, they reached the other side.

For the next hour they followed the trail as it weaved up and down forested slopes and across gorges until finally the trees began to thin ahead. They topped a crest and almost immediately heard the rumble of diesel engines and the beep-beep-beep of trucks backing up.

"Down!" Sam rasped, and dropped to his belly, dragging Remi with him.

"What?" she said. "I didn't see anything—"

"Directly below us."

He gestured for her to follow, then turned his body left and crawled off the trail into the underbrush. After twenty feet he stopped, glanced back, and curled his finger at Remi. She crawled up beside him. Using his fingertips, Sam parted the foliage.

Directly below them was a football-shaped earthen

pit, forty feet deep, two hundred yards wide, and nearly a quarter mile long. The sides of the pit were perfectly vertical, an escarpment of black soil dropping away from the surrounding forest as though a giant had slammed a cookie cutter into the earth and scooped out the center. In the center of the pit itself, yellow bulldozers, dump trucks, and forklifts moved to and fro on well-worn paths, while along the edges teams of men worked with shovels and picks around what looked like horizontal shafts that disappeared into the ground. At the far end of the pit, an earthen ramp led up to a clearing and, Sam and Remi assumed, the main service road. Construction trailers and Quonset-style huts lined the sides of the clearing.

Sam continued to look around the site. "I've got guards," he muttered. "Stationed in the trees along the rim and in the clearing."

"Armed?"

"Yes. Assault rifles. Not your run-of-the-mill AK-47s, though. I don't recognize the model. Whatever it is, it's modern. This isn't like any exploratory mine site I've ever seen," Sam said. "Outside of a banana republic, that is."

Remi stared at the steep slope of the pit. "I count thirteen . . . no, fourteen side tunnels. None of them are big enough for anything but men and hand tools."

The bulldozers and trucks seemed to be skirting the edges of the pit. Occasionally, however, a forklift would approach one of the tunnels, pick up a tarp-covered pallet, then scale the ramp and disappear from view.

"I need the binoculars," Remi said.

Sam dug them out of his pack and handed them over. She scanned the pit for half a minute, then handed them back to Sam. "Do you see the third tunnel from the ramp on the right side? Hurry, before they cover it up."

He panned the binoculars. "I see it."

"Zoom in on the pallet."

Sam did so. After a few seconds, he lowered the binoculars and looked at Remi. "What the hell is that?"

"It's not my area of expertise," Remi said, "but I'm pretty sure it's a goliath ammonite. It's a type of fossil, like a giant nautilus. This isn't a mining camp, Sam. This is an archaeological dig."

13

Langtang Valley, Nepal

"A dig?" Sam repeated. "Why would King be conducting a dig?"

"No way to tell for sure," Remi said, "but what's going on here breaks about a dozen Nepalese laws. They take archaeological excavation very seriously, especially anything dealing with fossils."

"Black market trade?" Sam speculated.

"That's the first thing that popped into my head," Remi replied.

In the last decade, the illegal excavation and sale of fossils had become big business, especially in Asia. China in particular had been cited as a primary offender by a number of investigative bodies, but all of them lacked the teeth to enforce penalties within her borders. The previous year, a report by the Sustainable Preservation

Initiative estimated that of the thousands of tons of fossil artifacts sold on the black market, less than one percent of them are intercepted—and, of these, none led to a single conviction.

"It's big money," Remi said. "Private collectors are willing to pay millions for intact fossils, especially if it's of one of the sexier species: *Velociraptor*, *Tyrannosaurus rex*, *Triceratops*, *Stegosaurus* . . ."

"Millions of dollars is pocket change to King."

"You're right, but there's no denying what's in front of us. Wouldn't this qualify as leverage, Sam?"

He smiled. "It would indeed. We're going to need more than pictures, though. How do you feel about a bit of skullduggery?"

"I'm a big fan of skullduggery."

Sam checked his watch. "We've got a few hours until nightfall."

Remi turned around and retrieved their digital camera from her pack. "I'll make the most of what daylight we have left."

Whether a trick of light or a genuine phenomenon, twilight seemed to last hours in the Himalayas. An hour after Sam and Remi hunkered down in the foliage to wait, the sun began dipping toward the peaks to the west, and for the next two hours they watched dusk ever so slowly settle over the forest until finally the bulldozers' and trucks' headlights popped on.

"They're finishing up," Sam said, pointing.

Along the perimeter of the pit, digging crews were emerging from the tunnels and heading toward the ramp.

"Working from dawn till dusk," Remi remarked.

"And probably for pennies an hour," replied Sam.

"If that. Maybe their pay is not getting shot at."

To their right they heard a branch snap. They froze. Silence. And then, faintly, the crunch of footsteps moving closer. Sam gestured to Remi with a flattened palm, and together they pressed themselves against the ground, their faces turned right toward the sound.

Ten seconds passed.

A shadowed figure appeared on the trail. Dressed in olive drab fatigues and a floppy jungle hat, the man carried his assault rifle diagonally across his body. He walked to the edge of the pit, stopped, and gazed down. He raised a pair of binoculars to his eyes and scanned the pit. After a full minute of this, he lowered his binoculars, then turned, stepped off the trail, and disappeared from view.

Sam and Remi waited for five minutes, then rose up onto their elbows. "Did you see his face?" she asked.

"I was too busy waiting to see if he was going to step on us."

"He was Chinese."

"Are you sure?"

"Yes."

Sam considered this. "Looks like Charlie King's got himself some partners. One bit of good news, though."

"What?"

"He wasn't carrying night-vision binoculars. Now all we have to worry about is bumping into one of them in the dark."

"Ever the optimist," Remi replied.

They continued to watch and wait, not only for the last of the men and equipment to make their way up the ramp and out of sight but also for any signs of further patrols.

An hour after night had fully fallen, they decided it was safe to move. Having decided against bringing rope of their own, they tried the organic approach and spent ten minutes quietly rummaging about the forest floor until they found a vine long enough and strong enough for their needs. After securing one end to a nearby tree trunk, Sam dropped the coil over the side into the pit.

"We'll have a drop of about eight feet."

"I knew my paratrooper training would come in handy someday," Remi replied. "Give me a hand."

Before Sam could protest, Remi was wriggling sideways, sliding her lower body over the edge. He grasped her right hand as she clamped onto the vine with her left.

"See you at the bottom," she said with a smile and dropped from sight. Sam watched her descend to the bottom of the vine, where she let go, hit the ground, and performed a shoulder roll that brought her back to her knees.

"Show-off," Sam muttered, then went over the side.

He was beside her a few moments later, having performed his own roll, though not as gracefully as his wife. "You've been practicing," he told her.

"Pilates," she replied. "And ballet."

"You never did ballet."

"I did as a little girl."

Sam grumbled and she gave him a conciliatory kiss on the cheek. "Where to?" she asked.

Sam pointed to the nearest tunnel entrance fifty yards to their left. Hunched over, they dashed along the pit's earthen side and followed it to the entrance. They crouched just inside.

"I'll have a peek," Remi said, then slipped inside.

A few minutes later she reappeared beside him. "They're working on a few specimens, but nothing earth-shattering."

"Moving on," Sam replied.

They sprinted to the next tunnel and repeated the drill, with similar results, then moved on to the third tunnel. They were ten feet from the entrance when, on the far end of the pit, a trio of pole-mounted klieg lights glowed to life, casting half the pit in stark, white light.

"Fast!" Sam said. "Inside!"

They skidded to a halt inside the entrance and dropped to their bellies. "Did they spot us?" Remi whispered.

"If they had, we'd be taking fire right now," Sam replied. "I think. One way or another, we'll know shortly."

They waited, breaths held, half expecting to hear the pounding of footsteps approaching or the crack of gunshots, but neither happened. Instead, from the ramp area they heard a woman's voice shout something, a barked command.

"Did you catch that?" Sam asked. "Is it Chinese?"

Remi nodded. "I missed most of it. Something like 'Bring him,' I think."

They crawled forward a few inches until they could see around the corner of the entrance. A group of two dozen or so workers were walking down the ramp flanked by four guards. At the head of the column was a small female figure in a black jumpsuit. Once the group reached the bottom of the pit, the guards herded the workers into a line facing in the direction of Sam and Remi's hiding spot. The woman continued walking.

Sam grabbed his binoculars and zoomed in on her. Sam lowered the binoculars and looked sideways at Remi. "You're not going to believe this. It's Crouching Tiger, Scary Lady herself," he said. "Zhilan Hsu."

Remi grabbed her camera and stared snapping pictures. "I don't know if I got her," she said.

Hsu stopped suddenly, whirled on the assembled workers, and began shouting and gesticulating wildly. Remi closed her eyes, trying to catch the words. "Something about thieves," she said. "Stealing from the site. Missing artifacts."

Hsu stopped abruptly, paused, then pointed an accusatory finger at one of the workers. The guards were on him immediately, one slamming the butt of his rifle into the small of the man's back, sending him sprawling forward, a second guard heaving him back to his feet and half dragging, half walking him forward. The pair stopped a few feet before Hsu. The guard released the man, who fell to his knees and began chattering.

"He's begging," Remi said. "He has a wife and children. He stole only one small piece . . ."

Without warning, Zhilan Hsu drew a pistol from her waistband, took a step forward, and shot the man in the forehead. The man toppled sideways and lay still.

Hsu began speaking again. Though Remi was no longer translating, it took little imagination to understand the message: if you steal, you die.

The guards began shoving and prodding the workers back up the ramp. Hsu followed, and soon the pit was empty again save the man's corpse. The klieg lights flickered out.

Sam and Remi were silent for a few moments. Finally he said, "Whatever sympathy I'd developed for her just went out the window."

Remi nodded. "We need to help these people, Sam."

"Absolutely. Unfortunately, there's nothing we can do tonight."

"We can kidnap Hsu and feed her to—"

"With pleasure," Sam interrupted, "but I doubt we could do that without raising the alarm. We wouldn't make it a mile before we'd be caught. The best we can do is blow the whistle on King's operation."

Remi considered this, then nodded. "Pictures won't be enough," she reminded him.

"Agreed. One of those trailers up there has to be an

office. If there's any hard documentation, that's where we'll find it."

After waiting until they were fairly certain the commotion had died down, they visited each of the tunnels in turn, Sam standing watch as Remi took pictures.

"There's a *Chalicotherium* specimen in there. It's in almost pristine condition."

"A what?"

"*Chalicotherium*. It's a three-toed ungulate from the Lower Pliocene era—a long-limbed horse-rhino hybrid. They died out about seven million years ago. They're very interesting, really—"

"Remi."

"What?"

"Maybe later."

She smiled. "Right. Sorry."

"How valuable?"

"I'd just be guessing, but maybe half a million dollars for a good specimen."

Sam scanned the ramp and clearing for signs of movement but could see only one guard patrolling the area. "Something tells me they're not so worried about people getting in as they are about people getting out."

"After what we just saw, I'd have to agree. What's our plan?"

"If we stay low, we've got a blind spot almost to the top of the ramp. We stop there, wait for the guard to pass, then sprint to that first trailer on the left and dive under. From there, it's just a matter of finding the office."

"Just like that, huh?"

Sam gave her a grin. "Like taking a fossil from a billionaire." He paused. "Almost forgot. Can I borrow your camera?"

She handed it over. Sam sprinted into the middle of the pit and knelt beside the corpse. He searched the man's clothes, then rolled him over, took a picture of his face, then sprinted back to Remi.

He said, "By morning, Hsu will have the body buried in this pit. It's a long shot, but perhaps we can at least let his family know what happened to him."

Remi smiled. "You're a good man, Sam Fargo."

They waited for the roving guard to again disappear from view, then slipped from the tunnel and ran along the pit's wall to where it met the ramp. They turned again and followed this route to the base. Thirty seconds later they were lying on their bellies near the top.

They now had a mostly unobstructed view of the entire clearing. On either side of it were eight trailers, three in a line to the left, five in a wide crescent to the right. The curtained windows of the left-hand trailers were lit, and Sam and Remi could hear the murmur of voices coming from inside. Of the five trailers to the right, the closest three showed lights and the last two were dark. Directly ahead of where Sam and Remi lay were four warehouse-style Quonset huts; between these, the main road leaving the camp. Mounted above the door of each hut was a sodium-vapor lamp, casting the road in sickly yellow light.

"Garages for the equipment," Remi guessed.

Sam nodded. "And if I had to put money on which one of these trailers is the office, I'd go with one of the dark ones."

"I agree. Getting there is going to be the tricky part."

Remi was right. They did not dare head straight for the trailers in question. All it would take was the sudden appearance of a guard or a glance out a window, and they'd be caught.

"We'll take it slow and use the first three trailers for cover."

"And if the office is locked?"

"A bridge we'll cross if we have to." Sam checked his watch. "The guard should be along anytime now."

As predicted, twenty seconds later the guard walked around the corner of the nearest Quonset hut and headed for the trio of trailers on the left. After scanning each trailer with a flashlight, he walked across the clearing, repeated the routine with the other five, then disappeared from view.

Sam gave him twenty more seconds, then nodded at Remi. In unison, they stood up, jogged up the remainder of the ramp, then veered right for the first trailer. They stopped at its back wall and dropped down, using one of the trailer's support pylons as cover.

"See anything?" Sam asked.

"All clear."

They stood up and crept along the back wall to the next trailer, where they stopped again, looked and listened, before moving on. When they were stopped behind the third trailer, Sam tapped his watch and mouthed the word "guard." Through the wall above their heads they could hear voices speaking in Chinese and the faint strains of radio music.

Sam and Remi spread themselves flat on the ground and went still. Their wait was a short one. Almost precisely on time, the guard walked into the clearing to their left and began his flashlight scan. As he drew even with their trailer, they watched, collective breath held, as the flashlight beam skimmed over the ground beneath the trailer.

The beam stopped suddenly. It tracked backward to the support pylon shielding Sam and Remi, then stopped again. They were lying side by side, their arms pressed against each other, when Sam gave Remi's hand a reassuring squeeze. *Wait. Don't move a muscle.*

After what seemed like minutes but was probably less than ten seconds, the beam moved on. The crunch of the guard's boots on the gravel faded away. Cautiously, Sam and Remi got back to their feet and circled the trailer. Looking left and right for signs of movement, they crept around the front of the trailer and picked their way to the steps of what they hoped was the office.

Sam tried the knob. It was unlocked. They shared a

relieved smile. Sam eased open the door and peeked inside. He pulled back, shook his head, and mouthed, "Supplies." They moved to the next trailer. Again, thankfully, the door was unlocked. Sam checked inside, then stuck his arm back through the door and gestured for Remi to enter. She did, and carefully swung the door shut behind her.

The back wall of the trailer was dominated by filing cabinets and storage shelves. A pair of battered gray-painted steel desks with matching chairs flanked the door.

"Time?" Remi whispered.

Sam checked his watch and nodded.

A few moments later the guard's flashlight beam flickered through the trailer's windows, then disappeared again.

"We're looking for anything with detail," Sam said. "Company names, account numbers, manifests, invoices. Anything investigators could sink their teeth into."

Remi nodded. "We should leave everything as is," she said. "If anything goes missing, we know who'll get the blame."

"And a bullet. Good point." He checked his watch. "We've got three minutes."

They began with the filing cabinets, checking each drawer, each folder and file. Remi's camera could hold thousands of digital pictures, so she photographed anything that looked remotely important using the ambient light from outside the trailer.

As the three-minute mark approached, they stopped

and went still. The guard passed by, performed his scan, and was gone again. They resumed their search. Four more times they repeated the cycle until satisfied they'd collected all they could.

"Time to go," Sam said. "We'll retrace our steps to the Rover and—"

Outside, an alarm began whooping.

Sam and Remi froze for a moment, then he said, "Behind the door!"

They pressed themselves flat against the wall. Outside, doors banged open, footsteps pounded on gravel, voices shouted.

Sam asked Remi, "Can you make out anything?"

She closed her eyes, listening intently. Her eyes sprung open again. "Sam, I think they found the Range Rover."

· 14 ·

Langtang Valley, Nepal

Before Sam could reply, the trailer door swung open. Using his fingertips, Sam stopped the door a few inches from their faces. One of the guards stepped across the threshold, his flashlight skimming through the space. The guard stopped. Sam saw his shoulders begin to pivot, signaling a turn in their direction.

Sam hip-bumped the door closed, took a single stride forward, then lashed out with a toe kick that struck the guard behind the knee. As he fell, Sam grabbed his collar and heaved forward, smashing the man's forehead on the edge of the desk. He groaned and went limp. Sam pulled him backward and dragged him behind the door. He knelt down, checked the man's pulse.

"He's alive but won't be waking up anytime soon."

He rolled the man over, tugged the slung rifle off his shoulder, and stood up.

Wide-eyed, Remi stared at her husband for several seconds. "That was very James Bond–ish."

"Dumb luck and a steel desk," he replied with a shrug and a smile. "An unbeatable combination."

"I think you deserve a reward," Remi replied with a smile of her own.

"Later. If there is a later."

"I'd like there to be a later. You have a plan?"

"Auto theft," Sam replied.

He turned around, moved to the nearest of the trailer's rear windows, and pulled back the curtain. "A tight squeeze, but I think we can make it."

"You check the front," Remi said, "I'll get the back window."

Sam walked to the front window, fingered back the curtain, and peeked outside. "The guards are assembling in the clearing. About ten of them. I don't see the Dragon Lady."

"She probably just stopped by to do King's dirty work."

"It looks like they're trying to decide what to do. We'll know in a second if they realize they're missing a man."

"Window's open," Remi said. "It's about an eight-foot drop to the ground. There are some thick trees about ten feet away."

Sam let the curtain slip back into place. "We might

as well go now before they have a chance to get organized." He unslung the rifle and examined it. "This is state-of-the-art."

"Can you handle it?"

"Safety, trigger, magazine . . . hole where the bullet comes out. I think I'll manage."

Abruptly the alarm went silent.

Sam walked to the front door and locked it. "It might delay them," he explained.

He grabbed the nearest chair and carried it to the rear window. Remi climbed up and began squeezing out the window. Once she was down and clear, Sam followed.

They ducked into the tree line and began picking their way toward the Quonset hut. When the rear wall came into view through the trees, they stopped and took a few moments to scan their surroundings. In the distance they could hear the guards still shouting over one another.

Sam and Remi moved forward, Sam in the lead, his rifle lowered and tracking back and forth. They reached the Quonset hut. Remi whispered, "Door," and pointed. Sam nodded. Remi now in the lead, they slid along the wall until her shoulder bumped the jamb. She tried the knob. It was open. She opened the door silently and peeked her head through. She pulled back.

"There's two trucks inside, parked side by side. They look military—green, double tires, canvas sides, a tailgate."

"Feel up to driving?" asked Sam.

"Sure."

"You get behind the wheel of the one on the left. I'll disable the other one, then join you. Be ready to start the engine and tear out."

"Got it."

Remi opened the door just wide enough for them to slip through. They were halfway to the trucks when they heard footsteps pounding on the road outside. Sam and Remi skidded to a halt against the right-hand truck's tailgate. Sam peeked around the corner.

"Four men," he said. "They're climbing into the trucks, two in each cab."

"Part of their emergency plan?" Remi suggested.

"Probably," Sam replied. "Okay, Plan B. We stow away."

Almost in unison, the trucks' engines rumbled to life.

Stepping carefully lest their shifting weight alert the guards, Sam and Remi mounted the truck's bumper, then high-stepped over the tailgate. With a loud thunk, the transmission engaged, and the truck surged ahead. Arm in arm, Sam and Remi stumbled and fell face-first into the bed.

Their truck was in the lead. Lying flat in the relative darkness of the bed, with the second truck's headlamps glowing green through the tailgate's canvas flap, Sam and Remi allowed themselves to take a full breath for the first time in ten minutes. On either side of them, wooden crates of various sizes were strapped to eyebolts in the truck's bed.

"We made it," Remi whispered.

"Cross fingers."

"What's that mean?"

"I'm pretty sure this is a Chinese Army truck."

"You're not suggesting what I think you're suggesting, are you?"

"I am. It seems clear King is in bed with someone in the Chinese military. The guards are Chinese, and so are their weapons probably. And we know what's in these crates."

"How far to the border?"

"Twenty miles, maybe twenty-five. Four hours, give or take."

"Plenty of time to make our exit."

"The question is, how far from civilization will we be?"

"You're starting to spoil my otherwise sunny disposition," she said, then lay back in the crook of Sam's shoulder.

Despite the hardness of the truck's bed and the constant jostling, Sam and Remi found the muffled growl of the engine soothing. They half dozed in the twilight, Sam occasionally waking to check his watch.

After an hour of traveling, they were jolted awake by the squeal of the truck's brakes. The following truck's headlights enlarged and brightened through the rear flap. Sam sat up and pointed the rifle toward the tailgate. Remi sat up beside him, her eyes questioning, but she said nothing.

The truck slowed, then ground to a halt. The following truck's headlights went dark. Cab doors opened, slammed shut. From either side of the bed came the crunch of footsteps. They stopped at the tailgate, and voices began murmuring in Chinese. Sam and Remi could smell cigarette smoke.

Sam turned his head and whispered in Remi's ear. "Stay perfectly still." She nodded.

Moving slowly, carefully, Sam curled his legs beneath him, then rose into a crouch onto the balls of his feet. He took two crab steps toward the tailgate and turned his head to listen. After a moment, he turned back to Remi and held up four fingers. Four guards were standing on the other side of the tailgate. He pointed to his rifle, then in the direction of the soldiers.

She handed him the rifle. Sam laid it across his legs, then pressed his wrists together, indicating he planned to take the men prisoner. She nodded. He gestured for her to lie flat. She did so.

Sam made sure the rifle's safety was off, adjusted himself, and took a deep breath, then reached up with his left hand, grasped the canvas, and jerked it aside.

"Hands up!" he shouted.

The two soldiers closest to the bumper spun around while simultaneously backpedaling. They stumbled into their comrades, who were struggling to unsling their rifles.

"Don't!" Sam said, and raised his rifle to his shoulder.

Despite the language gap, the soldiers got the message and stopped moving. Sam gestured with the barrel of his rifle several times until the men got the message. Slowly each man unslung his rifle and let it drop to the ground. Sam backed them up a few feet, then climbed over the tailgate and hopped down.

"All clear," he said to Remi.

She dropped to the ground beside him.

"They look terrified," she said.

"Perfect. The more terrified they are, the better for us," Sam said. "Would you do the honors?"

Remi collected their rifles and dumped all but one into the truck bed. Sam said, "Safety off?"

"I think . . ."

"Lever switch above the trigger on the right side."

"Got it. Okay."

Sam and Remi and the four Chinese soldiers stared at one another. For ten seconds, no one spoke. Finally Sam asked, "English?"

The soldier on the far right said, "Small English."

"Right. Okay. You are my prisoners."

Remi sighed heavily. "Sam . . ."

"Sorry. I've always wanted to say that."

"Now that you've got that out of your system, what do we do with them?"

"We tie them up and . . . Oh, no. That's not good."

"What?" Remi glanced at her husband. Sam's narrowed eyes were staring over the heads of the soldiers toward the cab of the second truck. She followed his gaze and saw a silhouetted figure sitting in the cab. The figure ducked down suddenly.

"We miscounted," Sam muttered.

"I see that."

"Get in the driver's seat, Remi. Start the engine. Check for—"

"You can be sure of it," she replied, then turned on her heel and sprinted toward the front of the truck. A moment later the engine started. The four soldiers shuffled nervously and glanced at one another.

"All aboard!" Remi shouted out the cab window.

"Coming, dear!" Sam replied without turning.

Sam shouted at the soldiers, "Move, move!" and gestured with the rifle. The men sidestepped away, leaving Sam a clear shot at the truck's radiator. He raised his rifle and took aim.

The fifth man, until now hidden in the second truck's cab, suddenly stuck his torso out the driver's window. Sam saw the silhouette of his rifle coming around toward him.

"Stop!"

The man kept twisting his body, the rifle coming around.

Sam adjusted his aim and fired two shots through the windshield. The soldiers scattered, diving into the underbrush bordering the road. Sam heard a crack. Something thudded into the tailgate beside him. He ducked down, lurched sideways around the opposite bumper, turned again, and snapped off a trio of shots into what he hoped was the truck's radiator or engine block. He turned, raced to the truck's passenger's door, jerked it open, and climbed in.

"We've worn out our welcome," he said.

Remi put the truck in gear and mashed the accelerator.

They hadn't gotten a hundred yards before realizing Sam's gunshots had either missed their mark or been insufficient. In the side mirrors, he and Remi saw the truck's headlights pop on. The four soldiers scrambled from cover and hopped aboard, two in the cab, the other two in the bed. The truck surged forward.

Remi called, "Narrow bridge ahead!"

Sam looked. Though still a couple hundred yards away, the bridge in question looked not just narrow but barely wider than their truck's girth. "Speed, Remi," he warned.

"I'm going as fast as I can."

"I meant, slow down."

"Joking. Hold on!"

The truck hit a rut in the road and slewed sideways, lurched upward, then slammed back down. The bridge loomed in the windshield. Fifty yards to go.

"Oh, of course," Remi said, annoyed. "It had to be one of these."

Though wider and more heavily buttressed, the bridge was simply a larger version of the one they'd crossed on foot earlier that day.

The truck lurched again. Sam and Remi were bounced from their seats, heads hitting the cab's roof. Remi grunted, wrestling with the steering wheel.

The bridgehead was almost upon them. At the last second, Remi slammed on the brakes. The brakes squealed, and the truck skidded to a stop. A cloud of dust enveloped them.

Sam heard the clank-clank of gears and looked over to see his wife shifting the transmission into reverse. "Remi, what's on your mind?" he asked.

"A little reverse chicken," she said with a grim smile.

"Risky."

"As opposed to everything else we've done tonight?"

"Touché," Sam conceded.

Remi slammed down on the accelerator. With a groaning whir from the engine, the truck started backing up, slowly at first but rapidly gaining speed. Sam glanced in the side mirror. Through the dust cloud created by Remi's hasty stop, all he could see of the second truck were headlights. He leaned out the window and fired a three-round burst, then a second. The truck slewed sideways, out of Sam's view.

Eyes fixed on her own mirror, Remi said, "They're stopping. They see us. They're backing up."

Over the roar of the engine they heard the pop-pop-pop of gunfire. They ducked down. With her head below the dashboard, Remi leaned sideways for a better view of her mirror. The pursuing truck was in full reverse mode now, but the combination of Remi's collision-course ploy and Sam's gunfire had clearly rattled the driver. The truck careened from one side to the other, the tires bumping over the berm alongside the road.

"Brace for impact!" Remi shouted.

Sam leaned back in his seat and jammed his feet against the dashboard. A moment later the truck jolted to a stop. Remi glanced at her mirror. "They're off the road."

"Let's not stick around," Sam prompted.

"Right."

Remi shifted back into drive and pressed the gas pedal. Once again the head of the bridge appeared.

"It didn't take," Remi announced. "They're back on the road."

"Persistent, aren't they? Hold the truck steady for a bit," he said, then opened his door.

"Sam, what are—"

"I'll be in back if you need me."

He slung the rifle around his neck and then, using the cab's doorframe for support, climbed down onto the running board. With his free hand he grabbed the canvas side cover and jerked, ripping free the snap enclosures. He grabbed the vertical brace, hooked his left leg over the side, then pulled himself into the bed. He crawled to the cab's rear wall and slid back the slot window.

"Hi," he said.

"Hi, yourself. Hold tight, I'm closing your door."

Remi jerked the truck to the right, then to the left. Sam's open door banged shut. She asked, "What's your plan?"

"Sabotage. How close are they?"

"Fifty yards. We hit the bridge in ten seconds."

"Got it."

Sam crawled to the tailgate. In the dim light, he groped along the truck bed until his hand found one of the other rifles. He picked it up and dropped his own, then hurriedly collected the other magazines.

"Bridge!" Remi shouted. "Slowing down!"

Sam waited until he heard the overlapping thud of the truck's tires bumping over the planking, then stuck his upper torso through the rear flap, aimed the rifle at the bridge deck, and opened fire. The bullets thudded into the wood, punching through the gaps and sending up plumes of wood chips. He ducked back through the flap, changed magazines, then opened fire again, this time alternating between the bridge deck and the oncoming truck, which had just crossed onto the bridge. Their truck swerved left, bumped into the side rail, then straightened out. Sam saw an orange muzzle flash from the window. A trio of bullets slammed into the tailgate below him. He threw himself backward onto the bed. Another salvo of gunfire shredded the rear flap and peppered the cab wall.

"Sam?" Remi called.

"It didn't work!"

"So I gathered!"

"How do you feel about the wanton destruction of fossil artifacts?"

"Generally against it, but this is a special occasion!"

"Buy me some time!"

Remi began braking, then speeding up, in hopes of spoiling the shooter's accuracy. Sam flipped over onto his belly, groped until he found the first ratchet strap securing the crates, and hit the Release button. In short order he had the remainder of the straps free. He crawled to the tailgate and flipped the release; it crashed down.

"Bombs away," Sam called, and shoved the first crate out. It bounced off the bridge deck, slammed squarely into the truck's bumper, and burst open. Wood shards and packing hay went flying.

"No effect," Remi called.

Sam waddled backward, put his shoulder to the entire stack of crates, then braced his feet against the cab wall and began pushing. With a groan, the stack began sliding along the bed. Sam paused, coiled his legs, and shoved hard, like a linebacker going after a blocking sled.

The line of crates slid off the tailgate and began tumbling toward the pursuing truck. Sam didn't wait to see the results but instead sidestepped to the other stack of crates and repeated the process.

From behind came the squeal of brakes. Shattering glass. The crunch of metal impacting wood.

"That did the trick!" Remi called. "They're stopped dead in their tracks!"

Sam rose to his knees and looked through the slot at Remi. "But for how long?"

She glanced at him, offered a quick smile. "However long it takes them to dislodge a half dozen crates from under their chassis."

15

Hyatt Regency Hotel,
Kathmandu, Nepal

Sam stepped out of the bathroom with a towel wrapped around his waist and rubbing his hair with another. "You hungry for a nice breakfast?"

"Famished," replied Remi. She was sitting at a table in front of a mirror, tying her hair into a ponytail. She wore the standard white towel of the hotel.

"Room service or go down to the dining room?"

"The weather is perfect. Let's dine out on the balcony."

"Sounds good." Sam walked over to an end table, picked up the phone, and dialed room service. "I'd like one salmon and a bagel, one eggs Benedict, a bowl of fruit, and sourdough toast and coffee." He waited until the voice in the kitchen repeated the order correctly. Then he rang off and called the bar.

When the bartender answered, Sam asked, "I'd like two Ramos Fizzes. Yes, a Ramos Fizz."

"You know how to treat a lady," said Remi.

"Don't get your hopes up. He doesn't know how to make one." Sam tried again.

"How about a Harvey Wallbanger. Wallbanger. It's made with vodka, Galliano, and orange juice. I see, no Galliano." Sam shook his head and tried once more. "All right, send up a bottle of Veuve Clicquot."

Remi laughed. "You really know how to treat a lady."

"That's the best you can do?" said Sam into the phone. "Okay, send it up well chilled."

He set the receiver back in its cradle. "No champagne. The only thing left after a political convention is a sparkling white from China."

"I didn't know the Chinese made anything sparkling." She looked at him with a sarcastic smile. "Is that the best you can do?"

Sam shrugged. "Any port in the storm."

The phone rang. Sam picked it up. "One moment." He switched on the speaker.

"Morning, Rube," Sam said into the speakerphone.

"For you, maybe," Rube replied. "It's dinnertime here. I hear you and your lovely bride are enjoying yet another relaxing vacation."

"Everything is relative, Rube," Remi replied. "How're Kathy and the girls?"

"Great. They're at Chuck E. Cheese's right now. Your call saved me from going."

"Don't let us keep you," Sam said with a half smile. "We can talk later."

"Oh, no, my friend. There's nothing more important than this. Trust me. Okay, brief me. Are you in jail? How many local laws have you broken?"

"No. And none that we're aware of," Remi replied. "I'll let Sam explain."

Though aware Rube had already received some information from Selma, Sam started at the beginning, with Zhilan Hsu boarding their boat near Pulau Legundi and ended with their escape from King's covert archaeological site.

The night before, after leaving their pursuers stalled on the bridge, Sam had driven through the darkness, looking for signs or landmarks that Remi could match to her map. After several hours of fruitless turns and dead ends, they finally crossed a recognizable mountain pass—the Laurebina—and not long after pulled into the outskirts of Pheda, some twenty miles due east of the camp. Predictably, they'd found the village dark and lifeless, save for a cinder-block and tin-roofed building that turned out to be the local pub. After breaking through the considerable language barrier, they managed to make a trade with the owner: their truck for his car—a thirty-year-old orange-and-primer-gray Peugeot—and directions back to Kathmandu. Just before dawn, they pulled into the Hyatt Regency's parking lot.

Rube listened to Sam's story without speaking. Finally he asked, "Let me make sure I understand this: you snuck into King's camp, witnessed a murder, wreaked havoc with what was probably a guard contingent of Chinese soldiers, then stole one of their trucks that happened to be loaded with black market fossils, which you then used as depth charges to stop your pursuers. Does that about cover it?"

"More or less," Sam said.

Remi added, "And the thirty or so gigabytes of intelligence we collected."

Rube sighed. "You know what I did last night? I painted our master bathroom. You two . . . Okay, send me your data."

"Selma's already got it. Contact her, and she'll give you a link to a secure online storage site."

"Got it. I know my bosses at Langley will be interested in the Chinese angle, and I'm sure we can find someone at the FBI interested in King's black market fossil operation. I can't promise any of it will pan out, but I'll run with it."

"That's all we ask," Sam said.

"There's a better-than-average chance that King's already ordered the site shut down. By now, it could be just an abandoned pit in the middle of the forest."

"We know."

"What about your friend Alton?"

"We're half hoping, half guessing we've found what King wants," Remi replied. "Or at least enough to get his attention. We're calling him after we hang up with you."

"King Charlie is scum," Rube warned. "People have

been trying to take him down all his life. They're all dead or ruined, and he's still standing."

Remi replied, "Something tells us what we've got is very personal for him."

"The Theurock—"

"Theurang," Remi corrected. "The Golden Man."

"Right. It's a gamble," Rube replied. "If you're wrong and King doesn't give a damn about the thing, all you've got are allegations of black market fossil trade—and, like I said, there's no guarantee anything will stick to him."

"We know," Sam replied.

"And you're going to roll the dice anyway."

"Yes," said Remi.

"Big surprise. By the way, before I forget, I've learned a little more about Lewis King. I assume you've both heard of Heinrich Himmler?"

"Hitler's best friend and Nazi psychopath?" Sam asked. "We've heard the name."

"Himmler and most of the upper echelon of the Nazi Party were obsessed with the occult, especially as it pertained to Aryan purity and the Thousand Year Reich. Himmler was arguably the most intrigued by it. Back in the thirties and throughout World War Two, he sponsored a number of scientific expeditions to the world's darkest corners in hopes of finding evidence to support the Nazis' claims. One of them, organized in 1938, a year before the war started, was dispatched to the Himalayas in search of evidence of Aryan ancestry. Care to guess the name of one of the lead scientists?"

"Lewis King," Remi replied.

"Or, as he was known then, Professor Lewes Konig."

Sam said, "Charlie King's father was a Nazi?"

"Yes and no. My sources tell me he probably joined the party out of necessity, not zealousness. Back then, if you wanted government funding, you needed to be a party member. There are plenty of accounts of scientists joining and doing perfunctory research into Nazi theories so they could conduct pure scientific research on the side. Lewis King was a perfect example of this. By all accounts, he was a dedicated archaeologist. He didn't give a damn about Aryan bloodlines or ancestry."

"So why did he go on the expedition?"

"I don't know, but what you found in the cave—this Golden Man business—is a strong possibility. Unless King was lying, it sounds like soon after Lewis King immigrated to the U.S. he started his globe-trotting."

"Maybe he found something on Himmler's expedition that piqued his interest," Sam speculated.

"Something he didn't want to end up in the hands of the Nazis," Remi added. "He kept it to himself, bided his time through the war, then picked up his work again years later."

"The question is," Rube said, "why is Charlie King picking up where his father left off? From what we know about him, he never showed the slightest interest in his father's work."

"Maybe it's the Theurang," Sam said. "Maybe to him, it's just another fossil to sell."

"You could be right. If the description of this thing is even remotely accurate, it would be worth a fortune."

Remi asked, "Rube, do we know whether any Nazi accusations against Lewis ever impacted Charlie?"

"Not that I could find. I think his success speaks for itself. And given how ruthless he is, I doubt anyone has the guts to bring it up anymore."

"That's about to change," Sam said. "Time to push King Charlie's comfort zone."

They hung up, talked strategy for a few minutes, then Sam dialed King's direct line. The man himself picked up on the first ring. "King."

"Mr. King. Sam Fargo here."

"I was wonderin' when you'd get around to callin'. Your pretty wife with you?"

"Safe and sound," Remi replied sweetly.

"It seems our partnership has hit a rocky patch," King said. "My kids tell me you ain't playin' ball."

"We're playing ball," Sam replied. "Just a different game than you are. Charlie, did you have Frank Alton kidnapped?"

"Kidnapped? Why would I do somethin' like that?"

"That's not an answer," Remi pointed out.

"I sent Frank Alton out there to do a job for me. He got himself in over his head, pissed off the wrong people. I have no idea where he is."

"Another nonanswer answer," Sam said. "Okay, let's move on. All you have to do is listen. We've got what you're after—"

"And what's that?"

"You're not listening. We've got what you're after—what your dad spent his lifetime hunting for. And, as you probably guessed, we paid a visit to your concentration camp in the Langtang Valley."

"I got no idea what you're talkin' about."

"We collected thousands of photos—mostly of documents we found lying around in an office trailer—but a few of them of your wife, or concubine, or whatever you call her in the privacy of your Gulfstream. As luck would have it, when we took the pictures, she was murdering one of your employees. We've got a picture of his face as well."

Charlie King did not respond for a long ten seconds. Finally he sighed. "I think you're fulla horse crap, Sam, but clearly somethin's got you excited. You've got my attention."

"First things first. Release Frank—"

"I told you I don't—"

"Shut up. Release Frank Alton. When we get a call from him saying he's safe and unharmed in the comfort of his home, we'll meet with Russell and Marjorie and reach an understanding."

"Now who's sayin' a lot without sayin' much?" King replied.

"It's the only deal you're going to get," Sam replied.

"Sorry, friend, I'm goin' to decline. I think you're bluffin'."

"Suit yourself," Sam said, and hung up.

He laid the phone on the coffee table. He and Remi looked at each other. She asked, "Odds?"

"Sixty–forty it rings in under a minute."

She smiled. "No bet."

At the fifty-second mark, Sam's phone trilled. He let it go off three more times, then picked up. Charlie King said, "You'd make a decent poker player, Sam Fargo. Glad we could reach an understanding. I'll make some calls and see what I can find out about Frank Alton. Can't promise nothin', of course, but—"

"If we don't hear from him in twenty-four hours, the deal is off."

Charlie King was silent for a few beats. Then, "Keep your phone nearby."

Sam disconnected.

Remi asked, "What if King thinks we've got the evidence with us?"

"He knows better than that."

"Do you think he'll follow through?"

Sam nodded. "King's smart enough to have insulated himself. Whoever took Frank probably made sure their faces were hidden. There'll be no trail leading back to King, so he's got nothing to lose and everything to gain by going along."

"Then why do you look so worried?" Remi asked her husband.

"Do I?"

"You've got the squinty-eyed thing going on."

Sam hesitated.

"Tell me, Sam."

"We just got done beating up on one of the world's richest men, a sociopathic control freak who got where he is by crushing his enemies. He'll release Frank, but something tells me King is sitting in his office planning a counterattack."

HOUSTON, TEXAS

Eight thousand miles away, Charles King was doing just that.

After hanging up the phone, he paced his office, staring straight ahead but seeing nothing beyond his rage. Muttering to himself, King stalked to his office window and stared out over the city. To the west, the sun was setting.

"Fine, Fargos," he rasped. "Round goes to you. Enjoy it. Ain't gonna happen again." He walked to his desk and stabbed the Intercom button. "Marsha, get me Russell and Marjorie."

"Yes, Mr. King, one moment."

Thirty seconds passed, then, "Dad—"

"Shut up and listen. Is Marjorie there?"

"I'm here, Daddy."

"Zhilan?"

"Yes, Mr. King."

"What in blazes do you three idiots think you're doin' out there! The Fargos just called me and whipped me from pillar to post. They say they got pictures of you, Zee, killin' some local at the Langtang site. What went on there?"

Russell answered, "I got a call this morning from the head of site security. He said they found a suspicious vehicle and raised the alarm. They found one man unconscious, but nothing appeared to be missing."

"How'd he get knocked out?"

"They're not sure. He may have fallen."

"Bull! Did we have any pendin' shipments?"

"Two trucks," replied Marjorie. "As soon as the alarm was raised, they were evacuated by Colonel Zhou's men. It's standard procedure, Daddy."

"Don't lecture me, girl. Did the trucks arrive at the transfer point?"

Russell replied, "We haven't gotten confirmation yet, but allowing for delays—"

"You're assumin'. Don't assume. Pick up the phone and find those trucks."

"Yes, Daddy."

"Zee, what's this about a killin'? Is it true?"

"Yes. One of the workers was caught stealing. I had to set an example. His body has already been disposed of."

King paused, then grunted. "Okay, then. Good work. As for you two morons . . . The Fargos told me they've got the Golden Man."

"How?" Marjorie asked. "Where?"

"They've got to be lying," Russell added.

"Maybe so, but this kind of stuff is their bailiwick. It's why we brought 'em into this. Guess we underestimated them. Figured Alton would be enough to keep 'em in line."

Marjorie said, "Don't be too hard on yourself, Daddy."

"Shut up. We gotta assume they're tellin' the truth. They want Alton set loose. Is there any way he could've seen anything or could identify anybody?"

Zhilan answered, "I looked into it when I got here, Mr. King. Alton knows nothing."

"Okay. Go rescue him. Feed 'im, clean 'im up, and put 'im on the Gulfstream. The Fargos said as soon as Alton's home, they'll meet with Russell and Marjorie and talk about handin' over the whatchamacallit."

"We can't trust them, Daddy," said Russell.

"I know that, dummy. Just put Alton on the jet and leave the rest to me. The Fargos wanna play hardball? They're about to see what real hardball feels like."

16

Jomsom Village,
Dhawalagiri Zone, Nepal

The single-engine Piper Cub banked sharply and descended through three thousand feet. Sitting on opposite sides of the aisle, Sam and Remi watched the chalky gray cliffs rise up, seemingly swallowing the plane as it lined up for the final approach to the airstrip. Above and beyond the cliffs rose the dark snow-veined peaks of the Dhawalagiri and Nilgiri ranges, their upper reaches half hidden in clouds.

Though they'd left Kathmandu only an hour earlier, their arrival here was just the beginning of the journey; the remainder would take another twelve hours by road. As with everything in Nepal, distances measured on a map were all but useless. Their ultimate destination, the former capital of the Kingdom of Mustang, Lo Monthang, lay only a hundred forty miles northwest of

Kathmandu but was inaccessible by air. Instead, their chartered plane would drop them here, in Jomsom, a hundred twenty miles due northwest of Kathmandu. They would then follow the Kali River Valley north for fifty miles to Lo Monthang, where they would be met by Sushant Dharel's local contact.

For Sam and Remi, it felt good to be far from the relative bustle of Kathmandu and, hopefully, beyond the reach of the King clan.

The plane continued to descend, rapidly bleeding off airspeed until it was, Sam estimated, flying only a few knots above stall speed. Remi looked at her husband questioningly. He smiled and said, "Short runway. It's either bleed airspeed up here or slam on the brakes when we're down."

"Oh, joy."

With a squelch and a shudder, the landing gear kissed the tarmac, and soon they were coasting toward a cluster of buildings at the southern end of the runway. The plane braked to a stop, and the engines began winding down. Sam and Remi collected their backpacks and headed for the door, which was already open. A ground crewman in dark blue coveralls smiled and gestured to the stepladder below the door. Remi climbed down, followed by Sam.

They started walking toward the terminal buildings. To their right, a cluster of goats nibbled at brown grass beside the hangar. Beyond them, on a dirt road, they could see a line of musk ox being herded by an old man in a red beanie and green trousers. Occasionally, he tapped a wayward ox with a switch while making a clucking sound with his mouth.

Remi gathered the collar of her parka closer to her neck and said, “I think this qualifies as brisk.”

“I was going to go with bracing,” Sam replied. “We’re at about ten thousand feet, but there’s a lot less cover.”

“And a lot more wind.”

As if to punctuate Remi’s point, a gust whipped across the tarmac. Clouds of ochre dust obscured their vision for a few seconds before clearing, revealing in greater detail the scenery behind the airport buildings. Several hundred feet tall, the taupe-colored cliffs were deeply grooved from top to bottom, as though carved by giant fingertips. Smoothed by time and erosion, the patterns looked almost man-made—like the walls of some ancient fortress.

Behind them a voice said, “Most of Mustang looks like that. At least the lower elevations.”

Sam and Remi stopped and turned to see a mid-twenties man with shaggy blond hair smiling at them. He asked, “First time?”

“Yes,” Sam replied. “But not yours, I’m betting.”

“Fifth. I’m a trekking junkie, I guess you could say. Jomsom’s sort of the base camp for trekking in this region. I’m Wally.”

Sam introduced himself and Remi, and the trio continued walking toward the terminal buildings. Wally pointed to several groups of people standing along the tarmac's edge. Most were dressed in brightly colored parkas and standing beside heavy-duty backpacks.

"Fellow trekkers?" asked Remi.

"Yep. A lot of familiar faces too. We're part of the local economy, I guess you could say. Trekking season keeps this place alive. Can't go anywhere here without being attached to a guide outfit."

"And if you'd prefer not to?" asked Sam.

"There's a company of Nepalese Army troops stationed here," Wally replied. "It's a bit of a racket, really, but you can't blame them. Most of these people make less in a year than we make in a week. It's not so bad. If you prove you know what you're doing, most of the guides just tag along and stay out of the way."

From a nearby group of trekkers a woman called, "Hey, Wally, we're over here!"

He turned, gave her a wave, then asked Sam and Remi, "Where are you headed?"

"Lo Monthang."

"Cool place. It's downright medieval, man. A real time machine. You already got a guide?"

Sam nodded. "Our contact in Kathmandu arranged one."

Remi asked, "How long should it take to get there? According to the map, it's—"

"Maps!" Wally replied with a chuckle. "They're not bad, fairly accurate on the horizontal, but the terrain here is like a piece of wadded-up newspaper that's only been half flattened out. Everything changes. One day you could pass a spot that's nice and flat, the next day it's half choked by a landslide. Your guide will probably follow the Kali Gandaki River ravine most of the way—it should be mostly dry right now—so you should figure sixty miles total. At least twelve hours' drive time."

"Which means overnight," Sam replied.

"Yep. Ask your guide. He'll either have a nice tent set up or a trekkers' hut reserved for you. You're in for a treat. The trail that follows the Kali Gandaki ravine is the deepest in the world. On one side, you got the Annapurna mountains; the other, the Dhawalagiri. In between, eight of the twenty highest mountains in the world! The ravine trail is like a cross between Utah and Mars, man! The stupas and caves alone are—"

The woman called again, "Wally!"

He said to Sam and Remi, "Hey, I gotta go. Nice meeting you. Travel safe. And stay out of chokes after dusk."

They shook hands all around, and Wally starting jogging toward his group.

Sam called, "Chokes?"

"Your guide will tell you!" Wally called over his shoulder.

Sam turned to Remi, "Stupas?"

"Most commonly known as chortens here. They're essentially reliquaries—mound-like structures containing sacred Buddhist artifacts."

"How big?"

"They can range from the size of a garden gnome to

a cathedral. One of the largest is back in Kathmandu, in fact. The Boudhanath."

"The dome draped in all the prayer flags?"

"That's the one. Mustang's got a huge concentration of them, mostly of the gnome-sized variety. Some estimates put the number in the low thousands, and that's just along the Kali Gandaki River. Up until a few years ago, Mustang was all but off-limits to tourism for fear of desecration."

"Fargos!" a male voice called. "Fargos!"

A bald Nepalese man in his mid-forties picked his way through a crowd of milling trekkers and trotted toward them, panting, "Fargos, yes?"

"Yes," Sam replied.

"I am Basanta Thule," the man replied in decent English. "I am your guide, yes?"

"You're a friend of Pradhan's?" Remi said.

The man's eyes narrowed. "I do not know who that is. I was asked by Mr. Sushant Dharel to meet you. You were expecting someone else? Here, I have identification . . ." Thule began reaching into the side pocket of his jacket.

"No, that's fine," Sam replied with a smile. "Good to meet you."

"And you, and you. Here, I will take those."

Thule grabbed their backpacks and gestured with his head toward the terminal buildings. "My vehicle is this way. Follow, if you will." He trotted off.

Sam said to Remi, "Very tricky, Mizz Bond."

"Am I growing paranoid in my advancing age?"

"No," Sam replied with a smile. "Just more beautiful. Come on, let's catch up or we're going to lose our guide."

After a cursory stop at the customs desk to satisfy what Sam and Remi guessed was Mustang's firm if tacit belief in its semiautonomous status, Sam and Remi stepped outside and found Thule at the curb beside a white Toyota Land Cruiser. Judging by the dozens of nearly identical vehicles lining the street, each of which seemed to bear a unique trekking-company logo, Toyota was the four-wheeler of choice for the region. Thule smiled at them, shoved the remainder of Sam's backpack in the Toyota's cargo area, and slammed shut the hatch.

"I have arranged accommodations for the night," Thule announced.

"We're not leaving for Lo Monthang immediately?" Remi asked.

"No, no. Very bad luck to start a journey at this time of day. Better to start tomorrow morning. You will eat and rest and enjoy Jomsom, and then we will depart first thing in the morning. Come, come . . ."

"We'd prefer to leave now," Sam said, not moving.

Thule paused. He pursed his lips, thinking for a moment, then said, "It is your choice, of course, but the landslide will not be cleared until morning."

"What landslide?" replied Remi.

"Yes, between here and Kagbeni. We would not get more than a few kilometers up the valley. And then there will be the traffic jam, of course. Many trekkers in Mustang now. Better to wait until morning, yes?" Thule opened one of the Toyota's rear passenger doors and flourished his arm toward the backseat.

Sam and Remi looked at each other, shrugged, then stepped into the SUV.

After ten minutes of the Toyota winding through the narrow streets, Thule brought it to a stop before a building a few miles southeast of the airstrip. The brown-on-yellow sign read "Moonlight Guest House. Tub Baths—Attached Bathrooms—Common Bathrooms."

With a smile and a raised eyebrow, Remi said, "It appears bathrooms are the big draw in Jomsom."

"And monochromatic architecture," Sam added.

From the front seat Thule said, "Indeed. Jomsom offers the best accommodations in the area."

He got out, hurried around to Remi's door, and opened it. He offered his hand to her. She graciously took it and climbed out, followed by Sam.

Thule said, "I will collect your luggage. You go inside. Madame Roja will assist you."

Five minutes later they were in the Moonlight Guest House's Royal Executive Suite, complete with a queen bed and a sitting area filled with an assortment of wickeresque lawn furniture. As Madame Roja had promised, their bathroom was in fact attached to their suite.

"I will return for you at eleven o'clock tomorrow morning, yes?" Thule said from the doorway.

"Why so late?" Sam asked.

"The landslide will have—"

"The traffic jam," Sam finished. "Thanks, Mr. Thule. We'll see you then."

Sam shut the door. From the bathroom he heard Remi say, "Sam, look at this."

He found a wide-eyed Remi standing beside a gigantic copper claw-foot tub. "It's a Beasley."

"I think the more common term is 'bathtub,' Remi."

"Very funny. Beasleys are rare, Sam. The last one was made in the late nineteenth century. Do you have any idea what this is worth?"

"No, but something tells me you do."

"Twelve thousand dollars, give or take. This is a treasure, Sam."

"And it's the size of a Studebaker. Don't even think of trying to fit it into your carry-on."

Remi tore her eyes from the tub and looked at him mischievously. "It is big, isn't it?"

Sam returned her smile. "Indeed."

"Care to be my lifeguard?"

"At your service, madam."

An hour later, clean and happy and prune skinned, they settled into the sitting area. Through the balcony windows they could see the peaks on Annapurna in the distance.

Sam checked his phone. "Voice message," he said. He listened to it, gave Remi a wink, and redialed. Selma's voice came over the speaker thirty seconds later: "Where are you?"

"In the land of wicker and copper," Sam replied.

"Pardon?"

"Nothing. Do you have good news for us?"

"Here, hang on."

A moment later a male voice came on the line. It was Frank Alton. "Sam, Remi . . . I don't know how you did it, but I owe you my life."

"Nonsense," Remi replied. "You saved ours in Bolivia a few times over."

"Are you okay?" Sam asked.

"A few bumps and bruises, but nothing permanent."

"Have you seen Judy and the kids?"

"Yes, as soon as I got home."

Sam said, "Selma, how are things?"

"Absolutely awful," she replied.

"Glad to hear it."

Based on a healthy respect of Charles King's reach, and perhaps a tinge of paranoia, Sam and Remi had instituted the "duress rule": had Selma or any of them been at gunpoint or otherwise in jeopardy, an answer other than "awful" would have raised the alarm.

Remi said, "Frank, what can you tell us?"

"Not much more than you already know, I'm afraid. Selma's brought me up to speed. While I agree King's a snake and he's not telling the whole truth, I have no proof he was behind my kidnapping. I was knocked out and snatched off the street. I never saw them coming. Can't tell you where I was held. When I woke up, I was blindfolded until they shoved me out of the van again. When I took the blindfold off, I was standing before the stairs to a Gulfstream jet."

"Speaking of eerie, did you meet the King twins?"

"Oh, those two. They were waiting for me at the airport. I thought I'd walked into a Tim Burton remake of *The Addams Family*. I'm guessing they're the product of King and his Dragon Lady?"

"Yes," Sam replied. "What's your take on Lewis King?"

"A hundred-to-one that he's been dead for decades. I think I was just bait for you two."

"Our thought as well," Remi agreed. "We're still working out the details, but we think it has something to do with an old Himalayan legend."

"The Golden Man," replied Frank.

"Right. The Theurang."

"From what little I was able to gather before I was taken, that's what Lewis King was after when he disappeared. He was obsessed by it. Whether the thing is real or not, I don't know."

"We think it is," Sam replied. "We're going to see a man in Lo Monthang tomorrow. With any luck, he'll be able to shed more light on the mystery."

17

Kali Gandaki Gorge,
Dhawalagiri Zone, Nepal

For the fourth time in an hour, Basanta Thule brought the Toyota Land Cruiser to a stop, the knobby tires crunching on the gravel that blanketed the valley floor. Above, the sky was a cloudless royal blue. The crisp air was perfectly still.

"More stupas," Thule announced, pointing out the side window. "There . . . and there. You see."

"We do," Sam replied, he and Remi glancing out Sam's rolled-down window. Shortly after leaving Jomsom that morning, they'd made the mistake of expressing an interest in chortens; since then, Thule had made it his mission to point out each and every one. They'd covered less than two miles so far.

For politeness's sake, Sam and Remi climbed out, walked around, and took a few pictures. While none of the chortens were taller than a few feet, they were nonetheless impressive—miniature temples painted snow-white sitting atop the ridge lines overlooking the gorge like silent sentries.

They climbed back into the Toyota and set out again, driving in silence for some time before Remi said, "Where's the landslide?"

There was a long pause. "We passed it some time ago," Thule replied.

"Where?"

"Twenty minutes ago . . . the slope of loose gravel beside the boulder we saw. It does not take much to block the way, you see."

After another pause for lunch—and a chorten-viewing stop that Sam and Remi tactfully declared their last—they continued north, following the serpentine course of the Kali Gandaki and passing a series of hamlets that were largely indistinguishable from Jomsom. Occasionally they would spot trekkers in the foothills above, ant-like against the mountains in the distance.

Shortly after five o'clock, they entered a narrower section of the gorge. The cliffs towering fifty feet above them closed in, and the sun dimmed. The air wafting through Sam's open window grew chilled. Finally, after slowing to a walking pace, Thule steered them through an archway of rock barely wider than the Toyota and then into a winding tunnel. The tires sloshed through the stream and echoed off the walls.

Fifty yards later they rolled into an elongated clearing, measuring forty feet wide and a quarter mile long. At the northern end of the ravine was a second slot opening in the rock. To their right, the river gurgled through an undercut section of the cliff.

Thule steered left, made a wide circle so the Toyota's nose was pointed back the way they'd come, and then braked to a stop. "We will camp here," he announced. "We will be protected from the wind."

"Why so early?"

Thule turned in his seat and gave them a broad smile. "Here night falls quickly, along with the temperature. Best to have the shelters erected and the fire started before dark."

With the three of them working together, they quickly had the shelters—a pair of older Vango siege-style tents—set up and ready for occupancy, complete with eggshell mattress pads and subzero sleeping bags. As Thule got a small fire started, Sam ignited a trio of kerosene lanterns that hung from poles at the edge of their camp. Flashlight in hand, Remi was taking a tour of the ravine. Thule had mentioned that trekkers had in the past found Kang Admi tracks in this area of the gorge. Translated loosely as "snowman," the term was one of dozens used to describe the Yeti, the Himalayan version of Bigfoot. While not necessarily a blind believer in the legend, the Fargos had encountered enough oddities in their travels that they knew better than to discount it out of hand; Remi had decided to indulge her curiosity.

After twenty minutes, she wandered back into the yellow glow of lanterns around the camp. Sam handed her a wool cap and asked, "Any luck?"

"Not so much as a toe track," Remi replied, tucking a few strands of loose auburn hair beneath the cap.

"Do not give up hope," Thule remarked from beside the fire. "We may hear the beast's call during the night."

"And what are we listening for?" Sam asked.

"That depends upon the person, yes? As a child, I heard the cry once. It sounded like . . . part man, part bear. In fact, one of the Tibetan words for Yeti is *'Meh-teh'*—'man-bear.'"

"Mr. Thule, this sounds like a tall tale designed to enthrall tourists," Remi said.

"Not at all, miss. I heard it. I know people who have seen it. I know people who have found its tracks. I personally have seen a musk ox whose head had been—"

"We get the picture," Remi interrupted. "So, what's for dinner?"

Dinner consisted of prepackaged dehydrated meals that when combined with boiling water morphed into a goulash mélange. Sam and Remi had tasted worse, but by only a narrow margin. After they finished eating, Thule redeemed himself with steaming mugs of tongba, a slightly alcoholic Nepalese millet tea, which they sipped as night enveloped the gorge. They chatted, and sat in silence for another thirty minutes, before dimming the camp lanterns and retreating to their respective tents.

Once nestled into their sleeping bags, Remi sat reading a trekker's guide she'd downloaded onto her iPad while Sam studied a map of the area under the beam of a flashlight.

Remi whispered, "Sam, remember what Wally mentioned at the airport about 'the chokes'? We never asked Thule about it."

"In the morning."

"I think now would be better," she replied, and handed Sam her iPad. She pointed to a section of text. He read:

> Known colloquially as "the chokes," these narrow ravines found along the length of the Kali Gandaki Gorge can be treacherous in the springtime. At night, meltwater runoff from the surrounding mountains frequently flash floods the ravines with little notice, rising to a height of—

Sam stopped reading, handed the iPad back to Remi, and whispered, "Pack your gear. Just the essentials. Quietly." Then aloud, he called, "Mr. Thule?"

No answer.

"Mr. Thule?"

After a few moments' delay, they heard the scuff of a boot on gravel, followed by, "Yes, Mr. Fargo?"

"Tell us about the chokes."

A long pause. "Uh . . . I am afraid I am not familiar with that phrase."

More scuffing on gravel, the distinctive click of one of the Toyota's doors being opened.

Hurrying now, Sam unzipped his sleeping bag and rolled out. Already mostly clothed, he grabbed his jacket, slipped it on, and quietly unzipped the tent. He crept out, looked left and right, then stood up. Thirty feet away he could just make out Thule's silhouette leaning through the Toyota's driver's-side door. He was rummaging around the interior. On his feet, Sam began creeping toward the Toyota. He was twenty feet away when he stopped suddenly and cocked his head.

Faintly at first, then more distinctly, he heard the rush of water. Across the ravine he could see the stream was roiling, white water lapping at the sides of the cliff.

From behind, Sam heard a *tsst* and turned around to see Remi poking her head from the tent flap. She gave him a thumbs-up, and he replied with a palm out: *Wait.*

Sam crept toward the Toyota. When he'd closed the gap to ten feet, he ducked down and continued on, stooped over, around the rear bumper to the driver's side of the vehicle. Sam stopped, peeked around the corner.

Thule was still leaning into the Toyota, with only his

legs visible. Sam eyed the distance between them: five feet. He extended his leg, carefully planted his foot, and began shifting his weight forward.

Thule whipped around. Clutched in his hand was a stainless-steel revolver.

"Stop, Mr. Fargo."

Sam stopped.

"Stand up." Thule's charmingly stunted speech had vanished. Only a slight accent remained.

Sam stood up. He said, "Something tells me we should have checked your ID when you offered."

"That would have been wise."

"How much did they pay you?"

"For rich people like you and your wife, a pittance. For me, five years' worth of wages. Do you want to offer me more?"

"Would it do any good?"

"No. The people made it clear what would happen to me if I betrayed them."

Out of the corner of his eye, Sam could see the river had begun expanding outward, and, far behind, the rush of water was gaining in volume. Sam knew he needed to play for time. Hopefully, the man before him would let down his guard, if only momentarily.

"Where's the real Thule?" Sam asked.

"Two feet to your right.

"You killed him."

"It was part of the task. Once the waters recede, he will be found along with you and your wife, his head crushed by the rocks."

"Along with you."

"Pardon?"

"Unless you have a spare spark ignition wire laying around," Sam replied, patting his jacket pocket.

On impulse, Thule's eyes darted toward the Toyota's interior. Anticipating this, Sam had started moving even as he'd patted his pocket. He was in midleap, his hands a foot from Thule, when the man spun back around, the barrel of his revolver lashing out; it caught Sam high on the forehead, a glancing blow that nevertheless gashed his scalp. He stumbled backward and dropped to his knees, gasping.

Thule stepped forward and cocked his leg. Sam saw the kick coming and braced himself while trying to roll away. The top of Thule's foot slammed into his side and flipped him onto his back.

"Sam!" shouted Remi.

He rolled his head to the right and saw Remi sprinting toward him.

"Get the gear!" Sam croaked. "Follow me!"

"Follow you? Follow you where?"

The Toyota's engine grumbled to life.

Moving on instinct, Sam rolled onto his belly, pushed himself onto his knees, then got to his feet. He stumbled toward the nearest lantern, six feet to his left. Through his pain-hazed vision he saw, down the ravine, a twenty-foot-tall wave of white water churning through the slot. Sam snatched the lantern off the pole with his left hand, then turned back toward the Toyota and forced his legs into a shuffling sprint.

The Toyota's transmission engaged, the wheels sprayed gravel, peppering Sam's lower legs. He ignored it and kept moving. As the Toyota lurched forward, Sam jumped. His left leg landed on the rear bumper; he clamped his right hand on the roof rack's rail.

The Toyota surged ahead, fishtailing on the gravel and jerking Sam from side to side. He held on, pulled himself closer to the cargo hatch. Thule straightened the Toyota out and sped toward the ravine entrance, now fifty yards away. Sam stuck the lantern's handle between his teeth and used his left hand to turn the wick knob. The flame guttered, then brightened. He grasped the lantern in his left hand again.

"One chance," Sam muttered to himself.

He took a breath, let the lantern dangle at arm's length for a moment, then heaved it like a grenade. The lantern twirled upward over the Toyota's roof and crashed onto the hood, shattering. Flaming kerosene splashed across the windshield.

The effect was immediate and dramatic. Startled by the wave of fire across his windshield, Thule panicked, jerking the wheel first left, then right, the double slewing motion sending the Toyota up on two wheels. Sam lost his grip. He felt himself flying. Saw the ground rushing toward him. He curled himself into a ball at the last instant, smashed into the ground on his hip, and let himself roll. Dully in the back of his mind he heard a crash, glass shattering and the crunch of metal. He rolled over, blinked his vision clear.

The Toyota had crashed with its hood wedged into the narrow rock arch.

Sam heard footsteps, then Remi's voice as she knelt beside him: "Sam . . . Sam! Are you hurt?"

"I don't know. I don't think so."

"You're bleeding."

Sam touched his fingers to his forehead and looked at the blood. "Scalp wound," he muttered. He grabbed a handful of dirt from the ground and patted it on the wound.

Remi said, "Sam, don't—"

"See? All better."

"Anything broken?"

"Not that I can tell. Help me up."

She ducked under his shoulder, and they stood up together.

Sam asked, "Where's the—"

In answer to his question, water washed across their feet. Within seconds, it rose to their ankles.

"Speak of the devil," Sam said. In unison, they turned around. Water was rushing through the northern end of the ravine.

The water was roiling around their calves.

"That's cold," Remi said.

"Cold doesn't even begin to describe it," Sam replied. "Our gear?"

"Everything worthwhile is in my pack," Remi replied, turning her shoulder so he could see it. "Is he dead?"

"Either that or unconscious. If not, I think he'd be shooting at us by now. We need to get that thing started. It's our only chance to outrun the flood."

They headed toward the Toyota, Remi in the lead and Sam limping behind her. She slowed as she reached the vehicle's rear bumper, then crept around to the driver's door and peeked inside.

She called, "He's out."

Sam shuffled up, and together they opened the door and dragged Thule out. He plunged into the water.

To Remi's unspoken question Sam said, "We can't worry about him. In a minute or so this is all going to be underwater."

Remi climbed into the Toyota and across to the passenger's seat. Sam followed and slammed the door shut behind him. He turned the key. The starter whined and clicked, but the engine refused to start.

"Come on . . ." Sam muttered.

He turned the key again. The engine caught, sputtered, died.

"One more time," Remi said, gave him a smile and held up crossed fingers.

Sam closed his eyes, took a breath, and turned the key again.

The starter clicked over, the engine coughed once, then again, then roared to life.

Sam was about to shift into gear when they felt the Toyota lurch forward. Remi turned in her seat and saw water lapping at the lower edge of the door.

"Sam . . ." Remi warned.

Eyes on the rearview mirror, Sam replied, "I see it."

He shifted into reverse and pressed the accelerator. The Toyota's four-wheel drive bit down. The vehicle began inching backward, the quarter panels shrieking as they were dragged along the rock walls.

They were shoved forward again.

"I'm losing traction," Sam said, worried that the rising water would drown the engine.

He pressed the accelerator again, and they felt the tires grab hold, only to give way again.

Sam pounded the steering wheel. "Damn!"

"We're afloat," Remi said.

Even as the words left her mouth, the Toyota's hood was being shoved deeper into the slot. Nose-heavy from the engine, the vehicle began tipping downward as the tide shoved the rear upward.

Sam and Remi were silent for a moment, listening to the water rush around the car and bracing themselves against the dashboard as the Toyota continued pitching downward.

"How long would we last in the water?" Remi asked.

"Providing we're not instantly crushed to pulp? Five minutes until the cold gets us; past that, we lose motor control and go under."

Water began gushing through the door seams.

Remi said, "Let's not do that, then."

"Right." Sam closed his eyes, thinking. Then: "The winch. We've got them on each bumper."

He searched the dashboard for the controls. He found a toggle switch labeled Rear and flipped it from

Off to Neutral. He said to Remi, "When I give the word, flip that to Engage."

"You think it's powerful enough to drag us?"

"No," Sam replied. "I need a headlamp."

Remi rummaged around the backpack and came out with the headlamp. Sam settled it on his head, gave her a quick peck on the cheek, then climbed over the seat, using the headrest as a handhold. He repeated this maneuver until he was wedged into the Toyota's cargo area. He unlatched the glass hatch, shoved it open, then, lying with his back pressed against the seat, mule-kicked the hatch until the glass tore free from its hinges and plunged into the water. He stood up.

Below, the water churned over the Toyota's undercarriage. Icy mist billowed around him.

Remi called, "The engine's dead."

Sam hinged forward at the waist, reached down, and grabbed the winch hook with both hands. Hand over hand, he began taking up the slack.

The winch froze.

"Climb up to me!"

Remi scrabbled over the front seat, reached back, retrieved the backpack, and handed it to Sam, then used his extended arm to climb into the cargo area.

"No!" she cried.

"What?"

Sam looked down. The beam of his headlamp illuminated a ghostly white face pressed against plastic sheeting.

"Sorry," Sam said. "I forgot to tell you. Meet the real Mr. Thule."

"Poor man."

The Toyota shuddered, slid sideways a few feet, then stopped, wedged tightly in the rock archway and standing perfectly upright.

Remi tore her eyes off the dead man's face and said, "I assume we're climbing again."

"With any luck."

Sam peeked over the tailgate. The water had enveloped the rear tires.

"How long?" she asked.

"Two minutes. Help me."

He turned his body sideways, and Remi helped him don the backpack. Next, he flipped his right leg over the tailgate, then his left, then slowly stood up, arms extended for balance. Once steady, he shone his headlamp over the rock face beside the Toyota.

It took him three passes before he found what he needed: a two-inch-wide vertical fissure fifteen feet above them and three feet to the right. Above that, a series of handholds that led to the top of the cliff.

"Okay, hand it up," Sam said to Remi.

She extended the winch hook toward him. He leaned down, grabbed it. His foot slipped, and he crashed onto one knee. He regained his balance and stood erect again, this time with his left arm braced on the Toyota's roof rack.

"Go get 'em, cowboy," Remi said with a brave smile.

Winch hook dangling from his right hand, Sam swung the cable like a propeller until he'd gained enough momentum, then let it fly. The hook clinked against the rock face, slid sideways over the fissure, and plunged into the water.

Sam retrieved the hook and tried again. Another miss.

He felt cold water envelop his left foot. He looked down. The water was past the bumper and was now lapping up against the tailgate.

"We've sprung more leaks," Remi said.

Sam tossed the hook again. This time it slid cleanly into the fissure and bit down momentarily before coming free.

"Fourth time's the charm, right?"

"I think the phrase is—"

"Work with me, Fargo."

Sam chuckled. "Right."

Sam took a moment to tune out the churning water and the pounding of his heart. He closed his eyes, refocused, then opened his eyes and began swinging the cable again.

He let go.

The hook sailed upward, clanked off the rock, and began sliding toward the fissure. Sam realized the speed was too great. As the hook skipped over the crack, he snapped the cable sideways. The hook snapped backward like a striking snake and wedged itself in the fissure.

Gently, Sam gave the cable a tug. It held. Another

tug. The hook slipped, then bit down again. Then, hand over hand, he began taking up tension on the cable until the hook was buried up to its eyelet.

"Yee-haw!" Remi called.

Sam extended his hand and helped Remi over the tailgate. Water was sloshing over their feet and tumbling into the Toyota's interior. Remi nodded toward the corpse of Mr. Thule.

"I don't suppose we could take him with us?"

"Let's not push our luck," Sam replied. "We will, however, add him to the list of things Charlie King and his evil spawn have to answer for."

Remi sighed, nodded.

Sam gestured grandly to the cable. "Ladies first."

· 18 ·

Lo Monthang,
Mustang, Nepal

Twenty hours after Sam and Remi climbed over the cliff top and left the Toyota to the waters of the Kali Gandaki, the pickup truck in whose bed they were riding coasted to a stop at a fork in the dirt road.

The driver, Mukti, a gap-toothed Nepali with a crew cut, called through the back window, "Lo Monthang," and pointed at the road heading north.

Sam gently shook Remi awake from her curled position against a bag of goat feed and said, "Home sweet home."

She groaned, pushed aside the coarse cotton, and sat up, yawning. "I was having the weirdest dream," she said. "Something similar to *The Poseidon Adventure*, but we were trapped inside a Toyota Land Cruiser."

"Truth is stranger than fiction."

"Are we there?"

"More or less."

Sam and Remi thanked the driver, climbed out, and watched as the truck turned onto the south fork and disappeared around the bend. "Too bad about the language barrier," Remi said.

With only a smattering of Nepali words and phrases between them, neither Sam nor Remi had been able to tell their driver that he had possibly saved their lives. For all he knew, he'd simply picked up a pair of wayward foreigners who'd somehow lost their tour group. His indulgent smile suggested this was not a rare event in these parts.

Now, exhausted but thankfully warm and dry, they stood on the outskirts of their destination.

Surrounded by a tall wall of patchwork rock, brick, and mud-thatch mortar, the ancient capital of the once-great Kingdom of Mustang was small, occupying a half mile square in a shallow valley surrounded by low rolling hills. Inside Lo Monthang's walls, most of the structures were also constructed from a mishmash of mud and brick, all of them painted in shades of white ranging from grayish to brownish and bordered with layered thatch roofing. Four structures rose above the rest: the Royal Palace and the red-roofed Chyodi, Champa, and Tugchen temples.

"Civilization," Remi said.

"Everything is relative," Sam agreed.

After they had wandered the wilds of Mustang for what seemed like days, the otherwise medieval Lo Monthang seemed positively metropolitan.

They started walking up the dirt road toward the main gate. Halfway there, a boy of eight or ten appeared and sprinted toward them, calling, "Fargos? Fargos?"

Sam raised his hand in greeting and called in Nepali, *"Namaste. Hoina."* Hello. Yes.

The boy, now beaming, skidded to a stop before them and said, "Follow, yes? Follow?"

"Hoina," Remi replied.

After leading them through the winding alleys of Lo Monthang under the curious gaze of hundreds of villagers, the boy stopped before a thick wooden door set in a whitewashed wall. He lifted the tarnished brass knocker, rapped twice, then said to Sam and Remi, *"Pheri bhetaunla,"* then scampered off down a side alley.

They heard footsteps clicking on wood from inside the building, and a few seconds later the door swung open, revealing a frail mid-sixties man with long gray hair and a matching beard. His face was heavily lined and brown. To their surprise, he greeted them with an upper-crust British accent:

"Good morning. Sam and Remi Fargo, I presume?"

After a moment's hesitation, Sam said, "Yes. Good morning. We're looking for a Mr. Karna. Sushant Dharel from Kathmandu University arranged a meeting."

"Indeed he did. And indeed you have."

"Pardon?" Remi replied.

"I am Jack Karna. Well, where are my manners? Please come in."

He stood aside, and Sam and Remi stepped inside. Similar to the exterior of the building, the interior walls were whitewashed, and the floor was constructed with old but well-scrubbed wooden planks. Several Tibetan-style rugs covered the floor, and the walls were dotted with tapestries and framed bits of parchment. Along the west wall, beneath thick casement windows, was a seating area with cushions and pillows and a low coffee table. Against the east wall was a potbellied stove. A small hallway led out of the room and into what looked like a sleeping area.

Karna said, "I was about to send out a search party for you. You look a bit travel worn. Are you quite all right?"

"We had a bit of a hiccup in our travel plans," Sam offered.

"Indeed you did. News reached me a few hours ago. Some trekkers found a guide vehicle destroyed in one of the chokes south of here. Two bodies washed ashore near Kagbeni. I feared the worst." Before they could answer, Karna ushered them toward the pillows, where they sat down. "The tea is ready. Give me just a moment."

A few minutes later he placed a silver tea service on the table, along with a plate piled high with scones and crustless cucumber sandwiches. Karna poured tea and then sat down across from them.

"Now. Do tell me your tale," Mr. Karna prompted.

Sam recounted their journey, beginning with their arrival in Jomsom and ending with their arrival at Lo Monthang. He left out nothing, including King's likely involvement in the assassination attempt. Through it all, Karna asked no questions, and, aside from a few arches of his eyebrow, gave no reaction.

"Extraordinary," he said at last. "And you have no idea of this impostor's name?"

"No," said Remi. "He was in a bit of a hurry."

"I can imagine. Your escape is the stuff of Hollywood."

"Par for the course, unfortunately," Sam said.

Karna chuckled. "Before we go on, I should make the local brahmins—the council—aware of what happened."

"Is that necessary?" Sam asked.

"Necessary, and of benefit to you. You are in Lo Monthang now, Mr. and Mrs. Fargo. We may be a part of Nepal, but we are quite autonomous. Have no fear, you will not be held responsible for what happened, and unless the council considers it absolutely necessary, the Nepalese government will not be involved. You are safe here."

Sam and Remi considered what he had said, then gave their assent.

Karna picked up a brass bell from the floor beside his cushion and rang it once. Ten seconds later the boy who greeted them on the approach road appeared from the side hallway. He stopped before Karna and bowed sharply.

In what sounded like rapid-fire Lowa, Karna spoke to

the boy for thirty seconds. The boy asked a single question, then bowed again, walked to the front door, and stepped out.

Karna said, "Fear not. All will be well."

"Forgive us," Remi said, "but the curiosity is killing us: your accent is—"

"Oxford through and through, yes. I am in fact British, though I haven't been home for . . . fifteen years, I suppose. I have lived in Mustang for thirty-eight years this summer. Most of that time, in this very house."

"How did you come to be here?" Sam asked.

"I came as a student, actually. Anthropology, mainly, with a few side interests. I spent three months here in 1973, then went home. I wasn't there for two weeks before I realized Mustang had gotten under my skin, as they say, so I returned and never left. The local priests believe I am one of them—reincarnated, of course." Mr. Karna smiled, shrugged. "Who can say? Without doubt, though, I have never felt more at home anywhere else."

"Fascinating," Sam replied. "What do you do?"

"I suppose I am an archivist of sorts. And an historian. My main focus is documenting Mustang's history. Not the history you read on Wikipedia, though." He saw Remi's confused expression and said with a smile, "Yes, I know about Wikipedia. I have satellite Internet here. Quite extraordinary, given the remoteness of the place."

"Quite," Remi agreed.

"I am—and have been for nearly twelve years—writing a book that will, with any luck, serve as a comprehensive history of Mustang and Lo Monthang. A hidden history, if you will."

"Which explains why Sushant thought you were the person we should see," said Sam.

"Indeed. He told me you were particularly interested in the legend of the Theurang. The Golden Man."

"Yes," replied Remi.

"He did not, however, tell me why." Karna was now serious, his eyes peering hard at Sam and Remi. Before they could answer, he went on: "Please understand. I mean no offense, but your reputation has preceded you. You are professional treasure hunters, are you not?"

"It's not the term we prefer," Sam replied, "but it's technically accurate."

Remi added, "We keep none of what we find for ourselves. Any financial compensation goes to our foundation."

"Yes, I read that. Your reputation is in fact quite good. The trouble is, you see, I have had visitors before. People after the Theurang for what I fear were nefarious reasons."

"Did these people happen to be a young man and woman?" Sam asked. "Caucasian twins with Asian features?"

Karna's left eyebrow arched. "Spot-on. They were here a few months ago."

Sam and Remi shared a glance. Silently, they agreed they could and should trust Karna. They were in as remote a location as they'd ever been, and the attempt on their lives the day before told them Charles King had taken the gloves off. Not only did they need Karna's knowledge but they needed a trustworthy ally.

"Their names are Russell and Marjorie King. Their father is Charles King—"

"King Charlie," Karna interrupted. "I read an article about him in the *Wall Street Journal* last year. Bit of a cowboy, I gather. A bumpkin, yes?"

"A very powerful bumpkin," Remi replied.

"Why on earth does he want you dead?"

"Why, precisely, we're not sure," Sam replied, "but we're convinced he's after the Theurang."

Sam went on to recount their affiliation with Charles King. He left nothing out. He told Karna what they knew, what they suspected, and what remained a mystery.

"Well, one mystery I can address immediately," Karna said. "These evil twins, the King children, clearly gave me a bogus name. But during their visit, they did mention the name Lewis 'Bully' King. When I told them what I'm about to tell you, they reacted with no apparent shock. Strange, given who they are."

"What did you tell them?"

"That Lewis King is dead. He died in 1982."

19

Lo Monthang,
Mustang, Nepal

Shocked, Sam and Remi didn't speak for several moments. Finally Remi said, "How did he die?"

"Fell into a crevasse about ten miles from here. In fact, I helped recover his body. He is buried in the local cemetery."

"And you told the King twins this?" Sam asked.

"Indeed. Their reaction was one of . . . disappointment, I suppose. Now, knowing who they are, it seems particularly coldhearted, doesn't it?"

"In keeping with the family character," Remi replied. "Did they tell you why they were looking for him?"

"They were very evasive, which is why I found an excuse to cut our visit short. All I could gather was, they were looking for King and had an interest in the

Theurang. I didn't much care for the cut of their jib. It's nice to know my instincts were right. So, it seems clear that Charles King knew his father was dead when he contacted you."

"And knew it when he hired Alton," Sam said. "The report about the photo showing Lewis here was another fabrication."

"All designed to get you involved in the hunt for the Golden Man," Karna added. "Not much of a deep thinker, this King, is he? He expected you would come here to find your friend, then pick up the hunt for the Theurang without getting suspicious, then lead the twins straight to it."

"So it seems," Remi said. "The best-laid plans . . ."

"Of country cretins and loathsome offspring," Karna finished. "The larger question is, why is the Theurang so important to King? You don't suppose he's some kind of closet Nazi, do you, picking up the banner of his father's expedition?"

"We don't think so," said Sam. "We've started to wonder if it's simply an obsession or a side business like his black market fossil endeavors. Either way, the Kings have kidnapped and murdered for the Theurang."

"Not to mention enslaved," Remi added. "The people at the dig site can't come and go as they please."

"That too. Regardless of his motives, we can't let the Golden Man fall into his hands."

Karna picked up his teacup and raised it in salute. "It's decided, then: we are at war with the King family. All for one?"

Sam and Remi raised their cups and said in unison, "And one for all."

"Tell me more about the burial chamber you found," Karna said. "Leave nothing out."

Remi briefly described the alcove they'd found in the Chobar Gorge cave, then retrieved her iPad from the backpack and brought up the gallery of photos she'd taken during their exploration. She handed it to Karna.

Fascinated by the iPad, he spent a minute turning it over in his hands and playing with the interface before looking up, wide-eyed, at Sam and Remi.

"I really must get one of these. All right . . . to business." He spent the next ten minutes studying Remi's photos, panning and zooming the iPad's interface, clicking his tongue and muttering words like "wondrous" and "astonishing." At last, he handed the iPad back to Remi.

"You have both made history," Karna said. "While I don't imagine the larger world will realize the significance of the find, the people of Mustang and Nepal certainly will. What you have there, in fact, is the final resting place of a Sentinel. The four characters engraved into the top of the box . . . Do you have a better photo of them?"

"No, sorry."

"Where is the box right now?"

Sam replied, "In San Diego, with Selma, our chief researcher."

"Oh, goodness. Is she—"

"Fully qualified," Remi said. "She's trying to open it—carefully, without damaging it."

"Very good. I may be able to help her with that."

"Do you know what's inside?"

"I may. I'll come to that shortly. How much did Sushant tell you about the Sentinels and the Theurang?"

"A good overview," Remi said, "but he made it clear you're the expert."

"That's very true. Well, Sentinels were guardians of the Theurang. The honor was handed down from father to son. They were trained from the age of six for one purpose and one purpose alone. The Himanshu Decree of 1421 was one of four times the Theurang has been evacuated from Lo Monthang. The previous three instances, all of which preceded an invasion, ended favorably, and the Theurang was subsequently returned to the capital. The invasion of 1421 was different, however. The Marshal of the Army at the time, Dolma, convinced the King and his advisers that this invasion would be different. He was certain it would spell the beginning of the end of Mustang. Not to mention the prophecy."

"Prophecy?" Sam prompted.

"Yes. I'll spare you the particulars, most of which involve Buddhist legend and numerology, but the prophecy stated that a time would come when the Kingdom of Mustang would fall, and the only way it would ever rise again was if the Theurang was returned to its birthplace."

"Here?" Remi said. "That's what Sushant told us."

"My dear friend is mistaken. Not his fault, really. The popular history of Mustang and the Theurang is spotty at best. First, you must understand something: the people of Mustang never considered themselves owners of the Golden Man but rather its caretakers. How exactly did Sushant describe the nature of the Theurang?"

"Its appearance?"

"No, its . . . nature."

"I think the term he used was 'life giver.'"

Karna considered this for a moment, then shrugged. "As a metaphor, perhaps. Mrs. Fargo, you're an anthropologist by training, are you not?"

"That's right."

"Good, good. Give me just a moment." Karna stood up and disappeared down the side hall. They heard what sounded like books being shuffled on a shelf, then Karna returned carrying two leather-bound tomes and an inch-thick manila folder. He sat back down, leafed through the books until he found the pages he was looking for, then set them aside, facedown, on the floor.

He said, "The Kingdom of Mustang was never a grand place. The architecture is more functional, more modest—like its people—but long ago they were quite learned, far ahead of the Western world in many ways."

Karna turned to Remi. He asked, "You're an anthropologist, what do you know about Ardi?"

"The archaeological find?"

"Indeed."

Remi thought for a moment. "It's been a while since

I read the reports, but this is what I remember: Ardi's the nickname given to a four-and-a-half-million-year-old fossil found in Ethiopia. As I recall, the scientific name is *Ardipithecus ramidus.*

"Though there's a lot of debate surrounding the find, the consensus is that Ardi is something of a missing link in human evolution—a bridge between higher primates, like monkeys, apes, and humans, and their more distant relatives, like lemurs."

"Very good. And its characteristics?"

"Skeleton similar to a lemur's but with primate attributes: grasping hands, opposable thumbs, clawless digits with nails, and short limbs. Did I miss anything?"

"Top marks," replied Karna. He opened his manila folder, pulled out an eight-by-ten color photograph, and handed it to Sam and Remi. "This is Ardi."

As Remi had described, the fossilized creature, lying on its side in the dirt, looked like a cross between a monkey and a lemur.

"Now," Karna said, "here's a popular artist's rendering of the Theurang."

He withdrew a piece of paper from his folder and handed it across. The color printout showed a drawing of a gorilla-like creature with massive arms and a squat head dominated by a wide fang-filled mouth and an enormous jutting tongue. Instead of having legs, it was supported by a column of muscle that ended in a single webbed foot.

"Notice any similarities to Ardi?" Karna asked.

"None," Sam replied. "This looks like a cartoon."

"Indeed. It comes from a legend involving Tibet's first King, Nyatri Tsenpo, who was said to have descended from the Theurang. In Tibet, over the millennia, the Theurang became something of a boogeyman. The Mustang version, however, is quite different." Karna picked up one of the books and handed it to Sam and Remi.

The page was open to a crude but highly stylized drawing. The tone was decidedly Buddhist in nature, but there was no mistaking the subject of the rendering.

Remi murmured, "Ardi?"

"Yes," Karna answered. "As if suddenly animated. This, I believe, is the most accurate portrayal of the Theurang. What you're looking at, Mr. and Mrs. Fargo, is the Golden Man."

Sam and Remi were silent for a full minute as they stared at the drawing and tried to absorb Karna's words. Finally Sam said, "You're not suggesting this creature was—"

"Alive in contemporary Mustang? No, of course not. I suspect the Theurang is a distant cousin of Ardi's, probably a much later missing link, but certainly millions of years old. I have other drawings that show the Theurang with all of Ardi's attributes: the grasping hands, the opposable thumbs. Other drawings show it with more primate-like facial features."

"Why is it called the Golden Man?" asked Sam.

"Legend has it that when on display in Lo Monthang's Royal Palace, the Theurang was fully assembled and articulated in such a way that it appeared human. In 1315, shortly after Lo Monthang was founded, the first King of Mustang—Ame Pal—decided the Theurang's aspect wasn't sufficiently glorious. He had the bones gilded with gold and the eye sockets adorned with gems, along with the fingertips. The teeth, which were said to have been mostly intact, were covered in gold leaf.

"He must have been quite a sight," Remi said.

"'Gaudy' is the word I use," Karna replied, "but who am I to argue with Ame Pal?"

Remi said, "Are you suggesting the people here developed a theory of evolution before Darwin did?"

"Theory? No. A firm belief? Absolutely. In the nearly thirty years I've spent here, I've found texts and artwork that make it clear the people of Mustang firmly believed man sprang from earlier creatures—primates in particular. I can show you cave murals that depict a distinct line of progression from lower forms to modern man. More important, despite popular belief, the Theurang was revered not in a religious sense but rather an historical one."

"Where did the legend originate?" Sam asked. "Where and when did they find the Theurang?"

"No one knows—or, at least, no one I've found. It's my hope that before I die, I can answer that exact question. Maybe your discovery will be the lost puzzle piece."

"Do you think the Theurang is in the box we found?"

"Not unless a terrible mistake had been made. One of the skills the Sentinels had to master was celestial navigation. No, I'm quite certain you found the Sentinel where you did because that's where he was ordered to go."

"Then what do you think is inside?"

"Either nothing or a clue to the Theurang's birthplace—the location to which it was allegedly taken in 1421."

"What kind of clue?" asked Remi.

"A disk, roughly four inches in diameter, hewn from gold and engraved with symbols of some kind. The disk, when used in conjunction with two other disks and a special map, would pinpoint the Theurang's final resting place."

"You know nothing else about it?" Sam said.

"I know the name of the place."

"Which is?"

"The ancient translation is a bit complicated, but you would know it by its popular moniker: Shangri-La."

20

Lo Monthang,
Mustang, Nepal

Karna said, "I can see by your expressions you think I'm winding you up."

"You don't strike us as a winding-up kind of guy," Sam said, "but you have to admit that Shangri-La is a bit of a fairy tale."

"Is it? What do you know about it?"

"It's a fictional utopia, a valley located somewhere in the Himalayas, filled with ridiculously happy and worry-free people."

"You forgot immortal," Remi said.

"Right, sorry. Immortal."

"That's Shangri-La as depicted in the novel: James Hilton's 1933 *Lost Horizon*. Another example of popular culture shanghaiing and adulterating a fascinating—and possibly true—tale."

"You have our attention," Remi said.

"Mention of Shangri-La, and its analogues, can be found in many cultures in Asia. Tibetans refer to it as Nghe-Beyul Khimpalung. They believe it is in the Makalu Barun region or the Kunlun Mountains or, the most recent candidate, the ancient city of Tsaparang in western Tibet. Several places in India have also been proposed as the true location, as well as dozens in China, including Yunnan, Sichuan, Zhongdian . . . Add to the list Bhutan and the Hunza Valley in northern Pakistan.

"Now, here's the truly interesting part: as you know, the Nazis were a bit mad for the occult. The expedition Lewis 'Bully' King was a part of in 1938 . . . One of its objectives was to find Shangri-La. They felt certain it would be home to an ancient master race, Aryans unspoiled by time and genetic impurities."

"We didn't know that," Remi said.

"Perhaps King Charles isn't after the Theurang alone but Shangri-La as well," Karna said.

"Anything's possible," Sam replied. "But King doesn't strike me as a big believer in the fantastic, true or otherwise. If he can't touch it, see it, or smell it—"

"Or sell it," Remi added.

"Or sell it, he's not interested," Sam finished. "What do you believe, Karna? I assume you believe it's real? Of all the possibilities you presented, which one fits?"

"None of the above. My research and my instincts tell me that for the people of Mustang, Shangri-La represented a wellspring—both the birthplace and the eternal resting place of the Theurang, a creature they believed was their universal ancestor. I suspect what we today call Shangri-La was where the Theurang was originally discovered. How long ago, I cannot say, but that's what I believe."

"And if you had to place money on its location?" Remi asked.

"I think the Tibetan etymology holds the key: *shang*, which is also *tsang*, combined with *ri*, together means 'mountain,' and *la*, means 'pass.'"

"So, Tsang Mountain Pass," Remi said.

"Not quite. In the royal dialect of ancient Mustang, *la* also means 'gorge' or 'canyon.'"

"The Tsangpo Gorge," Sam replied. "That's a lot of territory. The river that runs through it—the Yarlung Tsangpo—is how long? A hundred twenty miles?"

"One hundred fifty," Karna answered. "Bigger than your Grand Canyon, in many ways. And the mountains are thickly forested. Some of the most daunting terrain in the world."

"If you're right about the location and the legend," Remi said, "it's no wonder Shangri-La's remained hidden all this time."

Karna smiled. "As we sit here together, we may be closer to finding it—and the Golden Man—than anyone else in history."

"Closer, perhaps," Sam replied, "but not there. You said we need all three disks. Let's say the chest Selma has contains one of them. We'll still need the other two."

"And the map," said Remi.

"The map is the least of our hurdles," Karna said.

"I've located four candidates, one of which I'm certain will serve our purposes. As for the other two disks . . . How do you feel about the Balkans?"

Sam and Remi exchanged glances. Remi said, "We once had some bad lamb in Bulgaria, but, aside from that, we have nothing against it."

"Glad to hear it," Karna said with a mischievous smile. "What I'm about to tell you I've never shared with anyone. Despite the high regard in which I'm held here, I am not sure how my adopted countrymen would welcome my theory."

"Again, you have our attention," Sam said.

"Three years ago, I uncovered some texts I believe were written by the personal secretary to the King in the weeks leading up to the 1421 invasion."

"What kind of texts?"

"A personal diary of sorts. The King had of course been informed of the strength of the invading army, and he agreed with the prophecy that Mustang's demise was at hand. Further, he had his doubts that the Sentinels could carry out their duties. He felt the odds against them were overwhelming. He was also convinced someone from within his inner circle had turned traitor and was feeding the enemy information.

"In secret, he assigned the finest of the Sentinels—a man known as Dhakal—the task of transporting the Theurang to Shangri-La. In two of the three chests ostensibly containing the disks, he placed fakes. One was genuine."

"And the other two disks?" asked Remi.

"Given to a pair of priests from the Eastern Orthodox Church."

Neither Remi nor Sam spoke immediately. Karna's non sequitur was so abrupt, they weren't sure they'd heard him correctly.

"Say that again," said Sam.

"A year before the invasion, Lo Monthang was visited by a pair of priests from the Eastern Orthodox Church."

"This was the fifteenth century," Remi said. "At that time, the nearest outpost of the Church would have been . . ." She trailed off with a shrug.

"In present-day Uzbekistan," Karna replied. "Fourteen hundred miles from here. And to answer your question, no, I have found no mention in Church histories referring to missionaries traveling that far east. I have something better. I'll get to that shortly.

"As the King's diary tells, he welcomed the missionaries into his court, and they soon became friends. A few months after they arrived, an attempt was made on the King's life. The priests came to his aid, and one of them was wounded. He became convinced these two foreigners were part of the prophecy, sent to ensure the Theurang could one day be returned to Lo Monthang."

"So he gave each of them a disk for safekeeping and

sent them back to their home countries before the invasion," Remi guessed.

"Exactly so."

"Please tell me you found references to them somewhere," Sam asked.

Karna smiled. "I did. Fathers Besim Mala and Arnost Deniv. Both names appear in Church records from the fifteenth century. Both men were dispatched to Samarkand, Uzbekistan, in 1414. With the death of Genghis Khan, the weakening of the Mongol Empire, and the rise of Tamerlane, the Eastern Orthodox Church was keen on spreading Christianity to the heathens, as it were."

"What became of our intrepid priests?" Remi asked.

"Mala died in 1436 on the Albanian island of Sazan. Deniv died six years after that in Sofia, Bulgaria."

"The time line fits," said Sam. "If they left Lo Monthang in 1421, they would have made it back to the Balkans a year or so later."

Sam and Remi fell silent, each lost in thought.

Karna said, "A bit fantastic, isn't it?"

"I'm glad you said it," Sam replied. "I didn't want to be rude."

"I'm not offended. I know how it sounds. And you're right to be skeptical. I myself spent the first year after I found the diary trying to debunk it, with no success. Here's what I propose: I will turn over my research notes to this Selma of yours. If she can disprove my theory, so be it. If not, then . . ."

"Balkans, here we come," Remi said.

From his living quarters, Karna retrieved his laptop, an Apple MacBook Pro with a seventeen-inch screen, which he placed on the coffee table before them. He connected one end of an Ethernet cable to the laptop's port and the other to a wall jack leading up to what Sam and Remi guessed was Karna's satellite dish.

Soon, Selma's face appeared in the iChat window. Standing behind her, looking over each shoulder, were Pete Jeffcoat and Wendy Corden, and, behind them, the workspace in the Fargos' San Diego home. Predictably, Selma was in her uniform of the day: horn-rimmed glasses on a neck chain and a tie-dyed T-shirt.

Accommodating a three-second satellite transmission delay, Remi made the introductions, then brought Selma and the others up to speed. As was her way, Selma asked no questions during Remi's report, and was silent for a full minute afterward as she mentally collated the information.

"Interesting," was all she said.

"That's it?" Sam asked.

"Well, I assume you've already told Mr. Karna, in your own diplomatic way, how far-fetched this sounds."

At this, Jack Karna chuckled. "They did indeed, Ms. Wondrash."

"Selma."

"Jack, then."

"Do you have your research material digitized?"

"Of course."

Selma gave Karna a link to the office's server, then said, "Upload it there, and I'll start working through it. In the meantime, I'll turn the chest over to Pete and Wendy. The three of you can see about opening it."

It took twenty minutes to upload all of Karna's research notes. Once done, and after badgering Sam and Remi into having a nap in his guest room, Karna, Pete, and Wendy went to work on the box. Karna first asked to see enhanced pictures of the chest, including a close-up of the engraved characters.

He peered at them on his laptop screen, tilting his head first one way, then the other, until muttering something under his breath. He stood up suddenly, marched down the hallway, and returned a minute later with a tiny book bound in red-dyed textile. This he flipped through for several more minutes before calling, "Aha! Just as I thought: the characters are a derivation of Lowa and yet another royal dialect. The inscription is meant to be read vertically, from right to left. Roughly translated, it says:

"Through fulfillment, prosperity
"Through resistance, anguish . . ."

Wendy said, "I think I read that in a self-help book once."

"I have no doubt," Karna said, "but in this case it's

intended as a warning—a curse. I suspect these characters were inscribed on each of the Sentinels' boxes."

Pete said, "In short, 'Take this to its destination, and you'll find happiness; interfere with or impede that, and you're screwed.'"

"Impressive, young man," said Karna. "Not the words I would use, of course, but you arrested the gist of the message."

"Would this have been intended for the Sentinels?" Wendy asked.

"No, I don't think so. It was designed for the enemy or anyone who came into possession through illicit means."

"But if the dialect is that obscure, who aside from Mustang royalty would have been able to understand the warning?"

"That's beside the point. The curse stands, ignorance be damned."

"Harsh," said Pete.

"Let's take a closer look at this box, shall we? In one of Remi's pictures, I noticed the tiniest of seams along a bottom edge of the box."

"We noticed that too," Wendy replied. "Hold on, we've got a close-up . . ."

A few clicks of the mouse later, the image in question filled Karna's screen. He studied the photo for several minutes before saying, "Do you see the seam I'm talking about? The one that looks like a series of eight dashes?"

"Yes," said Pete.

"And the full seam opposite that?"

"Got it."

"Forget that one. It's a decoy. Unless I miss my guess, the dashed seam is a combination lock, of sorts."

"The gaps are almost paper-thin," said Wendy. "How can—"

"Two millimeters, I would say. You'll need a shim, of sorts; a thin but strong type of metal or alloy. Inside each of those dashes will be a brass or bronze flange, each with three vertical depression settings: up, middle, and fully down."

"Hold on," Wendy said. "I'm doing the math . . . That's over sixty-five hundred possible combinations."

"Not overly daunting," Pete said. "With enough patience, and time, you could eventually pick it."

Karna said, "True, if not for one fact: you only get one crack at it. Enter the wrong combination, and the internal mechanism locks itself."

"That does complicate things."

"We've not yet begun to unravel the complications, my boy. Once past the combination, the real challenge begins."

"How?" Wendy said. "What?"

"Have you ever heard of a Chinese puzzle box?"

"Yes."

"Think of what you have before you as the mother of all Chinese puzzle boxes. As it so happens, I believe I have the combination to the initial locking mechanism. Shall we get started . . . ?"

Three hours later Sam and Remi, now awake, refreshed, and armed with cups of tea, joined Karna before his laptop just in time to hear Pete exclaim through the iChat window, "Got it!" On-screen, he and Wendy were leaning over the worktable, the Sentinel box between them. It was brightly illuminated by an overhead halogen lamp.

Another iChat screen popped up on the screen, this one displaying Selma's face: "Got what?"

"It's a Chinese puzzle box," replied Wendy. "Once we got past the combination, a narrow panel popped open. Inside were three tiny wooden switches. Following Jack's directions, we flipped one. Another panel opened, then more switches, and so on . . . How many moves now, Jack?"

"Sixty-four. One more to go. If we've done our job, it'll open. If not, we may lose the contents forever."

"Explain that," Sam said.

"Oh, goodness, I didn't mention the booby trap, did I? So sorry."

"Mention it now," Remi said.

"If the box contains a disk, it will be suspended in the middle of the primary compartment. Set into the sides of that compartment will be glass vials filled with corrosive liquid. If your last move is the wrong one or you try to force the compartment open . . ." Karna made a hissing sound. "You get an unidentifiable lump of gold."

"I hope I'm wrong," said Selma, "but I don't think there's a disk in there."

"Why?" asked Pete.

"Odds. Sam and Remi stumble upon the only Sentinel box ever found and it just happens to contain the one genuine disk in the bunch?"

Karna said, "But they didn't 'stumble' upon it, did they? They were following in the footsteps of Lewis King—a man who had spent at least eleven years chasing the Theurang. Whatever his motives, I doubt he was on a goose chase that day at Chobar Gorge. It appears he never found the Sentinel's burial chamber, but I suspect he wasn't there for an empty box."

Selma considered this. "Logical," was all she said.

"One way to find out," Sam said. "Who's going to do the honors? Pete . . . Wendy?"

Pete said, "I'm nothing if not chivalrous. Go ahead, Wendy."

Wendy took a deep breath, reached into the box, and flipped the appropriate switch. An inch-wide rectangular hatch slid open beside her fingers.

Karna said softly, "Now gently slide your pinkie finger up along the inside of the box until you feel a square button."

Wendy did so. "Okay, got it."

"Slide that button . . . let me see . . . slide it to the right—no, left! Slide it to the left."

"Left," Wendy repeated. "Are you sure?"

Karna hesitated a moment, then nodded firmly. "Yes, left."

"Here I go."

Through the laptop's speaker Sam and Remi heard a wooden snick.

Wendy cried, "The top's open!"

"Now carefully lift the lid straight upward. If it's there, the disk will be suspended from the underside."

Moving with exaggerated slowness, Wendy began lifting the lid an inch at a time. "It's got some heft to it."

"Don't let it swing," Karna whispered. "A little more . . ."

Pete rasped, "I can see a cord hanging down. Looks like catgut or something similar."

Wendy kept lifting.

The halogen light reflected off something solid, a curved edge, a glint of gold.

"Be ready, Peter," said Karna.

Wendy lifted the lid the rest of the way. The remainder of the cord rose from the box. Dangling at its end: the prize, a four-inch-wide golden disk.

With latex-gloved hands, Pete reached out. Wendy lowered the disk into his palms, and he transferred it to a foam-lined tray on the table.

The group let out a collective breath.

"Now comes the hard part," Karna said.

"What?" Wendy said with exasperation. "That wasn't the hard part?"

"I'm afraid not, my dear. Now we must ascertain whether we do in fact have the genuine article."

21

Vlorë, Albania

The Fiat's dashboard clock clicked over to nine a.m. just as Sam and Remi passed the welcome sign for Vlorë. Albania's second-largest city, of a hundred thousand souls, sat nestled on a bay on the west coast, overlooking the Adriatic with its back to the mountains.

And with any luck, Sam and Remi hoped, Vlorë was still home to one of the Sentinel disks.

An hour after Wendy and Pete had extracted the Theurang disk from the box and set about determining its provenance with Karna, Selma's face reappeared in an iChat window on Karna's laptop's screen.

In her characteristically curt manner she said, "Jack, your research methods are impeccable. Mr. and Mrs. Fargo, I think his theory about the two priests holds water. Whether we can find them and the other two disks is another matter."

"What else have you been able to discover?" asked Sam.

"At the time of their deaths, both Besim Mala and Arnost Deniv had risen to the rank of Bishop and were highly respected in their communities. Both had helped found churches and schools and hospitals throughout their home countries."

"Which suggests their burial sites could be more elaborate than a six-foot-deep rectangle in the earth," Karna said.

"I found no mention of the particulars, but I can't fault your reasoning," replied Selma. "In the fifteenth and sixteenth centuries, the EOC—"

"The what?" asked Remi.

"Eastern Orthodox Church. The EOC—especially those based in the Balkans and southern Russia—tended to make a big deal of such deaths. Crypts and mausoleums appear to be the customary method of interment."

"The question is," Karna said, "where exactly were they laid to rest?"

"Still working on Deniv, but Church records state that Bishop Besim Mala's final posting was in Vlorë, Albania."

With time to kill until Selma could give them a more specific target area, Sam and Remi spent an hour touring

Vlorë, marveling at its beautifully blended architecture that felt at once Greek, Italian, and medieval. Shortly before noon, they pulled into the parking lot of the Hotel Bologna, overlooking the blue waters of the harbor, and took a seat in a palm tree–lined outdoor café.

Sam's satellite phone trilled. It was Selma. Sam put the phone on speaker.

"I have Jack here as well," Selma said. "We have—"

"If this is going to be a bad news/good news call, Selma, just give it to us," Remi said. "We're too tired to choose."

"Actually, this is an all-good-news call—or potentially good news, that is."

"Shoot," said Sam.

Jack Karna said, "The Sentinel disk is genuine, I believe. I can't be one hundred percent sure until I can check it against the wall maps I mentioned, but I'm optimistic."

Selma said, "As for the final resting place of Besim Mala, I can narrow your search grid to about a half mile square."

"Is it underwater?" Sam asked, skeptical.

"No."

"An alligator-infested swamp?" Remi chimed in.

"No."

"Let me guess," Sam said. "A cave. It's in a cave."

Karna said, "Strike three, to appropriate an American phrase. Based on our research, we believe Bishop Mala was laid to rest in the graveyard of the Monastery of Saint Mary on Zvernec Island."

"Which is where?" asked Remi.

"Six miles north, up the coast. Find a Wi-Fi hot spot, and I'll download the particulars to your iPad, Mrs. Fargo."

They took a short time to relax in the hotel's café. Sam and Remi ordered a flavorsome Albanian lunch of ground lamb meatballs scented with mint and cinnamon, baked dough with spiced spinach, and grape juice enhanced with sugar and mustard. As luck would have it, the café had free Wi-Fi, so between bites of a delicious lunch they perused their travel packet, as Selma called it. Predictably, it was exhaustive, with driving instructions, local history, and a map of the grounds of the monastery. The only detail she could not find was the actual location of Bishop Mala's grave site.

After paying the bill, Sam and Remi pointed the Fiat's hood north. After ten miles, they pulled into the village of Zvernec and followed a lone sign to Narta Lagoon. The lagoon was large, nearly twelve square miles.

Upon turning onto the dirt road encircling the lagoon, Sam drove north until they came to a gravel parking lot on a patch of land jutting into the lagoon. The lot was empty.

Sam and Remi got out and stretched. The weather was unseasonably warm, seventy degrees, and sunny, with only a few billowy clouds inland.

"I take it that's our destination," Remi said, pointing.

At the shore, a narrow pedestrian bridge led to Zvernec Island, eight hundred feet away, which was home to the Monastery of Saint Mary, a collection of four medieval-style church buildings occupying a two-acre triangle of grass on the shoreline.

They walked to the head of the bridge, where Remi paused. She stared at the bridge nervously. The ramshackle crossings they'd encountered first in Chobar Gorge, then again on their way to King's secret dig site in the Langtang Valley, had clearly made more of an impact than she'd realized.

Sam walked back to where she was standing and wrapped an arm around her shoulders. "It's solid. I'm an engineer, Remi. This monastery is a tourist attraction. Tens of thousands of people cross this bridge every year."

Eyes narrowed, she looked at him sideways. "You're not humoring me, are you, Fargo?"

"Would I do that?"

"You might."

"Not this time. Come on," he said with an encouraging smile. "We'll cross together. It'll be like strolling along a sidewalk."

She nodded firmly. "Back on the horse."

Sam took her hand, and they started across. Halfway there, she stopped suddenly. She smiled. "I think I'm all better."

"Cured?"

"I wouldn't go that far, but I'm okay. Let's keep moving."

Within a couple minutes they'd reached the island. From a distance, the church buildings appeared almost pristine: sun-bleached rock walls and red-tiled roofs. Now, standing before the structures, it was clear to Sam and Remi the buildings had seen better days. The roofs were missing tiles, and several of the walls were either sagging or partially crumbling. One belfry was missing a roof altogether, its bell slouching sideways from its support beam.

A well-groomed dirt path wound its way through the grounds. Here and there, pigeons sat clustered on eaves, cooing and staring unblinkingly at the island's two new visitors.

"I don't see anyone," Sam said. "You?"

Remi shook her head. "Selma's brief mentioned a caretaker but no tourist office."

"Then let's explore," Sam said. "How big is the island?"

"Ten acres."

"Shouldn't take long to find the cemetery."

After taking a cursory stroll through each of the buildings, they followed the path into the pine forest beyond the clearing. Once they were inside the tree line, the sun dimmed, and the trunks seemed to tighten around them. This was old-growth forest, with knee-high tangles of undergrowth and enough rotting logs and stumps to make passage a bit of a challenge. After a few hundred yards, the path forked.

"Of course," Remi said. "No sign."

"Flip a mental coin."

"Left."

They took the left-hand fork and followed the winding trail before coming to a rickety, half-rotted dock overlooking a marsh.

"Bad flip," Remi said.

They backtracked to the fork and began heading down the right-hand path. This took them generally northeast, deeper into the forest and toward the wider end of the island.

Sam jogged ahead on a scouting mission, turned and called back to Remi, "Spotted a clearing!" A few moments later he appeared from around a bend in the trail and stopped before her. He was smiling. Broadly.

"You generally don't get this excited about clearings," Remi said.

"I do if the clearing has tombstones."

"Lead on, bwana."

Together, they walked down the path to where the pine forest parted. Oval-shaped and roughly two hundred feet across, the clearing was indeed a cemetery, but almost immediately Sam and Remi realized there was something very wrong here. On the far side was a jumbled stack of pine logs; beside this stack, several house-high bales of withered boughs and branches. The earth in the clearing was pockmarked, as though it had undergone an artillery bombardment, and about half of the graves appeared to have been freshly churned.

To the east was a second opening in the trees, this

one a nearly straight corridor, at the end of which they could see the waters of the lagoon.

Of the dozens of tombstones visible, only a few were undamaged; all the others were either cracked or partially uprooted from the ground. Sam and Remi counted fourteen mausoleums. All of these showed signs of damage as well, either canted on their foundations or their walls and roofs caved in.

"What happened here?" Remi asked.

"A storm, I'm guessing," said Sam. "Came off the ocean and ripped across the island like a chain saw. It's a shame."

Remi nodded solemnly. "On the bright side, it may make our job easier. We won't technically be breaking into Mala's mausoleum."

"Good point. But there is one more hurdle," Sam said to Remi.

"What?"

"Let's look first. I don't want to jinx us."

They split up, Sam taking the east side and moving north, Remi taking the west side and moving north. Skipping grave markers, each headed for the nearest mausoleum, stopping only long enough to read the name engraved on the stone facade.

At last, Remi reached the graveyard's northeast corner, near the jumble of pine logs. As she approached the last mausoleum in her line, it seemed to be the least damaged of the lot, with only a few cracks showing in the walls. It was also uniquely decorated, she realized, her heart skipping a beat.

She called, "Sam, I think we may have a winner."

He walked over. "Why do you think so?"

"That's the biggest cross I've seen. You?"

"Yes."

The wall closest to them bore a four-by-five-foot Eastern Orthodox cross, with its three crossbars—two horizontal ones close together near the top and one near the bottom canted sideways.

"I've seen a lot of those, but none this big. I'm curious: why the slanted bottom crosspiece? I assume it's symbolic of something?"

"Ah, the mysteries of religion," said Sam.

They walked the last few feet to the mausoleum, then split up, each walking around a side to the front, which they found was surrounded by a calf-high wrought-iron fence. One side was smashed flat against the ground. At the bottom of three stone steps, the mausoleum door was open—or, to be more accurate, gone. Beyond that, the interior was dark.

Carved into the pediment beneath the mausoleum's sloped roof were four letters: MALA.

"Nice to finally find you, Your Eminence," Sam murmured.

Sam stepped over the fence, followed by Remi, and descended the steps. They stopped before the opening; the stench of mildew filled their nostrils. Sam dug into his pocket and came out with his micro LED flashlight. They stepped onto the threshold, and Sam clicked on the light.

"Empty," Remi murmured.

Sam panned the beam around the interior, hoping there was a lower antechamber, but he saw nothing. "Do you see any markings?" he asked.

"No. That smell isn't normal, Sam. It's like . . ."

"Stagnant water."

He clicked off the flashlight. They turned around and climbed the steps. Sam said, "Somebody took him somewhere. All the mausoleums I checked were also empty."

"Mine too. Someone disinterred these people, Sam."

Back on the monastery grounds, they spotted a man atop a wooden ladder leaning against the damaged belfry. He was middle-aged, stocky, and wearing a black bicycle-racing-style cap. They walked over.

"Excuse me," Remi said in Albanian.

The man turned and looked down at them.

"A flisni anglisht?" Do you speak English?

The man shook his head. *"Jo."*

"Damn," Remi murmured, and pulled out her iPad.

The man called out, "Earta?"

A little blond girl scampered around the edge of the building and skidded to a stop before Sam and Remi. She smiled at them, then up at the man. *"Po?"*

He spoke to her in Albanian for a few seconds, then she nodded. To Sam and Remi she said, "Good afternoon. My name is Earta. I speak English."

"And very well," Sam said, then introduced himself and Remi.

"Very nice to meet you. You would like to ask my father a question?"

"Yes," Remi said. "Is he the caretaker?"

Earta's brows furrowed. "Care . . . taker? Caretaker? Oh, yes, he is the caretaker."

"We were curious about the graveyard. We were just there, and—"

"A shame about what happened, yes?"

"Yes. What did happen?"

Earta put the question to her father, listened to his answer, then said: "Two months ago, a storm came in from the bay. Heavy winds. There was much damage. The next day, the sea rose and flooded the lagoon and part of this island. The graveyard was underwater. Much damage there too."

Sam said, "What happened to the . . . occupants?"

Earta asked her father, then asked them, "Why do you ask?"

Remi replied, "I may have distant relatives from here. My aunt told me one of them was buried here."

"Oh," Earta said with some consternation. "I am sorry to hear that." She spoke to her father again, who replied at length. Earta said to Remi, "About half of the graves were undamaged. The others . . . when the water receded, the people were no longer under the ground. My father, my sisters, and I were finding them for several days afterward." Earta's eyes brightened, and she smiled. "There was even a skull in a tree! Just sitting there. It was funny."

Remi stared at the beaming girl for a moment. "Okay, then."

"The government came and decided the bodies should be taken away until the cemetery can be . . . um . . . fixed. Is that the right word?"

Sam smiled. "Yes."

"Come back next year. It will be much nicer then. Less stinky."

"Where are the remains now?" said Remi.

Earta asked her father. She nodded at his explanation, then said to Sam and Remi, "Sazan Island." She pointed toward the Bay of Vlorë. "There is an old monastery there, older than this one even. The government took them all there."

22

Vlorë, Albania

"Well, that's a bit of bad luck," Selma said a few minutes later when Sam and Remi shared the news. They were sitting on the hood of their Fiat in the parking lot. "Hang on, let me see what I can find out about Sazan Island."

They heard thirty seconds' worth of keyboard clicking, then Selma was back: "Here we go. Sazan Island, largest island in Albania at two square miles, strategically located between the Strait of Otranto and the Bay of Vlorë in Albania. Unpopulated, as far as I can tell. The waters around the island are part of a National Marine Park. It's changed hands a number of times throughout the centuries: Greece, Roman Empire, Ottoman Empire, Italy, Germany, then back to Albania. Looks like Italy put some fortifications on it during

World War Two, and . . . Yes, here it is: they converted the Byzantine-era monastery into a fortress of some kind." Selma paused. "Oh, well, this could be trouble. Looks like I was mistaken."

"Caves," Sam predicted.

"Swamps, alligators—oh, my," Remi chimed in.

"No, about it being uninhabited. There's a Park Rangers installation on the island. It's home to three or four patrol boats and about three dozen Rangers."

"Therefore, off-limits to civilians," Remi added.

"I would imagine, Mrs. Fargo," agreed Selma.

Sam and Remi were silent for a few moments. Neither had to ask the other about what came next. Sam simply said to Selma, "How do we get there without being sunk by Marine Park Rangers?"

After skipping Selma's first and predictable suggestion of "Don't get caught," they began exploring their options. First, of course, they would need transportation, an easy enough task, Selma assured them.

Leaving Selma to her task, Sam and Remi drove the Fiat south back to Vlorë, where they regrouped at their de facto headquarters: the outdoor café at the Hotel Bologna. From their seats they could see in the distance Sazan Island, a speck of land rising from the Adriatic's blue waters.

Selma called an hour later. "How do you feel about kayaks?"

"As long as they're nice to us," Sam quipped.

Remi swatted Sam on the arm. "Go ahead, Selma."

"On the northern tip of the peninsula there's a recreation area: beaches, rock climbing, sea caves, coves for swimming, that sort of thing. From the tip of the peninsula to Sazan Island it's just over two miles. Here's the catch: they don't allow motorized craft in the area, and it closes at dusk. I presume you would prefer to do your skullduggery at night?"

"You know us so well," Sam replied. "You've found a trustworthy kayak emporium, I assume."

"I have. I've taken the liberty of renting a pair for you."

"What about weather and tides?" said Remi.

"Partly cloudy and calm tonight, with a quarter moon; but there's a storm moving in tomorrow morning. Based on the online nautical charts I've been able to find, the current within the bay is fairly gentle, but go too far east of Sazan Island and the peninsula and you're in the Adriatic. From what I've read, the current there is unforgiving."

Sam said, "In other words, a one-way trip south to the Mediterranean Sea."

"If you even get that far without being—"

"We understand, Selma," Remi interrupted. "East is bad."

Sam and Remi looked at each other and nodded. Sam said, "Selma, how long until dusk?"

As it turned out, the approach of nightfall was the least of their worries. While the shop—located in Orikum, a resort municipality ten miles south of Vlorë in the crook of the bay—had a wide selection of injection-molded plastic kayak models available, none of them came in anything but retina-burning reds, yellows, or oranges, or a Jackson Pollockesque mix of the three. With no time to shop for stealthier color schemes, they bought the best pair of the lot, along with double-ended oars and life jackets.

After a quick stop at a hardware store, they returned to Vlorë. Having had good luck with them since Kathmandu, they found a military surplus store and bought an all-black outfit for each of them: boots and socks, long underwear, wool pants, a knit cap, and an oversized long-sleeved turtleneck sweater to cover the neon orange life jacket. A bag of just-in-case odds and ends and a pair of dark rucksacks rounded out the spree. Then they set out.

Sam drove around the recreation area for several minutes, but they saw no one. The parking lots and beaches were empty. From a cliff overlook, they scanned the waters below and again saw no one.

"Probably too early in the year," Sam said. "School's still in session."

"We should assume there'll be patrols," Remi said. "Park Rangers or local police."

Sam nodded. "Good point." If found, the Fiat would either be ticketed or towed. In either case, it was a complication they didn't need. Worse still, the local authorities might push the panic button and assume they had a pair of vacationers lost at sea, which would undoubtedly attract the attention of the Navy and/or Coast Guard—the very thing Sam and Remi were trying to avoid.

After twenty minutes of tooling around the recreation area's dirt roads, Sam found a brush-choked drainage ditch into which he backed the Fiat. Under Remi's careful eye for detail, they rearranged the brush until the vehicle was invisible from the road.

Together they stepped back to admire the job.

"They could have used you in England before D-day," Sam remarked.

"It's a gift," Remi agreed.

Rucksacks on their backs, they dragged their kayaks down the hill to a secluded cove they'd spotted earlier. Measuring less than forty feet wide, with a shallow white sand beach, the inlet leading out to sea was two hundred yards long and curved, protecting them from prying eyes.

With forty-five minutes of light remaining, they set about camouflaging the kayaks. Using cans of black and gray marine spray paint, they emblazoned the sides, tops, and bottoms of the craft in jagged overlapping stripes until not a sliver of neon plastic showed. Sam's paint job, while functional, lacked the artistic flair of Remi's work. Her kayak bore a striking resemblance to the slashed camouflage pattern found on World War I warships.

He stepped back a few paces, studied each kayak in

turn, then said, "Are we sure you aren't reincarnated from some OSS operative?"

"Not entirely." She nodded at his kayak. "Do you mind?"

"Have at it."

A couple of minutes and half a can of spray paint later, Sam's kayak looked almost identical to her own. She turned to him: "What do you think?"

"I feel . . . unmanned."

Remi walked over and kissed him. She smiled. "If it helps, I think your kayak is bigger than mine."

"Very funny. Let's get changed."

After they donned their surplus clothes, their regular clothes went into the rucksacks, which in turn each went into the bow compartment of each kayak.

With nothing else to do, they sat together in the sand and watched the sun's descent, watched as the shadows lengthened over the water, and darkness slowly engulfed the inlet.

When night had fully fallen, they dragged the kayaks down to the water, each shoving halfway out before climbing in and pushing off with the tip of an oar. Soon they were moving through the inlet. They took ten minutes to practice maneuvering the kayaks, getting a feel for the oars and the balance, until they were confident they were ready.

With Sam in the lead, Remi behind and to his right,

they paddled down the inlet, oars making a barely perceptible hiss as they cut through the water. Soon the mouth of the inlet came into view; beyond that, a vast dark carpet of water. As Selma had predicted, the sky was partially overcast, with only the faintest moon glow reflecting off the water. Two miles ahead, almost due north, they could see the dark lump of Sazan Island.

Sam suddenly stopped paddling. He held up a closed fist: *Stop.* Remi took her oar out of the water, laid it across her lap, and waited. Using exaggerated and slow movements, Sam pointed to his ear, then up toward the top of the cliff to the right.

Ten seconds passed.

Then Remi heard it: an engine, followed by the soft squeal of brakes.

Sam looked back at Remi, pointed to the rock wall, then put his oar back in the water and headed in that direction. Remi followed. Sam turned his kayak parallel with the cliff, then rotated in his seat, placed a hand on Remi's bow, and steered her in.

"Ranger?" Remi whispered.

"Let's hope so."

They sat still, eyes cast upward.

At the edge of the cliff a match flared, then went out and was replaced by the glowing tip of a cigarette. In the faint glow Sam glimpsed the brim of a military-style cap. For five minutes they sat motionless, watching as the man finished his smoke. At last he turned and walked back the way he'd come. A car door opened, then slammed shut. The engine started, and the car began moving away, tires crunching on the gravel.

Sam and Remi waited another five minutes in case of a double back, then set out again.

A quarter mile into the bay, it became clear that Selma's tide prediction was similarly accurate. While neither Sam nor Remi were surprised, they also knew the ocean was a fickle beast; even a relatively gentle one-knot eastward current would have made the crossing twice as hard, forcing them to make constant course adjustments to compensate for the surge. Fail at this, and they could easily find themselves caught in the Adriatic and on their way to Greece.

Soon they found their rhythm, stroking in unison and quickly eating up the distance to Sazan. At the halfway point they stopped for a break. Remi brought her kayak alongside Sam's, and they sat in silence for a few minutes, enjoying the gentle rocking of the waves.

"Patrol," Remi said suddenly.

To the northeast a large speedboat came around the island's headland from the direction of the base. It kept turning, bow coming about until it was pointed directly at them. Sam and Remi sat frozen, watching and waiting. Though well-camouflaged, their kayaks wouldn't escape the attention of a spotlight a quarter mile away.

On the boat's bow a spotlight popped on, skimmed

over the island's southern shoreline, then went dark again. The patrol boat kept coming toward them.

"Come on," Sam muttered. "Go take some shore leave."

The boat swerved to the east.

Remi said, "Good boy. Keep going."

It did. They watched for a few more minutes as the boat's navigation lights grew more distant, then finally merged with the light clutter of Vlorë in the distance.

Sam looked at his wife. "Ready?"

"Ready."

They covered the remaining mile in about twenty minutes. Having already done a virtual reconnaissance of the island with Google Earth, Sam had picked out their landing point.

Measuring roughly three miles from north to south and a mile at its widest point, Sazan resembled, Sam thought, a misshapen guppy. The park station was on the guppy's back, a cove on the northeastern coast, while their landing site was the guppy's tail, at the extreme southern tip, near the old World War II–era fortifications.

Mostly devoid of vegetation save ground brush and a few patches of dwarf pines, the rocky terrain was dominated by two high hills near the island's center. It was on one of these hills that they hoped to find the old monastery and, if Earta's information was accurate, the occupants of the Zvernec Island graveyard, including the late Bishop Besim Mala.

As was normal for Sam and Remi, they were traveling far and jumping through a lot of hoops based on a big "if." Such was the life of professional treasure hunters, they'd learned during their years of searching.

As they neared the shore, the waves got choppy, crashing on jutting rocks and half-submerged coquina flats. The plastic kayaks performed admirably, bouncing off the rocks and skidding over shoals, until Sam and Remi were able to half paddle, half push themselves into the shallows, where they climbed out and waded ashore.

They crouched down to catch their breath and survey their surroundings.

The rock-strewn beach was barely deeper than their kayaks were long and was backstopped by a four-foot-tall rock wall; beyond this wall, a steep hill dotted with green scrub. Halfway up the hill, a garage-sized structure was built into the hillside.

"Pillbox," Sam whispered.

Higher up the hill stood what looked like a stone shack—a lookout post, perhaps—and higher still, a hundred yards away on the crest of the hill, was a three-story brick barracks-style building. Black glassless window openings stared out over the sea.

After five minutes of looking and listening, Sam whispered, "Nobody home. Anything catch your eye?"

"No."

"I don't see any graffiti," Sam remarked.

"Does that mean something?"

"If I were a kid living in Vlorë, I doubt I could resist sneaking out here. While it wasn't my thing as a teenager, I knew plenty of guys who would've spray-painted the hell out of that pillbox just to prove they'd been here."

Remi nodded. "So either Albanian youth are particularly law abiding or . . ."

"Nobody who sneaks over here stays free long enough to make mischief," Sam finished.

23

Sazan Island, Albania

Under the light of a half-moon, they began slogging their way up the hill road. Though the crest was only a crow's flight mile away and a few hundred feet higher than the barracks, the road's serpentine path doubled the actual distance.

Finally they reached the last bend in the road. Once around it, they spotted the crest of the hill. Sam gestured for Remi to wait, then ducked off the road and picked his way through the scrub brush until he could see over the crest. He gave her an *All clear* wave, and she joined him.

She said, "The promised land."

"A promised land that's seen much better days," Sam replied.

Though before leaving for the peninsula they'd

studied the structure on Google Earth, the overhead view had shown the church as merely an unremarkable, cross-shaped building. Now, up close, they could see a conical belfry, tall boarded-up windows, and a once-red tiled roof bleached pink from centuries of sunlight.

They found the main double doors locked, so they circled the church. On the north side they found two items of interest: a waist-high ragged hole in the brick wall and an unrestricted view of the northern half of Sazan, including the Park Rangers station half a mile below, situated on a man-made breakwater cove illuminated by pole-mounted lights. Sam and Remi counted three boats and three buildings.

Remi said, "Let's find Bishop Mala and get out of here."

24

Sazan Island, Albania

As soon as they ducked through the hole in the wall, they realized their task was going to be much harder than they'd anticipated. Instead of stepping into an open space, they found themselves standing in a labyrinth.

On either side and ahead of them, eroding wooden coffins were stacked eight high and four deep, forming a corridor that was barely wider than their shoulders. Headlamps illuminating the way, they walked to the end of the corridor. They found themselves at a T-turn. To the left and right, more coffins.

"Are you keeping count?" Sam whispered.

"A hundred ninety-two so far."

"The Zvernec graveyard isn't that big."

"It is if they were packing them shoulder to shoulder

and stacking them. We know Mala died in 1436. Even if his was the first burial, we could be talking about five-plus centuries."

"I just got a shiver down my spine. Left or right?"

Remi chose left. They walked a few paces. Ahead, Sam's headlamp washed over an exterior brick wall.

"Dead end," he said.

"Was that a pun?"

"Freudian slip."

They turned around, and, with Remi in the lead, proceeded past the T-turn and down the adjoining corridor. At the end of this, a right turn, followed by another sixty-four coffins, followed by a left turn and more coffins. The pattern continued through another five turns until the body count exceeded six hundred.

At last they entered an open space. Here the coffins were also stacked eight high, all the way to the vaulted ceiling's crossbeams. Sam and Remi turned in a circle, headlamps sweeping over walls of white pine.

"There," Sam said suddenly.

On the western wall, behind a mountain of rotting pine, was a row of stone sarcophagi. "Fourteen," Remi said. "The same as the number of mausoleums in the graveyard."

"That's a bit of good luck," Sam replied. He counted the coffin wall behind the sarcophagi. "Unbelievable," he murmured. "Remi, there are over a thousand corpses in this building."

"Earta must have been mistaken. After the storm and

flood, they must have taken all the bodies. Zvernec isn't so much a graveyard as it is a charnel pit."

"There's no smell."

"According to Selma, the last burial was in 1912. Even with embalming, there's probably little flesh left."

Sam smiled and sang softly, "Dem bones . . . dem bones . . . dem dry bones."

"Don't give up your day job. Let's check for markings. Mala's mausoleum bore a huge patriarchal cross; maybe they did the same for his sarcophagus."

A quick check of the end of each sarcophagus showed no crosses. Sam and Remi walked along the row, using their headlamps to peer at the top of each stone coffin. Of the fourteen, three had been chiseled with the Eastern Orthodox Church symbol.

They sat together on the floor and stared at them. Remi asked, "How heavy do you think each one is?"

"Four, five hundred pounds." Then, after a moment: "But the lid . . . that's a different story. Crowbar."

"Pardon?" Remi asked with a smile. She was used to her husband's cerebral non sequiturs; they were his way of working through problems.

"We forgot a crowbar. That lid weighs a hundred pounds at most, but prying open that seam while the sarcophagus is wedged in there . . . Damn, I knew I had that *We're forgetting something important* feeling."

"Luckily, you have a plan."

Sam nodded. "Luckily, I have a plan."

Having long ago learned the universal value of three

items—rope, wire, and duct tape—Sam and Remi rarely went into the field without them even when the specific task or journey didn't obviously call for any of them. This time, in a hurry to beat nightfall, they'd forgotten one of the trio in addition to the crowbar: wire. The fifty-foot coil of climbing rope and the duct tape would be enough, Sam hoped.

It took only a few minutes of scrabbling over the church's crossbeams before they found what they needed: a loose L bracket. After twisting it free, Sam used his body weight to smash it closed over the rope's center point. Next he crawled over the sarcophagus and wriggled the bracket into the rear seam beneath the lid. Then, grasping the rope like reins, he tugged until the L bracket was firmly seated in place. Finally he and Remi tossed the ends of the rope over a beam and used their combined body weight to slowly take up the slack until the far end of the lid began rising.

"I've got it." Remi said through clenched teeth, taking Sam's end. "Go ahead."

Sam hurried forward, bent over the lid, and slipped his fingers under its near side. He leaned backward and straightened his legs. The lid popped up and slid free between his legs. The L bracket popped free with a metallic twang.

Together, they stepped around the lid and leaned forward, their headlamps panning over the sarcophagus's contents.

"Bones, bones, and more bones," Remi said.

"And not a glint of gold in sight," Sam replied. "One down, two to go."

Though neither of them voiced the worry, Sam and Remi both had the gut feeling that whichever sarcophagus they chose next, it too would be the wrong choice. Similarly, neither of them dared acknowledge the nagging voice of doubt in the back of each's head—that Father/Bishop Besim Mala had not been faithful to the King of Mustang's request and that the second Theurang disk had been long ago discarded or lost, along with the Golden Man and, if Jack Karna were right, the location of Shangri-La.

Thirty minutes and a second sarcophagus lid later, they found themselves staring at a second set of bones and a second strikeout.

Ninety minutes after they entered the church, they slid back the lid of the third and final sarcophagus. Exhausted, Sam and Remi sat before it and took a minute to catch their breath.

"Ready?" Sam said.

"Not really, but let's get it over with," replied Remi.

On hands and knees, they crawled forward, went on either side of the stone lid, and, after taking a deep breath, peeked over the edge into the sarcophagus.

From the blackness a sliver of gold winked back at them.

25

Sofia, Bulgaria

Shortly after dawn, exhausted but triumphant, they were back on the peninsula and on their way to the hotel in Vlorë.

Having already expressed to Selma concern over shipping the Theurang disk back to San Diego via standard means, Sam and Remi found their chief researcher had, predictably, made alternative arrangements. Rube Haywood, their old CIA friend, had given her the name and address of a reliable and discreet courier service in Sofia. Whether the service was somehow affiliated with his employer, Rube declined to say, but the sign over the building's door, which read "Sofia Academic Archivist Services Ltd," told Sam all he needed to know.

"It'll be there no later than noon tomorrow local time," Sam told Remi. "You have directions for me?"

Remi smiled and held up her iPad. "Plugged in and ready to go."

Sam put the Fiat into gear and pulled out.

When they got to within a half mile of their destination, Remi's iPad became unnecessary. Signs in both Cyrillic and English led them down Vasil Levski Street, then past the Parliament building and the Academy of Sciences, then into the plaza encircling Sofia's religious heart, the Alexander Nevsky Cathedral.

The cross-domed basilica dominated the square, its gold-plated central dome rising a hundred fifty feet above the street and its bell tower twenty-five feet above that.

Reading from her downloaded tourist guide, Remi said, "Twelve bells at a total weight of twenty-four tons, ranging in weight from twenty pounds to twenty-four thousand pounds."

"Impressive," Sam replied, following the flow of vehicles around the cathedral. "And deafening, I would imagine."

They circled the tree-lined square twice before Sam pulled onto a side street and found a parking spot.

Their stop at Alexander Nevsky Cathedral would merely be a launching pad, they both knew. While both Selma and Karna agreed that Bishop Arnost Deniv had died in Sofia in 1442, neither had been able to find any details about his final resting place. They hoped the head librarian at Alexander Nevsky would be able to point them in the right direction.

They got out and walked into the square, following the stream of locals and tourists to the cathedral's west side, where they mounted the steps headed toward the massive wooden doors. As they approached, a blond woman with a bobbed haircut smiled at them and said something in Bulgarian—a question, based on the inflection. They caught the word "English," assumed the gist of the query, and repeated: "English."

"Welcome to Alexander Nevsky Cathedral. How may I help you?" she said.

"We would like to speak with the head of your library," replied Remi.

"Library?" the woman repeated. "Oh, you mean archivist?"

"Yes."

"I am sorry, there is no archivist here."

Sam and Remi exchanged puzzled glances. Remi got out her iPad and showed the woman the PDF file Selma had sent them, a brief on Bulgaria's Eastern Orthodox Church. Remi pointed out the passage, and the woman read it, her lips moving silently.

"Ah," she said sagely. "This is old information, you see. That person now works in the Palast of the Synode."

The woman pointed to the southeast, at a building surrounded by a copse of trees. "It is there. You go there, and they will help."

"And what is the Synode?" asked Sam.

The woman slipped into tour-guide-speak: "The Synode is home to a group of Metropolitans, or Bishops, who in turn elect Patriarchs and similarly important officials of the Bulgarian Orthodox Church. The tradition of the Synode goes back to the days of the Apostles in Jerusalem."

With that, the woman smiled, and tilted her head as if to ask *Is there anything else?*

Sam and Remi thanked the woman, turned around, and walked to the Palast. Once inside, and standing before the lobby information desk, they explained the reason for their visit—research for a book on the history of the Eastern Orthodox Church—and they were told to be seated. After an hour, a black-robed priest with a long salt-and-pepper beard appeared and escorted them to his office, where it quickly became clear he spoke little English, and Sam and Remi even less Bulgarian. An interpreter was summoned. They repeated their story, then produced the publisher's letter of introduction Wendy had created for them using Photoshop. The priest listened intently as the interpreter read the letter, and he sat back and stroked his beard for a full minute before answering.

"I am afraid we cannot help you," the interpreter said for him. "The records you seek are not kept at the Palast. The person you spoke with at the cathedral was mistaken."

"Does he know where we might look next?" Sam said.

The interpreter put the question to the priest, who pursed his lips, stroked his beard a bit more, then picked up the phone and spoke to someone on the other end. After some back and forth, he hung up. The translator told Sam and Remi, "Personnel records for that period are housed in the Sveta Sofia . . . I'm sorry, the Hagia Sophia Church."

"And where would we find that?" asked Remi.

"Directly east of here," the translator replied. "One hundred meters, on the other side of the square."

Sam and Remi were there ten minutes later, where they again waited, this time for a mere forty minutes, before being ushered into yet another priest's office. This one spoke English very well, so they had their answer in short order: not only was the guide at Alexander Nevsky Cathedral mistaken but the priest at the Palast of the Synode was as well.

"Records prior to the first Bulgarian Exarch, Antim I, who reigned until the outbreak of the Russo-Turkish War in 1877, are maintained in the Methodius."

Sam and Remi looked at each other, took a breath, and asked, "What exactly is the Methodius?"

"Why, it's the National Library of Bulgaria."

"And where would we find it?"

"Just east of here, opposite the National Gallery for Foreign Art."

Two hours after leaving their car, Sam and Remi found themselves back standing beside it and standing across the street from the Bulgarian National Library. Without realizing it, they'd parked ten paces from their ultimate destination.

Or so they thought.

This time, after a mere twenty minutes with a librarian, they learned that the Methodius had no record of a Metropolitan named Arnost Deniv dying in the early fifteenth century.

After apologizing, the librarian left them sitting alone at a reading table.

"Our shell game with the coffins on Sazan is starting to feel like a cakewalk," Sam said.

"This can't be the end," Remi said. "We know Arnost Deniv existed. How can there be no record of him?"

From the table beside theirs, a smooth, basso voice said, "The answer, my dear, is there are several Arnost Denivs in the history of the Bulgarian Orthodox Church and most of them lived prior to the Russo-Turkish War."

Sam and Remi turned and found themselves looking at a silver-haired man with twinkling green eyes. He gave them an easy, open smile and said, "Apologies for eavesdropping."

"Not at all," Remi replied.

The man said, "The trouble with the library is, they're in the middle of digitizing their records. They haven't fully cross-referenced the catalog. Consequently, if your request is not painstakingly specific, you miss the mark."

"We're open to any and all advice," Sam said.

The man gestured for them to move to his table. Once they were seated, and he had restacked the books piled around him, he said, "As it happens, I'm working on a little history myself."

"Of the Eastern Orthodox Church?" asked Remi.

The man smiled knowingly. "Among other things. My interests are . . . eclectic, I suppose you could say."

"Interesting that our paths would cross here," Sam said, studying the man's face.

"Truth is stranger than fiction, I believe. This morning, while I was researching the Ottoman rule of Bulgaria, I came across the name Arnost Deniv—a Metropolitan from the fifteenth century."

Remi replied, "But the librarian said there was no—"

"She said they had no record of a Metropolitan by that name dying during that period. The book in which I found him hasn't been digitized yet. You see, when the Ottoman Empire—which was devoutly Muslim—conquered Bulgaria, thousands of clergy were killed. Often, those who survived were demoted or exiled, or both. This was the case with Arnost Deniv. He was quite influential, and this worried the Ottomans.

"In 1436, after returning from missionary work in the East, he ascended to the level of Metropolitan, but four years later he was demoted and exiled. Under pain of death, he was ordered by the Ottomans to restrict his ministrations to the village in which he died two years later."

"And let me guess," Sam said. "The Ottomans did their best to destroy much of the EOC's history during that period."

"Correct," the man said. "As far as many of the history texts of that time are concerned, Arnost Deniv was never more than a lowly priest in a tiny hamlet."

"Then you can tell us where he's buried?" asked Remi.

"Not only can I tell you that but I can show you where all his worldly possessions are on public display."

· 26 ·

Sofia, Bulgaria

Their benefactor's instructions were simple: drive ten miles north to the town of Kutina, in the foothills of the Stara Planina Mountains. Find the Kutina Cultural History Museum, and ask to see the Deniv exhibit.

They pulled into Kutina shortly after one in the afternoon and stopped at a café for lunch. Using cobbled-together phrases, Sam and Remi were able to get directions to the museum.

"By the way," Sam said as he opened the Fiat's driver's door, "did you get that man's name? For the life of me, I can't remember."

With her own door half open, Remi paused. Her brows furrowed. "That's funny . . . neither can I. Something that began with a *C*, I think."

Sam nodded. "Yes, but was that his first name or his last name? Or both?"

Having seen more than their fair share of Eastern Orthodox churches, Sam and Remi were relieved to find the museum was located in an old butter yellow farmhouse overlooking the Iskar River. On either side of the structure was lush green horse pasture.

They parked in the museum's gravel turnaround, got out, and climbed the porch steps. In the front door's mullioned window was a universal "Be Back At" clock sign but in Cyrillic. The hands were pointed at two-thirty.

"Twenty minutes," Sam said.

They sat down on the porch swing and rocked back and forth, chatting and killing time. A light rain began to fall, pattering on the roof above.

Remi asked, "Why don't we have one of these? It's relaxing."

"We do," Sam replied. "I bought it for you for Arbor Day four years ago." Sam liked to surprise his wife with gifts on obscure holidays. "I haven't had the time to put it together yet. I'll move it to the top of my to-do list."

Remi hugged his arm. "Oh, that's right. Arbor Day? Are you sure it wasn't Groundhog Day?"

"No, we were in Ankara on Groundhog Day."

"Are you sure? I could have sworn Ankara was in March . . ."

At 2:28 an old green Bulgaralpine coasted into the turnaround and pulled to a stop on the lawn. A lanky woman in granny glasses and a beret climbed out, saw them on the porch, and waved. *"Sdrawei!"* she called.

"Sdrawei!" Sam and Remi replied in unison. "Hi, there!" and "Do you speak English?" were two phrases they tried to commit to memory whenever they visited a new country.

Sam now used the second phrase as the woman started up the porch steps. She replied, "Yes, I speak English. My sister, she lives in America—Dearborn, Michigan, America. She teaches me over the Internets. I am Sovka."

Sam and Remi introduced themselves.

Sovka asked, "You have come to see the museums?"

"Yes," said Remi.

"Good, then. Follow in, please." Sovka unlocked the front door and stepped inside. Sam and Remi followed. The interior smelled of old wood and cabbage, and the walls were painted in a similar tone as the exterior: faded butter yellow. After hanging up her coat in the foyer closet, the woman led them into a small office in the converted front room.

"What brings you to this museums?" the woman asked.

Sam and Remi had discussed their approach on the way to Kutina and had decided on directness. "We're interested in Father Arnost Deniv. Someone at the Bulgarian National Library in Sofia suggested you might have some artifacts related to him."

Sovka's eyes widened. "The Methodius? They know about our museums at the Methodius? In Sofia?"

Remi nodded. "Indeed they do."

"Oh, I will be putting this into our soon news flyer paper. What a proud moment for us. To answer question: no, you are mistaken. We do not have *some* of Father Deniv's personal matters. We have *all* of his personal matters here. May I ask, why are you interested with him?" Sam and Remi explained their book project, and Sovka nodded solemnly. "A dark time for the Church. Good that you are writing about it. Come."

They followed Sovka out of the office, down the hall, then up a set of switchback steps to the second floor. Here the walls had been torn down, turning what looked like a thousand square feet of bedrooms into an open space. Sovka led them to the southeast corner of the house, where a cluster of glass display cases and hanging tapestries had been arranged to form an alcove. Ceiling pot lights shone down on the cases.

Remi saw it first, followed a moment later by Sam. "Do you see—"

"I do," he replied.

Sovka asked over his shoulder, "Pardons me?"

"Nothing," Remi replied.

Even from ten feet away, the curved edge of gold seemed to leap out at them from the case near the wall. Hearts pounding, Sam and Remi stepped into the alcove. There, on the top shelf, resting on a folded jet-black cassock trimmed in burnt orange, was the Theurang disk.

Sovka spread her arms with a flourish and said, "Welcome to the Deniv Collections. Everything in his possessions at the time of death is here."

Sam and Remi tore their eyes from the disk and looked around. In all, there were perhaps twenty items, most of it clothing, grooming tools, writing instruments, and a few scraps of correspondence mounted in shadow boxes.

"What's this item here?" Remi said as casually as possible.

Sovka looked at the Theurang disk. "We are not to be certain. We believe it is a keepsake of sorts, perhaps from within his missionary quest in savage lands."

"It's fascinating," Sam said, leaning closer. "We'll just have a look around, if you don't mind."

"Of course. I am over here, if help is needed."

Sovka wandered off but never strayed out of eyesight.

"This complicates matters," Remi whispered to Sam.

Relieving Besim Mala of his Theurang disk had been an easy decision. Here, however, Arnost Deniv's disk was a part of recognized history. Breaking into the museum after hours would be easy enough, they knew, but neither Sam nor Remi felt good about that option.

"Let's confer with our experts," Remi suggested.

They told Sovka they would be back shortly, then stepped out onto the porch. They dialed Selma, asked her to conference in Jack Karna, then waited through two minutes of squelches and clicks as she made the appropriate connections. Once Karna was on the line, Sam explained their situation.

Remi asked, "Jack, what exactly do you need from the disks to make them compatible with the mural map? Is it the disk itself or the markings on it?"

"Both, I suspect. Is there any chance she would lend it to you?"

"Doubtful," Sam replied. "This is her pride and joy. And I'm worried that if we ask, she'll get suspicious. Right now, she's helpful and cooperative. We don't want that to change."

Selma asked, "Jack, how similar in size and shape are the disks?"

"From my research, I would say nearly identical. You'll know for sure when you compare the one Sam and Remi just sent you with the one you retrieved from the chest."

Remi said, "Selma, what are you thinking?"

"Too early to say, Mrs. Fargo, but if you'll all hold for a bit . . ." The line clicked and went silent. True to her word, Selma was back in three minutes: "I can build one," she said without preamble. "Well, not me, but I have a friend of a friend who can replicate one with tool-and-die CAD/CAM precision. If we supply him with enough of the right kind of pictures, he can model the missing disk."

Sam said, "I assume you have a specifications list?"

"Sending it to you right now."

After securing Sovka's agreement to let them photograph the Deniv Collection in return for a small donation to the museum's "New Roof Fund," Sam and Remi drove back to Sofia, and, following both Selma's directions and her shopping list, they collected what they needed: two professional-quality triangle-scale rulers, a lazy Susan turntable, a black inch-high display stand on which the disk could rest, and lights and a tripod for Remi's camera.

They were back in Kutina by four and shooting thirty minutes after that. Careful to pay the right amount of attention to every artifact in the collection lest Sovka become too interested, they photographed each in turn, leaving the Theurang disk for last. Having become bored with the process, Sovka had disappeared into her downstairs office.

"This would be much easier if we were unscrupulous," Sam observed.

"Think of it as good karma. Besides, who knows what the penalty for historical artifact theft is in Bulgaria."

"Both valid points."

With the light box erected and white linen backdrop in place, Sam set up the lights according to Selma's instructions. Once done, Remi placed the display stand on the turntable, then the disk flat on the stand. Finally the scaled rulers were put in place, forming an L around the disk.

After taking a series of test shots and making some adjustments to the camera, Remi began shooting: five pictures for each eight-degree turn of the turntable, for a total of forty-five turns or two hundred twenty-five pictures in all. They repeated the process for the disk's opposite side, then shot another series with it standing upright on its stand. Then, last, a series of close-ups of the disk's twin faces, concentrating on the symbols.

"Eight hundred pictures," Remi said, straightening up from her tripod.

"How big is the file?"

Remi checked her camera's LCD screen. "Wow. Eight gigabytes. Far too big for standard e-mail."

"I think I know how we can get around that," Sam replied. "Let's pack up and get going."

After a quick call to Selma, who in turn called Rube, who in turn called his friends at the Sofia Academic Archivist Services Ltd, Sam and Remi found the office open when they arrived back in Sofia at six-thirty. As with his first visit, Sam was asked only to identify himself and offer a code phrase—this one different than the first—before he was led to an adjoining office and a computer terminal. The office's high-speed Internet line made short work of the picture files, uploading them to Selma's storage site in less than three minutes. Sam waited for the confirmation message, then returned to the Fiat and Remi.

"Where to now?" she asked.

Sam hesitated. Frowned. They'd been moving so fast since arriving in Kathmandu, they'd had no chance to consider the question.

Sam said, "I vote we go home and regroup."

"Seconded."

27

Goldfish Point, La Jolla, California

"Great . . . thanks. We'll look for him."

Selma hung up the phone and turned to the group gathered around the maple worktable: Sam, Remi, Pete, and Wendy.

Selma said, "That was George. The Theurang disk model is done. He's sending it over by bike messenger."

"Can't wait to see what eight hundred photos look like in three dimensions," Remi said.

Arriving home after their Sofia–Frankfurt–San Francisco–San Diego flight, Sam and Remi had made their greetings, then promptly gone to bed for a blissful ten hours. Refreshed, and their bodies mostly realigned with California time, they'd met the team in the workroom for a get-up-to-speed meeting.

"No matter how good the model is," Pete said, "it can't compare to the real thing."

Resting in their formfitting black foam trays, the two genuine Theurang disks gleamed under the hard glare of the halogen pendant lights.

"In looks, yes," Sam replied. "But in utility value . . . As long as it helps point us where we need to go, it's golden to me."

Selma asked, "Do you believe any of it?"

"Which parts?"

"The prophecy, Jack's theory about the Theurang being an evolutionary missing link, Shangri-La . . . all of it."

Remi answered, "Well, Jack admitted it himself: we only have drawings of the Theurang, and there's no telling how much they're based on myth and how much on direct observation. I do think his argument is compelling enough that we should see this through to the end."

Sam nodded his agreement. "As for Shangri-La . . . A lot of legends are based on a kernel of truth. In modern popular culture, Shangri-La is synonymous with paradise. For the people of Mustang, it may have been nothing more than where the Theurang was originally found—and where it should rightfully be laid to rest. Place names are trivial. It's the meaning we attach to them that counts."

"Sam, that's almost poetic," Remi said.

He smiled. "I have my moments."

The intercom buzzed. Selma answered it, then walked out. She returned a minute later carrying a cardboard box. She opened the box, examined the contents, then removed them. She placed the modeled Theurang disk on the foam tray.

The disk was nearly indistinguishable from its mates.

"I'm impressed," Sam said. "Good call, Selma."

"Thank you, Mr. Fargo. Should we call Jack?"

"In a bit. First, though, I think it's time we touch base with King Charlie. I'd like to get him riled enough to talk."

"What do you mean?" asked Wendy.

"Depending on how reliable his sources in Mustang are, he may believe his plan to drown us in the Kali Gandaki succeeded. Let's see if we can rattle his cage. Selma, can you get me a secure line on the speaker here?"

"Yes, Mr. Fargo. One moment."

Soon the line clicked open and began ringing. Charlie King answered with a gruff, "King here."

"Good morning, Mr. King," said Sam. "Sam and Remi Fargo here."

Hesitation. Then a boisterous, "Morning to you too! Haven't heard from you for a while. I was gettin' a bit worried you two were renegin' on our deal."

"Which deal is that?"

"I got your friend released. Now you're gonna turn over to me what you've found."

"You're experiencing a case of wishful memory, Charlie. The deal was that we'd meet with Russell and Marjorie and reach an understanding."

"Well, dammit, son, what'd you think that meant? I give you Alton, and you give me what I want."

Remi said, "We've decided you're in breach of contract, Charlie."

"What're you talkin' about?"

"We're talking about the bogus tour guide you hired to kill us in Mustang."

"I did no such—"

Sam interrupted: "Difference without a distinction. You ordered your children or your wife to get it done."

"You think so, huh? Well, go ahead and prove it."

"I think we can do better than that," Sam replied. Beside him, Remi mouthed, *What?* Sam shrugged and mouthed back, *I'm playing it by ear.*

King said, "Fargo, I been threatened by tougher and richer men than you. I hose their blood off my boots just 'bout every day. How 'bout you just give me what I want and we'll part company friends."

"It's too late for that—the friends part, that it. As for the prize you're after—the prize your father spent most of his adult life hunting for—we've got it. It's sitting right in front of us."

"Bull."

"Mind your manners, and we might send you a picture. First, though, why don't you explain your interest in it?"

"How 'bout you tell me what you think you found."

"A wooden chest, shaped like a cube, in the possession of a soldier who'd been dead for half a millennium or so."

King didn't respond immediately, but they could hear him breathing on the line. Finally, in a hushed tone, he said, "You really have it."

"We do. And unless you start telling us the truth, we're going to open it and see what's inside for ourselves."

"No, hold it right there. Don't go doin' that."

"Tell us what's inside."

"Could be one of a couple things: a big coin-shaped thing or a bunch a bones. Either way, they won't mean much to you."

"Then why do they mean so much to you?"

"None of your business."

From across the table, Selma, standing behind her laptop, held up an index finger. Sam said, "Mr. King, can you hold for just a moment?"

Without waiting for a response, Pete reached over to the speakerphone and tapped the Mute button.

Selma said, "Forgot to tell you: I've been doing a little more digging into King's teen years. I came across a blog written by a former reporter at the *New York Times*. The woman claims that during an interview with King three years ago, she asked him a question he didn't like. After staring daggers at her, he terminated the interview. Two days later she was fired. She hasn't been able to find a legitimate job in journalism since then. King blackballed her."

Remi asked, "What did she ask him?"

"She asked why in King's high school yearbook everyone referred to him by the nickname Adolf."

"That's it?" said Sam. "That's all?"

"That's it."

Wendy said, "We already know Lewis King was a Nazi in name only, and Charlie had nothing to do with any of it, so why would—"

"Kids being kids," Remi replied. "Think about it: Lewis King was largely absent from Charlie's life from an early age. On top of that, everywhere Charlie went he probably got teased mercilessly about his Nazi roots. It doesn't sound like much from our perspective, but for a kid, for a teenager . . . Sam, this could be King's hot button. Back then, he was a petulant child with no power. Now he's a petulant billionaire with more power than many heads of state."

Sam considered this. He nodded at Pete, who unmuted the phone. "Apologies, Charlie. Where were we? Oh, that's right: the box. You said it could contain a coin or some bones, correct?"

"That's right."

"And your father wanted them for what? Some obscure Nazi occult ritual? Something Himmler dreamed up with Adolf?"

"Shut up, Fargo!"

"Your dad spent his life hunting for this. How can you be sure he didn't have some ties to a secret postwar Nazi organization?"

"I'm warnin' you . . . Shut your mouth!"

"Is that why you want the Golden Man, Charlie? Are you trying to finish what your goose-stepping dad couldn't?"

From the speaker came the sound of something heavy crashing down on wood followed by jumbled static. King's voice came back on the line: "I ain't no Nazi!"

"The apple never falls far from the tree, Charlie. Here's how I think it happened. Your dad learned about the existence of the Theurang during the 1938 expedition, then after the war the family moves to America, where he continues your Nazi indoctrination. In your twisted minds, the Theurang is some kind of Holy Grail. Lewis disappeared trying to find it, but he taught you well. You're not going to—"

"That bastard! That idiot! He traipses off, leaving my mother back in Germany, then does the same damned thing when she gets here! When my mom swallows a bottle of pills, he don't even bother comin' back for the funeral. He killed her and he don't even have the decency to show up!

"Good ol' eccentric Lewis! He don't give a damn what they say about him, and he can't understand why it'd bother me. Every day, every damned day, I had to listen to them whispering behind my back, giving me that damned Heil Hitler! All that, and I still beat 'em. Beat 'em all! I could buy and sell every single one of 'em now.

"You think I'm after the Golden Man 'cause it meant

so much to my dad? You think I'm some kind of duty-bound son? What a joke. When I get my hands on that thing, I'm going to crush it into dust! And if there's a God in heaven, my dad will be watching!" King paused, and let out a forced chuckle. "Besides, you two have been thorns in my paw since day one. I'll be damned if you're gonna take what's rightfully mine."

Sam didn't respond immediately. One look at Remi told him they were of like minds: for the child Charlie King they felt absolute pity. But King was no longer a child, and his insane mission to exact revenge on his long-dead father had cost people their lives.

Sam said, "That's what this is? A tantrum? King, you've murdered, kidnapped, and enslaved people. You're a sociopath."

"Fargo, you don't know what you're—"

"I know what you've done. And I know what you're capable of doing before this is all over. I'm going to make you a promise, King: not only are we going to make sure you don't get the Golden Man, but we're going to make sure you go to prison for what you've done."

"Fargo, you listen to me! I will kill—"

Sam reached out and hit the Disconnect button.

The line went dead.

There was silence around the worktable.

Then, softly, from Selma: "Well, he sounds a tad peeved."

Her gross understatement broke the tension. They all broke out in laughter. When it died away, Remi said,

"The question is, if we follow through on our promise, will King end up in prison or a rubber room?"

TRISULI, NEPAL

Colonel Zhou had agreed to the late-night meeting partially out of curiosity, partially out of necessity. His arrangement with the strange-faced American *zázhǒng*—half-breeds—had thus far been lucrative, but now that he knew their true identities, and that of their father, Zhou was anxious to change the terms of their partnership. What Charles King was doing in Nepal didn't bother Zhou. What annoyed him was how little he had charged them in . . . handling fees, as the Americans say. Getting the fossils to Lhasa and through customs was easy enough, but finding and securing trustworthy distributors for such banned merchandise was far trickier—and, as of tonight, much pricier.

A few minutes before midnight, Zhou heard the growl of an SUV engine outside. The two soldiers behind the colonel rose from their chairs and brought their assault rifles to the low ready position.

"I've ordered them searched this time," he told his men. "Still, do not let your guards down."

One of the exterior guards stepped across the threshold, gave Zhou a nod, then disappeared. A moment later Marjorie and Russell King stepped out of the darkness into the flickering glow of the kerosene lantern. They were not alone. A third figure, a willowy, grim-faced

Chinese woman, stepped into the room. The King children's body language told Zhou this new woman would be speaking for the trio.

And then he saw it, the similarities in the eyes and nose and cheekbones. Mother and children, Zhou thought. Interesting. He decided to play out the hand. He rose from his seat at the trestle table and nodded respectfully at the woman. "Shall I call you Mrs. King?"

"No. Hsu. Zhilan Hsu."

"Please, sit down."

Zhilan took the bench, her hands folded neatly on the table before her. The King children remained standing, mirroring the at-attention posture of Colonel Zhou's soldiers. Zhou sat down.

"To what do I owe the pleasure?" he asked.

"My husband requires something of you."

"Does he?"

"Yes. First he requires that you understand this: we know that your name is not Zhou, and you are not a colonel in the People's Liberation Army. Your name in fact is Feng, and you are a general."

General Feng felt like his stomach had turned to a block of ice. It was an act of will to keep the panic from showing on his face. "Is that so?"

"It is. We know everything about you, including all of your other illicit activities: small-arms dealing, heroin smuggling, and so on. We also know who in your chain of command is an ally of yours and who is an enemy. In fact, my husband is on quite good terms with a certain general named Gou. Do you know the name?"

Feng swallowed hard. He felt his world crumbling around him. He managed a barely perceptible, "I do."

"General Gou is not fond of you, is he?"

"No."

"Have I made my point?" Zhilan Hsu asked.

"You have."

"Let's talk about our partnership. My husband, in fact, is pleased with the services you have provided and would like to offer you a fifteen percent increase on all transactions."

"That's very generous."

"My husband is aware of that. He also asks a favor of you."

Even as the words were leaving his mouth, Feng was cursing himself. "A favor suggests no compensation."

Zhilan's hard obsidian eyes stared at Feng for a few moments before she answered. "I misspoke. Perhaps 'task' is a better word. Of course, he is happy to compensate you in the amount of two hundred thousand U.S. dollars. But only if you succeed."

Feng struggled to keep the smile from his face. "Of course. That is only fair. What's the nature of this task?"

"There are people—two of them, to be specific—who are threatening our business interests here. We expect that they will be traveling along the border in the coming weeks, perhaps even crossing into the TAR," Zhilan said, referring to the Tibet Autonomous Region. "We want you to intercept them."

"You will need to be more specific."

"Captured and held for us or killed. I will give you the order when the time comes."

"How close to the border will they be traveling?"

"In some places, less than a few miles."

"The border is many hundreds of miles long. How would one find two individuals in all of that?"

"Don't be obtuse," Zhilan said, her voice taking on a harder edge. "You have under your command fourteen Harbin Z-9 helicopters equipped with infrared radars, night-vision cameras, and missiles, both anti-air and anti-tank."

Feng sighed. "You are extraordinarily well informed."

"Your command also maintains seventy-nine observation posts along the border. Is this also correct?"

"Yes."

"We suspect the people will have to use a helicopter to transit some of the more remote areas. There are a limited number of charter companies in Nepal that offer such services. In order to make your task easier, we will be monitoring these companies."

"Then why not intercept these people before they board?"

"We will allow them to . . . complete their mission before you take action against them."

"What is their mission?"

"They are looking for something. We want them to succeed."

"What are they looking for?"

"You do not need to know that. General, I have explained what is required of you; I have given you all the information you need to make a decision. So decide, please."

"I accept. I will need information on the targets."

Zhilan reached into the front pocket of her parka and withdrew an SD card. She slid it across the table to Feng, then stood up. "Make sure you are ready when I call."

28

Jomsom, Nepal

Acutely aware that, in Charles King, they'd enraged a lion that had thus far only been annoyed, Sam and Remi had instructed Selma to find them an alternate route to Mustang.

Everyone involved knew the Theurang was somewhere in the Himalayas, and King now knew that the Fargos, possessing a significant lead in the race, would have to return to Nepal. Sam and Remi had no doubt that Russell and Marjorie King, along with their mother, Zhilan Hsu, would be on the lookout for them. Only time would tell what other forces King would bring to bear, but they intended to walk very carefully until this odyssey was over.

A series of marathon flights eventually took them to New Delhi, India, where they drove two hundred fifty miles southeast to the city of Lucknow, where they picked up a single-engine charter flight another two hundred miles northeast to Jomsom. They'd left the trekker's hub less than a week earlier, and as the plane's wheels squealed on the airstrip tarmac both Sam and Remi felt a sense of déjà vu. This sensation was only heightened as they headed for the terminal amid throngs of trekkers and guide service reps vying for their business.

As Jack Karna had promised, they slipped through customs unmolested and unquestioned. Waiting for them at the curb outside the terminal was another blast from the past: a Nepali man standing beside a white Toyota Land Cruiser and holding a sign bearing their name.

"I think you're looking for us," Sam said, extending his hand.

The man shook both their hands. "I am Ajay. Mr. Karna asked me to tell you, 'Selma's newest fish is called a *Apistogramma iniridae.*' Have I pronounced that correctly?"

"You have," Remi replied. "And its name is?"

"Frodo." In their lengthy discussions, Selma and Jack Karna had discovered they were both avid fans of the Lord of the Rings trilogy. "Yes? Okay?" Ajay asked with a smile.

"Okay," Sam replied. "Lead on."

Not surprisingly, Ajay was not only a better tour guide than their previous one but he was also a better driver, negotiating the Kali Gandaki's innumerable twists, turns, and hazards with expertise. A mere twelve hours after leaving Jomsom they were standing before Jack Karna's door in Lo Monthang.

He greeted them each with a warm hug. Hot tea and scones were ready and waiting in the cushioned seating area. Once they were settled and had warmed themselves, Sam and Remi retrieved the Theurang disks and placed them on the coffee table before Karna.

For a full minute, he simply stared at them, eyes agog and a half smile on his face. Finally he picked up each disk in turn, examining it carefully. He seemed only slightly less impressed by the model.

"Aside from the symbols, it's almost identical to the genuine article, isn't it? Your Selma . . . she is quite a woman, I must say."

Remi gave Sam a sideways glance and smile. Her woman's intuition had told her there was a bit of spark growing between Selma and Jack. Sam had dismissed the idea. Now he gave her a nod of recognition.

"She's one of a kind," Sam said. "So, you think these will work?"

"I have no doubt. To that end, Ajay will be taking us to the caves tomorrow morning. With any luck, by the end of the day we will have found a match. From there, it will simply be a matter of following the map to Shangri-La."

"Nothing is ever that simple," Remi said. "Trust us."

Karna shrugged. "As you say." He poured them more tea and passed around the plate of scones. "Now, tell me more about Selma's love of tea and tropical fish."

They were up before dawn the next morning for a full English breakfast served by Karna's houseboy: streaky bacon, eggs, black pudding, grilled tomatoes and mushrooms, fried bread, sausages, and seemingly bottomless mugs of tea. When they could take no more, Sam and Remi pushed away their plates.

"Is this your regular morning fare?" Remi asked Karna.

"Of course."

"How do you stay trim?" Sam said.

"Lots of hiking. Not to mention the cold and the altitude. You burn calories at a massive rate here. If I don't consume at least five thousand a day, I start shedding weight."

"Perhaps you should start a fitness boot camp," Remi suggested.

"There's a thought," Karna said, standing up. He clapped his hands and rubbed them together. "Right! Ten minutes until departure. Ajay will meet us at the gate!"

True to his word, Karna was ushering them out the door a few minutes later, and soon they were in the Land Cruiser heading southeast toward the foothills. Two miles out of the city, as they topped a crest, the landscape began to change dramatically. The rolling hills steepened, and their outline grew more jagged.

The soil slowly morphed from grayish to an olive brown, and what little scrub brush dotted the terrain grew even more sparse. The Land Cruiser began jostling from side to side as Ajay navigated the now boulder-strewn tract. Soon Sam's and Remi's ears began popping.

From the front seat Karna said, "There are two cases of bottled water in the cargo boot. Make sure to stay hydrated. The higher we go, the more fluid you'll need."

Sam grabbed two pairs of bottles, handed one to Remi and two to Karna in the front seat, then asked Karna, "How far from the Tibetan border are we?"

"Seven miles or so. Try to remember: along with most of the rest of the world, we may think of it as the Tibetan border, but the Chinese do not. It's a distinction they zealously enforce. The official name may be the Tibet Autonomous Region, but as far as Beijing is concerned it's all China. In fact, if you keep a sharp eye out, you'll begin to see outposts on the ridges. We may even encounter a patrol or two."

"A patrol?" Sam repeated. "As in, the Chinese Army?"

"Yes. Both ground units and aircraft routinely wander into Mustang, and not by accident. They know Nepal can do nothing but lodge a formal complaint, which means nothing to the Chinese."

"And what happens if someone strays over their side of the border? A lost trekker, for example."

"Depends on the place. Between here and the northern tip of Myanmar there are almost two thousand miles of border, much of it over remote and rugged terrain. As for here, on rare occasions the Chinese not so politely shoo wayward souls back across the border, but usually interlopers are arrested. I know of three trekkers in the last year who were snatched up."

In the driver's seat, Ajay silently held up four fingers.

Karna said, "I stand corrected: four trekkers. All but one of them was eventually released. Have I got that right, Ajay?"

"Right."

"Define 'eventually,'" Remi said.

"A year or so. The one they kept has never been heard from again. The Chinese are keen on setting examples, you see. Letting an invader go too early would be bad form. Next thing you know, you've got hordes of Western agents disguised as trekkers flooding over the border."

"Is that how they really see it?" asked Sam.

"Some in the government do. But I suspect it's mostly for show. There are swaths along China's southern border that are impossible to cover from the ground, so China is strict on what areas it can control. I have it on good authority"—Karna gave a comical jerk of his head toward Ajay—"that trekkers in northern India frequently slip across the border; in fact, there are tourism companies that specialize in it. Isn't that right, Ajay?"

"Right, Mr. Karna."

"Not to worry, Fargos. Ajay and I have been doing this together for years. Our GPS unit is perfectly calibrated, and we know this area intimately. We won't be stumbling into the clutches of the Chinese Army, I can assure you."

Another hour's drive brought them to a gorge hemmed in by cliffs so deeply eroded they looked like tiered rows of massive anthills. Ahead was a castle-like structure that appeared to be partially embedded in the cliff. The ground floor's outer walls were painted the same burnt red color they'd seen in Lo Monthang, while the upper two stories, stacked upon jutting horizontal beams, were progressively smaller and seemed hewn from the rock itself. Faded prayer flags strung between two of the conical roofs flapped in the breeze.

"Tarl Gompa," Karna announced.

"We've heard that name several times," Remi said, "but the definition seems . . . indefinable."

"An accurate way of putting it. In one sense, gompas are fortifications of a sort—outposts for education and spiritual growth. In another sense, they are monasteries; in yet another, military posts. Much depends on the period of history involved and the people occupying the gompa."

"How many of these are there?"

"In Nepal alone, over a hundred that I know of. Probably triple that number remain undiscovered. If you expand the area to Tibet and Bhutan, there are thousands."

"Why are we stopping at this one?" asked Sam.

"Mostly out of respect. Wherever there are sacred caves, a council of elders is formed to watch over them.

The caves here are not yet well known, and the elders are very protective of them. If we don't pay the proper respect, we'll find ourselves staring down the barrels of about a dozen rifles."

They climbed out of the car. In Nepali, Karna called out toward the gompa, and a few moments later an elderly man in khaki pants and a bright blue parka stepped from the darkened doorway. His face was nut brown and deeply lined. From beneath wiry eyebrows he scrutinized his guests for several seconds before breaking into a wide smile.

"*Namaste*, Jack!" the man called.

"*Namaste*, Pushpa. *Tapaai laai kasto chha?*"

Karna walked forward, and the two men embraced and then began talking in low tones. Karna gestured toward Sam and Remi, and they instinctively came forward.

Ajay stopped them: "Better if you wait here. Pushpa is a *sgo-nyer*—a doorkeeper. Mr. Karna is well known to these people, but they are suspicious of outsiders."

Karna and Pushpa continued to talk for several minutes before the old man nodded and clapped Karna on both arms. Karna walked back to the Land Cruiser.

"Pushpa has given us permission to proceed. He will inform a local guide to meet us at the first caves."

"Inform the guide how?" Remi asked. "I don't see any—"

"By word of foot," Karna replied.

He pointed to one of the rocky shark's teeth atop

the opposite cliff. There, a figure was standing. As they watched, Pushpa raised his arm and formed a sequence of shapes with his hand. The figure signaled back, then disappeared behind the cliff.

Karna said, "By the time we get there, all the locals will know to expect us and that we have permission."

"In other words, no angry villagers with pitchforks."

"Rifles," Sam corrected.

Karna smiled reassuringly. "Neither. Shall we go?"

Leaving Tarl Gompa in their rearview mirror, they continued heading generally east, following the gorge for two miles, before emerging on a dry riverbed. A quarter mile away, across a bridge, a collection of gompa-like structures sat at the foot of another anthill cliff, this one several hundred feet high and stretching to the north and south as far as the eye could see.

Ajay guided the Land Cruiser over the river bottom to the bridge, then across. As they neared the village, the terrain changed from scree and boulders to a fine rusty brown sand. Ajay halted the vehicle beside a low stone wall on the village's perimeter. They all climbed out into a brisk wind. Sand pelted their jackets.

"It's got a bite to it, doesn't it?" Karna said.

Sam and Remi, in the middle of pulling up their hoods, nodded back. Sam called over the rush, "We're walking from here?"

"Yes. Into those." Karna pointed toward the anthills. "Come on."

Karna led them through a gap in the wall and started down a stone-lined path. At the end of this path they found a thick hedgerow of scrub brush. He followed the hedge to the left, then through a natural pergola. They emerged in a small cobblestoned square centered around a bubbling fountain. Around the perimeter, planter boxes overflowed with red and purple flowers.

"They divert a bit of the river for irrigation, plumbing, and fountains," Karna explained. "They love fountains."

"It's beautiful," Remi said.

It took little imagination to see how Shangri-La legends began here, she thought. In the middle of some of the bleakest terrain she and Sam had ever encountered, they'd found a tiny oasis. The juxtaposition was pleasantly jarring.

Seated nearby on a wooden bench was a short middle-aged man in a plaid sweater-jacket and a baseball cap emblazoned with the Chicago Bears logo.

He raised a hand toward them and walked over. Karna and the man embraced and spoke for a bit before Karna turned to introduce Sam and Remi.

"Namaste . . . namaste," the man said with smile.

Karna said, "This is Pushpa." Before they could ask, Karna added, "Yes, it's more or less the same as the man at the gompa. To us, it sounds exactly the same; to them, the inflection makes all the difference. Pushpa will lead us to the caves. We'll take some tea with Pushpa, and then we'll get down to business."

· 29 ·

Jomsom, Nepal

Packs settled on their backs, they retraced their footsteps past the Land Cruiser, then followed Pushpa along the wall, first south, then east, around the village to the foot of the anthill cliffs.

"I suddenly feel very small," Remi said over her shoulder to Sam.

"Very."

Upon their first seeing the cliffs, both distance and the fantastical geology had combined to make them seem less than real, as though they were a backdrop from a science-fiction movie. Now, with Sam and Remi standing in the anthills' shadow, they were simply awe inspiring.

At the head of the line, Pushpa had stopped, waiting patiently until Sam and Remi finished gawking and taking pictures before setting out again. Ten more minutes of hiking brought them to a fissure in the rock that was barely taller than Sam. One by one, they slipped through the opening and onto a tunnel-like path. Over their heads, the smooth rusty brown walls curved inward, almost touching, leaving only a sliver of distant blue sky above.

Ever eastward the path zigzagged and spiraled until Sam and Remi had lost track of how far they'd traveled. Pushpa called a halt with a barked word. Behind them at the rear of the line Ajay said, "Now we climb."

"How?" Remi asked. "I don't see any handholds. And we don't have any gear."

"Pushpa and his friends have made a way. The sandstone here is very fragile; standard pitons and rock screws cause too much damage."

Ahead, they could see Pushpa and Karna talking. Pushpa disappeared into an alcove on the left side of the cliff, and Karna picked his way back down the path to where Sam and Remi were standing.

"Pushpa is going up first," he said, "followed by Ajay. Then you, Remi, followed by you, Sam. I'll bring up the rear. The steps look daunting, but they're quite sturdy, I assure you. Just go slow."

Sam and Remi nodded, and then Karna and Ajay changed positions.

Ajay stood at the head of the line, neck craned backward for several minutes before he too stepped into the alcove and disappeared from view. Sam and Remi stepped forward and looked up.

"Oh, boy," Remi murmured.

"Yep," Sam agreed.

The steps Karna had mentioned were in fact wooden stakes that had been pounded into the limestone to form a series of staggered hand- and footholds. The ladder rose a hundred feet up a chimney-like slot before curving out of sight behind a hanging wall of rock.

They watched Ajay scramble over the rungs until they could no longer see him. Remi hesitated for only a moment, then turned to Sam, smiled, kissed him on the cheek, and offered a cheerful, "See you at the top!"

With that, she mounted the first rung and started climbing.

When she was halfway up, Karna said over Sam's shoulder, "She's a dynamo, that one."

Sam smiled. "You're preaching to the choir, Jack."

"Much like Selma, then, right?"

"Right. Selma is . . . unique."

Once Remi had rounded the bend, Sam started upward. Immediately he could feel the solidity of the rungs, and after a few test movements to compensate for his pack's weight, he settled into a steady rhythm. Soon the walls of the chimney closed in around him. What little sunlight had filtered its way to the path below dimmed to twilight. Sam reached the hanging wall and paused to peek around the bend. Twenty feet away, above and to his left, the rungs ended at a horizontal wooden plank nailed to a row of stakes. At the end of this plank was a second, this one angling behind another hanging wall. Remi was standing at the junction; she gave him a wave and thumbs-up.

When Sam reached the plank, he found it not nearly as narrow as it had looked from below. He boosted himself onto the platform, found his footing, and walked toe to heel down the plank, then around the corner. Four more planks brought him to a rocky shelf and an oval-shaped cave. Inside, he found Pushpa, Ajay, and Remi seated around a Jetboil stove supporting a miniature teakettle.

The water had just started boiling when Karna slipped into the cave entrance. He sat down. "Oh, good, tea!"

Wordlessly, Pushpa dug five red enamelware mugs out of his pack, passed them out, then poured the tea. The group sat huddled together, sipping the brew and enjoying the silence. Outside, a gust of wind occasionally whistled past the entrance.

Once everyone was finished, Pushpa deftly packed away the mugs, and then they set off again, this time with their headlamps on. Once again, Pushpa was in the lead while Ajay brought up the rear.

The tunnel curved to the left, then the right, then stopped suddenly at a vertical wall. Straight ahead, a chest-high archway was carved out of the limestone. Pushpa turned and spoke with Karna for a few seconds, then Karna told Sam and Remi:

"Pushpa understands that you are not Buddhists, and he understands that our work here may be a bit complicated, so he won't ask us to observe all Buddhist customs. He only asks that when you first enter the main chamber, you circle the perimeter once, in a clockwise direction. Once you've done this, you can move about as you please. Understood?"

Sam and Remi nodded.

Pushpa ducked through the archway and stepped to the left, followed by Remi, Sam, and Ajay. They found themselves in a corridor. Painted on the wall before them were faded red-and-yellow symbols unfamiliar to Sam and Remi, along with hundreds of lines of text in what they assumed was a dialect of Lowa.

Whispering, Karna told them, "This is a greeting of sorts, essentially a historical introduction to the cave system. Nothing specific to the Theurang or Shangri-La."

"Is all this natural or man-made?" Remi asked, gesturing to the walls and ceiling.

"A bit of both, actually. At the time these caves were constructed—about nine hundred years ago—the Loba in this area believed that sacred caves were revealed by nature in their embryonic stage. Once the caves were found, the Loba could excavate them according to their spiritual will."

Following Pushpa, the group continued down the corridor, walking stooped over until they reached another arched entrance, this one a few inches taller than Sam.

Over his shoulder Karna said with a smile, "We're here."

At first glance, the main chamber seemed to be a perfect dome, ten paces in diameter and eight feet high, with the ceiling tapering to a rounded point. The wall opposite the entrance was dominated by a mural that stretched around the chamber and from the floor to the domed ceiling. Unlike on the mural in the corridor, the symbols, text, and drawings here were painted in vibrant shades of red and yellow. The contrast against the mocha-colored walls was startling.

"It's magnificent," Sam said.

Remi, nodding, stared at the mural. "The detail . . . Jack, why is the color so different here?"

"Pushpa and his people have been restoring it. The pigment they use is a long-held secret. They won't even share it with me, but Pushpa assures me it's the same recipe that was used nine centuries ago."

Standing at the center of the chamber, Pushpa was gesturing toward them. Karna said to Sam and Remi, "Let's make our circuit. No talking. Head bowed."

Karna led them clockwise around the space, stopping again at the archway. Pushpa nodded to them and smiled, then knelt by his pack. He pulled out a pair of kerosene lanterns and hung one from a peg in each side wall. Soon the chamber was filled with an amber glow.

"What can we do to help?" Remi asked.

"I'll need the disks and some quiet. The rest I must do myself."

Sam dug the Lexan case containing the Theurang disks from his pack and handed it to Karna. Armed with the disks, a spool of string, a tape measure, a parallel rule, an architect's compass, and a directional compass, Karna stepped up to the mural. Pushpa hurried forward carrying a rough-hewn wooden step stool, which he placed beside Karna.

Sam, Remi, and Ajay took off their packs and sat down, their backs against the entrance wall.

For almost an hour, Karna worked without pause, silently measuring symbols on the mural and jotting in his notebook. Occasionally he would step back, stare at the wall while muttering to himself, and pace back and forth.

Finally he said something to Pushpa, who had been standing to one side, hands clasped before him. Pushpa and Karna knelt down, opened the Lexan case, and spent a few minutes examining the Theurang disks, fitting them together with the flanged outer ring in various patterns before finding an apparently satisfactory configuration.

Next, Pushpa and Karna placed the disks over certain symbols, measured distances with the tape measure, and murmured to each other.

Finally Karna stepped back, hands on hips, and gave the mural a final once-over. He turned to Sam and Remi.

"Selma tells me you two are fond of good news/bad news scenarios."

Sam and Remi smiled at each other. Sam replied, "Selma's having a little fun at your expense. She enjoys those; us, not so much."

"Go ahead anyway, Jack," said Remi.

"The good news is, we need go no further. My hunch was correct: this is the cave we needed."

"Fantastic," said Sam. "And . . . ?"

"Actually it's good/good/bad news. The second bit of good news is we now have a description of Shangri-La—or at least some signs that will tell us if we're close."

"Now the bad news," Remi prompted.

"The bad news is, the map offers only the path that the Sentinel Dhakal would have taken with the Theurang. As I suspected, it leads east through the Himalayas, but in all there are twenty-seven points marking the path."

"Translation, please," said Sam.

"Shangri-La could be at any one of twenty-seven locations stretching from here all the way to eastern Myanmar."

30

Kathmandu, Nepal

"Are you sure you won't change your mind, Jack?" asked Remi. Behind her, on the dirt tarmac, was a blue-on-white Bell 206b LongRanger III helicopter, its engine whining as the rotors spun up for takeoff.

"No, my dear, I'm sorry. And apologies for abandoning you. I have a hate-hate affair with all flying contrivances. The last time I flew back to Britain, I was under extreme sedation."

After leaving the cave complex the day before, the group had returned to Lo Monthang to regroup and brainstorm their next move. There was only one, they knew: follow Dhakal the Sentinel's path east across Nepal, eliminating the locations Karna had gleaned from the mural map.

The altitude and remoteness of the target areas left

them only one transport option—a charter helicopter service—which in turn brought them back to Kathmandu and into the lion's den, as it were. With luck, Sam and Remi would find what they needed within a few days, before King could discover their route.

"And if the Kings follow our trail?" asked Sam.

"Goodness, didn't I tell you? Ajay here is ex–Indian Army—and a Gurkha, in fact. Quite the tough bloke. He'll look after me."

Standing behind Karna's shoulder, Ajay gave them a shark-like smile.

Karna handed them the laminated map he'd spent the previous night annotating. "I've managed to eliminate two points from today's search grid that are improbable, both from summits that would have been covered in ice and snow at the time of Dhakal's journey . . ."

Karna's research into the "real" Shangri-La had led him to believe it was in a comparatively temperate location with regular seasons. Unfortunately, the Himalayan range was rife with such hidden valleys, little slivers of near-tropical paradise nestled amid the forbidding peaks and glaciers.

"That leaves six targets to search," Karna finished. "Ajay's given your pilot the coordinates." On the tarmac, the Bell's rotors were accelerating. Karna shook their hands and shouted, "Good luck! We'll meet you back here this evening!"

He and Ajay trotted off to Ajay's Land Cruiser.

Sam and Remi turned and headed for the helicopter.

Their first target lay thirty-two miles northeast of Kathmandu, in the Hutabrang Pass. Their pilot, a former Pakistani Air Force flier named Hosni, took them directly north for ten minutes, pointing out peaks and valleys and letting Sam and Remi get the lay of the land, before veering east toward the coordinates.

Hosni's voice came over their headsets: "Entering the area now. I'll circle it clockwise and try to get as low as possible. The wind shear can be treacherous here."

In the cabin behind Hosni, Sam and Remi each scooted sideways for a better view out the window. Remi said to Sam, "Eyes open for mushrooms."

"Aye, Captain."

Karna's translation of the cave mural had offered a vague but hopefully useful description of Shangri-La's most prominent feature: a mushroom-like rock formation. As the mural predated flight, the shape would likely only be recognizable from the ground. Exactly how large the formation was, or whether Shangri-La was supposed to be on it, in it, or simply nearby, the mural didn't specify. Sam and Remi hoped/assumed that the planners of the Golden Man's evacuation had chosen a formation large enough to stand out from its neighbors.

In anticipation of numerous landings and takeoffs, they were paying Hosni almost double his usual fee, and had booked him for five days, with a nonrefundable deposit for five more.

The Bell passed over a forested ridge, and Hosni nosed over, descending into the valley below. Three hundred feet over the treetops, he leveled off and decreased his airspeed.

"In the zone now," he called.

Binoculars raised, Sam and Remi began their scan of the valley. Remi radioed, "Remind me: how accurate did Jack say the coordinates were?"

"Half a kilometer. About a third of a mile."

"That doesn't help me." Though adept at it, Remi was not a fan of math; gauging distances especially vexed her.

"About four hundred fifty yards. Imagine a standard running track."

"Got it. Imagine it, Sam: that Sentinel was required to hit each of these coordinates almost dead-on."

"A remarkable bit of orienteering," Sam agreed. "Karna said it, though: these guys were the equivalent of today's Green Berets or Navy SEALs. They trained for this their whole lives."

Hosni flew on, dropping as close to the trees as he dared. The valley, which the Bell traversed from end to end in less than two minutes, yielded nothing. Sam ordered Hosni to proceed to the next set of coordinates.

The morning wore on as the Bell continued ever eastward. The going was slow. Though many of the coordinates were but a few miles apart, the Bell's ceiling constraints forced Hosni to skirt some of the higher peaks, flying through alpine cols and passes that lay below sixteen thousand feet.

Shortly after one in the afternoon, as they were flying northwest to avoid a peak in the Ganesh Himal range, Hosni called, "We have company. Helo at our two o'clock."

Remi scooted over to Sam's side, and they peered out the window at the aircraft.

"Who is it?" Remi asked.

Hosni called back, "PLA Air Force. A Z-9."

"Where's the Tibetan border?"

"About two miles on the other side of them. No worries, they always send up eyes to watch helicopters out of Kathmandu. They are simply flexing their muscles."

"Anywhere else and that would be called an invasion," Sam observed.

"Welcome to Nepal."

After a few minutes of paralleling the Bell, the Chinese helicopter peeled away and headed north toward the border. They soon lost sight of it in the clouds.

Twice in the afternoon they asked Hosni to land near a rock formation that looked promising, but neither panned out. As four o'clock approached, Sam put a red grease pencil X through the last point on the day's map, and Hosni headed for Kathmandu.

The morning of the second day began with a forty-minute flight to the Budhi Gandaki Valley northwest of Kathmandu. Three of Karna's coordinates for the day lay within the Budhi Gandaki, which followed the western edge of the Annapurna range. Sam and Remi were treated to three hours of beautiful scenery—thick pine forests, lush meadows exploding with wildflowers, jagged ridgelines, churning rivers, and tumbling waterfalls—but little else, aside from a formation that, from above, looked mushroom-like enough to warrant a landing but turned out to be merely a top-heavy boulder.

At noon they landed near a trekker's stop in a village called Bagarchhap, and Hosni entertained the local children with tours of the Bell while Sam and Remi ate sack lunches.

Soon they were airborne again and heading north through the Bintang Glacier and toward Mount Manaslu.

"Eighty-one hundred meters high," Hosni called, pointing to the mountain.

Sam translated for Remi: "About twenty-four thousand feet."

"And five thousand less than Everest," Hosni added.

"It's one thing to see these in pictures or from the ground," Remi said. "But, from up here, I can see why they call this place the rooftop of the world."

After lingering so Remi could take some pictures,

Hosni turned the Bell west and descended into another glacier—the Pung Gyen, Hosni called it—which they followed for eight miles before turning north again.

"Our friends are back," Hosni said over the headset. "Right side."

Sam and Remi looked. The Chinese Z-9 was indeed back, again paralleling their course; this time, however, the helicopter had closed the gap to only a few hundred yards.

Sam and Remi could see silhouettes staring back at them through the cabin windows.

The Z-9 shadowed them for a few more miles, then veered off and disappeared into a cloud bank.

"Next search area coming up in three minutes," Hosni called.

Sam and Remi got situated near the windows.

As had become routine, Hosni lifted the Bell's nose over a ridgeline, then banked sharply into the target valley, bleeding off altitude as he went. He slowed the Bell to a hover.

Sam was the first to notice the valley's surreal landscape below. While the upper slopes were thick with pine trees, the lower reaches looked as if they had been carved by a rectangular cookie cutter, leaving behind sheer cliffs plummeting into a lake. Jutting from the opposite slope and encircling one end was an ice-covered plateau. A runnel of churning water sliced through the shelf and cascaded to the waters below.

"Hosni, how deep do you think this is?" Sam asked. "The valley, I mean."

"From the ridgeline to the lake, perhaps eight hundred feet."

"The cliffs are half that at least," said Sam.

Hosni eased the Bell forward, following the slope, as Sam and Remi scanned the terrain through their binoculars. As they drew even with the plateau, and Hosni came about, they saw that the plateau was deceptively deep, narrowing for a few hundred yards before ending at a towering wall of ice bracketed by vertical cliffs.

"That's a glacier," Sam said. "Hosni, I didn't see this plateau on any maps. Does it look familiar?"

"No, you are right. This is relatively new. You see the color of the lake, the greenish gray?"

"Yes," said Remi.

"You see that after glacial retreat. This section of the valley is less than two years old, I would estimate."

"Climate change?"

"Most definitely. The glacier we passed earlier—the Pung Gyen—lost forty feet last year alone."

Pressed up against her window, Remi suddenly lowered her binoculars. "Sam, look at this!"

He slid over to her side and peered out the window. Directly below them was what looked like a wooden hut half buried in a waist-high ice shelf.

"What in the world is that?" Sam asked. "Hosni?"

"I have no idea."

"How close to the coordinates are we?"

"Not quite a kilometer."

Remi said, "Sam, that's a gondola."

"Pardon?"

"A wicker gondola—for a hot-air balloon."

"Are you sure?"

"Hosni, set us down!"

31

Northern Nepal

Hosni crabbed the Bell sideways over the plateau until he found a spot he decided was solid enough to bear the helicopter's weight, then touched down. Once the rotors had spooled down, Sam and Remi climbed out and donned their jackets, caps, and gloves.

Hosni called, "Step carefully! There will be many crevasses in an area like this."

They waved their understanding and started across the plateau toward the object.

"Here, wait . . ." Hosni called. They walked back. He climbed out of the cockpit and stooped beside the tail storage compartment. He removed what looked like a foldable tent pole and handed it to Sam. "Avalanche probe. Works as well with crevasses. Best to be safe."

"Thanks." Sam gave the probe a flick, and it snaked outward, the inner bungee cord snapping the sections into place. "Nifty."

They set off again, this time with Sam probing as they walked.

The ice sheet that partially covered the plateau was rippled like waves frozen in place, leftover, they assumed, by the glacier's slow grinding retreat up the valley.

The object in question lay near the far edge of the plateau, sitting kitty-corner to the rest of the plateau.

After five minutes of careful walking, they stood before it.

"I'm glad I didn't bet you," Sam said. "That's a gondola, all right."

"Upside down. That explains why it looked like a hut. They don't make them like this anymore. What in the world is it doing here?"

"No idea."

Remi took a step forward; Sam halted her with a hand on her shoulder. He probed the ice in front of the gondola, found it solid, then began poking around what should have been its sides.

"There's more," Sam said.

They continued sidestepping left, paralleling the gondola, probing as they went, until they reached the end.

Sam frowned and said, "Curiouser and curiouser."

Remi asked, "How long is it?"

"Roughly thirty feet."

"That's impossible. Aren't most maybe three feet by three feet?"

"More or less." He slid the probe over the gondola's upturned bottom as far as he could reach. "Nearly eight feet wide."

Sam handed her the probe, then knelt down and crawled forward, hands sliding through the snow along the gondola's side.

"Sam, be care—"

His arm plunged into the snow up to his elbow. He froze.

"I can't be entirely sure," he said with a grin, "but I think I found something." He laid himself flat.

"I got you," Remi replied. She grabbed his boots.

Sam used both hands to punch a basketball-sized hole in the ice, then poked his head inside. He turned back to Remi. "A crevasse. Very deep. The gondola's half straddling it diagonally."

He took another peek through the hole, then wriggled back away from the crevasse and pushed himself to his knees. He said, "I've found the answer to how it got here."

"How?"

"It flew. There's rigging still attached to the gondola—wooden stays, some kind of braided cord . . . I even saw what looked like a fabric of some sort. The whole tangled mess is hanging in the crevasse."

Remi sat down beside him, and they stared at the gondola for a bit. Remi said, "A mystery for another time?"

Sam nodded. "Absolutely. We'll mark it and come back."

They stood up. Sam cocked his head. "Listen."

Faintly in the distance came the chopping of helicopter rotors. They turned around, trying to localize the sound. Standing beside the Bell, Hosni had heard it too. He stared up at the sky.

Suddenly to their left an olive green helicopter popped over the ridgeline, then dropped into the valley and turned in their direction. On the aircraft's door was a five-pointed red star outlined in yellow.

The helicopter drew even with the plateau and slowed to a hover fifty feet from Sam and Remi, nose cone and rocket pods pointed directly at them.

"Don't move," Sam said.

"Chinese Army?" asked Remi.

"Yes. Same as the Z-9 we spotted yesterday."

"What do they want?"

Before Sam could answer, the helicopter pivoted, revealing an open cabin door. In it, a soldier crouched behind a mounted machine gun.

Sam could sense Remi's body go tense beside him. He slowly grasped her hand in his. "Don't run. If they wanted us dead, we'd already be dead."

Out of the corner of his eye Sam saw movement. He glanced toward the helicopter and saw Hosni opening the side door. A moment later he emerged. In his hands was a compact machine gun. He raised it toward the Z-9.

"Hosni, no!" Sam shouted.

Hosni's machine gun bucked, and the muzzle flashed orange. Bullets peppered the Z-9's windshield. The helicopter banked sharply right, then accelerated away, skimming over the lake's surface toward the ridgeline, where it banked again until its nose was aimed at the Bell.

"Hosni, run!" Sam shouted, then to Remi: "Behind the gondola! Go!"

Remi spun into a sprint, with Sam close on her heels.

"Remi, the crevasse!" Sam called. "Veer left."

Remi did, then pushed off with both legs, diving headfirst onto the gondola. Sam hit it a moment later, then pushed himself to his knees and helped Remi onto the ice shelf. They tumbled down the backside and landed in a sprawling heap.

From across the plateau they heard the chattering of Hosni's machine gun. Sam stood up and peeked over the ice. Hosni was standing defiantly at the edge of the plateau, firing at the oncoming Z-9.

"Hosni, get out of there!"

The Z-9 stopped in a hover a hundred yards away. Sam saw a flash from the left-hand rocket pod. Hosni saw it as well. He turned and began sprinting toward Sam and Remi.

"Faster!" Sam shouted.

With a brilliant flash of light and a plume of smoke, a pair of rockets burst from the Z-9's pod. In a split second they reached the Bell, one striking the ground beneath the tail, the other slamming into the engine compartment.

The Bell convulsed, leapt upward, then exploded.

Sam ducked and threw himself over Remi. They felt the blast ripple through the plateau, felt the ice crackle beneath them. A wave of shrapnel pelted into the gondola and through the ice shelf a foot above their heads.

Then silence.

Sam said, "Follow me," and crawled down the length of the ice shelf to the end of the gondola. On his belly, he wriggled forward and peered around the corner.

The plateau was strewn with the shattered remains of the Bell. Jagged chunks of the fuselage, still rocking from the concussion, sat amid a sheet of burning aviation fuel. Splintered lengths of rotor blade jutted from the snowbanks.

The Z-9 had retreated across the lake to the ridgeline, where it hovered, rocket pods still pointed menacingly at the plateau.

Remi said, "Do you see Hosni?"

"I'm looking."

Sam spotted him lying beside a ragged piece of the Bell's windshield. The body was charred. Then Sam spotted something else. Directly ahead of them, twenty feet away, was Hosni's machine gun. It looked intact. He pulled back and faced Remi.

"He's gone. Never felt a thing."

"Oh, no."

"I spotted his machine gun. I think I can reach it."

"Sam, no. You don't even know if it works. Where's the Z-9?"

"Hovering. Probably radioing their base for instructions. They've already spotted us; they'll be coming in for a closer look."

"You can't hope to hold them off for long."

"My guess is they want us alive. Otherwise, they would be pounding this plateau with missiles."

"Why, what are they after?"

"I have a hunch."

"Me too. We'll compare notes later, if we're alive. What's your plan?"

"They can't land, not with all the debris, so they'll have to hover above the plateau and fast-rope soldiers down. If I can catch them at the right moment, maybe . . ." Sam let his words trail off. "Maybe," he added. "What's your vote? Fight and perhaps die here or surrender and end up in a Chinese prison camp?"

Remi smiled gamely. "You really have to ask?"

Half hoping, half expecting the Z-9 would make a reconnaissance pass before putting men on the ground, Sam sent Remi back along the ice shelf, where she buried herself in the snow between a pair of drifts. Sam crouched beside the gondola and readied himself.

For what seemed like several minutes, but was likely less than one, Sam listened for the sound of the Z-9 approaching. When it came, he waited until the chopping sound was deafening. He risked a peek around the corner of the gondola.

The Z-9 had stopped in a hover, just off the edge of the plateau and a few feet above it. The helicopter slid sideways like a dragonfly waiting for its prey to appear. In the side door, Sam could see the door gunner bent over the machine gun.

Suddenly the Z-9 veered away and dropped out of sight below the plateau. Seconds later Sam saw it streaking back across the lake. Sam didn't think but reacted, scrambling from behind cover and running, hunched over, to Hosni's gun. He snatched it up and sprinted back to the gondola.

"Made it," Sam called to Remi, then began checking the machine gun. The wooden stock was partially splintered, and the fore stock charred by flames, but the working parts seemed in order and the barrel unscathed. He ejected the magazine; thirteen rounds left.

Remi called, "What are they doing?"

"Either leaving or waiting for enough of the aviation fuel to burn off so they can come in for a fast rope."

The Z-9 reached the edge of the lake and swooped upward along the slope to the ridgeline. Sam watched, fingers mentally crossed that the helicopter would keep going.

It didn't.

As had become its pattern, the Z-9 banked over the ridge, reversed course, and came streaking back across the lake.

"They're coming back," Sam announced.

"Good luck."

Sam mentally rehearsed his plan. Much would depend on whether the Z-9 presented him an open door as the soldiers prepared for their fast-rope descent. Firing into the aircraft's fuselage was pointless; Hosni's attack had proven that. What Sam needed was a chink in the armor.

The rush of the Z-9's engine drew nearer, and the rhythmic chop of the rotors rattled Sam's eardrums. He waited, head down and watching the ice a few feet from the gondola.

Wait . . . wait . . .

Snow began whipping across the ice.

Sam peeked around the corner.

The Z-9 was hovering thirty feet above the plateau.

"Come on, turn," Sam muttered. "Just a little bit."

The Z-9 pivoted slightly, bringing the door gunner around so he could cover the soldiers' descent. Two thick black ropes uncoiled from the door and hit the ice. The first pair of soldiers stepped up to the door. Sam could just make out the pilot's seat diagonally behind them.

Sam took a breath, set his teeth. He clipped the fire selector to Single Shot, then ducked out. In a crouch, he brought the machine gun to his shoulder and took aim at the Z-9's open doorway, then shifted left, placing the sight over the door gunner's helmet. He fired. The gunner crumbled. Sam switched the fire selector to Three Round, adjusted his aim again, and fired a burst into the doorway. Hit, one of the soldiers stumbled backward; the other ducked and dropped to his belly. Sam now had a clear view of the pilot's seat—but that would last only a second or two, he knew. Even as he readjusted his aim he could see the pilot's arm moving, adjusting controls, trying to make sense of the chaos around him.

Sam focused on the seat back. He took a breath, let it out, then pulled the trigger. A trio of bullets peppered the Z-9's interior. Sam pulled the trigger again, then once more. The machine gun let off an empty click; the magazine was empty.

The Z-9 pitched sideways, nose spiraling down and toward the plateau. Through the open cabin door the lifeless body of the door gunner slid out, followed by a second soldier. Arms flailing for handholds, two more soldiers tumbled through the door. One managed to snag the Z-9's landing skid, but the other plummeted to the ground. Now fully out of control, the pilotless Z-9 hit the plateau, crushing the hanging soldier beneath it.

Sam tore his eyes free, ducked behind the gondola, and sprinted to where Remi was lying. "More shrapnel coming!" he shouted, and dove on top of her.

Two of the Z-9's rotors struck the ice first, shearing off and hurling away a quarter second before the fuselage struck. Pressed flat in the snow, Sam and Remi waited for a fiery explosion but none came. They heard a high-pitched grinding sound followed by a trio of grenade-like whumps.

On impulse, Sam stood up and glanced over the gondola.

It took a full two seconds for his brain to register what he was seeing: the Z-9, skidding, hurtling toward him, the mangled fuselage, half sliding, half lurching, as the remaining rotor blades splintered on the ice and propelled it forward. It looked like a crippled bug in the throes of death.

Sam felt a hand clamp onto his. With surprising strength, Remi jerked him back to the ground. "Sam, what do you think you're—"

The Z-9 slammed into the gondola, shoving it backward into Sam and Remi, who began backpedaling, feet scrabbling over the ice.

The gondola stopped moving. The grinding thud-thud-thud of the helicopter's skid continued for a few seconds, then suddenly died save the stuttering coughs of the engine turbine.

That too stopped, and Sam and Remi found themselves in perfect silence. They got to their feet and peeked over the gondola.

"Well, that's not something you see every day," Sam said drily.

32

Northern Nepal

It took ten seconds for Sam and Remi to piece together the scene that lay before them.

After bouncing off the gondola, the crippled Z-9 had reversed course and skidded toward the runnel that cut through the plateau, where, like a pinball caught in a groove, it had slid to the edge of the plateau, then over—or partially over. The Z-9's tail, a few inches narrower than the runnel itself, had become lodged in the trough.

The helicopter's cabin sat suspended over the edge, water cascading over the fuselage and through the open cabin door.

"We should see if anyone's left alive," Remi prompted.

Wary of the still-hot engine, they picked their way

over to the Z-9. Sam knelt down beside the runnel and crawled on hands and knees to the edge. The fuselage was crushed to half its height, and the windshield was missing. He could see nothing through the doorway, so thick was the cascading water.

"Anyone in there?" he shouted. "Hello!"

Sam and Remi listened but heard nothing.

Twice more Sam called out, but still there was no response.

Sam stood up and rejoined Remi. He said, "Lone survivors."

"That sounds both wonderful and terrifying. What now?"

"First, we can't climb out of here. And even if we managed to without getting injured, we're thirty miles from the nearest village. Between the subzero temperatures at night and no shelter, we'd have little chance. For that matter, we need to start thinking about surviving tonight."

"Cheery," Remi said. "Go on."

"We have no idea how long before Karna declares us overdue and a search party is mounted. And even more important, we have to assume the Z-9 was in contact with its base after Hosni opened fire. When they don't make contact again and don't return, the base will send another helicopter, probably two."

"Any guesses on how soon?"

"Worst case, a matter of hours."

"Best case?"

"Tomorrow morning. If it's the former, we may have

an advantage: nightfall's coming. It'll make it easier for us to hide. I need to get inside that thing."

"What, the Z-9?" Remi said. "Sam, that's—"

"A really bad idea, I know, but it's got supplies we need, and, if we're very lucky, the radio may still work."

Remi considered this for a few moments, then nodded. "Okay. But first let's see what we can scrounge from the Bell's wreckage."

This took but a few minutes. There was little of value left, mostly charred bits and pieces from their packs, including a half-shredded section of climbing rope, a smattering of items from a first-aid kit, and a few tools from the Bell's tool kit. Sam and Remi picked up anything that could be of use, whether recognizable or not.

"How's the rope look?" Sam asked.

Kneeling beside their pile of supplies, Remi examined the rope. "It'll need some splicing, but I think we've got eighteen or twenty feet of usable line here. You're thinking a belay for the Z-9?"

Sam smiled, nodded. "I may be a bit thick at times, but there's no way I'm crawling onto that death trap without a safety line. We're going to need something piton-like."

"I may have just the thing."

Testing the ground as she went, Remi moved off across the plateau and soon returned. In one hand she was holding a shard of helicopter rotor, in the other a fist-sized rock. She handed them to Sam and said, "I'll start on the rope."

Sam used the rock to first smooth the edges of the shard's upper half, then to taper and sharpen the lower half. Once done, he found a particularly thick patch of ice a couple paces from the edge of the plateau just to the right of the Z-9. Next, he began the painstaking process of hammering the makeshift piton into the ice. When he finished, the shard was buried a foot and a half in the ice and angled backward at forty-five degrees.

Remi walked over, and they used their combined weight to wrench and pull the belay until they were confident it would hold. Remi uncoiled the spliced rope—into which she'd tied knots at two-foot intervals—and secured one end to the piton with a bowline knot. After shedding his jacket, gloves, and cap, Sam used the loose end to fashion a rope seat, with the knot tight against his lower back.

"If this thing starts going over the edge, get clear," Sam said.

"Don't worry about me, I'll be fine. Concentrate on you."

"Right."

"Do you hear me?"

"I hear you," he said with a smile.

He kissed her, then walked toward the Z-9's upturned tail assembly. After giving the aluminum side a few test shoves, he climbed up and began crawling toward the cabin.

"Getting close," Remi called. "A couple more feet."

"Got it."

As he reached the edge of the plateau, he slowed down, testing each of his movements before continuing on. Aside from a few heart-skip-inducing creaks and groans, the Z-9 didn't budge. Foot by foot, he crawled forward until he was perched atop the Z-9's belly.

"How's it feel?" Remi called.

On his hands and knees, Sam shifted his weight from side to side, slowly at first, then more vigorously. The fuselage let out a shriek of tearing aluminum and shifted to one side.

"I think I found its limits," Sam called.

"You think so?" Remi shot back. "Keep moving."

"Right."

Sam moved sideways until his hip was up against the landing skid. He grasped this with both hands and leaned over the side as though looking for something.

"What are you doing?" called Remi.

"I'm looking for the rotor mast. There it is. We're in luck; it's jammed into the runnel. We've got a bit of an anchor."

"Happy day," Remi said impatiently. "Now, get in there and get out."

Sam gave her what he hoped was a reassuring grin.

After adjusting the rope so it ran straight back to the piton, Sam grasped the skids with both hands and lowered his legs down along the fuselage. The spewing water immediately drenched his lower body. Sam groaned, clenched his teeth against the cold, then kicked his legs, trying to gauge his position over the door.

"I'm going in," he called to Remi.

Sam kicked forward, swung his legs backward, then repeated the process until he'd built up a steady rhythm. At the right moment, he let go. The momentum carried him through the cascade and into the cabin, where he slammed into the opposite door and landed in a heap on the floor.

He went still, listening to the Z-9 groan around him. A shudder coursed through the fuselage. Everything went still. Sam looked around, trying to orient himself.

He was sitting in icy water up to his waist. Part of the flow was seeping out around the closed door, the other part flooding into the cockpit and out through the shattered windshield. A few feet away, the body of a soldier lay lifeless. Sam eased forward until he could see between the cockpit seats. The pilot and copilot were dead, whether from his bullets or the impact, or both, he couldn't tell.

He could now see that the cockpit had suffered more damage than he'd realized. In addition to most of the windshield, a section of the nose cone and dashboard, including the radio, was gone, probably somewhere at the bottom of the lake by now.

The helicopter dropped beneath him.

Sam's stomach rose into his throat.

The movement stopped, but now the helicopter was resting at an angle; through the cockpit, he could see the waters of the lake far below.

Running out of time . . .

He turned around, eyes darting around the cabin. Something . . . anything. He found a partially full green canvas duffel bag. He didn't bother examining the contents, but instead began snatching up loose items from inside the cabin, paying little attention to what they were. If they felt useful and would fit in the bag, he took them. He searched the dead soldier, found a lighter but nothing else of use, then turned his attention to the pilot and copilot. He came away with a semiautomatic pistol and a kneeboard stuffed with paperwork. Out of the corner of his eye, he spotted a half-open hatch at the rear of the cabin. He climbed up to it, stuck his hand inside. His fingers touched canvas. He pulled the object free: a lumbar pack. He stuffed it into the duffel.

"Time to go," he muttered, then shouted through the door, "Remi, can you hear me?"

Her reply was muffled but understandable: "I'm here!"

"Is the piton still—"

The helicopter lurched again; the nose tipped downward. Sam was now half standing on the pilot's seat back.

"Is the piton still firm?" he shouted again.

"Yes! Hurry, Sam, get out of there!"

"On my way!"

Sam zipped the duffel closed and shoved the looped handles down over his head so the bag was dangling from his neck. He closed his eyes, said a silent *One . . . two . . . three . . .* then dove through the open door.

Whether his shove off from the pilot's seat was the cause, Sam would never know, but even as he broke clear of the sheet of water he heard and felt the Z-9 going over. He resisted the urge to look over his shoulder, instead concentrating on the wall of rock rushing toward him. He arched his head backward, covered his face with both arms.

The impact was similar to slamming one's chest into a tackling dummy. The duffel bag had acted as a bumper, he realized. He felt his body spinning, bumping over the wall several times, before he settled into a gentle swing.

Above him, Remi's face appeared over the edge. Her panicked expression switched to a relieved smile. "An exit worthy of a Hollywood blockbuster."

"An exit born of desperation and fear," Sam corrected.

He looked down at the lake. The Z-9's fuselage was slipping beneath the surface; the rear half was missing. Sam looked left and saw the tail section still jutting from the runnel. Where the fuselage had torn free, only ragged aluminum remained.

Remi called, "Climb up, Sam. You're going to freeze to death."

He nodded wearily. "Give me just a minute—or two—and I'll be right with you."

33

Northern Nepal

Exhausted and shaking with adrenaline, Sam slogged his way up the rope until Remi could reach over and help him the rest of the way. He rolled onto his back and stared at the sky. Remi flung her arms around him and tried to hide her tears.

"Don't you ever do that again." After a deep sigh, she asked, "What's in the duffel?"

"A whole bunch of I'm not sure. I was grabbing anything that looked useful."

"A grab bag," Remi said with a smile. She gently lifted the duffel's handle over Sam's head. She unzipped it and began rummaging inside. "Thermos," she said, and brought it out. "Empty."

Sam sat up and donned his jacket, cap, and gloves. "Good. I've got a mission for you: take your trusty thermos and go scoop up every drop of unburned aviation fuel you can find."

"Good thinking."

Sam nodded and grunted, "Fire good."

Remi slowly moved off and began kneeling beside depressions in the ice. "Found some," she called. "And here."

Once she was done, they met back at the gondola. "How'd you do?" Sam asked, jogging in place. His pants were beginning to stiffen with ice.

Remi replied, "It's about three-quarters full. The melted ice partially diluted it, though. We need to get you warmed up."

Sam knelt by the pile of debris they'd collected from the Bell and began sifting through it. "I thought I saw . . . Here it is." Sam held up a length of wire; at each end was a key ring. "Emergency chain saw," he told Remi.

"That's an overly optimistic name for it."

Sam examined the gondola, walking down its length, then back again. "It's half tipped into the crevasse, but I think I've found what we need."

He knelt beside the near corner of the gondola, where a series of wicker stays had popped free. As though threading a needle, Sam slipped one end of the saw through the wicker, then out the other. He grasped both rings and began sawing. The first section took five minutes, but now Sam had an opening in which to work. He kept sawing chunks from the end of the gondola until he had a good-sized stack.

"We need flat rocks," he told Remi.

These they found in short order; they fit the rocks together to form a hearth. On top of this went the wicker chunks, stacked in a pyramid. While Remi balled paper from the pilot's kneeboard into kindling, Sam retrieved the lighter from the duffel. Soon they had a small fire going.

Arm in arm, they knelt before the flames. The warmth washed over them. Almost immediately they felt better, more hopeful.

"It's the simple things in life," Remi remarked.

"I couldn't agree more."

"Tell me your theory about the Chinese."

"I don't think the Z-9 showing up was a coincidence. One shadowed us the first day, then again today. Then one shows up here just minutes after we touch down."

"We know King is smuggling artifacts over the border; it follows that he's got a Chinese contact. Who would have that much freedom of movement, that much clout?"

"The PLA. And if Jack's right, King probably guessed the general area in which we'd be searching. With King's reach, all he had to do is call his Chinese contact, then sit back and wait for us to show up."

"The question is, what did this Z-9 have in mind? If Hosni hadn't opened fire, what would they have done?"

"I'm only speculating, but this is the closest we've come to the border; it's about two miles to the north. Maybe the opportunity was too good to pass up. They take us prisoner, slip across the border, and we're never heard from again."

Remi hugged Sam's arm more tightly. "Not a happy thought."

"Sadly, here's another one: we need to assume they're coming back—and sooner rather than later."

"I saw the pistol in the duffel bag. You're not thinking of trying to—"

"No. This time, it was mostly pure luck. Next time, we'd have no chance. When reinforcements arrive, we need to be gone."

"How? You said yourself we can't climb out."

"I misspoke. We need to appear to be gone."

Remi said, "Tell me." Sam outlined his plan, and Remi nodded, smiling. "I like it. The Fargo version of the Trojan Horse."

"Trojan Gondola."

"Even better. And, with any luck, it'll keep us from freezing to death tonight."

Using the rope and the makeshift piton as a grappling hook, they slid the gondola a few feet from the crevasse, a task made easier by the ice. The tangled rigging Sam had spotted earlier trailed from beneath the gondola down in the crevasse. Sam and Remi looked over the edge but could see nothing beyond ten feet.

"Is that bamboo?" Remi said, pointing.

"I think so. There's another one, that curved piece

there. It would certainly make our job easier if we cut it all free, but something down there might be of use to us."

"Piton?" Remi suggested. "Cut it free and tie it off."

Sam knelt down and gathered some of the cordage in one hand. "Some kind of animal sinew. It's in amazing condition."

"Crevasses are nature's refrigerator," Remi replied. "And if all this was covered by that glacier, the effect is even more dramatic."

Sam collected some more of the rigging and gave the mess a tug. "It's surprisingly light. It would take me hours to get through all this sinew, though."

"We'll pull it along, then."

Using the avalanche probe, Sam measured first the width of the gondola, then the width of the crevasse.

"The crevasse is four inches wider," he announced. "My gut tells me it'll get wedged, but if I'm wrong, we lose all our firewood."

"Your gut has never steered us wrong."

"What about that time in the Sudan? And in Australia? I was way off that time—"

"Shush. Help me."

With one of them stationed at each end, they crouched together and grasped the bottom edge of the gondola. On Sam's signal, they heaved, trying to straighten their legs. It was no good. They let go and stepped back.

"Let's concentrate our power," Sam said.

Standing an arm's length from each other at the gondola's center point, they tried again. This time, they got the gondola two feet off the ground.

"I'll hold it," Sam said through clenched teeth. "Try a leg press."

Remi rolled onto her back, wriggled beneath the gondola, then pressed her feet against the edge. "Ready!"

"Heave!"

The gondola rolled up and over onto its side.

"One more time," Sam said.

They repeated the drill, and soon the gondola was sitting upright. Remi peered inside. She gasped and backed away.

"What?" Sam asked.

"Stowaways."

They walked up to the gondola.

Lying at the far end of the wicker bottom amid a jumble of rigging and bamboo tubes was a pair of partially mummified skeletons. The remainder of the gondola, they could now see, was divided into eighths by wicker cross struts wide enough to also serve as benches.

"What's your guess?" Remi asked. "Captain and copilot?"

"It's possible, but a gondola this size could hold fifteen people at least—it might take that many to handle all this rigging and the balloons as well."

"Balloons . . . as in plural?"

"We'll know more when I see the rest of the rigging, but I think this was a full-on dirigible."

"And these were the sole survivors."

"The rest may be . . ." Sam jerked his head toward the crevasse.

"That's no way to go."

"We can speculate later. Let's keep going."

After securing the rigging so it would hang off the end of the gondola and not get wedged against the crevasse wall, Sam and Remi took up stations on either end of the gondola and pushed in unison until the wicker bottom began sliding over the ice. As they neared the crevasse, they picked up speed, then gave the gondola a final shove. It slid the last few feet, bumped over the edge, and disappeared from view. Sam and Remi ran forward.

"Always trust your instincts," Remi said with a smile.

The gondola sat wedged between the crevasse's walls about a foot below the edge.

Sam climbed in and, careful to avoid the mummies, walked the length of the gondola. He proclaimed it solid. Remi helped him back up.

"Every home needs a roof," she said.

They walked the plateau together collecting pieces of the Bell's aluminum exterior large enough to bridge the crevasse, then began layering them over the gondola until only a narrow slot remained.

"You've got a flair for this," Sam told her.

"I know. One last touch: camouflage."

Using a bowl-like chunk of the Bell's windshield, they collected about five gallons of water from the runnel, which they poured over the gondola's aluminum roof, followed by several layers of snow.

They stepped back to admire their handiwork.

Sam said, "Once it freezes, it'll look like part of the ice sheet."

"One question: why the water?"

"So the snow would stick to the aluminum. If our hunch is correct and we're visited by another Z-9 to-night, we don't want the rotor downwash exposing our shingles."

"Sam Fargo, you're a brilliant man."

"That's the illusion I like to create."

Sam looked up at the sky. The sun's lower rim was dropping behind a jagged line of peaks to the west.

"Time to hunker down and see what the night brings."

With their supplies either stuffed into the duffel or buried in the snow, Sam and Remi retreated to their shelter. In the quickly dwindling twilight, they took inventory of the duffel's contents.

"What's this?" Remi asked, pulling out the lumbar pack Sam had snagged just before leaping from the Z-9.

"That's a—" He stopped, frowned, then smiled. "That, my dear, is an emergency parachute. But to you and me, it's about a hundred fifty square feet of blanket."

They extracted the chute from the pack and soon they were huddled tightly inside a white fabric cocoon.

Relatively warm and so far safe, they chatted quietly, watching the light fade into complete darkness.

They slowly drifted off to sleep.

Sometime later Sam's eyes sprung open. The blackness around them was complete. Wrapped in his arms, Remi whispered, "Do you hear it?"

"Yes."

In the distance came the chopping thud of helicopter rotors.

"What are the chances it's a rescue party?" Remi asked.

"Virtually none."

"Thanks for playing along."

The sound of the rotors slowly increased until Sam and Remi were certain the helicopter had dropped into the valley. A few moments later a bright spotlight swept over the crevasse; blinding white slivers of light arced through the gaps in the roof.

Then the light was gone, fading as it skimmed over the plateau. Twice more it returned and went away.

Then, suddenly, the helicopter's engine changed in pitch.

"Coming in to hover," Sam whispered.

Sam grabbed the pistol from where he had tucked it beneath his leg and switched it to his right hand.

The downwash came. Jets of icy air and swirling snow filled the gondola. Based on the shadows cast by the searchlight, the helicopter seemed to be crabbing sideways over the plateau, pivoting this way, then that way, either looking for them and/or survivors among their missing comrades.

Sam and Remi had left the Z-9's tail jutting from the runnel as a clue to the helicopter's fate. Anyone lucky enough to survive a plunge to the lake would have certainly drowned soon after. It was a conclusion that Sam and Remi prayed this search party would make.

Doggedly, their visitors made three more passes over the plateau. Then, as suddenly as it had appeared, the spotlight went dark, and the rotors faded into the distance.

34

NORTHERN NEPAL

Despite the extreme cold, their gondola cave served them well, the snow-covered roof not only protecting them from the wind but also trapping a precious fraction of their body heat. Ensconced in the parachute canopy, their parkas, caps, and gloves, they slept deeply, if sporadically, until the sun peeking through the aluminum shingles woke them.

Though wary of another visit from the Chinese, Sam and Remi knew that to survive they would have to find a way out of the valley.

They climbed out of the gondola and set about making breakfast. From the Bell's wreckage, they'd also managed to scrounge nine tea bags and a half-torn bag of dehydrated Stroganoff. From the Z-9, Sam had unknowingly picked up a packet of rice crackers and three cans of what looked like baked mung beans. They split one of these and shared a cup of tea, the water for which they boiled inside the empty can.

They both agreed it was one of the best meals they'd ever had.

Sam took his last sip of tea, then said, "I was thinking last night—"

"And talking in your sleep," Remi added. "You want to build something, don't you?"

"Our mummified friends in the gondola got here by hot-air balloon. Why don't we leave the same way?" Remi opened her mouth to speak but Sam pushed on. "No, I'm not talking about resurrecting their balloon. I'm thinking more along the lines of a . . ." Sam searched for the right term. "Franken-Balloon."

Remi was nodding. "Some of their rigging, some of ours . . ." Her eyes brightened. "The parachute!"

"You read my mind. If we can shape it and seal it up, I think I have a way of filling it. All we need is enough to lift us out of this valley and onto one of those meadows we saw to the south—four or five miles at most. From there we should be able to walk to a village."

"It's still a long shot."

"Long shots are our specialty, Remi. Here's the truth of it: in these temperatures, we won't survive for more than five days. A rescue party might come before that, but I've never been a big fan of 'might.'"

"And there's the Chinese to consider."

"And them. I don't see any other option. We gamble on rescue or we get ourselves out of here—or die trying."

"No question: we try. Let's build a dirigible."

The first order of business was inventory. While Remi took careful stock of what they had scrounged, Sam carefully reeled the old rigging up from the crevasse. He found only shreds of what had once been the balloon—or balloons, in this case.

"There were at least three of them," Sam guessed. "Probably four. You see all the curved pieces of wicker, the way they come to a point?"

"Yes."

"I think those might have been enclosures for the balloons."

"This material is silk," Remi added. "It's very thick."

"Imagine it, Remi: a thirty-foot-long gondola suspended from four caged silk balloons . . . wicker-and-bamboo struts, sinew guylines . . . I wonder how they kept it aloft. How did they funnel the heated air into the balloons? How would they—"

Remi turned to Sam, clasped his face between her hands, and kissed him. "Daydream later, okay?"

"Okay."

Together, they began separating the tangled mess, setting guylines to one side, bamboo-and-wicker struts to the other. Once done, they carefully lifted the mummies from the gondola and began untangling them from the last bit of rigging.

"I'd love to know their story," Remi said.

"It's obvious they'd been using the upturned gondola as a shelter," Sam said. "Perhaps the crevasse split open suddenly, and only these two managed to hold on."

"Then why stay like that?"

Sam shrugged. "Maybe they were too weak, by that point. They used the bamboo and rigging to build a small platform."

Kneeling beside the mummies, Remi said, "Weak and crippled. This one's got a broken femur, a compound by the looks of it, and this one . . . See the indentation in the hip? That's either dislocated or fractured. It's awful. They just laid in there and waited to die."

"It won't be our fate," Sam replied. "A fiery balloon crash, maybe, but not this."

"Very funny."

Remi stooped over and picked up one of the bamboo tubes. It was as big around as a baseball bat and five feet long. "Sam, there's writing on this. It's scratched into the surface."

"Are you sure?" Sam looked over her shoulder. He was the first to recognize the language. "That's Italian."

"You're right." Remi ran her fingertips over the etched words while rotating the bamboo in her opposite hand. "This isn't, though." She pointed to a spot near the tip.

No taller than a half inch, a square grid framed four Asian symbols. "This can't be," Remi murmured. "Don't you recognize them?"

"No, should I?"

"Sam, they're the same four characters engraved on the lid of the Theurang chest."

· 35 ·

NORTHERN NEPAL

Sam opened his mouth to speak, then clamped it shut. Remi said, "I know what you're thinking. But I'm sure, Sam. I remember drinking tea and staring at these characters on Jack's laptop screen."

"I believe you. I just don't see how—" Sam stopped and furrowed his eyebrows. "Unless . . . When we landed here, how far were we from the last set of coordinates?"

"Hosni said less than a kilometer."

"Maybe a half mile from the path Dhakal would have taken on his journey. What if he died near here, or ran into trouble and lost the Theurang chest?"

Remi was nodding. "And then our balloonist friends come along centuries later. They crash-land here and find the box. When was the earliest manned balloon flight?"

"Just guessing . . . late sixteenth–early seventeenth century. But I've never heard of a dirigible from that period as advanced as this one. This would have been way ahead of its time."

"Then at the earliest, it crashed here almost three hundred years after Dhakal left Mustang."

"It's plausible," Sam admitted, "but hard to swallow."

"Then explain these markings."

"I can't. You say they're the Theurang curse, and I believe you. I'm just having trouble wrapping my brain around it all."

"Join the club, Sam."

"How's your Italian?"

"A bit rusty, but I can give it a try later. Right now let's concentrate on getting out of here."

They devoted the morning to checking the guylines, setting aside those that looked too frayed or decayed; these Sam cut away with his Swiss Army knife. They repeated the process with the wicker-and-bamboo struts (all of which Remi checked for engravings but found none), then turned their attention to the silk. The biggest piece they found was only a few inches wide, so they decided to braid the usable fabric into cordage, should it be needed. By lunchtime, they had a respectable pile of construction materials.

For added stability, they decided to fasten eight of the dirigible's balloon-cage struts to the interior of the dome. This job they accomplished in assembly-line fashion: Sam, using his knife's awl, poked double holes in the canopy where each strut was to go followed by Remi inserting twelve-inch lengths of sinew thongs into the holes. Once done, they had three hundred twenty holes and one hundred sixty thongs.

By late afternoon Sam began cinching the thongs closed using a boom hitch. He'd secured almost a quarter of the thongs when they decided to call it a night.

They were up with the sun the next day and returned to the dirigible's construction.

During the five hours of usable afternoon light they turned their attention to sewing closed the mouth of the parachute/balloon with strips of silk knotted around a barrel-sized ring Sam had fashioned from curved pieces of wicker.

After savoring a few crackers each, they retired to the gondola cave and settled down for what they knew would be a long night.

"How long until we're ready?" Remi asked.

"With luck, we'll have our basket ready by late morning tomorrow."

As they labored, Sam had been working and reworking the engineering problem in the back of his mind. They had slowly been cannibalizing the gondola for firewood, which they used not only to cook but to occasionally warm themselves throughout the day and before going to bed at night.

As it stood, they had ten feet of gondola left. Based on Sam's calculations, the remaining wicker combined with the chemical concoction he had in mind would be enough to get them aloft. Much less certain was whether they could ascend high enough to clear the ridgeline.

The one factor Sam was not worried about was wind. So far, what little they'd gotten had come from the north.

Remi voiced yet another concern, one that had also been nagging at Sam: "What about our landing?"

"I'm not going to lie. That could be our bridge too far. There's no way to tell how well we'll be able to control the descent. And we'll have virtually no steering."

"You have a Plan B, I'm guessing?"

"I do. Do you want to hear it?"

Remi was silent for a few moments. "No. Surprise me."

Sam's timetable estimate was close. It wasn't until noon that they had the basket and risers completed. While "basket" was an overly optimistic word for their construction, they were nevertheless proud of it: a two-foot-wide bamboo platform bound together and secured to the risers by the last of the sinew.

They sat and ate lunch in silence, admiring their creation. The craft was rough-hewn, misshapen, and ugly—and they loved every inch of it.

"It needs a name," Remi said.

Sam of course suggested *The Remi*, but she dismissed the idea. He tried again, "I had a kite when I was a kid called *High Flier*."

"I like it."

The afternoon was spent implementing Sam's scheme for a fuel source. Except for a three-foot section in which they would huddle that night, Sam used the wire saw to dismantle the remainder of the gondola, cutting away as he stood inside it and handing up chunks to Remi. They managed to lose only three pieces to the bowels of the crevasse.

Using a stone, Remi began grinding the wicker and the remaining sinew into a rough pulp, the first palmful of which Sam dropped into a bowl-shaped section of the Bell's aluminum skin. To the pulp he added lichen they'd scraped from every stone and clear patch of granite they could find on the plateau. Next came dribbles of aviation fuel followed by dashes of gunpowder Sam had extracted from the pistol's bullets. After thirty minutes of trial and error, Sam presented Remi with a crude briquette wrapped inside a swatch of silk.

"Do the honors," he said, and handed Remi the lighter.

"Are you sure it won't explode?"

"No, not at all sure."

Remi gave him a withering stare.

He said, "It would have to be packed inside something solid."

At arm's length, Remi touched the lighter's flame to the brick; with a barely perceptible whoosh, it ignited.

Grinning broadly, Remi leapt up and hugged Sam. Together, they sat crouched around the brick and watched it burn. The heat was surprisingly intense. When the flames finally sputtered out, Sam checked his watch: "Six minutes. Not bad. Now we need as many as we can make but bigger—say, about the size of a filet mignon."

"Did you have to use that analogy?"

"Sorry. The moment we get back to Kathmandu we'll head for the nearest steakhouse."

Buoyed by the success of their ignition test, they made rapid progress. By bedtime, they had nineteen bricks.

As the sun began to set, Sam finished the brazier by notching into its base three short legs, which he then attached to a double-thick aluminum bowl by crude flanges. As a final step, he cut a hole into the side of the cone.

"What's that for?" asked Remi.

"Ventilation and fuel port. Once we get the first brick going, airflow and the shape of the cone will create a vortex of sorts. The heat will gush through the top of the cone and into the balloon."

"That's ingenious."

"That's a stove."

"Pardon?"

"It's an old-fashioned backpacking stove on steroids.

They've been around for a century. At last my love of obscure knowledge pays off."

"In spades. Let's retreat to our bunker and try to rest up for the maiden—and final—flight of the *High Flier*."

They slept fitfully for a total of two hours, kept awake by exhaustion, lack of food, and excitement. As soon as there was enough light to work by, they climbed out of the gondola and ate the last of their food.

Sam dismembered the remainder of the gondola save the last corner, which they pried free with the piton and knotted rope. Once the sawing was done, they had a pile of fuel that was as tall as Sam.

Having already chosen a spot on the plateau that was virtually free of ice, they carefully dragged the balloon to the launchpad. Onto the platform they stacked ballast rocks. In the center they placed the brazier, then secured it to the platform with sinew thongs.

"Let's get cooking," Remi said.

They used wads of paper and lichen as tinder, on top of which they placed a tripod of wicker chunks. Once they had a solid bed of coals, they continued to feed wicker into the brazier, and slowly flames began licking upward.

Remi placed her hand over the brazier's flue. She jerked it back. "Hot!"

"Perfect. Now we wait. This is going to take a while."

One hour turned into two. The balloon filled slowly,

expanding around them like a miniature circus tent, as their fuel supply dwindled. Beneath the canopy the sunlight seemed ethereal, hazy. Sam realized they were fighting time and thermal physics, as the air cooled and seeped through the balloon's skin.

Just before the third hour, the balloon, though still lying perpendicular to the ground, lifted and floated free. Whether reality or perception, they weren't sure, but this seemed to be a watershed moment. Within forty minutes the balloon was standing upright, its exterior growing more taut by the minute.

"It's working," Remi murmured. "It's really working."

Sam nodded, said nothing, his eyes fixed on the craft.

Finally he said, "All aboard."

Remi trotted to their supply pile, snatched up the engraved length of bamboo, slid it down the back of her jacket, then jogged back. She removed rocks one by one until she had room to kneel, then sit. The opposite side of the platform was now hovering a few inches off the ground.

Having already stuffed the emergency parachute pack with some essentials, and the duffel bag with their bricks and the last armload of wicker, Sam grabbed both, then knelt beside the platform.

"You ready?" he asked.

Remi didn't blink an eye. "Let's fly."

· 36 ·

Northern Nepal

The flames leapt up in the brazier's interior, disappearing through the balloon's mouth, until Sam and Remi were floating at knee height above the plateau.

"When I say so, push with everything you've got," Sam said.

He stuffed the last two pieces of wicker into the brazier and watched, waited, eyes darting from the brazier to the balloon to the ground.

"Now!"

In unison, they coiled their legs and shoved hard.

They surged upward ten feet. Then descended just as rapidly.

"Get ready to push again!" Sam called.

Their feet struck the ice.

"Push!"

Again they shot upward and again they returned to earth, albeit more slowly.

"We're getting there," Sam said.

"We need a rhythm," Remi replied. "Think bouncing ball."

So they began bouncing over the plateau, each time gaining a bit more altitude. To their left, the edge of the cliff loomed.

"Sam . . ." Remi warned.

"I know. Don't look, just keep bouncing. Fly or swim!"

"Lovely!"

They shoved off once more. A gust of wind caught the balloon and shoved them down the plateau, their feet skipping over the ice. Remi's leg slipped off the edge of the cliff, but she kept her cool, giving one last united shove with the other leg.

And then, abruptly, everything went silent save the wind whistling through the guylines.

They were airborne and climbing.

And heading southeast toward the slope.

Sam reached into the duffel and withdrew a pair of bricks. He fed them into the brazier. They heard a soft whoosh as the brick ignited. Flames shot from the flue. They began rising.

"Another," Remi said.

Sam dropped a third brick into the brazier.

Whoosh! The balloon climbed.

The pine trees were a few hundred yards away and closing fast. A gust of wind caught the balloon and spun it. Sam and Remi clutched at the guylines and tightened their legs around the platform. After three rotations, the platform steadied and went still again.

Looking over Remi's shoulder, Sam gauged the distance to the slope.

"How close?" Remi asked.

"About two hundred yards. Ninety seconds, give or take." He looked her in the eye. "It's going to be razor thin. Go for broke?"

"Absolutely."

Sam stuffed a fourth brick into the brazier. *Whoosh!*

They both looked over the side of the platform. The tops of the pine trees seemed impossibly close. Remi felt something snag at her foot, and she tipped sideways. Sam leaned forward, grabbed her arm.

He added another brick. *Whoosh!*

Another. *Whoosh!*

"A hundred yards!" Sam called.

Another brick. *Whoosh!*

"Fifty yards!" He grabbed a brick from the duffel, shook it in his cupped hands like dice, and extended it toward Remi. "For luck."

She blew on it.

He dropped the brick into the brazier.

Whoosh!

"Raise your feet!" Sam shouted.

They felt and heard the tip of a pine tree clawing the underside of the platform. They were jerked sideways.

"We're snagged!" Sam called. "Lean!"

In unison, they tipped their torsos in the opposite direction, hanging over the edge while clutching a guy-line. Sam kicked his leg, trying to free them from whatever lay below.

With a sharp crack the offending branch snapped. The platform righted itself. Sam and Remi sat up, looking down and around and up.

"We're clear!" Remi shouted. "We made it!"

Sam let out the breath he'd been holding. "Never doubted it for a second."

Remi gave him the look.

"Okay," he said. "Maybe for a second or two."

Now clear of the ridge, the wind slackening slightly, they found themselves heading south at what Sam estimated was ten miles per hour. They had traveled less than a few hundred yards before their altitude began bleeding off.

Sam dug another brick out of the duffel. He dropped it through the feed hole and it ignited. They began rising.

Remi asked, "How many do we have left?"

Sam checked. "Ten."

"Now might be a good time to tell me your landing Plan B."

"On the off chance we don't manage a perfect, feather-soft touchdown, our next best chance is pine trees—find a tight cluster and try to fly straight in."

"What you've just described is a crash landing without the land."

"Essentially."

"Exactly."

"Okay, exactly. We hold on tight and hope the boughs act as an arresting net."

"Like on aircraft carriers."

"Yes."

Remi considered this. She pursed her lips and puffed a strand of auburn hair from her forehead. "I like it."

"I thought you would."

Sam dropped another brick into the brazier. *Whoosh!*

With the late afternoon sun at their backs, they glided ever southward, occasionally feeding bricks into the brazier while keeping a sharp eye out for a landing spot. They'd traveled approximately four miles and had so far seen only scree valleys, glaciers, and copses of pine trees.

"We're losing altitude," Remi said.

Sam fed the brazier. They continued to descend.

"What's happening?" she asked.

"Dissipation, I think. We're losing the sun, along with the temperature. The balloon's bleeding heat faster than we can put it in."

Sam dropped another brick through the hole. Their descent slowed slightly, but there was no denying it: they were on an irreversible downward glide path. They began gaining speed.

"Time to make a choice," Sam said. "We're not

going to make a meadow, but we've got a Plan B coming up."

He pointed over Remi's shoulder. Ahead and below was a stand of pine trees. Past that lay another boulder-strewn valley.

Sam said, "Or we can stuff the rest of the bricks into the brazier and hope we find a better spot."

"We've pushed our luck too far. I'm ready for terra firma. How do you want to do this?"

Sam checked the approaching tree line, trying to gauge speed, distance, and their angle of approach. They had three minutes, he guessed. They were traveling at perhaps fifteen miles per hour, and that would likely double by the time they reached the trees. While a survivable crash inside a car, on this platform their chances were fifty-fifty.

"If only we had an air bag," Sam muttered.

"How about a shield?" asked Remi, and tapped their bamboo platform.

Sam immediately grasped what she was suggesting. "Dicey."

"A lot less dicey than what you were just mulling over in your head. I know you, Sam, I know your expressions. What do you put our odds at?"

"Fifty percent."

"This may give us a few more points."

Sam's eyes darted to the tree line, then back to Remi's eyes. She smiled at him. He smiled back. "You're a hell of a woman."

"This, I know."

"We don't need this anymore," Sam said. He sliced the straps holding the brazier and shoved it off the platform. Amid a plume of sparks, it hit the ground, tumbled down the valley, then crashed into a rock.

Sam scooted across the platform until he was snug against Remi. She was already grasping the guylines in both hands. Sam grabbed another with his left hand, then leaned backward, laid the blade of his Swiss Army knife against one of the risers, and started sawing. With a twang, it parted. The platform dipped slightly.

Sam moved to the second riser.

"How long until we hit?" he asked.

"I don't know—"

"Guess!

"A few seconds!"

Sam kept sawing. Pitted and slightly bent from overuse and Sam's attempts to sharpen it on rocks, the knife's blade was dull. He clenched his teeth and worked harder.

The second guyline snapped. Sam moved to the third.

"Running out of time," Remi called.

Twang!

The opposite end of the platform was dangling by a single riser now, fluttering like a kite in the wind. With both hands clutching guylines, Remi was all but hanging, with only one foot perched on the edge of the platform. Sam's left hand was grasping the line beside hers like a talon.

"One more!" he shouted, and started sawing. "Come on . . . Come on . . ."

Twang!

The end of the platform swung free, now hanging vertically below them. Sam was about to drop his knife when he changed his mind. He folded the blade closed against his cheek. He clamped his right hand on a guyline.

Remi was already lowering herself down the risers so her body was behind the platform. Sam climbed down toward her. He peeked around the edge of the platform and saw a wall of green rushing toward him.

Their world began tumbling. Though having taken a good portion of the impact, the clawing branches immediately spun the platform around. They found themselves hurtling through a gauntlet of whipping boughs. They tucked their chins and closed their eyes. Sam unclenched his right hand from the riser and tried to cover Remi's face with his forearm.

On instinct she shouted, "Let go!"

Then they were falling through the tree, their fall softened by branches.

They jolted to a stop.

Sam opened his mouth to speak but all that came out was a croak. He tried again. "Remi!"

"Here," came the faint reply. "Below you."

Lying faceup and diagonally across a pair of boughs, Sam carefully rolled onto his belly. Ten feet below, Remi was lying on the ground in a pile of pine needles. Her face was scratched as though someone had swiped her with a wire brush. Her eyes brimmed with tears.

"How bad are you?" he asked.

She forced a smile and gave him a weak thumbs-up. "And you, intrepid pilot?"

"Let me lie here for a bit and I'll let you know."

After a time, Sam began the task of climbing down.

"Don't move," he told Remi. "Just lie there."

"If you insist."

Sam felt as though he'd been pummeled by a bat-wielding gang, but all of his major joints and muscles seemed to be working properly, if sluggishly.

Using his right hand, Sam lowered himself from the last branch and dropped in a heap beside Remi. She cupped his face with a hand and said, "Never a dull moment with you."

"Nope."

"Sam, your neck."

He reached up and touched the spot Remi had indicated. His fingers came back bloody. After a bit of probing he found a three-inch vertical gash below his ear.

"It'll coagulate," he told her. "Let's check you out."

Their clothes had likely saved them, he quickly realized. The parkas' thick padding and high collars had protected their torsos and throats, and the knit caps had served as a crucial bit of cushion for their skulls.

"Not bad, all things considered."

"Your shield idea saved the day."

She waved her hand dismissively. "Where's *High Flier*?"

"Tangled in the tree."

"Do I still have the bamboo?"

Sam saw the end of it jutting from her collar. "Yes."

"Does my face look as bad as yours?" Remi asked.

"You've never looked more lovely."

"Liar—but thank you. The sun is setting. What now?"

"Now we get rescued. I build you a fire, then go find some friendly villagers who will offer us cozy beds and hot food."

"Just like that?"

"Just like that."

Sam pushed himself to his feet and stretched his limbs. His entire body hurt, a throbbing pain that seemed to be everywhere at once.

"Be right back."

It took him only a few minutes to find the emergency chute pack, which had been ripped off his back during the crash. It took longer to find the duffel bag, however; it had fallen when the platform's last riser had given way. Of the seven or so bricks that had been left, he found three.

He returned to Remi and found she had managed to sit upright with her back against the tree. Soon he had a brick burning in a small dirt circle next to her. He placed the two remaining bricks beside her.

"I'll be back in a flash," he said.

"I'll be here."

He gave her a kiss, then headed off.

"Sam?"

He turned. "Yes?"

"Watch out for Yetis."

37

Goldfish Point, La Jolla, California

"I have a translation for you," Selma said, walking into the solarium. She walked to where Sam and Remi were reclined on chaise longues and handed Remi the printout.

"That's fantastic," Remi replied with a wan smile.

Sam asked Selma, "Did you read it?"

"I did."

"Would you mind giving us the *Reader's Digest* condensed version? Remi's pain meds have left her a bit . . . happy."

As it had turned out, Sam's search for rescuers in the high Himalayas had, in fact, been a simple affair. In retrospect, given what they'd gone through to get this far, Sam considered it poetic justice. Without realizing it, they had crashed less than a mile from a village called

Samagaun, the northernmost settlement in that region of Nepal.

In the dimming twilight, Sam had shuffled his way down the valley until he was spotted by an Australian couple on a trekking vacation. They took him to Samagaun, and in short order a rescue party was organized. Two villagers, the Australian couple, and Sam rode as far up the valley as possible in an ancient Datsun truck, then got out and walked the rest of the way. They found Remi where Sam had left her, in the warm glow of the fire.

For safety's sake they placed her on a piece of plywood they'd brought along for that very purpose, then made their way back to Samagaun, where they found the village had mobilized on their behalf. A room with twin beds and a potbellied stove was arranged, and they were fed *aloo tareko* (fried potatoes) and *kukhura ko ledo* (chicken with gravy) until they could take no more. The village doctor came in, examined them both, and found nothing life threatening.

The next morning they awoke to find a village elder had already sent word of their rescue down the valley via ham radio. Soon after Sam gave the village elder Jack Karna's contact information, a more robust SUV arrived to take them south. In Gorkha they found Jack and Ajay waiting to take them the rest of the way to Kathmandu.

Jack had in fact reported them missing and was wading through the Nepalese government bureaucracy trying to organize a search party when word came of their rescue.

Under the watchful eye of Ajay, Sam and Remi spent

a night in the hospital. Remi's X-rays revealed two bruised ribs and a sprained ankle. For their bumps and bruises Sam and Remi got prescription painkillers. The scratches on their faces, though ugly, were superficial and would eventually fade.

Five days after crash-landing in their balloon, they were on a plane headed home.

Now Selma gave them the edited version. "Well, first of all, Jack has confirmed your hunch, Mrs. Fargo. The symbols carved into the bamboo were identical to those on the lid of the Theurang chest. He's as dumbfounded by it as you are. Whenever you're ready to talk, call him.

"As for the rest of the markings, you were right again: it's Italian. According to the author, a man named"—Selma scanned the printout—"Francesco Lana de Terzi—"

"I know that name," Sam said. Since returning home, he had immersed himself in the history of dirigibles.

Remi said, "Tell us."

"De Terzi is widely considered the father of aeronautics. He was a Jesuit, and professor of physics and mathematics, in Brescia—northern Italy. In 1670 he published a book called *Prodomo*. For its time, it was groundbreaking, the first solid analysis of the math behind air travel. He laid the groundwork for everyone that followed him, starting with the Montgolfier brothers in 1783."

"Oh, them," Remi replied.

"The first successful balloon flight," Sam explained. "De Terzi was an absolute genius. He paved the way for things like the sewing machine, a reading device for the blind, the first primitive form of Braille . . ."

"But no airship," Selma said.

"His primary concept was something he called a Vacuum Ship—essentially, the same as the multiple balloon dirigible we found, but in place of fabric spheres you would have copper ones that had been evacuated of air. In the mid sixteen hundreds, the inventor Robert Boyle created a pump—a 'pneumatic engine,' as he called it—that could completely evacuate the air from a vessel. With it, he proved that air has weight. De Terzi theorized that once the ship's copper spheres were evacuated, the ship would be lighter than the air around it, causing it to rise. I won't bore you with the physics, but the concept has too many hurdles to be workable."

"So the Vacuum Ship was never built," said Selma.

"Not that we know of. In the late nineteenth century a man named Arthur De Bausset tried to get funding for what he called a vacuum-tube airship, but nothing came of it. As for De Terzi, according to history he kept working on his theory until he died in 1686."

"Where?"

Sam smiled. "In Brescia."

"After gallivanting around the Himalayas," Remi added. "Go on, Selma."

"According to the bamboo, De Terzi and his Chinese crew—he doesn't say how many—crash-landed during a test flight of an airship he was designing for the Kangxi Emperor. The Emperor had named the airship the

Great Dragon. Only De Terzi and two others survived the crash. He was the only one uninjured."

"The two mummies we found," Remi said.

"I checked the dates for the Kangxi Emperor," said Selma. "He ruled from 1661 to 1722."

"The time line fits," said Sam.

"Now, here's the good part: De Terzi states that while foraging for food he found a"—Selma read the printout—"'mysterious vessel of a design I had never seen, engraved with symbols both similar and dissimilar to those used by my benefactor.'"

Sam and Remi exchanged smiles.

Selma continued: "In the final part of the engraving, De Terzi wrote that he had decided to leave his crew-mates and head north, back toward the airship's launch base, something he referred to as Shekar Gompa."

Sam said, "Did you check—"

"I did. Shekar Gompa is only ruins now, but it's located about forty miles northeast of where you found the ship, in Tibet."

"Go on."

"If De Terzi made it back to Shekar Gompa, he himself would tell the tale of the journey. If he failed, his body would never be found. The bamboo was to be his testament."

"And the mysterious vessel?" said Sam.

"I left the best for last," Selma replied. "De Terzi claimed he was going to take the vessel with him as, and I quote, 'ransom to free my brother Giuseppe, held hostage by the Kangxi Emperor to ensure my return with the *Great Dragon*.'"

"He took it with him," Sam murmured. "He took the Theurang into Tibet."

Remi said, "I have so many questions, I don't know where to start. First, how much history do we have on De Terzi?"

"There's very little out there. At least not that I could find," Selma replied. "According to every source, De Terzi spent his life in Italy. He died there and is buried there. As Sam said, he spent his final years working on his Vacuum Ship."

"Both versions of his life can't be true," Sam said. "Either he never left Brescia and the bamboo is a hoax or he spent time in China working for the Kangxi Emperor."

"And perhaps died there," Remi added.

Sam saw the mischievous smile on Selma's face. He said, "Okay, out with it."

"There's nothing online about De Terzi, but there is a professor at the University of Brescia who teaches a class in late Renaissance–era Italian inventors. According to their online catalog, De Terzi figures prominently in the curriculum."

Remi said, "You really enjoy doing that, don't you?"

"Not in the slightest," Selma replied solemnly. "Just say the word, and I'll have you in Italy by tomorrow afternoon."

"Just say the word, and we'll get an Internet appointment for tomorrow."

GOLDFISH POINT, LA JOLLA,
CALIFORNIA

The next day, late afternoon Italian time, on iChat, Sam and Remi introduced themselves and explained, ambiguously, the gist of their interest in Francesco Lana de Terzi to the course's instructor, Professor Carlotta Moretti. Moretti, a mid-thirties brunette with owlish glasses, smiled at them from the computer screen.

"So nice to meet you both," she said in lightly accented English. "I am something of a fan, you know."

"Of ours?" Remi replied.

"*Sì, sì.* I read about you in the *Smithsonian* magazine. The Napoleon's lost cellar, and the cave in the mountains, the, uh . . ."

"Grand Saint Bernard," Sam offered.

"Yes, that is it. Please excuse my prying, but I must ask: are you both well? Your faces?"

"A hiking mishap," Sam replied. "We're on the mend."

"Oh, good. Well, I was fascinated, and then of course happy when you called. Surprised too. Tell me more of your interest in Francesco De Terzi and I will try to be of help to you."

"His name came up during a project," Remi said. "We've been able to find surprisingly little published about him. We were told you're something of an expert."

Moretti wagged her hand. "Expert, I do not know. I teach about De Terzi, and have had a curiosity about him since I was a little girl."

"We're primarily interested in the latter part of his life; say, the last ten years. First, can you confirm that he had a brother?"

"Oh, yes. Giuseppe Lana de Terzi."

"And is it true Francesco never left Brescia?"

"Oh, no, that is untrue. De Terzi traveled often to Milan, to Genoa, to other places too."

"How about out of Italy? Overseas, perhaps?"

"It is possible, though I could not say where exactly. Based on some accounts, mostly secondhand accounts of stories De Terzi was said to have told, he traveled distantly between the years 1675 and 1679. Though no historian I know of will confirm that."

"Do these stories talk about where he might have been?"

"Somewhere in the Far East," replied Moretti. "Asia, is one speculation."

"Why would he have gone there?"

The professor hesitated. "You must understand, this may all be fantasy. There is so little documentation to support any of this."

"We understand," Sam replied.

"The story goes that De Terzi could find no investors for his aircraft plan."

"The Vacuum Ship."

"Yes, that. He could find no one to give him money, not the government, not wealthy men here. He journeyed east hoping to find support so he might finish his work."

"And did he?"

"No, not that I am aware of."

"What happened when he returned in 1679?" Sam said.

"It is said he returned to Italy a changed man. Something bad had occurred during his travels, and Giuseppe did not return home. Francesco never spoke of that. Soon after, he resettled in Brescia, left the Jesuit Order, and moved to Vienna, Austria."

"In search of investors again?"

"Perhaps, but in Vienna he found only bad luck."

"How so?" asked Remi.

"Soon after he moved to Vienna he married, and then quickly followed a baby boy. Two years later came the big battle—the Siege and then the Battle of Vienna. Do you know of it?"

"Only vaguely."

"The Siege lasted for two months, the Ottoman Empire fighting the Holy League: the Holy Roman Empire, the Polish-Lithuanian Commonwealth, and the Venetian Republic. In early September of 1683, the final battle was fought. Many tens of thousands of people died, including Francesco De Terzi's wife and new son."

"That's awful," Remi said. "So sad."

"*Sì.* It is said he was terribly heartbroken. First his brother, and then his new family, all dead. Shortly afterward, De Terzi disappeared again."

"Where?"

Moretti shrugged. "Again, a mystery. He returned again to Brescia in October of 1685, and then died a few months later."

"Let me ask you what may sound like an odd question," Remi said.

"Please."

"Are you, or anyone, absolutely certain De Terzi returned to Brecia in 1685?"

"That is an odd question. I suppose the answer would be no. I know of nothing that certifies he was buried here—or that he returned, for that matter. That part of the story is, like the rest, based on secondhand information. Short of an . . ."

"Exhumation."

"Yes, an exhumation. Only that, and a DNA sample from his descendants, would be proof. Why do you ask? Do you have reason to believe—"

"No, not really. We're brainstorming."

Sam asked, "About these stories: do you believe any of them?"

"Part of me wants to believe. It is a thrilling adventure, yes? But, as I said, the official histories of De Terzi's life contain none of these accounts."

"A few minutes ago you said there is so little documentation. Does that mean there is *some* documentation?" Remi said.

"There are a few letters, but written by friends. None in De Terzi's own hand. It is what your justice system calls hearsay, *sì*? Aside from those, there is only one other source that may be related to the stories. I am reluctant to mention it."

"Why?"

"It is fiction, a short story written by De Terzi's sister a few years after his death. Though named differently, the protagonist is clearly intended to be Francesco. Most thought the sister was trying to make money on his fame by exploiting the rumors."

"Can you give us the gist of the story?"

"A fanciful tale, really." Moretti gathered her thoughts. "The hero of the story leaves his home in Italy. After braving many dangers, he is captured by a tyrant in a strange land. He is forced to build a flying ship of war. The ship crashes in a desolate place, and just the hero and two of his comrades survive, only to eventually die of their injuries. The hero then finds a mysterious treasure, which the natives tell him is cursed, but he ignores the warning and undertakes an arduous journey back to the tyrant's castle. Once there, he finds that his traveling companion, who the tyrant had been holding hostage, has been executed.

"The hero returns to Italy with the treasure only to find more tragedy: his family has been killed by the plague. The hero is now convinced the curse is real, so he sets out to return the treasure to where he found it and is never heard from again."

Sam and Remi struggled to keep their faces expressionless.

Sam said, "You don't happen to have a copy of this story, do you?"

"Yes, of course. I believe I have it in the original Italian as well as a very good English translation. As soon as we have finished our conversation, I will send you an electronic version."

38

Goldfish Point, La Jolla, California

With copies of "The Great Dragon" on each of their iPads, Sam and Remi thanked Professor Moretti for her help. Sam and Remi read the story and e-mailed copies to Selma, Wendy, and Pete. As Remi was sending a copy of the story to Jack, Selma connected with him via iChat.

"You two look absolutely giddy," Karna said. "Don't keep me in suspense. What have you found?"

Sam said to Remi, "You tell him."

Remi first recounted their conversation with Moretti, then gave everyone a summary of "The Great Dragon."

"Incredible," said Selma. "You've both read the story?"

"Yes," said Sam. "It should be in your e-mail. You too, Jack."

"Yes, I see it here."

"How closely does the story match the bamboo engraving?" asked Wendy.

"If you replace the clearly fictional bits of the story with De Terzi's alleged testament, you get what reads like a factual account: the crash, the number of survivors, the discovery of a mysterious treasure, the trek home . . . It's all there."

"And the time line fits," Remi said. "Between the secondhand accounts of De Terzi's comings and goings, he could easily have been traveling to and from China."

"I am flabbergasted," said Karna.

Pete, who was paging through the story on Sam's iPad, said, "What's this map on the frontispiece?"

"That's the hero's journey to return the treasure," replied Remi. "Jack, do you have that?"

"Looking at it right now. It appears De Terzi arrives from the west and first stops at what is labeled here as a castle. This, we can assume, is Shekar Gompa."

"The launch base for the airship," Sam said.

"And possibly the burial site for Giuseppe," added Remi.

Karna continued: "From Shekar Gompa, De Terzi travels east to the Great City. Based on the position of Shekar, the city could be Lhasa."

"Why would he go there?" asked Wendy. "The crash site is forty miles south of Shekar Gompa. Wasn't he trying to return the treasure?"

"Yes," Sam replied, "but in the story when he reaches the castle a local wise man tells him he must return the treasure to 'its rightful home.' He is told to seek out another wise man in the Great City to the east."

Karna picked up Sam's line of thought: "From the Great City, De Terzi continues eastward, eventually arrives at . . . I don't know. There's only an X here."

"Shangri-La," Remi suggested.

There were a few moments of silence from Karna, then: "You're going to have to excuse me. Apologies. I'll get back to you."

The iChat screen went dark.

Karna was back thirty minutes later. "There are some rough grid lines and other landmarks on this map I'll have to cross-reference, but using the distance from Shekar Gompa to Lhasa as a benchmark, the final leg of De Terzi's journey ended in an area that's known today as the Tsangpo Gorge."

"Your front-runner for the location of Shangri-La," said Sam.

"Yes indeed. Sam, Remi, you may have just solved a riddle six hundred years in the making."

Sam said, "Let's not get ahead of ourselves. How long will it take you to nail down the locations on the map?"

"I'll start right now. Give me a day."

· 39 ·

Arunachal Pradesh Region,
Northern India

"Jack!" Remi called. "I didn't really believe you'd show up."

Karna's SUV rolled to a stop, and he climbed out. Remi gave him a hug, Sam shook his hand. "Glad you're on board, Jack."

"As am I."

Standing behind Karna, Ajay nodded and smiled at them.

Karna said, "You two look better than when I last saw your faces. Remi, how's the foot? And the ribs?"

"Healed enough that I can get around without gritting my teeth. I've got ACE bandages, a good pair of hiking boots, and a bottle of ibuprofen."

"Outstanding."

"She'll outmarch all of us," Sam said.

"Any trouble getting here? Any tails? Suspicious people?"

Remi answered. "None of the above."

Since their last conversation with Charles King, they had neither seen nor heard from him, his children, or Zhilan Hsu. It was a development they found at once pleasing and unnerving.

"Jack, how did you conquer your fear of flying?" said Sam.

"I didn't, actually," Karna replied. "I was utterly terrified from the moment we lifted off from Kathmandu to the moment I stepped off the plane in Bangladesh. My excitement for our expedition temporarily overpowered my fear, and, voilà, here I am."

"Here" was the end of a five-hundred-mile overland journey Sam and Remi had finished just a few hours earlier. Situated on the banks of the Siang River, the quiet town of Yingkiong, population nine hundred, was the last outpost of any significant population in northern India. From there, the next city, Nyingchi, Tibet, was a hundred miles northeast, through some of the world's most forbidding jungles.

Ten days had passed since their iChat conversation. It had taken that long to make all the necessary travel arrangements. True to his word, Karna had contacted them the next day, having worked nonstop in hopes of deciphering the map from "The Great Dragon."

De Terzi's land navigation skills must have rivaled those of the Sentinels, Karna had explained. Both the bearings and distances on De Terzi's map were remarkably accurate, missing the real-world measurements by less than a mile and one compass degree. Once finished with his calculations, Karna was certain he had triangulated the location of Shangri-La down to a two-mile diameter. As he had suspected all along, the coordinates were in the heart of the Tsangpo River Gorge.

Sam and Remi had studied the area on Google Earth but had seen nothing but towering peaks, raging rivers, and thick forests. Nothing that looked like a mushroom.

Karna said, "What say we retire to a bar for a drink and a bit of chalk talk? It's best you understand the nastiness we're in for before we set out in the morning."

The tavern was a two-story building with a corrugated tin lean-to roof and clapboard walls. Inside, the lower level was devoted to a reception area and a restaurant that looked as if it had been stolen from a 1950s Hollywood Western: wooden floors, a long J-shaped bar, and vertical posts supporting exposed ceiling joists. Their rooms for the night, Karna told them, were on the second floor.

The tavern was surprisingly crowded. They found a trestle table against the wall beneath a flickering neon Schlitz sign and ordered four beers. They were ice-cold.

"Most of what I'm going to tell you I got from Ajay, but since he's not the loquacious type you'll have to rely on my memory. As I told you, these are Ajay's old stomping grounds, so we're in good hands. By the way, Ajay, what's the status of our transportation?"

"All arranged, Mr. Karna."

"Fantastic. Correct me if I get offtrack while I'm talking, Ajay."

"Yes, Mr. Karna."

Karna sighed. "Can't get him to call me Jack. Been trying for years."

"He and Selma play by the same handbook," Sam replied.

"Right. Here's the quick and dirty about Arunachal Pradesh: depending on who you ask, we're in China right now."

"Whoa! Say that again," Sam said.

"China officially claims most of this region as part of southern Tibet. Of course, to the people and the government here, Arunachal Pradesh is an Indian state. The northern border between Arunachal Pradesh and China is called the McMahon Line, drawn up as part of a treaty between Tibet and the United Kingdom. The Chinese never bought into it, and India never enforced the border until 1950. Bottom line, China and India both claim it but neither does much about it."

"What does that mean for a military presence?" asked Sam.

"Nothing. There are some Indian troops in the region, but the Chinese stay north of the McMahon Line. It's all fairly amicable, really."

"That's good for our team," Remi said.

"Yes, well . . . What isn't so wonderful is the ANLF—the Arunachal Naga Liberation Front. They're the latest and greatest terrorist group in the area. They've been keen on kidnapping as of late. That said, Ajay says we probably won't have any trouble with them; the Army has been cracking down."

Sam said, "According to the maps, our destination is twenty-five miles into China. Based on the landscape, I'm assuming there aren't any border checkpoints."

"You're correct. As I mentioned back in Mustang, the border is fairly open. Several hundred trekkers jaunt across it every year. Actually, the Chinese government doesn't seem to care. There's nothing of any strategic importance in the area."

"More good news," Remi said. "Now tell us the downside."

"You mean aside from the ridiculously rugged terrain?"

"Yes."

"The downside is that we will be, for all intents and purposes, invading China. If we're unlucky enough to get caught, we'll probably end up in prison."

"We've already faced the possibility once," Sam replied. "Let's do our best to avoid that, shall we?"

"Right. Okay, let's move on to snakes and venomous insects . . ."

After a quick supper that consisted of tandoori chicken, Sam and Remi retired for the evening. They found their rooms in keeping with the hostel's motif: Hollywood Western chic sans the chic. Though the outside temperature was a pleasant sixty degrees, the humidity was stifling. The room's creaking ceiling fan slowly churned the air, but after sunset the temperature began dropping, and soon the room was comfortable.

They were asleep by eight.

They awoke the next morning to the sound of Ajay knocking softly on their door and whispering their names. Bleary-eyed, Sam crawled out of bed in the darkness and shuffled to the door.

Ajay said, "Coffee, Mr. Fargo."

"No tea? This is a pleasant surprise. It's Sam, by the way."

"Oh, no, sir."

"What time is it?"

"Five a.m."

"Uh-oh," Sam murmured, and glanced over at Remi's sleeping form. Mrs. Fargo was not exactly a morning person. "Ajay, would you mind bringing us two more cups of coffee right away?"

"Of course. In fact, I will bring the carafe."

The group assembled in the tavern thirty minutes later for breakfast. Once they were done, Karna said, "We'd best pack. Our death trap should be here anytime now."

"Did you say 'death trap'?" Remi asked.

"You might know it by its common name: helicopter."

Sam chuckled. "After what we've been through, we

almost prefer your description. Are you sure you can handle it?"

Karna held up a softball-sized Nerf ball. It was riddled with finger holes. "Stress toy. I'll survive. The ride will be short."

With their gear assembled and packed, they soon regrouped at the northern edge of Yingkiong near a dirt clearing.

"Here he comes," Ajay said, pointing to the south where an olive green helicopter was skimming over the surface of the Siang.

"It looks positively ancient," Karna observed.

As it drew even with the clearing and slowed to a hover, Sam spotted a faded Indian Air Force roundel on the side door. Someone had tried and failed to paint over the orange, white, and green insignia. The group turned away from the rotor downwash and waited until the dust settled.

"Ajay, what is this thing?" asked Karna.

"A Chetak light utility helicopter, sir. Very reliable. As a soldier, I flew in these many times."

"How old?"

"Nineteen sixty-eight."

"Bloody hell."

"If I had told you, Mr. Karna, you would not have come."

"Oh, you're damned right. All right, all right, let's get on with it."

With Jack clawing furiously at his Nerf ball, the group packed their gear aboard, then took their seats. Ajay checked their five-point seat harnesses, then slid the door shut and gave the pilot a nod.

They lifted off, the nose tilted forward, and surged ahead.

Partially for ease of navigation and partially to increase their chances of rescue should the Chetak crash, the pilot followed the serpentine course of the Siang River. The few pockets of habitation that lay north of Yingkiong were situated along its banks, Ajay explained. With luck, someone would see the Chetak go down and report the incident.

"Oh, that's just fantastic!" Karna shouted over the rush of the engine.

"Squeeze your ball, Jack," Remi replied. "Ajay, do you know this pilot?"

"Oh, yes, Mrs. Fargo, very well. We served together in the Army. Gupta now runs a cargo business—brings supplies to the far parts of Arunachal Pradesh."

The Chetak continued north, skimming a few hundred feet above the brown waters of the Siang, and before long they found themselves flying through knife-edged ridges and plummeting valleys, all of it covered in jungle so thick Sam and Remi could see nothing but a solid carpet of green. In most places the Siang was wide and sluggish, but several times, as the Chetak passed through a gorge, the waters were a maelstrom of froth and crashing waves.

"Those are Class VI waters down there," Sam called, staring out the window.

"That's nothing," Karna replied. "Where we're headed, the Tsangpo River Gorge, is known as the Everest of Rivers. There are sections of the Tsangpo that defy classification."

Remi said, "Has anyone ever tried traversing those?"

"Oh, yes, a number of times. Mostly extreme kayakers, right, Ajay?"

Ajay nodded. "Many lives have been lost. Bodies never found."

"They don't wash downstream?" asked Sam.

"Bodies are usually either trapped forever in hydraulics, where they are ground into pulp along the bottom, or they are ground into pulp while being dragged down the gorges. There is not much left to find after that."

After they had traveled forty minutes, Gupta turned in his seat and called, "Coming up on Tuting Village. Prepare for landing."

Sam and Remi were surprised to find that Tuting had a dirt airstrip partially overgrown with jungle. They touched down, and everyone climbed out. To the east, higher up the valley, they glimpsed a few roofs peeking above the treetops. Tuting Village, Sam and Remi assumed.

"From here, we hike," Karna announced.

He, Sam, and Remi began unloading their gear.

"Pardon, just one moment," Ajay said. He was standing ten feet away with the pilot. "Gupta has a proposal he wishes you to consider. He asked me how far into China we are going, and I told him. For a fee, he will fly us very close to our destination."

"Isn't he worried about the Chinese?" asked Sam.

"Very little. He says they maintain no radar in the area, and from here to our destination the valleys only deepen, and that there is almost no habitation. He can fly unseen, he believes."

"Well, that's a damned sight better than a six-day march in and back," Karna observed. "How much does he want?"

Ajay spoke to Gupta in Hindi, then said, "Two hundred thousand rupees—or roughly four thousand U.S. dollars."

Sam said, "We don't have that much cash on us."

"Gupta assumed this. He says he will happily take a credit card."

They agreed to Gupta's terms, and in short order the pilot was on the helicopter's radio, transmitting Sam's Visa information to his home base in Itanagar.

"This is surreal," Sam said. "Standing here, in the back of beyond, while an Indian pilot runs our card."

"As I said back in Nepal, never a dull moment,"

Remi replied. "I know my ankle will appreciate this itinerary change."

Ajay called, "Gupta says you are approved. We can lift off whenever you are ready."

Airborne and heading north along the Siang again, they soon passed over the last Indian settlement before the border. Gengren disappeared behind them in a flash, and then Gupta announced, "We are crossing the McMahon Line."

"That's it," Sam said. "We've invaded China."

The crossing had been decidedly anticlimactic, but soon the landscape began to morph. As Gupta had predicted, the peaks and ridges traded their rounded appearance for exposed and serrated rock; the valley walls steepened and the forests thickened. The most startling difference was the Siang. Here, on the southern edge of the Tsangpo Gorge region, the river's surface roiled, the waves exploding against boulders and hanging rock walls, sending plumes of mist high into the air. Gupta kept the Chetak as close to the river as possible, and kept below the ridgeline. Sam and Remi felt as though they were on the wildest flume ride on earth.

"Fifteen minutes," Gupta called.

Sam and Remi shared an anticipatory smile. They'd come so far, gone through so much, and now their destination was only minutes away . . . they hoped.

Karna's reaction was intense. Jaw clenched, fingers

digging into the Nerf ball, he stared out the window with his forehead pressed against the glass.

"You okay, Jack?" Sam asked.

"Never better, mate. Almost there!"

"Approaching the outer edge of the coordinates," Gupta announced.

Ajay had given their pilot a datum point with a two-mile diameter. The area into which they were flying was dominated by a cluster of flat-topped obelisk peaks, each one varying in height, from a few hundred feet to a thousand feet to three thousand feet. In the gorges below, the Tsangpo River twined itself around the obelisks, a churning white ribbon enclosed by sheer cliffs.

"Haven't seen any kayakers," Sam observed. "Or anyone, for that matter."

Karna looked up from the map he was studying and replied, "I would be surprised if you did," Karna replied. "You've seen the terrain. Only the most determined—or insane—venture here."

"I can't decide if that's an insult or a compliment," Remi whispered to Sam.

"If we make it back victorious and alive, it's a compliment."

Karna called to Ajay, "Ask Gupta if he can give us a better look at these peaks. If my numbers are correct, we're right on top of the datum point."

Ajay relayed the request. Gupta slowed the Chetak to

thirty knots and began orbiting each of the obelisks in turn, adjusting his altitude so his passengers could make a closer examination. At her window, Remi had her camera shutter on rapid-fire.

"There!" Jack shouted, pointing.

A hundred yards beyond the window lay one of the medium-sized obelisks, at approximately a thousand feet high and five hundred yards wide. The vertical granite slopes were heavily laced with vines, foliage, and great swaths of moss.

"Do you see it?" Karna said, his index finger tracing along the glass. "The shape? Start at the bottom and go upward . . . Do you see where it begins to widen out and then, there, about a hundred feet below the plateau, it flares out suddenly? Tell me you see it!"

It took Sam and Remi several seconds to piece together the image, but slowly smiles spread over their faces.

"A giant mushroom," Remi said.

40

Tsangpo River Gorge, China

After making several aborted passes because of wind shear, Gupta managed to ease the Chetak sideways over the obelisk until Karna spotted a small clearing in the jungle near the edge of the plateau. Gupta slowed to a hover and then touched down. Once the rotors had stopped spinning, the group climbed out and grabbed their gear.

"Does this remind you of anything?" Sam asked Remi.

"Absolutely."

The plateau bore a striking resemblance to the paradise valleys they had spotted during their helicopter search of northern Nepal.

Beneath their feet was a carpet of moss, ranging in color from dark green to chartreuse. Here and there, the landscape was dotted with granite boulders speckled with lichen. Directly across from them stood a wall of thick jungle, unbroken save a few tunnel-like paths that disappeared into the growth, rough ovals that stared back at Sam and Remi like unblinking black eyes. The air seemed to buzz with the chattering of insects, and, unseen in the foliage, birds squawked. In a nearby tree a monkey hung upside down and stared at them for a few seconds before skittering off.

Jack and Ajay walked over to where Sam and Remi were standing. Karna said, "Thankfully, our search area is limited. If we split into two groups, we should be able to cover a lot of ground."

"Agreed," Sam said.

"One last thing," Karna said. He knelt beside his pack and rummaged inside and came up with a pair of snub-nosed .38 revolvers. He handed one each to Sam and Remi. "I've got one, of course. And as for Ajay . . ."

From a holster at the rear of his waistband Ajay pulled out a Beretta semiautomatic pistol, then quickly replaced it.

"Are we expecting trouble?" Remi asked.

"We're in China, my dear. Anything can happen: bandits, cross-border terrorist groups, the PLA . . ."

"If the Chinese Army shows up, these popguns are only going to make them mad."

"A bridge we'll cross if need be. Besides, we'll likely find what we're looking for and be back across the border before nightfall."

Sam said, "Remi and I will head east; Jack, you and

Ajay head west. We'll meet back here in two hours. Any objections?"

There were none.

After checking their portable radios for reception, the group split up. Headlamps on and machetes in hand, Sam and Remi chose one of the paths and started in.

Ten feet inside the jungle, the light dimmed to quarter strength. Sam slashed clear some of the vines growing across their path, then they paused to take a look around, panning their lights up, down, and to both sides.

"The yearly rainfall here must be mind-boggling," Sam said.

"A hundred ten inches. About nine feet," Remi replied, then smiled. "I know how you love trivia. I looked it up."

"I'm proud of you."

A few feet over their heads, and on both sides, was a tangled mass of vines so thick they could see nothing of the forest itself.

"This doesn't feel right," Remi said.

"No, it doesn't."

Sam jabbed the tip of his machete through the canopy. With a clang, his arm jolted to a stop. "That's stone," he murmured.

Remi swung her machete to the left and also got a clang. The same to the right. "We're in a man-made tunnel."

Sam unclipped the radio from his belt and pressed the Talk button. "Jack, are you there?"

Static.

"Jack, come in."

"I'm here, Sam. What is it?"

"Are you on a trail?"

"Just started."

"Swing your machete off the path."

"Okay . . ." *Clang!* Jack came back: "Stone walls. Fascinating development."

"Remember your hunch about Shangri-La being a temple or monastery? Well, I think you've found it."

"I think you're right. Amazing what a millennium of unchecked jungle can do, isn't it? Well, I don't think this changes our plan, do you? We search the complex, then regroup in two hours."

"Okay. See you then."

Now aware they were inside a man-made structure, Sam and Remi began examining their surroundings for architectural telltales. Vines and roots had infiltrated every square foot of the complex. In the lead, Sam tried to swing his machete in short arcs but couldn't avoid striking the stone walls occasionally.

They reached an alcove and stopped.

"Shut off your headlamp," Sam said, dousing his.

Remi did. When their eyes had adjusted to the darkness, they began to see slivers of dim sunlight through the foliage-covered walls and ceiling.

"Windows and skylights," Remi said. "This must have been an amazing sight in its day."

Sam and Remi started climbing a set of steps and soon reached a landing where the steps doubled back and rose to a second floor. Here, through an archway, they found a large open space. A patchwork of roots and vines arced above their heads to form a vaulted ceiling. Spanning the Great Room, as they dubbed it, were what looked like six half-rotted logs. Support beams, they decided, long ago decayed, the remnants held in place by a sheath of vines. Directly opposite the ramp/stairs they'd climbed was another set, leading upward into darkness.

Headlamps panning, Sam and Remi spread out to explore the space. Along the far wall Sam found a row of stone benches jutting from the wall, and, in front of these, six rectangular slots in the stone floor.

"Those are tubs," Remi said.

"They look like graves."

She knelt beside one and tapped the inside walls with her machete. She got back the familiar clang of steel on stone.

"Some more over here," Sam said, crossing to the other side.

They found a semicircle of stone benches enclosing a round basin wider than Sam was tall. Remi repeated her routine but could not touch the bottom. Sam found a chunk of stone that had fallen off a nearby bench and dropped it into the basin.

They heard a muffled thump.

"About ten feet deep," Sam said.

He crouched and shone his light down the shaft but could see nothing through the web of vines and roots. "Hello!" he called. There was no echo.

"Too much vegetation," Remi guessed.

Sam found another rock and prepared to drop it.

"What are you doing?"

"Indulging my curiosity. We didn't see any sign of this shaft on the floor below, which means it was behind a wall. It has to have a purpose."

"Go ahead."

Sam leaned over the shaft, angled his arm, then hurled the stone. Unseen, it thumped against the bottom, then again, then clattered against a hard surface.

Remi said. "Good call. It's got to lead somewhere. Do you want to—"

Sam's radio crackled to life. In between bursts of static, faint staccato voices came through the speaker. The snippets were hurried and overlapping.

"I think it's Gupta and Ajay," Remi said.

Sam pressed the Talk button. "Ajay, can you hear me? Ajay, come in!"

Static. Then Jack's voice: "Sam . . . Gupta . . . has spotted a . . . is taking off."

"He's leaving," Remi said.

They turned and ran down the stairs, Remi trailing with her slight limp. They crossed the den and headed down the tunnel.

Remi called, "What do you think he spotted?"

"Only one thing I can think of that would panic him," Sam replied over his shoulder: "Helicopter."

"I was afraid of that."

An oval of light appeared ahead. Sam and Remi skidded to a stop before reaching it and crouch-walked the last few steps. In the clearing, the Chetak's rotors were spinning rapidly; through the side window they could see Gupta furiously punching buttons and checking gauges. He grabbed the radio handset and started talking.

His voice burst through Sam's radio: "Sorry, I will try to return. Try to hide. They may go away."

Gupta then lifted the collective, and the Chetak lifted straight up. At thirty feet, it banked, nose down, and zoomed from view.

Out of the corner of their eyes Sam and Remi saw Karna and Ajay step from a tunnel entrance. Sam waved, caught their attention, then gestured at them to retreat. They slipped back out of sight.

Preceded by only a few seconds of thudding rotors, an olive green helicopter rose into view at the far edge of the plateau. Sam and Remi immediately recognized the nose cone and rocket pods: a Chinese PLA Harbin Z-9.

"Hello, old enemy," Remi muttered.

She and Sam backed up a few more feet.

The Z-9 continued to rise, then pivoted, revealing another fond memory: an open door and a soldier crouched over a mounted machine gun. The Z-9 slid sideways over the clearing and touched down.

"Let's go, Sam," Remi said. "We need to hide."

"Just wait."

A figure appeared in the doorway.

"Oh, no," Remi muttered.

They both recognized the lithe, willowy body shape. Zhilan Hsu.

She stepped down from the doorway. Dangling from her right hand was a compact submachine gun. A moment later two more figures stepped from the doorway to join her. Russell and Marjorie King, also armed with compact submachine guns.

"Behold, the Wonder Twins," Sam said.

Zhilan turned, said something to them, then stepped to the Z-9's side door, which opened to reveal a mid-forties Chinese man. Sam withdrew a pair of binoculars from his pack and zoomed in on the pair.

"I think we've found King's Chinese contact," Sam said. "He's definitely PLA. Very high ranking, either a colonel or general."

"Do you see any more soldiers inside?"

"No, just the door gunner. Between him, Zhilan, and the twins, that's all they need. I don't know why they haven't shut down the engine yet, though."

"How in God's name did they find us?"

"No idea. Too late to worry about it now."

The PLA officer and Zhilan shook hands, then he closed the door. The Z-9's engine rose in pitch, and then the helicopter lifted off. It pivoted so its tail was facing the plateau, then headed off.

"Our odds just improved," Sam said.

"What's Zhilan doing?"

Sam focused his binoculars on Zhilan in time to see

her pull a cell phone from her jacket pocket. She punched a series of numbers into the keypad, and then she and the twins turned and watched the helicopter recede into the distance.

In a mushroom of orange and red, the Z-9 exploded. Chunks of flaming debris plummeted toward earth and then out of sight.

Sam and Remi couldn't speak for several seconds. Finally Remi said, "That ruthless—"

"King is tying up loose ends," Sam said. "He's probably already shut down his black market fossil operation: the dig site, his transportation system—and now his contact in the government."

"We're the last loose ends," Remi said. "Can we shoot them from here?"

"No chance. Our snub noses aren't worth a damn beyond twenty feet or so."

In the clearing, Zhilan had traded her cell phone for a portable radio. She brought it up to her lips.

Over Sam's radio they heard, "Do you have him?"

"I have him." Ajay's voice.

"Bring him out."

Sam and Remi looked right. Jack Karna stepped from the tunnel entrance, followed by Ajay. The barrel of his gun was pressed against the base of Karna's skull. The other hand clutched the collar of his jacket.

Prodded by Ajay, the pair walked halfway to the clearing, then stopped. They were forty feet to Sam and Remi's right.

"Why, Ajay?" Karna asked.

"I am sorry, Mr. Karna. Truly I am."

"But why?" Karna repeated. "We're friends. We've known each other for—"

"They came to me in Kathmandu. It's more money than I would make in ten lifetimes. I can send my children to university, my wife and I can buy a new home. I am sorry. But she gave me her word. None of you will be harmed."

Karna replied, "She lied to you." Then louder to Zhilan: "Your spawn I've already met a few months ago in Lo Monthang. But I don't think we've been properly introduced."

Zhilan said, "My name is—"

"The Dragon Lady, I know. You're too late, you realize. This is not the place. The Theurang is not here."

"You're lying. Ajay, what do you say?"

"We only started searching, ma'am. Mr. Karna and the Fargos seem sure this is the location of Shangri-La."

Zhilan said, "Speaking of the Fargos . . . Come out, both of you! Your helicopter is gone! Come out now, help me find the Golden Man and I'll signal for our transportation. I will land you safely back in Yingkiong. You have my promise."

"You forget, Dragon Lady, Sam and Remi know you," Karna said. "Your promise is worthless."

"You are likely correct," Zhilan replied. "Mr. and Mrs. Fargo! Come out now or I will kill your friend!"

Remi whispered, "Sam, we've got to help him."

"That's what she wants," he replied.

"We can't just let her—"

"I know, Remi."

Karna called, "Dragon Lady, they can't hear you. All this behind me is a temple—a complex so big, it will take months to search. Right now, they probably don't even know you're here."

"They would have heard me on the radio."

"Not from inside. The reception is nonexistent."

Zhilan considered this. "Ajay, is that true?"

"About the radios, mostly true. As to the temple, it is vast. They may be unaware of your arrival."

"Then we'll have to go find them," Zhilan said.

"Besides," Karna added, "if they were watching, they would know what I wanted. I've spent my entire life searching for the Theurang. I would rather be dead and have them destroy it than give it to you."

Zhilan turned toward Russell, who was standing behind her right shoulder, and said something. In one smooth motion, Russell lifted the machine gun to his shoulder.

On an impulse he immediately regretted, Sam shouted, "Jack, duck!"

Russell's weapon bucked. The left side of Karna's neck exploded in blood; he crumpled to the ground. Russell fired again, a three-round burst that slammed into Ajay's chest. He stumbled backward and fell dead.

Zhilan shouted. "They are there! In that tunnel! Go after them!"

Machine guns raised, Russell and Marjorie began sprinting. Behind them, Zhilan began walking toward Karna's body.

Sam turned and grabbed Remi's shoulders. "Go! Hide!"

"What about you?"

"Right on your heels."

Remi spun around and took off down the tunnel in a limp-sprint. Sam raised his .38 and snapped off a round toward Russell and Marjorie. He had no illusion about hitting them, but the gunfire accomplished his goal. Russell and Marjorie split up, each diving behind a nearby boulder.

Sam turned and ran after Remi.

He was only halfway down the tunnel when he heard footsteps at the entrance behind him. "Fast bastards," Sam muttered, and kept going. Ahead, Remi had reached the end of the tunnel. She darted left into the den.

Bullets ricocheted off the wall to his left. Sam leapt right, bounced off the wall, half turned, saw a pair of headlamp beams bouncing down the tunnel, and fired at them. He turned again, kept running. Five more strides brought him to the den. Remi was crouched beside the near wall.

"Come on—"

From the clearing they heard a gunshot, a pause, then a second gunshot.

Sam took her hand, and they bounded up the ramp.

Bullets thudded into the steps behind them. They reached the landing and started up the next flight. Remi's foot slipped out from under her. She slammed chest first to the ground. She groaned.

"Ribs?" Sam asked.

"Yes . . . Help me up."

Sam lifted her to her feet, and they climbed the rest of the steps and stopped before the arch that led into the Great Room. Through clenched teeth Remi asked, "Ambush them?"

"We're outgunned, and they're not going to charge up the steps. Sit here for a second and catch your breath. I'm going to check the next stairs."

His left foot had just touched the first step when Remi screamed, "Sam!"

He turned to see Remi stooped over, running through the arch into the Great Room. To the right, a pair of figures appeared on the landing below and began charging up the steps.

"Mistake, Sam," he muttered.

He fired two shots, but the snub nose was worthless. Both bullets missed, sparking against the stone behind Russell and Marjorie. They ducked and backpedaled out of sight.

Remi's voice came through the archway: "Run, Sam! I'll be okay."

"No!"

"Just do it!"

Sam eyeballed the distance to and angle of the Great

Room's archway and instinctively knew he'd never make it. Russell and Marjorie would cut him down before he got halfway.

"Dammit," Sam rasped.

Russell and Marjorie popped up on the steps. The muzzles of their machine guns flashed orange.

Sam turned and charged up the steps.

Crouched in one of the tubs, her headlamp doused, Remi was just realizing her position was indefensible when the shots rang out.

Silence.

Then Russell's whispered voice: "She's in there. You take her, I'll take him."

"Dead or alive?" Marjorie replied softly.

"Dead. Mother says this is the right place. The Theurang is here. Once the Fargos are gone, we'll have all the time in the world. Go!"

Remi didn't think but acted. She climbed out of the tub and crab-walked to the shaft. She took a deep breath, let it out, then jumped.

One floor above Remi, Sam had found himself in a maze of small interconnecting rooms and corridors. Here, the roots and vines were much thicker, crisscrossing the spaces like monstrous cobwebs. Slivers of sunlight peeked through, casting the labyrinth in a greenish twilight.

Having left his machete back at the tunnel entrance, there was nothing for Sam to do but duck and weave his way forward and deeper into the maze.

Somewhere behind him he heard the crunch of footsteps.

He froze.

Three more steps. Closer now. Sam turned his head, trying to pin down the direction.

"Fargo!" Russell shouted. "All my father wants is the Theurang. He's decided not to destroy it. Do you hear me, Fargo?"

Sam remained silent. He stepped to the left, under a thigh-sized root and through a doorway.

"He wants the same thing you do," Russell shouted. "He wants to see the Golden Man in a museum, where it belongs. You and your wife would be co-discoverers. Imagine the prestige!"

"We're not in this for the prestige," Sam said under his breath. "Idiot."

To his right, farther down the corridor, a vine snapped, followed by a barely perceptible "Damn!"

Sam crouched down, switched the .38 to his left hand, and looked around the corner. Twenty feet away, a figure was charging toward him. Sam fired. Russell stumbled and almost went down but regained his footing and dodged right and through a doorway.

Sam stepped across the hall and crab-stepped over a root into the next room. He paused, flipped open the .38's cylinder.

He had one bullet left.

Remi landed hard at the bottom of the pit and tried to shoulder-roll to dissipate the impact but slammed into something solid. White-hot flames spread across her rib cage. She swallowed the scream and forced herself to be still. She was in pitch-blackness. She was belowground, she guessed.

From up the shaft came Marjorie's voice. "Remi? Come on out. I know you're hurt. Come out, and I'll help you."

Not going to happen, sister, Remi thought.

She cupped her hands around the headlamp, clicked it on, and took a quick scan. At her back was a wall; directly ahead, a wide, downward-sloping tunnel. Archways lined either side of the tunnel. Remi clicked off her lamp.

On hands and knees, she crawled ahead. When she'd put what she thought was enough distance between her and Marjorie, she turned her headlamp back on. One hand pressed against her ribs, Remi climbed to her feet. She chose an archway at random and stepped through it. To her left was another arch.

From the tunnel she heard a thump, then a grunt. She peered around the corner in time to see a headlamp turning toward her. Remi raised her pistol, took aim, and fired three quick shots. The muzzle of Marjorie's weapon mushroomed orange.

Remi backpedaled, turned, and darted through the next arch.

Sam knew Russell was behind him and across the corridor.

One bullet, Sam thought. Russell had more than that, and probably spare magazines as well. Sam needed to draw him in, ten feet or less, close enough that he couldn't miss.

Careful to keep the corridor in his mind's eye, Sam crept deeper into the room, then stepped left through an archway. He turned right, stepped up to the next arch, and risked a glance into the corridor.

Through the archway across from him Sam heard a snap. Russell.

Pistol raised to waist height, Sam back-stepped away from the door. When he drew even with the next arch, he turned to step through it.

Russell was standing in the corridor. Sam raised his gun, took aim. Russell took a step and disappeared. Sam took two large strides forward and, gun leading the way, sidestepped into the corridor.

He found himself standing face-to-face with Russell.

Sam knew that Russell was younger and stronger than him, and the King boy was also lightning fast. Before Sam could squeeze the trigger, Russell swung the butt of his machine gun upward, the stock arcing toward Sam's chin. Sam jerked backward. The butt struck a glancing blow. Sam's eyesight flashed red. On instinct, he charged forward, engulfing Russell in a bear hug that pinned his arms to his sides. They stumbled backward.

Russell planted his back foot and spun his body, taking Sam along with him. Sam found his footing again, drew his knee back, and slammed it forward into Russell's groin. Russell grunted. Sam kneed him again, then again. Russell's legs buckled, but he managed to stay upright.

Wrapped up, they stumbled into the next room, bounced off a wall, and then lurched into yet another room. Russell reared his head back, tucked his chin. Sam thought, Head butt, and tried to turn away from it, but it was too late. The top of Russell's forehead slammed into Sam's eyebrow. His eyesight flashed red again, then blackness began creeping in from the sides. Sam exhaled hard, drew in a deep breath, clenched his teeth, and held on. His vision cleared slightly. He drew his own head back, but the height difference made a face strike impossible. Sam chose instead Russell's collarbone. This time, Russell let out a yelp of pain. Sam head-butted again, then again. Russell's machine gun hit the ground.

They spun again, Russell trying to use his superior strength to either dislodge Sam or slam him against a wall.

Suddenly Sam felt Russell's balance change; he was backpedaling quicker than his feet could keep up. Sam's judo training took hold. He would capitalize on Russell's imbalance. Sam put everything he had into his legs and charged forward. Feet scrabbling over the vines and roots, he bulldozed Russell backward, picking up speed.

They bounced through an arch, and then they were back in the corridor. Sam kept pushing.

And then they were stumbling, Russell's balance having given out. They were enveloped by a curtain of foliage. Sam heard and felt vines snapping around them. Over Russell's shoulder he saw daylight. Sam released his death grip on Russell and snapped his head forward, catching him in the sternum. Russell disappeared through the curtain. Sam, trying to arrest his own momentum, pitched through the opening and into space.

Sam's vision was filled with sky, granite walls, a churning river far below—

He slammed to a stop. The impact knocked the wind out of him. He sucked in a couple lungfuls of air. All he saw was a black steel cylinder.

Gun, he thought numbly. He was still clutching his pistol.

He was lying, belly first, in the crook of a moss-covered tree. He looked around and pieced together what he was seeing. They'd fallen from a temple window. The tree, having grown half embedded in the temple's exterior wall, was rooted in a tiny patch of earth at the edge of the plateau. Over the edge was a thousand-foot drop into the Tsangpo Gorge.

Sam heard a groan below him. He craned his neck down and spotted Russell lying on his back next to the tree. His eyes were open and staring directly into Sam's.

His face twisted in pain, Russell sat up. His right hand slid down his pant leg and jerked it up his calf.

Strapped to his boot was a holster. Russell grabbed the butt of the revolver.

"Don't, Russell," Sam said.

"Go to hell."

Sam extended his arm and laid the .38's front sight over Russell's chest. "Don't," he warned again.

Russell unbuckled the holster and slid out the revolver.

"Last chance," Sam said.

Russell's hand began to rise.

Sam shot him in the chest. He let out a gasp, then fell backward, lifeless eyes staring at the sky.

Led by her wildly dancing headlamp, Remi charged through the archway. Bullets thunked into the stone around her. Remi spun, blindly fired two shots back the way she had come, then turned and kept running.

She stumbled back into the corridor. The pit was up the slope to her left. Remi turned right and continued on, half limping, half sprinting. Ahead, her headlamp flicked over a dark circle in the floor. It was another shaft. In pain, and with her injured ankle quickly failing her, Remi tried to swerve around the shaft but slipped and tumbled through the opening.

The fall was mercifully short, perhaps half the depth of the first pit. Remi landed hard on her butt. This time, the pain was too intense to contain. She screamed. She rolled over, looking for her gun. It was gone. She needed something . . . anything. Marjorie was coming.

Remi's headlamp came to rest next to a wooden object. Even before her conscious mind had told her what the object was, her senses were processing it: dark wood, thick black lacquer, no visible seams . . .

She reached out, snagged the edge of the box with her fingertips, and rolled it toward her. In the bright cone of light from her headlamp, Remi saw four symbols, four Lowa characters, in a grid pattern.

"Gotcha!"

Marjorie dropped from the opening above and landed like a cat at Remi's feet. Marjorie, having slung the machine gun across her back for the jump, now reached back and grabbed the stock. She brought it around toward Remi.

"Not today!" Remi shouted.

She grabbed the Theurang box with both hands, raised it over her head, then bolted upright and slammed it into Marjorie's forehead.

Pinned by Remi's headlamp beam, Marjorie's face went slack. With blood streaming down her forehead, her eyes rolled upward. She fell backward and went still.

Stunned, Remi scooted backward until she was pressed against solid stone. She closed her eyes.

Sometime later, a sound penetrated her half-conscious mind.

"Remi? Remi?"

Sam. "I'm here!" she shouted. "Down here!"

Thirty seconds later Sam's face appeared at the top of the shaft. "Are you okay?"

"I may need a little checkup, but I'm alive."

"Is that what I think it is?"

Remi patted the Theurang box beside her. "I just happened upon it. Pure dumb luck."

"Is Marjorie dead?"

"I don't think so, but I hit her pretty hard. She may never be the same again."

"An improvement, then. Are you ready to come up?"

Sam, now armed with Russell's machine gun, had made his way back to the main tunnel. Unsure of Zhilan's location, he simply grabbed his backpack and found his way to the second pit and Remi.

Thirty minutes later they were both back in the Great Room. Together, they reeled Marjorie's limp body up the shaft. Sam handed Remi the machine gun, then scooped up Marjorie and folded her across his shoulder.

"Keep an eye out for the Dragon Lady," he told Remi. "If you see her, shoot first and forget the questions."

As they neared the tunnel exit, Remi stopped. "Do you hear that?"

"Yes . . . Someone's whistling." A smile spread across Sam's face. "It's 'Rule, Britannia!'"

Cautiously, Sam and Remi stepped out of the tunnel.

Sitting twenty feet away, his back against a boulder,

was Jack Karna. He spotted them and stopped whistling. He gave them a cheery wave.

"Tallyho, Fargos. Oh, wait, that rhymes. How clever of me."

Dumbfounded, Sam and Remi walked toward him. As they drew nearer they could see tufts of white emergency dressing jutting from a scarf tied around Karna's neck. He was cradling Ajay's Beretta in his lap.

A few feet away, Zhilan Hsu lay flat on her back, her head propped up by Ajay's balled-up parka. Wrapped around the midpoint of each of her thighs was a bloody field dressing. Zhilan was awake. She glared at them but said nothing.

Remi said, "Jack, I think an explanation is in order."

"Quite. As it turns out, Russell is a good shot but not an expert marksman. I believe he was trying to shoot through me and get Ajay in the process. His damned bullet punched through that muscle . . . What's it called, between the shoulder and the neck?"

"Trapezius?" Sam offered.

"Yes, that's it. Two inches to the right and I'd be a goner."

"Are you in pain?" Remi asked.

"Of course, a monumental amount. Say, what's that you're carrying, lovely Remi?"

"A little something we found lying around."

Remi set it down beside Karna. He smiled and gave the lid a pat.

"What about her?" Sam asked.

"Ah, the Dragon Lady. Very simple, really. She thought I was dead; she let her guard down. As she approached, I grabbed Ajay's gun—this one here—and shot her in the right leg. Then again in the left leg for good measure. I think it took the wind out of her sails, don't you?"

"I'd say so."

Sam turned to Zhilan. He crouched down and dumped Marjorie on the ground beside her. Zhilan reached out and touched her daughter's face. Sam and Remi watched, stunned, as Zhilan's eyes brimmed with tears.

"She's alive," Sam told her.

"And Russell?"

"No."

"You killed him? You killed my son?"

"Only because he gave me no choice," said Sam.

"Then I will kill you, Sam Fargo."

"You can try. But think about this first: we could have left Marjorie in there to die. We didn't. Jack could have killed you. He didn't. You're here because of your husband. He sent you and your children to do his dirty work, and now one of them is dead.

"We're getting off this mountain and we're taking you with us. As soon as we get to a phone, we're going to call the FBI and tell them everything we know. You've got a choice to make: do you want to be a witness or a defendant alongside your husband? No matter what, you're going to jail, but depending on how you play your cards Marjorie might have a chance."

Remi said, "How old is she?"

"Twenty-two."

"She's got a long life ahead of her. It's largely up to you how she spends it: free, and out from under her father's thumb, or in prison."

Zhilan's hateful stare suddenly gave out. Her face went slack, as though she had just let down a heavy burden. She said, "What would I need to do?"

"Tell the FBI everything you know about Charles King's illegal dealings—every nasty thing he's ever done or ordered you to do on his behalf."

Remi said, "A smart lady like you, I'll bet you're a big believer in insurance. You have a very thick file on King stashed away somewhere, don't you?"

"What's it going to be?" Sam asked.

Zhilan hesitated, then nodded.

"Good choice. Jack, we seem to have misplaced our radios."

"I have mine right here."

"Get on the line and try to raise Gupta. It's time to get out of here."

EPILOGUE

Kathmandu, Nepal,
Weeks Later

Sam and Remi's rescue from the Shangri-La temple mountain had unfolded without any dilemma. As he had promised, Gupta had orbited the area, listening and waiting for their call. He returned and picked them up. Four hours after they left Chinese airspace, Gupta landed the Chetak at Itanagar Airport.

Since they were the only witnesses to what had occurred on the mountain, aside from the deceased Z-9 crew, no one in the Chinese government was aware of the incursion. As far as anyone knew, Gupta and his passengers had simply been on a sightseeing tour.

After a brief checkup at an Itanagar hospital, Sam and Remi were dismissed. Marjorie was kept overnight for observation. Like her father, she was hardheaded, suffering only a mild concussion from Remi's blow.

Karna refused medical attention until he was across the border in Nepal but had his entry and exit bullet wounds cleaned and dressed by Gupta.

After lengthy conversations with Rube Haywood, Sam arranged for Zhilan Hsu and Marjorie to be discreetly and securely transported to Washington, D.C., where special agents of the FBI were waiting for them. During interrogation, Zhilan Hsu held nothing back about Charles King. According to Rube, the FBI and the Justice Department had formed a task force devoted to unraveling King's many illicit operations. It was predicted that King would spend the rest of his life behind bars.

The Nepalese government and their scientific community kept the chest under close security while their chief anthropologist, Ramos Shadar, and his associates had time to study its contents. It was decided the discovery of the Golden Man and the Shangri-La temple's location should be kept secret until they were ready to be revealed to the world.

Now the time had come.

"Cheers!" Remi announced, holding up her glass of champagne.

The rest of the assemblage—Sam, Jack Karna, Adala Kaalrami, Sushant Dharel, and Ramos Shadar—echoed the toast and clinked glasses.

"Now it's time for the unveiling," said Shadar, smiling. "I'm sure you've all been anxious for this moment."

"To the Theurang," Remi said softly.

They climbed the stairs to the stage in Kathmandu University's marble-tiled exhibition hall. The official unveiling and media conference would not happen until the following evening, but Sam, Remi, and the others were being honored with a private viewing.

"Who's going to be the first of you to lift the lid and see the Golden Man?" asked Shadar, knowing well what lay inside and already amused at how the others would react. "Who would like the privilege of lifting the lid?"

"No question about it," Sam replied, "Jack deserves to be first."

"Mr. Karna," said Shadar, motioning toward the chest, "if you please."

Tears brimming in his eyes, Karna nodded his thanks to the group, then walked to a low, velvet-draped object. Slowly, with great reverence, he grasped the draw cord and pulled.

The chest of the Theurang lay open with the lid lying alongside. They all stared in awe, except Shadar.

Lying inside, curled in a fetal position, was a nearly complete fossilized skeleton completely gilded in gold. Under the overhead lights of the stage, the sight was awe inspiring. Everyone went silent for several seconds.

Finally Jack Karna muttered, "Why is he so small?"

"It looks like a little boy," said Remi softly. "No more than three years old."

"Can't be much over three feet tall," guessed Sam.

Shadar grinned, "Three feet two inches, to be exact. The weight we estimated at about fifty pounds. Its brain was about the size of a soft baseball."

"It must be fake," Adala Kaalrami spoke for the first time.

Shadar shook his head. "You may not believe it, but you're looking at a thirty-year-old human being. We can arrive at a reasonably close age by the wear on the teeth and bone structure."

"A dwarf?" Sam offered.

"Not a dwarf," answered Shadar, "but a separate species of human who lived between eighty-five thousand and fifteen thousand years ago. When it was found by my ancestors in a mountain cave, they gilded the bones and considered them sacred."

"And worshipped him for over a thousand years," added Sam.

Shadar's eyes took a sly gleam. "Not him," he said slowly, "but her."

There was a long moment for the revelation to sink in.

"Of course!" Remi snapped. "Life giver. The Mother of Mankind. The Theurang was a woman. No wonder they glorified her."

Sam shook his head, but with a twinkle in his eye. "Why is it," he asked, "that women always have to have the last word?"

The extraordinary new novel in the #1 *New York Times* bestselling NUMA® Files series

CONNECT ONLINE

www.cusslerbooks.com
www.clivecusslerfacebook.com

A MEMBER OF PENGUIN GROUP (USA) INC. • WWW.PENGUIN.COM

M1067JV0312

ALSO FROM #1 *NEW YORK TIMES*
BESTSELLING AUTHOR

CLIVE CUSSLER
WITH GRANT BLACKWOOD

SPARTAN GOLD

A Fargo Adventure

Thousands of years ago, two superpowers of the ancient world went to war, and a treasure of immeasurable value was lost to the shadows of history. In 1800, Napoleon Bonaparte stumbled across a startling discovery. Unable to transport it, he created an enigmatic map on the labels of twelve bottles of rare wine. When he died, the bottles disappeared.

Treasure-hunting husband-and-wife team Sam and Remi Fargo discover a World War II German midget torpedo submarine in a Maryland swamp. Inside, they find a wine bottle taken from Napoleon's famous "Lost Cellar." Fascinated, they set out to find the rest of the collection. But another connoisseur is searching for his own prize, and the Lost Cellar is his key to finding it—and the treasure will be his, *no matter what . . .*